I0615716

ALL THE
GOLD IN
CHINA

A novel of China's first republic

KATE ZENG

ISBN: 0615693849
ISBN 13: 9780615693842
Library of Congress Control Number: 2012916471
CreateSpace Independent Publishing Platform
North Charleston, South Carolina

For FS, who lets me be me, and makes it all possible

Those who dream by night,
in the dusty recesses of their minds,
wake in the day to find that all was vanity,
but the dreamers of the day are dangerous men,
for they may act their dream with open eyes,
and make it possible...

T.E. LAWRENCE

History made me who I am, yet I had no history.

My name is Jong Lin. It is a Chinese name, but I am only half Chinese. I was born in the old capital of Peking. I was a few days old when a prostitute found me on the street. She took me home and raised me as her son. This was all I knew about the beginning of my life. I never found out why it was decided that my mother was Chinese and my father Caucasian. And if it were true, where did he come from? America? Russia? One of the countries in Europe that forced China to open its door to the West? What spurred a man to leave home and go to the other side of the world at a time when international travel was prohibitively difficult? Why did he choose China? Did he come to preach or to pillage? Was he running away from something? The law? A girl? Himself? What about my mother? What attracted her to a foreigner? Rebellion? The promise of adventure? A better life? Did they love each other? Were they married or was I the outcome of an illicit encounter? What happened to them?

The question I wanted answered most was why they abandoned me. What made them leave their infant son out on a freezing night? Did they do so willingly or were they forced? Did they regret what they had done?

I came up with different scenarios that might explain what happened.

I was born at the time when Manchu royals were packing up and leaving the Forbidden City. Peking was in an uproar. Bandits and soldiers banded together. They raided and robbed and rioted. It was possible that my parents were caught up in a street scuffle and lost me in the frenzy. China had suffered humiliating defeats in the Opium Wars. Resentment of foreigners was raging. Neighbors who held a grudge against Westerners could have decided that throwing a half-Caucasian baby on the street would be a way of getting back at them. They broke into my parents' house and yanked me from my crib. The scenario I liked most was that my parents gave me up for a heroic purpose. A personal sacrifice for the greater good. For emperor and country. Like a plot out of a folktale.

Over time, I've accepted that I may never find out what happened. If I wanted to fill in the void, I would have to invent my own legend.

It would be tempting to explain my rise in the world by the usual attributes of self-made success: determination, cleverness, foresight. The truth was more humbling. For a half-breed orphan to become a political player in a country like China took more luck than will. The Chinese would put it down to joss. Karma.

I met my joss the month after I turned fifteen. The occasion was the wedding of Chiang Kai-shek and Soong May-ling. Chiang, who by then had cast himself in the role of de facto emperor, was acquiring the wife of his political dreams. Soong May-ling was well-connnected, American-educated and easy on the eyes. The wedding was the party of the century. National and international luminaries gathered at Shanghai's Majestic Hotel.

I was a tea boy. He was a guest of honor. There was no reason for him to pay attention to me. But he did.

My world changed.

Han.

His title was General Commando and Governor of Shansui Province. In some circles he is still revered as one of the founding fathers of China's first republic. To the rest of the country, his legacy is less exalted. He is more famous as one of the two richest men in China. The other was Soong Tse-ven, Minister of Finance and Chiang Kai-shek's brother-in-law. Han and Soong were believed to have owned more wealth than half the population combined. Fortunes of such magnitude are inevitably linked to dubious means. Soong got rich by stealing from the national treasury; Han by distributing opium for the British.

There was a noble purpose to his greed, Han believed. His wealth would save China from the road to modern ruin and return the country to its former imperial glory. He would make himself emperor of the second Han dynasty— his name was that of the dynasty that ruled from 206 B.C. to A.D. 220. The Chinese had a name for regional tyrants like him: *Chün Fa*. Bandit King.

He lived like one. His palace was more opulent than the Forbidden City, a sprawling Shangri-la guarded by its own great wall and a manmade forest the size of West Lake. The trees had been planted to form a maze, the foliage so dense sunlight couldn't penetrate. Below the architectural splendor lay the largest gold reserve in Asia. A subterranean vault warehoused profits from decades of dispensing opium to the Chinese population. Miles of shelves stacked with solid gold bullion. To keep the location secret, Han had the laborers executed the day they completed construction of the vault. Five hundred men were gunned down in one night, the bodies cremated, the ashes collected in wheel barrows and dumped into the river. Local folks claim that on the hour of their execution, hollowed faces float up from the riverbed.

Han had a fixation on pubescent girls, pretty young things coming into the first bloom of womanhood. A new girl every night. A young girl every hour when he was in the mood. Half of the province's female population had been deflowered by him. Psychologists would have come up with all kinds of theses and hypotheses. Sexual addiction. Pathological libido. Unfulfilled yearnings. I believe it had a simple explanation: Virgins fed the appetite of his imperial ego. Own their first, he loved to say, and I own them forever.

To the world, Han stood for everything that was wrong with China: decadent, cruel, corrupt. To me, he was the best father an orphan could hope for, kind, attentive, and generous.

Power and wealth. I was a heartbeat from the top.

One night Han vanished. The public assumed he had died, probably of unnatural causes. Han had plenty of enemies and his friends wouldn't have hesitated to kill him if they could get their hand on the gold. To this day his disappearance remains a mystery. The body has never been found. The gold has never been recovered. Thousands of gold buillon are buried in an unmarked grave, a tantalizing picture that keeps the Han myth alive.

All those gold buillon. Just lying there. Why can't they be found? Who owns the gold if Han was dead?

Many thought Han faked his death, as a ploy to deflect rivals. He had the means to bribe the gods and the devil a thousand times over. Sightings of Han have been reported, in Sri Lanka, Chiang Mai, Buenos Aires... Vivid narratives have accompanied snapshots of blurred profiles. Others believe the legend of Han's gold was a sham from the start. There isn't a shred of evidence that the vault existed. And if there *was* so damn much gold, why hadn't anyone seen it? The warlord made the whole thing up. His bluff was called and that's why he fled.

I am the only one who knows the truth. It had to do with a woman. Because of her, it had to do with me.

I never told anyone what happened and I never contradicted the rumors.

I left China after Chiang Kai-shek lost the country to Mao Tse-tung. I chose my new home nearby, in the British Colony of Hong Kong. The world was nursing a fragile peace after the war. Hong Kong was a young city with a troubled past and an uncertain future, an East-meets-West no man's land. The same was true of me. The city and I suited each other. The years I spent there turned out to be my best.

In 1997, the Treaty of Nanking that had ceded Hong Kong to the British expired. China was determined to take back the city lost by the war on opium. Flurries of diplomatic negotiations couldn't extend British rule. On the night of June 30, fireworks showered over Victoria harbor. The Union Jack came down and the Chinese flag went up. I watched the handover ceremony on television, feeling no sadness and no closure. Leaders of the two sovereigns spoke solemnly about legacies and promises, about the ending and the beginning of eras. The Opium War was not in the speeches. Nor the man who had brought the drug to China.

I turn opium into gold, Han said. I will turn the gold into a new China.

The new China arrived, heralding its own brand of socialism. It was not the China Han had in mind.

Perhaps it was good that he wasn't there, I thought.

Later that year, I moved to California, fulfilling an old dream of finding the Caucasian half of me. I have been living alone on the top floor of a highrise overlooking the Pacific. If the world were flat, I would see China from my balcony. Thankfully it isn't. The view is lovely in its stark simplicity. The vast expanse of the ocean and its endless reflection of the sky. A reminder that life goes on regardless of what, who, or why. I draw comfort from the space and the anonymity in my new country. A person of mixed race is not an object of curiosity in multi-ethnic California. Few know who I was; even fewer are interested in my past. Memories are abundant in the land of immigrants, even when the memories are framed in gold.

Gold is the essence of wealth, Han said time and time again. And he had all the gold in China.

I have one piece of Han's gold. It sits on my desk. Round with a cleft and a pointed base. The shape of a peach, the symbol of longevity in Chinese folklore. When the afternoon sun streams through the windows, scales of light transform it into a burst of golden rays. After so many years, I am still stirred by the sight. A glittering souvenir of a drug that weakened a nation. The last tangible tie to the man who made me who I am. The bright dot on my retina grows into a yellow haze and fills up the universe. In my mind's eye I see laborers toiling in a vast dungeon, young girls sobbing as they stagger from Han's bed, three hundred thousand people being slaughtered in the streets in Nanking, and the eyes of the girl who saw the gold and broke my heart...

Everything began and ended with the gold. It was the plot, Han was the player and China the stage. I was the stagehand who set up the scenes and stayed behind to clean up. I saw how the gold changed everyone who came too close.

A century has passed since the birth of China's first republic. The stage is occupied by a different troupe, performing a new play. The old cast is gone. I am the only one left.

Time to tell the world what happened.

Why now? Someone might ask, why give away the secrets I have been guarding all these years?

Because I promised her I would tell the truth. Because I am old.

Age has taught me that lies may morph and dissipate with time, but truth stays. The truth has been weighing on me, heavier now than when I was a younger man. Strange. One would expect memories to fade with the years. Mine don't. They are like images projected on a screen, made sharper by the gradual pulling of the focus. Clearer now than ever before. Perhaps it's my unconscious desire to keep Han in my head. Perhaps I'm still unwilling to acknowledge the woman I loved wasn't who I thought she was. Perhaps I am haunted by what I did and didn't do.

I am tired.

Too tired to analyze, to judge, or to grieve. I just want to be relieved of the past.

So, here's the story.

Here's the story.

It begins with the year the gold brought her to me.

1937

The imperial Ching Dynasty had ended. China's last emperor, Pu-yi, was exiled in Manchukuo. Mao Tse-tung's Communist Party was challenging the ruling Nationalist Party, the Kuomintang, headed by Chiang Kai-shek. Civil war was imminent. Japan had bombed Shanghai; their next target was the capital, where 300,000 people were to die in the Nanking Massacre.

In a province far from Nanking, a warlord watched and waited. He had amassed a vast fortune smuggling opium for the British. Gold. Mountains of it. Enough to buy China.

He was General Han. He was going to change history.

1

Emperors are lonely men, General Han thought.

With the resolute stride of someone who was ready to be the loneliest man in the world, he headed to the innermost sanctum of his palace, Crescent Moon Villa, popularly known as the Forbidden City of the South. He was inside Grand Hall, the largest structure on the site which housed his office and his private apartment. He walked along a narrow corridor, dark and airless like a tunnel. He didn't turn on the lights; he didn't need any. He knew the place like a childhood haunt. His footfalls echoed reassuringly like a heartbeat. One hundred and fifty paces to the door at other end. He pushed it open, stepped inside, and flipped a switch. The light revealed a small study. Desk, armchair, shelves holding a few books. As he closed the door behind him, his eyes located the two strands of black silk hanging over a corner of the desk that was directly in the path of entrance. An unaware intruder would have brushed them off. They were there. Exactly as he had left them. His caution was unnecessary. Access to Grand Hall was severely restricted. No one was permitted to go near Han's sanctum.

He lifted the stone inkwell and retrieved a key. At the shelf, he nudged a blue and white Ming vase a palm's width to the left. Click. The wall glided open to reveal a door. He unlocked it with the key, stepped back, and flipped the light switch again, on and off five times, to stop the poisoned blades from thrusting out from the door frame. From a drawer, he retrieved incense sticks and a box of matches. He pounded his fist eight times on a spot at eye level. The second wall receded like a stage curtain. He was at the top of a steep stairwell. Bending down, he fished a metal pick from a receptacle on the floor. He descended the fifty steps to the bottom landing and unlocked an iron gate with the pick.

It was as cavernous as an auditorium and very cold. The entire space was lined with concrete shelves, each five feet high and two feet deep. Rows of gold bars were stacked on them so tightly that they appeared to be solid banks of shining metal. Han strode down the aisle. A proud head of state inspecting his best troops.

The Hans were the first family of China's opium trade, pioneer of the lucrative enterprise that had begun more than a century ago. After the first Opium War, China had been forced by the British to sign the Treaty of Nanking. Among other concessions including the island of Hong Kong, Britain's right to export opium into China had been reinstated. This time the British had decided they would have a local partner to oversee the operations. An insider who knew China's ways, who had the connections to expand the trade to the far reaches of the country. More important, someone to blame in case things went wrong. Han's great-grandfather, a close friend of the chairman of the East India Company and a favorite of the Manchu court, had recognized the potential profitability of the alliance. He had offered his services to Queen Victoria and had become her comprador *extraordinaire*—in secret, so as not to jeopardize his standing with the Emperor in Peking. Resistance to the drug, led by upright officials who wanted to keep the poison out of the country, had remained strong. Distribution had been limited to the ports in the southern provinces. The first time Han's father had shown him the vault, most of the shelves were empty. The young Han had stared at the gaping holes, ashamed. Filling them had become his single purpose in life. It had taken twenty-five years, thousands of tons of opium and millions of new addicts to accomplish his goal. Han's opium empire had become the largest in the world, from the tropical forests of Indochina to the northern Chinese seaboard.

In the center of the vault, Han knelt. He planted the incense sticks in a floor recess and lit them with a match. Thin ribbons of smoke rose like magic cobwebs. Gold. The greatest, most revered treasure in the universe. The commodity of unquestioned worth. He bowed his head to the floor three times and prayed.

Help your favorite son to win. Give him the Mandate of Heaven. Give him China.

Crescent Moon Villa was situated in the shadow of Shansui's famous limestone mountains. Set on fifteen hundred acres, the compound had satellite palaces, pavilions, and ceremonial halls built around gardens and streams. There could be little doubt that its crimson façade, blue-tiled roofs, and marble plinths were modeled after those of the Forbidden City. Han claimed his palace was a vast improvement on the old structure in Peking, a claim unlikely to be challenged, as anyone who might be inclined to do so would not be invited to the premises.

The first rays of the sun were bursting behind the hills. Han mounted his favorite horse for his daily ride around the compound. Using archery gear that had belonged to Genghis Khan, Han aimed at random targets to practice his shooting. The curl of an eave. The tip of a branch. A bird in flight. He enjoyed the exhilaration of speed, the buoyancy of crisp morning wind, and the feeling of being master of his universe.

Approaching the final leg of the route, Han reined in the horse to a trot. Sunlight filtered through the treetops and cast webs of shadow on the ground. The day began to encroach on his thoughts. It would be a busy one.

After months of evasive responses, Pu-yi, China's last emperor resurrected as monarch of Japan-controlled Manchukuo, had accepted Han's invitation to visit Shansui. There couldn't be many activities on the former emperor's political or social calendar—the role of China's last Son of Heaven in Manchukuo was decorative. But not hard to understand that he wasn't eager to return to the country he had lost.

Something must have happened to change his mind, Han thought.

And there was the telegram from Generalissimo Chiang Kai-shek, head of the reigning Kuomintang Party, Han's boss. The message had been marked top priority and

4

top secret. For Han's eyes only. It had confirmed what Han already knew: The Kuomintang was relocating the capital from Nanking to Chungking.

Relocate? Retreat would be closer to the truth.

The Japanese were blatant in their intention to swallow China. The Land of the Rising Sun was made up of mountains, half of them volcanoes. Useable land was scarce. The population needed space to grow. So they decided they would take China, a country twenty-five times its size, with as many problems to match. They had started in the northeast, marching southward, heading to the capital of Nanking. Rather than facing up to the enemy, Chiang chose to run. As far away as he could. To Chungking. A smoggy dump in the middle of nowhere.

Coward.

In nine years as Party leader, Chiang's accomplishments consisted of kissing American behinds, looting the national treasury, and marrying the woman with the best connections in China. The man was barely literate, didn't know how to govern, and couldn't care less about people's welfare. The country was in worse shape now than the last days of the Ching Dynasty.

Han had been ready to tear up the telegram when he noticed the postscript.

To prevent hostile entities from taking advantage of the Central Government's transition to the new capital, Shansui units are to mobilize immediately and prepare for second-line defense. Stand by for orders...

Shansui was on the Chinese border, a distance from the major hubs. Its geographical isolation had ensured its independence; the province had been out of bounds to the ruling party for generations. Not even the mighty emperors of the Yuan and Ming dynasties had interfered with the local government. What made Chiang think he could order my troops to fight for him? Han thought. This had to be another one of his tired tricks. Han was expected to disobey and Chiang would call it an act of insubordination. A pretext to confiscate Han's gold.

"My soldiers are *my* soldiers. My gold is *my* gold," Han said aloud and gave the horse a whip.

Coming out of the trees, he heard music. A complex, abstract composition played on unfamiliar instruments. Classical, he had been told. Jong was playing the records he had brought back from the British colony of Hong Kong. Han knew Jong was fond of European music, though he only played the records in private, just as he kept his English books in his apartment and was never seen with them in public. Not too many people were aware that General Han's adoptive son read and spoke the language like a native.

Jong was half Chinese and half Caucasian, a fact Han sometimes forgot.

When I am with you, Jong had said, I am Chinese completely.

What about when you are not with me?

I'll always be with you.

Han wanted to make sense of this music. It bothered him that he was finding things in Jong's life he didn't share. When had the rift begun? What happened to the boy he had brought back from Shanghai more than a decade ago? Where was the pure adoration in the eyes that worshipped his every move? Han rarely saw that look any more. Boys grow into men—that's as inevitable as the change of seasons. But he missed the unquestioning love. Sorely.

Han held back the horse. He listened hard. If he could understand the music, he would understand the man.

It remained chaotic, incomprehensible. *Foreign.*

Was that why Jong played it day and night? Did he need nourishment for his Western soul? Why?

Why now?

The scroll dominated the suite like a royal ensign unfurled over a throne room. There was only one character on the fifteen-foot canvas: *longevity*. The calligraphy was rendered in ancient script; the word looked like an inky maze. Facing the scroll, a canopied bed rested on a rosewood plinth. Tapestry embroidered with a roaring dragon framed the bed like a stage curtain. The sheets were heavy silk brocade in imperial yellow. A matching comforter was rolled up at the foot of the mattress. The latest issues of *Life* magazine and a set of ivory opium pipes were arranged on the nightstand.

Han and Jong were inspecting the guest suite newly furnished for Pu-yi's visit.

"This should make our emperor feel at home," Han remarked.

"Probably more than the drafty house in Manchukuo he calls his palace," Jong replied.

Jong Lin was a startlingly handsome man. He stood six feet tall with a trim and muscular frame, graceful and godlike. Jet-black hair naturally wavy, strong cheekbones, square jaw. His eyes were the evidence of his non-Chinese half. They were blue.

"The fool still thinks of himself as the Son of Heaven," Han continued. "We'll indulge him—why not? Let him have some fun with his old props. Get him back in the imperial frame of mind and he'll believe the good old days can be brought back. Did you tell him why we want him here?"

"Nothing specific, General, only that you'd like to renew the friendship. He said you and he had met only once; he didn't think you were friends. And he was tired of traveling. Since moving out of the Forbidden City, he has been shuffled between hotels and rented mansions. Now that he has his own palace and his mandate restored, he wants to stay put for a while."

" 'Mandate.' Did he say that?"

"That was the word he used."

"The Japanese made him chief executive. Not emperor. They are using him to secure control of northeast China. He will be thrown out the moment the Japanese get what they want. Pu-yi has no more mandate than a Ginza geisha."

"It could be just his official line. He sounded guarded."

"What changed his mind?" Han asked.

"Snowstorms in Manchukuo. They were ferocious, the worst he has experienced. He couldn't step outside the palace. He said he would enjoy a change of scenery and warm weather."

" 'Couldn't step outside the palace.' Sounds like someone under house arrest."

"He made an oblique remark about having more soldiers than servants in the palace."

"He is being watched."

8

"That's quite likely. There has never been any real trust between him and the Japanese." Jong added, "He made the call himself."

"He didn't want his staff to know."

"He didn't want anyone to know until the itinerary was set."

"Did he say why he moved up the date?"

"He said he needs to be back for the New Year—the one on the Western calendar. There will be festivities he has to attend. I suggested the third week of December. He'll be traveling on our plane; it wouldn't be a problem to get him back in time. He insisted on coming as soon as arrangements are made."

"Interesting."

"He was worried about something—even afraid. It was in his voice."

"Any clue what that something is?"

"I made small talk with him, get him to relax and open up, but he was not forthcoming," Jong replied.

"He wouldn't dare speak up with Japanese soldiers hovering about. Pu-yi is a weak little man who is out of his depth."

"Nothing in his upbringing prepared him for what happened."

"No," Han agreed. "His situation can only get worse when the Japanese move further into China and Manchukuo loses its strategic importance. He won't be useful anymore. They'll throw him out. Pu-yi has nowhere to go. No one wants him. Not even his own people. What can they do with an emperor who has outlived his dynasty? Put him in a museum or an orphanage? The man has no assets, no troops, no friends." Han added with absolute certainty, "I will be his only option. I will be China's only option."

A shadow flitted across Jong's face.

Han turned to the sky outside the window, affirming his claim with heaven. "Nobody knows better than I what is good for China. Nobody is better than I to rule China."

Jong was quiet.

"If not me, who?" Han insisted, responding to Jong's silence. "I welcome a worthy opponent, but where is he? There are a few competent soldiers in the Party who may have a notion or two about solving the country's problems. If they teamed up, they might amount to something, but they don't trust each other, and they all despise their commander-in-chief."

"Strange relationship they have with Chiang. One moment they're in bed together; the next they're ready to gouge the other eyes out."

"They'll gouge each other's eyes out in bed. Just watch."

Standing at the foot of the calligraphy, Han examined the angular strokes. His face sobered as he seemed to realize that the word could refer to life's endless hazards as much as the promise of years.

"The Ching Dynasty lasted two hundred and sixty-seven years. Not long enough for Pu-yi's grandmother. She wanted eight hundred more. She drank turtle soup and had the word *longevity* displayed around the palaces so it would be always in her sight. She thought that would make her live forever. What a fool."

"They were irrational efforts to attain an impossible goal."

"What do you expect from a woman?" Han said. "But she was not as big a fool as our Generalissimo. He needed a reliable partner in crime, so he recruited his brother-in-law Soong Tse-ven to run the national treasury. It's like picking the hungriest rat and putting it in charge of the pantry. Soong is cleaning out the treasury as fast as he can move assets abroad. A corrupt government is like a house vandalized by its occupants. A piece here, a piece there— soon they don't have a home. The Kuomintang's days are numbered."

"They have the Americans on their side. It's a formidable source of support."

"They are foreigners. They have their own agenda and their own interests to protect. They are not going to bail out the Kuomintang forever."

"The Communists might take over, General."

"The Communists," Han repeated with a frown. "What strange ideas they have. Everyone works for the Party, sharing everything. No ownership. No personal enterprise. It's unnatural, bizarre. Definitely not Chinese."

"People are listening to them. Peasants are abandoning the fields to join the Communist Party."

"People are hungry and desperate. They listen to anyone who can spin a fairy tale. It's a temporary craze."

"It will last as long as times are bad. A new society where everyone is entitled to have their basic needs met is a tempting prospect to people who have nothing. It helps that the man advocating the ideas is a charismatic leader."

"Mao."

"He has gone far with what little he has."

"I don't deny there's something about him. It's as if he is more than a man, but a force." Han declared, "Mao will be my toughest rival *or* my strongest ally."

"Do you think he can be your ally?"

"Why not? Everyone has a price. Mao's should be cheap; the Communists are dirt poor. I'll make him an offer when the time is right."

With the gold, Jong thought. The perennial Han solution.

"Nothing and no one is going to stand in my way. Next year China will be mine."

Han's face was alighted with anticipated triumph. Jong sensed specific information behind the confidence. A secret alliance? A crucial piece of intelligence? A new arsenal? Whatever it was, Han didn't want to jinx it by talking. He ambled to the other side of the room.

"Yuan Dynasty?" he asked, looking at the painting of a warrior on horseback.

"Yes, Chan Meng-keng was the artist. Pu-yi collected his works. An agent who brokers pieces stolen from the National Museum found it in the black market."

"I like the muted tones and the simple lines. The horse appears to be moving. Very nice. Put it in Grand Hall after Pu-yi leaves."

"Yes, General." Jong joined Han. "Did you read the telegram?"

Han nodded.

"Are we sending troops to Nanking?"

"Absolutely not. The troops are mine. They will not serve anyone else."

"But…"

"What can Chiang do? Fire me? Arrest me? With the Japanese coming from the east and the Communists making trouble in the west, his hands are tied."

"The Generalissimo is someone who holds a grudge."

"I don't doubt he will find a way to get back at me. It's not as if he hasn't tried before."

"Our troops could and would make a difference," Jong said. "Protect the capital. Stop the Japanese momentum. That would be good for Shansui too."

"Shansui is a long way from Nanking."

"It would take a few days for our troops to get there, but it would help the soldiers in Nanking if they knew help was on the way."

Han snapped, "Chiang is bankrolled by the Americans. Let him fight his own war."

The finality in Han's voice was clear. Jong asked, "What should we do about a reply?"

"Nothing in black and white he can use against me. The man has a twisted mind. You give money to an orphanage and he would find a way to turn it into a crime."

"I can make a call to Nanking."

"No calls."

"A messenger?"

"No."

"We'll just ignore the order?"

"We never saw the damn thing. The same goes for future summons. Time to sever the tie. Put an end to the pretense that the Party and I are on the same side. No point in wasting time with this meaningless dance." Han had said all he wanted about Chiang. "Is everything ready for Pu-yi?"

"Yes, General. The agenda is on your desk."

Han turned his gaze to the scenery outside the window. The day was brightening, the mountain peaks splendid against a cloudless sky, sparkling in the crystal air.

"The poets were right. This is indeed the loveliest place under Heaven. Why emperors didn't choose to live here, I'll never understand," Han said with feeling. "What else did Pu-yi say?"

"He asked whether we have open pastures to play polo, and he reminded us about his preference for variety in meals."

"One hundred and twenty-eight dishes at every meal served in the Forbidden City, yet the Manchu royals were thin as matchsticks. Where did the food go?"

"Perhaps his former majesty would help us solve the mystery."

"What about Pu-yi's bedmates?" Han asked.

"He will have his choice of girls, boys, and eunuchs."

"You've prepared the girls?"

"They have been instructed to undergo a medical procedure before they are presented to the Emperor."

"I can count on the treatment to work?"

Jong hesitated. "It won't be a sure thing, General. The full impact of syphilis can take months or even years to present itself. How the disease behaves depends on the health of the victim. It's unpredictable."

"Give it six months. If nothing happens, find another way to disable him."

"With or without affliction, I doubt that Pu-yi will be an active partner."

"What makes you so sure?"

"Pu-yi's aptitude is that of a dull-witted fourteen-year-old," Jong explained. "He studied with palace tutors and a teacher from Britain. The scope of his schooling was limited. Basic vocabulary. Some history and geography. That was twenty years ago; he hasn't done anything to build on what he learned. He can barely read a newspaper. That's hardly sufficient training for a head of state in the modern world."

"Not even for a tribal chief."

"Weak intellect aside, the man is chronically lazy. He doesn't tie his own shoe laces, doesn't wipe his own bottom. That won't change if and when he joins our camp. He is and will always be the child emperor."

"Crowned at three and forced to abdicate at six. One could almost feel sorry for the man."

"There is another consideration, General," Jong said. "Since moving to Manchukuo, no female has shared Pu-yi's bed."

"What about the Empress?"

"They reside in separate quarters."

"Concubines?"

"They were disbanded after the royal entourage left the Forbidden City. Pu-yi seems to have given up any pretense that he's interested in women."

"We only need one quick coupling. The girls are pros. They know their way around a yang, even a disinterested one."

"We are infecting ten girls."

"Good to cast a wide net."

"It's a crippling affliction."

"So is the war."

"The war will end. The girls will have to live with the disease for the rest of their lives."

Han cast a knowing look. "You want to spare them?"

"I'd like to find another way to achieve the same result."

Han pushed the double door of the suite and stepped onto the veranda. Sunlight poured into the atrium garden, its rays bouncing on the marble surfaces. Han seemed to take the brightness along. Jong kept the customary three paces behind. Our positions are an apt metaphor for our relationship, Jong thought. Han is the sun and I a satellite. I move in Han's orbit, the trajectory of my existence guided and defined by him.

Han paused for Jong to catch up with him.

"In everything else, you are pragmatic and shrewd," Han said, as though he too had been assessing Jong in the brief silence. "But you have this soft spot for ordinary folk. You want to improve their lives and solve their problems. I don't mind if you act on your charitable impulses now and then. Why not? Philanthropy enhances one's standing with the gods. But not this time. I cannot give up what may be the only chance I have with Pu-yi under my roof. In their line of work, the girls would be infected sooner or later. At least for this they will be amply compensated."

Jong was quiet.

"I am going to put Pu-yi back on the dragon throne. As a symbolic head of state. He can call himself the Son of Heaven, but the mandate will not come from heaven. It will come from me. The man is a spoiled dimwit who knows better than anyone what it means to be emperor. He might get it into his head that he had his old mandate back. Even the semblance of power can be seductive. If he decides to behave like the ruling monarch, we will have a messy problem on our hands. There is nothing more dangerous than a cretin in power. Look at the damage the Empress Dowager inflicted on the country."

The Empress Dowager was a foolish woman, Jong thought. But it was feudalism that had made her and her evils possible. That was the soul of the monster. Yet you plan to bring it back. Resurrect the imperial corpse. With your gold. I, half Chinese and half I don't know what, a man of no history and no country, will be part of this madness.

"Syphilis is insurance. Double the girls' pay. Tell them whoever succeeds in coupling with the Emperor will be awarded a bonus. One catty of gold. Put it where everyone can see."

They walked past grottos and lawns, landscaped with miniature mountain ranges and valleys. The air was clean; the colors sharp. In the distance, crimson roofs shimmered against a blue sky.

"I should have been born a thousand years ago, when the Mandate of Heaven was in full force," Han reflected. "Not this twilight hour when bandits can pose as emperors."

"It may be a long twilight, General."

"It has been a long twilight. Time for the sun to rise. Right here."

For a while they listened to the small sounds around them: the gurgle of a waterfall, fish nipping at algae, breeze agitating a flowering wisteria.

Never pensive for long, Han shifted to a different task at hand. "The van for Henry. Did it leave?"

"It's on its way to Nanking, and should arrive at Henry's house on the afternoon of the birthday banquet."

"If Pu-yi hadn't moved up the date, I would have traveled to Nanking. See Henry and his family. See the capital while it's still the capital. And watch Chiang Kai-shek and Soong May-ling run in their socks. I heard she gives Roosevelt a robust rub of his yang every time she sits next to him—to show appreciation for the foreign aid checks. The woman would have made a first-class whore."

"Serving a *kweiloh* clientele."

Han laughed. "She did resemble your foster mother."

"Na-na looked like Madame Chiang?"

"Prettier. You should have seen her debut at Rain Flower Chamber. Her pimp knew he had someone special and sent invitations to his best customers. I would have made a bid if I had been free that night."

"You met Na-na back then?"

"Didn't I tell you? It was quite brief. There were a lot of people around. How is she?"

"She's getting by, though she's far from well."

"Tell her to move here. You can take care of her."

"I tried, but I can't change her mind. She won't leave Shanghai."

"Does she care that she is living in a war zone?"

"She said she has been running from one thing or another all her life. She just wants to live out the rest of her days quietly."

"It would be easier on you if she were here."

"I miss her, but there's not much I can do. She can be stubborn."

"Women."

Jong's thoughts went to the women in Han's life. Did he miss any of them? His mother, who had died when Han was a boy? His wife, who had committed suicide after two years of marriage? The string of concubines? Other men's wives he'd appropriated for a moment of pleasure? The hundreds of young girls he had abducted and raped? Some were sure to have gotten pregnant. What happened to those children? People were not kind to children born out of wedlock. How would they make it through life? It must have occurred to Han that he had fathered children. Yet he never looked for them. Why?

Han broke the silence. "Thinking about Nan-fei?"

"Only how fortunate she is to be in your thoughts." Jong bowed. "Please allow me to thank you on her behalf."

"When we are alone, Jong, you can do away with the formalities."

"One shouldn't take one's good fortune for granted."

"You are like a son to me. I want you to have everything you want."

"I do, General."

"You will have more." Han went on warmly, "After I restore the Middle Kingdom, you will have the first appointment of the new Han Dynasty."

"That would be an immense honor, General. But perhaps premature in light of my youth and inexperience."

"Is that what you think?"

"Yes, General."

"Your age and experience don't worry me, Jong," Han said with mild exasperation. "Your modesty does. After all these years, I would have expected my ambition to rub off on you. Another man would have taken advantage of the opportunities. Bolster his own position. Carve out his own domain. I know I would. But you are not moved by the temptations. Not even the trivial ones. I would gladly share the girls with you. It would be fun to invent a few games of our own."

"You know I'm not a monk when it comes to women. But something is missing when the coupling is performed without the heart's participation. I believe it will be different with the right woman. She hasn't come into my life yet."

Han shook his head. "This quest for the perfect woman. It's a Western obsession."

"Or the universal weakness to desire what one doesn't have."

"I am not in that universe."

"No," Jong agreed. "As to my lack of ambition, the reason is simple. When you found me in Shanghai, I was nobody and I had nothing. You made me who I am. You gave me a future. I vowed to spend my life serving you."

"Vows are made to be broken."

"Not mine."

"If that's what you believe, I can't ask for more."

"I hope I have shown that my loyalty is more than belief."

"You have."

"But you are not convinced, General."

Palm flat inside the front of his jacket, Han spoke quietly, "I know I can count on you to stand by me. That's probably the only thing I can count on in this treacherous world. But loyalty has its limits. Everything concerning men has its limits. More so between two strong-willed men. Like us. Who are as different as they come."

"My will is to serve yours, General."

"I know that's what you want, but it doesn't make us less different. You are a thinker, a man of ideas. I am a pragmatist, a man of action. You revel in the chess game of military maneuvers, but you abhor bloodshed. I kill and destroy if that's what it takes to get what I want. I am a passionate man with immense appetites. You are a compassionate man with concerns for the little people and the greater good. The compassion trait probably came from your missionary father—if that story about your parents is true. If it were up to you, conflicts would be settled by debates. Rich people would share their wealth with the poor. The just would win every time."

"You are describing a dreamer, General."

"An idealist who is a world-class diplomat. But you have to put off your true calling. At this point in history, war is the only way to make peace possible."

"I only hope the war will be over soon."

"What if it isn't over soon? What if bringing an end to the war requires a brutal fight and you have to take part in killing soldiers and civilians on a scale you've never imagined?"

"I'll cope when the time comes."

"Cope?"

"Do my best. Do what's right."

"I assume that means doing what I want?"

"Yes, General."

"What if what I want goes against your instincts and your principles? Will you follow my orders no matter what?"

"Yes."

"Think again."

"I will follow your orders no matter what."

Han shook his head. "That's what worries me."

"Why?"

"You should fight with me because you want to achieve the same goal as mine. Not because you want to follow my orders."

"A common goal, in due course, is likely to produce conflict. I am a contented follower. A contented man does not desire things beyond his reach. A follower does what his master wants. These simple truths sum up my life."

"Nothing is that simple. Not when this much is at stake."

"It is with me."

"You think I am reading too much into your modesty?"

"You know best, General."

They were at the entrance to the rock garden. In the pale light, the rocks resembled ancient animals frozen in time. Without warning, they might come alive and unravel the landscape.

"Do I know best?" Han said, studying the rocks. "I don't think so, Jong. Not when it comes to you. We are too close. I don't see you with my eyes and my mind. I see you with my heart, and the heart neither appraises nor judges. You are not my flesh and blood, yet you are part of my life. More so than anyone. I don't want you to change. What I want is to get inside your head and make you think and feel the way I do. But then you wouldn't be you and I wouldn't want that." They exchanged heartfelt smiles. "One thing I do not doubt: there is more in you than you let people see."

Han liked to spend late mornings with a concubine. The current favorite was Gin-lin, an eighteen-year-old waitress from Canton. She was a southern girl, with olive skin, thick luxuriant hair that turned deep auburn in the light and hearty laughs like a child's. A connoisseur of classic Soochow beauties, Han had found her vivacious ways refreshing. He had bought her contract and taken her back to Shansui. After a month, the infatuation was wearing off.

She was waiting in his private apartment inside Grand Hall.

"Good morning. How is my general today?" Gin-lin said as she moved up and began to untie the strings of his pantaloons.

"I'm not in the mood."

"You always like to make Clouds and Rain, General."

"I've got things on my mind."

"Gin-lin can help you forget them," she purred. "You know if you let her, she can take your mind off anything. Hasn't she satisfied your yang every time?" She slipped her hands into the curl of his arms. "A little birdie told Gin-lin someone important is coming. Is that what's on your mind, General?"

"What have you heard?"

"We have so few visitors. Naturally the servants are excited when there is one. This is such a gorgeous place. More people should see it. It will impress emperors and presidents."

"I don't need to impress anyone."

"Of course not. But you will let the world admire your palace?"

"Not yet."

"That means some day you will." Her eyes crinkled. "Gin-lin has guessed right. It will happen. Shansui will be your Peking and the Villa your Forbidden City. With your gold you can buy all the soldiers and the guns in the world. You will beat the Japanese and the *kweilohs*. You will rule China like an emperor."

"You talk too much. What I do outside this room is none of your business."

She pushed her body forward, pressing her breasts into his chest. "Poor Gin-lin pays attention because she is grateful. So grateful that she pinches herself every morning to make sure she is not in a dream, though it feels like one. One day poor Gin-lin was a miserable waitress. The next she is living in a palace and serving the great General Han." She untied her camisole and dropped it to the floor. She took his hands and pressed them on her breasts. "Remember the first night in Canton? You were sweet to poor Gin-lin. You touched every inch of her pitiful body. You made Clouds and Rain with her all night long. She will never forget."

He didn't seem to be listening.

"You remember, General? It wasn't very long ago."

"Long enough."

The unexpected rebuff smarted. "So sorry, General. I brought it up only because it was the happiest night of my life. You are not getting tired of poor Gin-lin, are you, General? There isn't someone else you like better, is there?"

"You'd better go. I want to be alone."

She was crestfallen. "Can Gin-lin come back later?"

"No."

"Tomorrow?"

"Only if I send for you."

"Has poor Gin-lin done something wrong? Tell her how she can make amends and she will make them. But please don't send her away. She is only happy when she is serving you." She covered her face with her hands and began to sob.

The wailing sounded genuine, though Han knew she was tough. It would take a lot to break her. She must have been feeling anxious, wondering if and when she would be made official concubine—a guaranteed livelihood, like the one the royal concubines in the Forbidden City enjoyed. Three thousand women for one emperor. Only a lucky few had made it to the royal bed. The rest had spent years waiting, never seen the emperor's face, never felt the touch of a man. Yet girls had lined up to be chosen. A palace position had meant security for life and prestige for the family. Han had no desire to follow the imperial model. He had never let any woman stay after he lost interest. Females starving for attention were trouble.

"You want to please me?" Han said.

Her hands slid down to reveal a tearless face. "I do, General."

"Make my guest feel welcome."

"Guest?"

"Pu-yi."

She gasped. "The *Emperor*?"

Han nodded.

"Pu-yi," she repeated under her breath. "How come I haven't heard?"'"

"Gin-lin, have you been spying on my affairs?"

"Gin-lin wouldn't dare."

"The Empress won't be coming along. He'll want some company. You have my permission to go to him."

"You mean…"

"You have served me well. This will be your reward. Do your best to please Pu-yi. He may make you a royal concubine. In Manchukuo."

It took a moment for her to realize her tenure with Han had been terminated. Another to see that no pleas would change her fate.

She knelt and bowed her head to the floor. "Thank you, General, for taking pity on poor Gin-lin and granting her favors she doesn't deserve."

"Find a room in the outer court and rest up. You will be sent for when Pu-yi is here."

"Yes, General."

"Pu-yi was brought up by eunuchs. The marriage is a sham; he and the Empress haven't shared a bed since the wedding night. He is inexperienced like a little boy. You'll need to be inventive with him. Think up some games to rouse his yang."

"Yes, General."

"Go to Mr. Lin. He'll arrange for you to see a physician. A procedure will be performed to make you more desirable."

"Yes, General."

"If it turns out Manchukuo is not in your future, I'll buy the restaurant in Canton for you."

"Thank you, General."

Glancing down, he caught the profile of her breasts, full and round like those of a Caucasian woman. They had been the first thing he'd noticed in the restaurant. Two trembling melons under the cotton top. When she refilled his wine cup he had squeezed to make sure they were genuine. Large breasts are a sign of fertility. She might bear me a son if I let her stay, he thought. But Gin-lin is not wife material. Not for the next emperor of China. My Fu-jen, if there is to be one again, will be a great beauty of impeccable breeding. And a virgin.

Virgin.

Nothing surpasses that glorious moment when my spear breaks the delicate shield. The luscious satisfaction of taking possession of an untouched Jade Well, feeling the power of my yang as it surges and surges…

His yang was rising in response to the thought.

Shouldn't let such magnificence go to waste.

"Come to bed," he said.

Gin-lin looked up uncertainly.

"We'll have a nice farewell."

2

Dawn. A mountain highway linking the northeastern provinces of Anhwei and Kiangsu. Clouds streaked across the sky in tufts. Patches of fog curled around the power poles. The road was deserted, the air still. Suddenly, shrieking birds shot out of treetops, shocking brittle branches to break off. Around the bend, a pair of headlights blazed. A van roared out of the fog, body grimy, tires encrusted with mud, unremarkable except for the circled star on the grille. A Mercedes Benz. One of the few in China. The make favored by the warlord of Shansui, General Han Tang-ming.

Seconds later, a jeep rolled out from behind the trees. It followed the van.

The two vehicles continued on, heading east. The jeep kept a steady half mile from the van. Above, a hawk glided along like a mascot. A gray sun peeped through the haze. The road wound down a slope. The forest thinned out to scrubland and open fields. At the crossing to Kiangsu

Province, they drove by a wide basin of smoldering ash. Villagers stood around the rim like attendees at a wake, gazing at the pile of charred columns of human remains. More signs of habitation appeared. Mules gnawing the remnants of a bad harvest. Clusters of dilapidated cottages. Women washing clothes in tiny gardens with toddlers by their side, their eyes following the vehicles until they were out of sight. A donkey cart came rattling down the side of the road. Behind it, a loaded bus whipped off a trail of dust. The van accelerated and thundered past them. The jeep did the same.

Morning fog had dissipated, revealing a long stretch of highway ahead. The faint outline of Nanking's ancient walls was visible in the distance. Ahead a roadhouse stood by the highway, an oversize shanty with thatched roof and bamboo awnings. A canvas banner with the customary "wine" character hung over the door, flapping in the wind. The van slowed down and pulled up to the front.

The driver needed a break.

Finally, thought the driver of the jeep.

His name was Tong and he was a member of the Blue Shirts, the most powerful crime ring in Shanghai. He watched the other driver get out of the van, lock the door, and walk toward the eatery. How does the man manage to go half a day without stopping? The jeep was running out of gasoline; his bladder was about to burst. It had to be the car, he decided. Mercedes vehicles were believed to be superior with features no other brand could match. He wouldn't be surprised if General Han had installed a contraption that could turn piss into gasoline. The warlord could afford the moon, and there seemed to be nothing the Westerners couldn't do with their machines.

Westerners.

Who were those pale-skinned, yellow-haired, big-nosed creatures? Why were they everywhere and throwing their weight around like they owned China? Russians, Jews, Germans, French, British… Tong hadn't realized there were that many different species in the human race until they showed up.

He turned the steering wheel sharply and the jeep skidded across the road. He stepped hard on the brakes and screeched to a stop just short of a tree. Cutting the engine, he jumped out and relieved himself. That is one grand feeling, he thought as he buttoned up his trousers. Pleasures in life were so few these days, not that there had been better times in recent memory. The Ching Dynasty was gone, the Forbidden City was vacant. Last Emperor Pu-yi was living off scraps from the Japanese. The Kuomintang promised rule by the people, for the people, but there were few signs that they intended to live up to the promises. Foreigners weren't the only ones making trouble. Anyone who could put together a makeshift army was grabbing a piece of the Middle Kingdom. The country was breaking up into smithereens… I'm glad I don't have children. Terrible to grow up in this stinking world. Tong shot a spit into the patch of wet dirt, a tribute to the moment of pleasure. Smoothing out his jacket, he assumed the pace of someone on his way to a well-deserved break.

The exterior of the roadhouse was weather-beaten. Most of the plaster had peeled off, exposing cracks and bricks. Boxes and crates were bundled with ropes and stacked on carts along the wall. The owner is getting ready to leave, Tong observed. Bombings must have started in Nanking.

As soon as the job is done, I'll get out.

Smell of fried grease. His stomach growled. Breakfast had been two wheat buns and cold tea. He could eat a horse. Better not. A full stomach would dull his reflexes and he needed to stay alert. Nanking was half an hour away. Once inside the city, things could get complicated. Traffic, crowds, gangsters. What if the driver of the van had backup in the capital?

The time to act was now.

He consoled himself that tomorrow he would be treated to a lavish banquet at Henry Li's house. Nanking banquets were famous for appetizers, fifteen varieties before the main course…

The banquet would be Li's last meal.

"*Li-Hen-ri*," Tong said aloud.

What kind of Chinese calls himself by the name of a foreign devil?

"Li is big time." The local Blue Shirt boss had said when he summoned Tong to brief him on his next job. "Professor at Nanking University. Old money, fancy education abroad, speaks a dozen languages. His wife is a Kung, first cousin to the Minister of the Treasury. That's how Li got a seat in the Kuomintang Cabinet."

"Like a Court Mandarin?"

"Better. Cabinet members sit at the same table with the Generalissimo."

"If he is family, why does the Generalissimo want him killed?"

"Li is a traitor, that's why. He has been stealing Party secrets and passing them to Shansui. No doubt being paid a fortune by Han. Everyone knows the warlord has been itching to cut loose from the Party. Some nerve Li has. Betraying the most powerful man in China right under his nose."

"He must be a slick operator."

"Very slick. Li has always been friendly with the warlord. No one made much of it. That's what politicians do. They pretend to be everybody's best friend. Get people to lose their guard so they can use them for their own purposes. Chiang must have assumed Li was cozying up to Han on the Party's behalf. No real bond, nothing to worry about. Chiang may not like the warlord, but Han is a formidable player. Someone has to keep the communication lines open between Nanking and Shansui; it might as well be Li. He being family gave him perfect cover."

"How was Li found out?"

"Last week an informant for the Japanese intercepted a wire sent from Li's house in Nanking to Han. An innocuous message that wouldn't have needed to be transmitted by wire. He suspected something fishy has been going on between the warlord and Li; he took it to the Japs. They cracked the code. The message was about a clandestine project the Kuomintang Army is working on that wouldn't involve a local chief like Han. It's an opportunity to stir up trouble; of course the Japs didn't pass it up. They presented the wire to the Generalissimo. He didn't take the Japs at their word—he had us investigate Li. More evidence surfaced. Circumstantial mostly, but the pieces fit. Most damaging was the discovery of Li's secret assets. He's probably the richest man this side of the Yangtze. A professor doesn't earn that kind of money. The Generalissimo was furious. He was ready to put Li in front of a firing squad."

"Why didn't he?"

"The Madame talked him out of it. She didn't want her cousin's husband arrested. It would mean admitting publicly that they had been fooled. Very bad for the Generalissimo's image. She isn't worried about the local press; they do what the Party wants. But she is concerned the foreign reporters might get wind of this. She can't control them."

"And being cousin to Li's wife, she would share the shame."

His boss nodded. "The Generalissimo would lose face overseas. It would jeopardize the profitable relationship with the Americans. That's why the Generalissimo wants the problem handled discreetly. This is your big break, Tong. Do a good job and he might offer you a position in the Party."

"I don't want a job in the Party."

"I thought you always wanted a regular job."

"There is nothing regular about working for the Kuomintang. At least the Blue Shirts are honest. We're professional criminals and we don't pretend to be anything else."

As the ruling criminal organization in Shanghai, the Blue Shirts doubled as Chiang's private mafia. Tong had been recruited a month after taking a job as a door guard at the Bank of Shanghai. In addition to his regular bank duties, Tong was to do the bidding of the local Blue Shirt boss. That had been it. No interview. No probation. No choice. He didn't want a career in crime, but he hadn't been able to say no. The Blue Shirts were more powerful than the police.

"When should I leave for Nanking?" Tong had asked.

"As soon as you're ready. Get there before Li finds out his cover is blown."

"Will I have help?"

"A backup if you want, but you won't be paid more. We prefer you to go solo. The fewer people involve, the easier to keep things under wraps."

"Is Li trained in the use of weapons?"

"I wouldn't think so. The man is a gentleman scholar. He makes his living reading books and making small talk at cocktail parties."

"Who else lives in the house?"

"Wife, daughter, a newborn infant, servants."

"Bodyguards?"

"I expect he has a few, but not many. He wouldn't want to draw attention that way."

"Solo it will be. I can use the money."

"That's what the big boss prefers." He handed Tong a wad of bills. "Half now, half when the job is done."

"Thanks."

"One more thing. You are to make it look like Han's people did it."

"How am I supposed to do that?"

"There is a delivery from Han to Li scheduled. Something important. We couldn't find out what, but we know where and when. This is how it will work. You will wait on the highway at Anhwei border, watch for a Mercedes van. The driver is Han's courier to Nanking..."

Through a window, Tong saw that the van driver had found a table. He was giving the waiter his lunch order. It would take a few minutes for the food to arrive and another few to eat. There should be enough time.

Keeping the same pace, Tong walked past the entrance to the back and looked around. The roadhouse sat on a knoll. The ground was part gravel, part dry grass. Only one tree in sight, and it was rotting on the stump. The kitchen was at the rear of the structure, the windowpanes thick with grease and soot. A half-opened door revealed a wood-burning stove and a cook's back. A plume of smoke rose from the chimney. On the other side of the knoll, there was a shack, the size of a closet, with a piece of soiled canvas hung over the entrance. The toilet. Tong smelled the stench as he approached. Behind the shack, it was scrub land to the edge of a slope strewn with garbage and dead leaves.

He knew what to do.

Back to the jeep, he retrieved a piece of wire and a knife wrapped in a handkerchief. He slipped them into his trouser pocket and then sauntered back to the eatery. The customers were coolies on their lunch break. They squatted on benches, noisily slurping food. The van driver sat facing a wall, his back to the door. The man had to be new, Tong thought. An experienced operator would have a seat where he had a full view of the room and the entrance. Tong picked a table where he could keep an eye on him. He told the waiter to bring him a bowl of plain noodles.

The driver's order arrived. Barbecued pork and fried eggs on steamed rice drizzled with soy sauce. A southern favorite.

The man was from a southern province.

Of course. Shansui is in the south. People in the south eat differently; they also speak differently. Damn. Why hadn't he thought of it? How could he convince Li he was from Shansui when he couldn't speak a word of the dialect? He had to come up with a cover before he knocked on Li's door. It had better be convincing; Li was undoubtedly pretty smart. His food came. Tong ate ravenously, needing to calm his nerves. Too late to pull out now. Punishment for a Blue Shirt member who aborted a job was death for himself and his family. He didn't want to die yet, nor would his wife, though after eighteen years each wished the other would. But no point in dying together if they couldn't stand living together.

The van driver finished his meal. He was pouring himself a cup of tea, taking a respite.

Tong put down his bowl and chopsticks. He left enough money on the table and headed to the door. Once outside, he hurried to the back. He hid behind the tree and waited.

In the sunlight, he saw his quarry's face for the first time. Clear eyes, soft jawline, pink lips. Handsome in an effeminate way. Tong knew the type. A sexual hybrid, voice like a bird and yang no bigger than a Szechuan pepper. He could be a young version of the film star who had been the reigning lead in Shanghai. Tong's wife was crazy about him. Three shows a day in the airless cinema until her eyes watered wasn't enough. She clipped photographs of the actor from magazines and pasted them over their bed. Every time Tong drove into her, he had to look at the sickeningly handsome face.

The young man was following a butterfly, chin up, mouth agape like a child marveling at the stars. A look of pure joy that enraged Tong. How could anyone find pleasure in something so frivolous? The man was a fool. Fools had no place in a tough world.

Tong reached into his pocket for the piece of wire and formed a noose. He slid out from behind the tree and moved carefully. The young man was heading to the shack, oblivious of his stalker. Inside the cubicle, an open gutter brimmed with raw sewage. He was unfastening his trousers when Tong's right hand shot out, pulled him around and punched him in the solar plexus. Before the driver knew what was happening, another punch. This one threw him off-balance. He staggered. Screamed. Before he could fight back, Tong delivered the final blow. Hard. The young man tripped backward, teetering, waving his arms like a drowning man. His mouth let out rasping sounds. Confusion and terror filled his eyes. He tilted his head for a look at his assailant. Lost his balance. Tong grabbed him before he stumbled into the sewer. He held him upright and locked the wire around his neck, the metal cutting into tender flesh. The man choked, gasped. He lurched about, hands pulling frantically at the wire, his urine a wild arc on the wall. Tong tightened the noose, kept at it until the man went limp.

Tong let go. The body slumped next to the gutter. He bent down and felt the driver's neck, avoiding the line of blood oozing around the throat. No pulse. That was quick. Even for the young, the line between life and death was thin. He was glad he didn't have to use the knife; the sight of more blood would have unnerved him. He peered out. The knoll was as empty as before. The noise in the dining room could have obscured the screams. The cook might have heard but decided not to get involved in the brawl. Tong pulled the body out of the shack, dragged it behind a tree, flipped it over, and went through the clothes, doing his best to ignore the trembling in his hands. The belongings were distributed evenly in the pockets: the key to the van; a badge with Han's insignia; a photograph of a girl, much smudged; a piece of low-grade jade shaped like a scythe; a lock of hair wrapped in a handkerchief embroidered with a pair of mandarin ducks; money; a map of the route from Shansui to Nanking with hand-drawn symbols of landmarks on the way. The possessions summed up the man: peasant stock, illiterate, and he had a sweetheart.

A novice of life, who believed good deeds deserved just rewards and happiness lay in a woman's eyes.

Tong shook off the young man's face, though he knew the image would stay with him for a long time. Why did it feel different this time? The man's youth? Or have I killed one man too many?

He hadn't grown numb to killing. Maybe that was a good thing.

He undressed the corpse. The feel of the smooth skin was hard to bear, soft like a child's; it evoked paternal feelings he had decided long ago he didn't possess. He took off his own jacket and put on the man's. It was tight; he had to squeeze into it. As he buttoned it up, he registered a scene of jasmine, undoubtedly from an affectionate farewell with the girl. The accumulating evidence of young love was getting tedious. He tore up the photograph and threw the pieces along with the lock of hair to the wind. He lugged the corpse to the edge of the slope. Pushed. Wiping his mouth with the back of his hand, he watched the body roll, gathering leaves and dirt, sluggishly at first until it hit a steep incline, then tumbling until it vanished out of sight.

He took the shortest way back to the road. He wouldn't be surprised if someone in the roadhouse noticed his change of clothes and the missing young driver. He wasn't concerned. The long war had numbed people to violence. Even if some fool decided to inform the police, nothing would happen to him. In this part of China, the Blue Shirts reigned supreme.

He unlocked the van. Its interior was like a rich man's den. The seats were nicely curved; the gear stick was made of polished wood and gleaming metal. There were twice as many knobs and switches as his jeep. He was studying the dashboard when something in the rear view mirror caught his eye. He got out and unlocked the back door.

A single trunk sat in the center like an altar in a sanctuary.

It was the size of a child's coffin, constructed of premium camphor wood and bolted with an intricate lock he knew he couldn't pick with the few tools he had. The trunk was held in place by neat stacks of sandbags, accompanied by a wheeled cart of identical size, custom made for easy transport. He gave the trunk a push. Heavy as a block of lead. What was being delivered to the spymaster in Nanking that required a special courier traveling across five provinces? Cash? Opium? Guns? The chopped-up body of a rival? Too bad the instructions didn't include examining the cargo.

Whatever it was, a motorcar would have been sufficient to haul it and would have saved two thirds the fuel, enough money to feed a family of four for a month. But then, General Han was famous for his excesses.

3

It was a gentleman's drawing room, the atmosphere redolent of polished mahogany and aged brandy. Gainsborough imitations brightened the dark paneled walls. Ripped leather club chairs gathered around green-shaded lamps. A raised hearth held a blazing fire. The windows looked out on a tangle of bare trees, lumps of gray snow weighing down the branches; and, as a reminder to the members of Nanking's Europe Club where they were, the gabled roof of a Chinese temple.

Lunch was long over; most guests had left. Those who remained sat in small groups, smoking cigars and drinking cognac. Three men, two Caucasian and one Chinese, sat by the fireplace.

"Four years in this godforsaken country, coming to an end," said Jeremias Van Gilder to his companions, Henry Li and John Rabe. "I'm going to miss this."

"Don't leave," Rabe said simply. "I'm staying. I'll tell the daikon-heads to go to hell. That's what everyone in Asia should do. The Japs are bullies. Bullies prey on the weak. Stand up to them and they crumble."

Van Gilder was in his late forties, blond, tall and broad-shouldered. He wore a black turtleneck sweater and brown wool trousers. An officer of the Dutch embassy, he had the title of commercial attaché. Key personnel had been ordered to leave the Chinese capital; Van Gilder would join the last group to depart. Rabe, a German, was brown-haired and medium-built, his dark suit well pressed and white shirt starched. Round-rimmed glasses rested on the bridge of his nose. He had worked for Siemens China Company for thirty years. The third man was Henry Li, professor of European history at Nanking University and a member of the local elite. He wore a tweed jacket, a maroon silk cravat, cashmere trousers, and leather wing tips. One of the few Chinese who conversed in fluent English and German, he was popular in the European community. It was the first day of Nanking University's winter break. Henry was lunching with his two closest friends.

"I go where I am assigned—that's the life of a Foreign Service officer," Van Gilder said. "My wife can't wait to leave. She's been complaining since we got off the ship. She thinks China is alien and sinful."

"But that's the attraction," Rabe remarked with a wink.

"You are not concerned about the bombings?" Henry asked Rabe.

"Of course I'm concerned, but I don't see leaving as a viable alternative. I've lived here most of my life. My family is here, my friends are here; everything I've worked for is in China."

"Germany and Japan are on good terms. You are a prominent citizen running an international company. They would leave you alone."

"I'm counting on that. And I want to do more. I'm going to ask for a Safety Zone for foreign residents," Rabe said.

"Only for foreign residents?"

"I'll call it that so it'll hard for the Japs to say no. But it'll be for anyone who needs help." To Henry: "When are you leaving with your Generalissimo?"

There was an inch of brandy left in his glass. Henry rolled the stem between his fingers and watched the liquid tremble like a golden lake in a storm.

"The date hasn't been set yet," he said quietly.

"No? It has to be soon. The Kuomintang is shutting down the offices. The Party chiefs are packing up. We heard Chiang and his Madame have already picked out their new palace in Chungking," Van Gilder said. "They're taking the National Museum with them."

The government hadn't announced the relocation to the public, but word had gotten out. The move involved the entire Kuomintang apparatus; it would be impossible to keep it secret. But the mention of the National Museum was unexpected. The transport of art objects had been done under tight security. Who was the Dutchman's source?

"It would be quite a feat to move the National Museum to Chungking," Henry said as calmly as before.

"We've never expected Chiang to admit openly that he won't put up a good fight, but does he believe he can bolt with truckloads of antiquities without being noticed? I thought you would give him better advice, Henry, as a member of his shadow cabinet."

"'Shadow' is the operative word," Rabe remarked half-teasingly. "Henry is not supposed to be anybody important and he is not supposed to have access to state secrets."

"My wife is related to the Generalissimo's brother-in-law. I get to attend the parties and drink the *mao-tai*. That's about it."

"You are among friends and you won't see one of us for a while. Why not tell us what you really do for your Generalissimo?"

"I advise him on matters related to my scholarly training: history of Europe, art, culture. Unimportant topics for a head of state who is engaged in a war. Quite useless, frankly. Kai-shek likes the idea of having an academician in his cabinet. He rarely calls on my services."

"What a waste of your talents."

"That suits me fine. I don't have much interest in politics."

Van Gilder's eyes were unblinking. "We've always assumed the cabinet position is a cover. You keep a low profile because your real work is done behind the scenes. And all these years we have been exchanging confidences with the spymaster of China."

Henry's heart missed a beat—it was the first time the Dutchman made the inference. It wouldn't surprise him that his friends suspected a covert role. He hoped Van Gilder assumed the spying was being carried out on behalf of the Kuomintang. Not for a warlord with plans to overthrow the government.

"You have an active imagination, Jerry."

"If you can't tell us what you do, we understand."

"You set the rules," Henry protested. "You made us promise not to talk about work here. So we never did, unless it was something in the papers. You know about my family, my students, and the books I read. But, my friend, how many secrets have you shared with us? You wouldn't even trust us with the name of your mistress."

Van Gilder took the bait and switched the topic. "I had to be discreet. Well, what does it matter now? Her name is Yuan-yuan."

"Where did you find her? Was it love at first sight? Is she ravishing? We want the details."

"I met her at the Peony Gardens during Winter Festival last year. The day my second life began. My lovely China doll. Dimples, long straight hair, skin soft like a young peach, and curves..." He trailed off. The thought of her warmed him. He rubbed the moisture on his brow with the tip of his napkin. "Go see her. Will you do that for me? Tell her to be patient. Tell her I'll come back for her as soon as I can."

"She would like it better if she heard from you."

"Don't I wish! We're leaving tomorrow, crack of dawn. Tell her I am a good man and I keep my promises. After the war, I'll put in a request to be reassigned here. I'll divorce my wife and marry her. We'll find a fabulous house on Purple Gold Mountain. Like the one you built, Henry. I am going to do the things I've always wanted to do. With my true love."

His declarations caused a moment of wistful speculation. The uncertain future returned to the forefront of their minds.

"I wonder what China will be like after the war."

"First, let's hope we survive the war."

"Few will if we don't. We are more fortunate than most."

Were they more fortunate? Henry wondered. The recent hailstorms had not been reassuring. Ice balls large as eggs were hitting the city at odd hours. In Chinese folklore, hailstones are precursors of disaster. The omen had proven accurate on past occasions. Everyone was worried. With or without a supernatural sign, the country was heading for a difficult war. Japanese bombings were escalating in the northeast. Like Shanghai, Nanking was expected to fall quickly.

"Maybe America will intervene and save China."

"America will sit on the fence as long as they can."

"Maybe God will intervene."

"Whose God? The Christians'? The Muslims'? What about the Buddhists and the atheists? We'd need more wars to sort that out."

They shared a nervous laugh, and then sadness came upon them, along with a sense of doom. Van Gilder emptied his glass in one pull and filled it up again. He passed the bottle to Rabe who did the same.

Rabe cradled his glass with both hands. "I hope this is the last war in our lifetime."

"Don't you wish you'd been born in a different period in history, when people went about their lives in peace, free of war and suffering?"

"Was there ever such a period in history?"

"Better yet, not to have been born at all."

"*Come what come may, time and hour run through the roughest day.*"

"Let's drink to that."

They clinked glasses.

A waiter approached the table. "Professor Li?"

"Yes?"

The waiter handed Henry an envelope. "This is for you."

Rabe and Van Gilder watched as Henry pulled out a piece of paper folded twice. After one glance, Henry slipped it into his pocket.

"Sorry, I have to go," Henry said. "Summons from my wife."

"Is everything all right?"

"She wants me home. She's nervous about the baby. You know how new mothers are."

"Too bad I'm going to miss your son's birthday banquet," Van Gilder said. "We would change our itinerary if we could, but everything is fully booked out of Nanking."

"We'll have a banquet when the war's over."

They stood in a small circle, shaking hands in turn.

"Have a safe journey home," Henry said to Van Gilder.

"I'll see you again, I know I will," Van Gilder said, thick in his throat. "And you, John, go easy on the Japs. They are just vicious little turds who kill without mercy."

The sky was overcast, a blend of sulfur yellow and charcoal. A typical December day in Nanking, though Henry knew it would be anything but typical for him. He had never been summoned at the Club. There was obvious risk in sending for him with the foreign elite looking on. It had to be bad news.

A black Ford sedan with curtained windows pulled up to the curb. He climbed in and nodded at the familiar face in the rear view mirror. Without a word, the driver rammed the car into gear and careened into traffic, heading to Hunan Road. Henry took out the note and read it again. Nothing except the code for a rush meeting.

The estate occupied an entire block. A three-story limestone surrounded by high walls topped with barbed wire. The architecture was part monastery, part barracks. The exterior was painted in gray, the windows trimmed in drab green. The garden was a flat lawn outlined by sharply trimmed hedges. Two sentries manned the front. At the sight of the car, they unbolted and pulled back the gate. The driver swung up to the entrance and let Henry out.

The door was nine feet tall, constructed of wood six inches thick and framed in steel. Henry pressed the bell. An armed guard opened.

No salute. No greeting. "Third floor, Mr. Li."

The black marble floor of the foyer was smudged with fresh footprints. A big gathering had been here. Henry listened as he climbed the stairs. No domestic noises. No meetings in session. He sensed a hushed tension, as though people were watching through keyholes and holding their breath.

Reaching the third floor, he knocked on the door in the center.

"Come in."

The sitting room was furnished like the reception area of an office. A long sofa, two chairs, a coffee table with a black telephone and an ashtray. A day calendar hung on the wall, a thin stack remaining for the year. The window looked out to ancient rooftops crumbling in the afternoon light. Chiang Kai-shek presided from the center of the sofa. He wore the gray robe of a Chinese patriarch, a black wool scarf bundled around his neck, his bald peanut-shaped head shiny in a ray of light. A glance might give the impression of a monk in a state of enlightenment, until one noticed the black stare and the rows of coarse hair above his lip. His American-educated wife, Soong May-ling, took the chair by his side. Hair done up and face flawlessly painted, she was dressed for a cocktail party. A pink cashmere throw was draped over a silk cheongsam in chartreuse; her stockinged legs were crossed to show off her signature open-toed pumps. She smiled like she was looking at cameras.

"Sit," Chiang ordered.

"Hello, Henry," Madame Chiang murmured in English as Henry took the other chair.

One look was enough. A fundamental shift in their relationship had taken place since the last time he saw his wife's cousins.

"How are you, Generalissimo and Madame?" Henry began politely. "I was having lunch with the Dutch commercial attaché and a German friend when your message came. I told them it was from my wife. The note said top priority. I wondered what…"

"I've asked General Tang Sheng-chin to be in charge of Nanking after we move the government to Chungking," Chiang announced without preamble.

Tang, an old timer from the days of Sun Yat-sen, had openly disputed Chiang's legitimacy as Party leader. What had prompted Chiang to pick him to guard the erstwhile capital? Why was this the first thing Chiang said to him?

"Has Tang accepted the offer?" Henry asked.

"He was ready to serve the moment I asked. This is a critical time. Tang and I have our differences, but we've put them aside. We are patriots and we must do what is best for the good of the country."

Henry decided that Tang's reaction could have a variety of meanings. He didn't know the man and had no way of figuring out the politics of the new position.

"Tang will oversee regional security. Policy decisions, of course, will continue to be made by the central government. Because of your proficiency in European languages, I want you to assist him in matters related to foreigners in the city. You will have the title of Provisional Minister of Foreign Communications for the City of Nanking. You will report to Tang."

"But I won't be here. We are going to Chungking…"

"I changed my mind. You will not be leaving Nanking. You will stay and join the defense team."

"I have no experience in defense. I won't be any use to Tang."

"Support from the international community will be critical in maintaining order. Tang will need an intermediary, someone who speaks their languages and knows their ways. You have the right skills and you will act as conduit between the municipal administration and the foreign communities. Experience in defense is not necessary."

"Aren't you already chummy with most of them?" Soong May-ling smiled broadly. "Darling of the Europe Club, I heard."

"What about my family?" Henry asked.

"They stay with you."

"For how long?"

"As long as it takes."

"It could be weeks, months."

"Not if you and Tang do your job. Get the Japanese out of Nanking quickly."

"To do that, we will need the full force of the Kuomintang army behind us."

"The Army will be protecting the new administration in Chungking. If you need help, you can convince your foreign friends to lend a hand."

"Su-chen and I are set to leave. The staff has been given notice. The house will be shut down." Henry couldn't keep the anxiety out of his voice. "Our baby. He is only a month old. I don't want him here when the Japanese come."

"Personal concerns have no place in a time of national crisis," Chiang said sharply. "You are an officer of the government. Your first duty is to defend the country."

You are the top officer of the government, yet it's clear that your first duty is to save your own skin.

Soong May-ling, who had never given birth to a child or reared one, declared with feeling, "Imagine having a second child after so many years. Poor Su-chen must be overwhelmed. I heard it was a difficult birth."

"It was. Su-chen is still recovering. She shouldn't be in a war zone."

"It's unnatural for a woman her age to bear children," she went on, admiring her red lacquered fingernails. "She is lucky to have survived the pregnancy and gotten herself a son. If her health suffers as a result, it's not the government's problem." A flutter of eyelashes. "I say things are turning out in her favor. She will be spared the difficulties of a long journey. She can rest in her own home and nurse the baby in comfort."

"We didn't expect the journey to be difficult."

"These are difficult times, Henry. One shouldn't take anything for granted."

Neither should you. Wait till the Japs follow you to Chungking. He asked, "When will General Tang arrive?"

"Soon."

"Is there a date?"

"You will be notified when his itinerary is finalized."

"May I ask when my appointment will begin?"

"The moment we leave Nanking," Chiang said.

"When will that be?"

"You'll know when it happens."

"I'd like to know now. I need to tell my family."

"You'll know when we tell you."

Soong May-ling said with perfect insincerity, "My sister will miss Su-chen. Your wife is wonderful company. Docile, agreeable, predictable. It's the traditional upbringing—turns women into perfect pets. Not like us. We studied in America and we saw the world. We have big ideas and we speak our minds. Well, Ai-ling will have to make do with me. When Su-chen feels better, she can visit us. Bring the baby too."

"Thanks, Madame. I'll tell Su-chen. She'll like that," Henry said. "And Yunna too, of course." It would be good to get the family out of harm's way, even if he was stuck here.

"Hold off on making those plans. A man's family should be with him," Chiang said, as if reading Henry's thoughts. "I don't want anyone leaving Nanking until things are settled with the Japanese."

We'll be dead before it happens, since once again you are counting on foreigners to defend the country for you, Henry thought bitterly. Didn't you order bombs dropped on civilians in Shanghai's international district? You thought that was the way to get the European powers involved. You didn't care that it was the middle of the day and the bombs fell on crowds. Three years ago, you struck a secret deal with the Japanese. You withdrew the troops from Hupei and let them move inland. All because you didn't have the guts to fight a real war. Just as you are about to leave half a million people to die. What kind of leader are you? What kind of man? I am so glad I've been giving your secrets to General Han, your rival and soon your nemesis. Over the years there have been moments of doubt—have I served the right master? Not anymore. From this day on, I will do everything I can to destroy you.

Henry replied in his calmest voice: "The new arrangement was a surprise. I haven't had time to think things through; I didn't react appropriately. You are right, Generalissimo. These are extraordinary times; we must put aside our personal concerns for the country. I am grateful to be given the opportunity to serve the people of Nanking. My family shall stay and I shall do my best to assist General Tang."

He caught Soong May-ling's eye. *She knows that I know we are playing roles in a farce.* He returned the smile, phony to phony.

"Shall I prepare an announcement on the central government's relocation?" Henry went on. "I'm sure the foreign press is expecting one."

"No announcement until we are in Chungking," Chiang said with a wave of hand. "I don't want the damn foreign press following us."

"Except *Time*, darling," Soong May-ling purred. "We must have our friends with us."

"You told the people at *Time*?" Chiang asked.

"I spoke to Henry—Henry Luce—that we need peace and quiet to conduct state business. The bombings around here are getting to be a nuisance. He was sympathetic—he always is. He said he supports us no matter where we are. Such a dear friend."

Chiang looked irritated for a moment, and then he seemed to acquiesce that America was his wife's concern and left it at that.

He turned to Henry. "What about the stuff from the National Museum? How much more packing needs to be done?"

"The inventory turns out to be larger than expected. Last week, we discovered more carvings in the basement that had not been cataloged, artifacts from the Sheng and Hsia dynasties. They are fragile and needed to be placed in special crates. Those have to be custom built from scratch. The schedule has to be revised."

"How much more time?"

"An extra week and a half."

"I want a precise date."

"Ten days."

Chiang asked, "Your son's banquet is tomorrow night?"

"Yes."

"Have the packing done by then."

"That's not possible!"

"Make it possible. It's an order."

Henry seethed with impotent rage. "Maybe there's a chance if I quadrupled the staff, have them work round the clock. But there's no guarantee that…"

"Go ahead, quadruple the staff. And I want a different crew to do the loading."

"A different crew will cause more delay."

"It will safeguard the process."

"Is there reason to suspect the current process is not safe?"

"If we found the reason, it would be too late." Chiang quoted a proverb: "A boat can sail on the wind of caution for ten thousand years."

"Since we are on the topic of caution, allow me to make the point again. Ten days' work will have to be done in two. People make mistakes when they are hurried. We are working with priceless objects that must be handled with care."

"Point noted."

"There are other issues."

"What issues?"

"Should the police keep an eye on the coolies when they move the art pieces from the warehouse to the dock, or should the Army supervise? What about using the Blue Shirts as escorts? Certainly we can count on them to be discreet. They have an excellent relationship with you, except that it would mean trusting criminals with priceless national treasures. What about the inventory list? Should I deposit a copy in the National Archives, or would you prefer to have the records destroyed?"

"You ask too many questions," Soong May-ling cried, smiles gone.

"I am concerned because the art objects belong to the Chinese people. They are priceless and irreplaceable. We wouldn't want them in the wrong hands. Would we?"

Chiang's black stare intensified. "Just pack the damn stuff."

"In view of the new deadline, I'd better excuse myself." Henry got up. He had an urgent need to put a great distance between himself and them. "There is a lot to be done. I shouldn't waste another minute."

"I want reports on your progress every hour. And deliver them here."

"Anything else?"

"Give me your word that you will show up for your new appointment."

"The appointment is an honor and a privilege. Why would I be anywhere else?"

"We'll be thinking about you in Chungking," said Soong May-ling.

It would be better if I were sacked, Henry thought as he hurried out of the house. He and his family would be able to leave as private citizens. The Japanese were closing in by the hour. An order to stay was nothing short of a death sentence. Why did his wife's cousins want him and his family dead? What was behind the new urgency to speed up the packing of the museum objects? Why was the deadline set by his son's birthday banquet? Last week they were on the short list to evacuate, his family was to ride on Chiang's personal plane to Chungking. What had changed?

4

Shanghai. Paris of the East.

Gone mad, Victor Maurier thought.

He was looking out from a corner booth at the Vienna Gardens, a fantasy of a European dance hall decorated by someone who had never seen the real thing. An octagon painted in cream illuminated by rose-shaped lamps mounted on the walls; half the bulbs had been out since last Christmas. Plaster angel heads hovered over the moldings. Dirt had accumulated in the recesses, outlining curly hair and hollow eye sockets, making them look like beheaded orphans from the slums. The stage was draped in crushed red velvet, purple lights blinking wildly along the platform. A five-man band was playing a medley of Benny Goodman tunes. Couples were moving to their own beat; the ones remaining at the tables were chatting noisily. No one seemed to mind that outside the swing doors, beggars lay crouched on the pavement, fighting with rats for food scraps, or that half the population of the city was dying of hunger and untreated wounds.

"Well, Mr. Shiozawa?" Victor said to the Japanese across the table.

Shiozawa was a comic book caricature of an Oriental bully: slit eyes, walrus moustache, and a strand of hair sprouting from a wart on his chin. His military jacket was covered with medals; they jingled like warning bells when he moved. He was feeding himself a slab of roast beef smothered in a thick sauce. Victor had ordered an English mixed grill, and had hardly touched the platter of chops and sausages.

"Quite an inventory," Shiozawa replied, wiping his mouth with a napkin. "It took my men hours to go over the list."

"Best stuff we've seen in years."

"Price?"

"Market rate. Sixty cents on the dollar."

"Wholesale?"

"Wholesale."

Shiozawa tossed the last morsel of beef into his mouth, chewing noisily. "The prevailing rate is forty."

"That gets you second-rate goods from secondhand markets. This is top-of-the-line merchandise from the Kremlin arsenal. Brand new. The best outside America."

Shiozawa frowned. " 'The best outside America.' Why do people assume America sets the standard for the rest of the world?"

"Because they are taking over the world; it certainly seems so from here."

Victor stared at his own haggard face in the mirror on the wall. Bags under the eyes, pallid cheeks with a three-day stubble, blond hair needing a wash. He looked like hell, as he should. He had spent the last thirty-six hours fielding prospective buyers for the Russian arsenal, dashing around Shanghai like a man on the run, living on coffee and cigarettes, barely sleeping. His boss Soong Tse-ven—T.V. Soong to the world—had ordered the deal closed before the weekend. It would be their final deal in Shanghai before they shut down the operation. The Japanese bombings were escalating. The high and mighty Soong family was ready to bolt.

So am I, he thought. I could use a holiday in the Lu Mountains, a good rest and a long soak in the hot springs before the Japs bomb out the country. I'll take my Chinese mistress along. Lillie. Beautiful and wild and insatiable. We'll make Clouds and Rain in the hot springs under the stars. It's the only way we haven't yet made love…

"Are the goods really from Moscow?" Shiozawa asked.

"Being unloaded from a Trans-Siberia train as we speak."

"Why are the Russians selling?"

"They are Soviet Big Brother's gift to the Chinese Communist Party. It happens that the supervising comrade general needs cash, fast. Don't know the circumstances. We didn't ask, never do. He fudged the communication lines and had a portion of the load detoured to the black market. He expected their Chinese Communist brothers would be too grateful as to run a check on the inventory; even if they did, they couldn't complain that part of the gift was missing."

"Clever."

"Too clever. We weren't convinced a Soviet general would take that kind of risk. Maybe some rank-and-file fabricated the story, trying to make a quick killing while the bosses weren't looking. Things can get messy without the proper authority backing up the deal—the Kremlin isn't your friendly neighborhood store. We asked for verification. A week later we got a ton of flimsies in Russian. Inventory certificates. Leave it to the Socialist bureaucrats to produce a paper trail for a black market deal."

"The Russians couldn't have forgotten Port Arthur and Liaoyang. You are sure there are no restrictions as to who can bid?"

"We weren't informed of any. The comrade general is a pragmatist. Cash is cash."

"Forty-five cents on the dollar."

"Not negotiable. Not this one."

"Everything is negotiable, as your boss likes to say." Shiozawa shot a glance at the door by the stage. "He is here, isn't he? He's always around for something this big. Never shows his face, though. Bet his name isn't on the bank accounts either. Shrewd man." He dabbed the napkin on his mouth. "All right, we'll up the offer to forty-eight cents. American dollars. The money will be deposited in the account in Hong Kong, following established procedure."

"We had an offer of fifty. It was turned down."

"From whom?"

"I am not at liberty to say."

"I'll bet it was Gold Fox Han. He's the only man who has this kind of cash in China. That gold mine of his must be worth more than the whole damn country. Wish we'd got into the opium business with the Brits. We'd have our own gold mine in Kyoto now." With mock regret, "But it wouldn't have worked. The Japanese people are committed to healthy living. We are not like the Chinese—eat anything, smoke anything, and fornicate with their slaves. And they have the nerve to claim their culture is superior to ours." Shiozawa rolled the brandy glass between his pudgy fingers. "Have you seen Han's gold?"

"No one has, from what I've heard."

"Hard to believe."

"Not even the coolies who moved the gold. Han had them executed on their way out. The place is miles underground and protected by lethal traps only the warlord can disarm." Victor blew out rings of smoke. "That's what people say. Who knows if it's true or not."

"Profit margin for opium is three thousand percent. It's Britain's chief export and makes up more than half the country's income. The Han family has been in the business for a good part of a century. Their cut may not be as big as the Brits', but it has to be damn close. Easy to do the arithmetic. It has to be true."

"Some people say Han has all the gold in China."

Shiozawa wet his lips. "I'd give anything to get my hands on it."

"So would everyone who heard of the gold."

"There must be a way to find out where it is and how to neutralize the traps."

"I'm sure there is. No one has found it yet."

"We could just bomb out the whole damn place."

Victor stubbed out his cigarette. A wisp of smoke rose from the ashtray. His eyes followed it briefly. "Wouldn't that also destroy the gold?"

Shiozawa concluded with absolute certainty, "There won't be any need to destroy anything. China will become a vassal state of Japan. Han's gold will be our gold."

The man is going from one fantasy to the next, Victor thought. China is weak, but it's a big country that has weathered centuries of upheavals. And the Americans might get into the war and change the game.

Shiozawa resumed bargaining. "You can't cut the deal with Han. If you sold the arsenal to the warlord, your Generalissimo would have a fit."

"Our goods are sold strictly to the highest bidder."

A wink. "Never mix politics with the more serious business of making money."

"What's your best offer?"

"Fifty cents."

"Fifty-eight."

"We are not raising it a cent. It's *the* best offer you will get. Take it or leave it."

The Japanese must have known he didn't have any real competition. Since Soong was not willing to sell in parcels, who else in Asia could afford an arsenal big enough to blow up a province? The Koreans were poor. The countries in Southeast Asia were in the dark ages. The other warlords in China couldn't afford the staggering sum. Shiozawa had guessed right. Han did put in a bid. One had to admire the warlord, Victor thought. It took guts to challenge a party backed by the Americans. No doubt it helped that the man owned a gold mine the size of Tai Shan. Han's offer was turned down as soon as it reached Soong. Victor knew Soong wouldn't mind doing business with his brother-in-law's rival—if he could keep the deal secret. But he couldn't trust Han to do the same. Han would find the opportunity to brag about scoring the new Russian arsenal from Soong. Just so Chiang would lose face.

Face, Victor had learned, is the supreme driving force in China. A man can abandon his wife and children. But he cannot lose face.

When it became clear that the Japanese were the last resort, a call had been made to Manchukuo and connections onward to Tokyo. A day later, Shiozawa had shown up at the International Airsea office on Sikiang Road, one of the dummy outfits set up to handle Soong's private enterprises. Shiozawa had requested a meeting at Vienna Gardens, the code for placing a bid.

In the end, what did it matter whether it was Han or the Japanese who get their hands on the weapons? They would be used on the Chinese people.

Rotten country. Rotten times.

"I'll sweeten the deal, Mr. Maurier. I'll make things easy for you. You won't need to deliver the merchandise further than Nanking."

"You want the weapons in the capital?"

Shiozawa nodded.

"Why?"

No answer.

"*Why?*"

"Why would you care if it's the capital or a village in Tibet?" Shiozawa said with deliberate casualness. "You are not Chinese."

No, I'm *kweiloh*. Foreign devil. Big nose barbarian. I arrived with lofty ideals. To save Chinese souls for the church. To bring this ancient country into the modern world. But Sin City converted me instead, turned my holy inspiration into unholy aspiration. I ruined my marriage, made mountains of money, and fell in love with Shanghai's number one singsong girl. Hell may be waiting for me, but I don't regret any of it.

"French, aren't you?" Shiozawa continued. "Food and sex are your two obsessions. Like the Shanghainese. Nothing personal, but I prefer the Germans. Disciplined, efficient, strong-willed. Like us. You are a long way from home. You miss your country?"

"Not much. China is my home now."

"Serious?"

"I'm comfortable here."

"Money can buy a lot of comfort. You must have made a fortune working for Soong."

"Creature comforts can only mean so much. I love the culture and the people," Victor said, feeling an intense distaste for Shiozawa.

"That's commendable, considering what you do for Soong," Shiozawa said contemptuously. "Han had to build his opium empire gold brick by gold brick. It took Soong only a few years to amass his fortune. He must be the second-richest man in China by now. American foreign aid turns out to be as big a cash crop as opium. Nice seed money for the Soong family's business ventures. Your boss has his finger in everything: banking, real estate, forestry, oil, shipping. Hard to keep track, Mr. Soong finds ingenious ways to hide his assets. Tell me, did he acquire his business savvy at Harvard, or from his sisters who married the three most powerful men in China?"

Victor kept quiet.

"The Soongs are simply phenomenal," Shiozawa went on, eyebrows raised in mock awe. "Imagine how much more we would have to do if they were halfway decent. They are practically handing their country to us. Well, *selling* would be more apt. Your boss isn't the type who does anything for free."

Victor recited the official line: "Mr. Soong has no part in this."

"Of course not. Pardon me. Too much brandy loosens the tongue." He'd hardly had a drop. "Business is business. Selling arms is no different from selling rice. We are men of the world. Cheers."

"Cheers."

Victor emptied his glass automatically. He was bone-tired. Tired from the long week. Tired of years following another man's orders. Tired of his own greed and hypocrisy.

"Do we have a deal?"

"A deal…"

"Fifty cents on the dollar."

Victor felt cold tremors; a small glacier was cracking inside his body. He reached for the cigarette. His fingers were shaking. An inch of ash tumbled down the front of his jacket. He stared at the trail of gray flecks. He wanted to brush them off but couldn't get his hand to aim.

"Fifty cents on the dollar," Shiozawa repeated. "I thought we agreed."

Victor felt numb. All over. No sensation. Just a crippling chill. His spinal column seemed to be turning into ice. The cold was radiating outward to his limbs.

"We don't have all night. Let's close the deal and I can report back to my bosses."

The Japanese was turning into a formless mass, pulsating and expanding, filling up Victor's field of vision.

Shiozawa was getting impatient. "A handshake to conclude the damn deal. Like we always do. No contract, no signature…"

His mouth was moving, but Victor couldn't hear a word. The room rocked like a boat on a rough sea. Lights blurred. Noises faded. A thundering silence enveloped him. He felt weightless, insubstantial, empty. Glimmers of moving shadows began to appear. Shapes crawling around, rodents, snakes, creatures of the night. Cobwebs everywhere, clinging like thick strands of fog. The air was damp and tepid. He was standing by a mass grave. A hollow in the ground filled with human remains. I am dying. I am already dead... He tried to breathe, swallow, and blink his eyes. Nothing. His body seemed to have dissolved away. How could this be? Two hours ago I was in Lillie's arms. Moments ago I was drinking brandy... I can still taste it. Wait. If I can taste the brandy, I can't be dead. He breathed again and managed a tiny gasp. He kept it up until he was drawing in air, taking in smells of cheap scent and cigarette smoke. His retina shimmered. His eyes began to clear. Images were pulling into focus. More air. He stretched his palms and forced them outward, fingertips feeling the curlicue in the wooden arms of the chair. I didn't die, thank God. It was a momentary blackout, that's all. It must be the stress. I need rest. And Lillie. We need to go away. From Shanghai. From China.

The chill had not left. He was shivering.

"Are you all right, Mr. Maurier?"

A nod.

"I wasn't sure what happened to you. You didn't respond to anything I said. I was about to ask the waiter if he could find a doctor."

"No need. I'm fine."

"You looked like you were seeing a ghost."

"Too much brandy on an empty stomach." Victor managed a smile and finished what was left in the glass. A retching cough followed.

"Let's get you some hot tea."

"Later." Victor staggered out of his chair. "Excuse me for a moment."

He steadied his gait and headed to the door by the stage.

Five knocks.

"Come in."

Victor stepped inside and closed the door. "He is offering fifty."

Soong looked up. The face was middle-aged and ordinary. The thinning hair was brushed back over a generous crown. The eyes behind dark rim glasses were black marbles set in shallow sockets; a thick nose. He was dressed formally, double-breasted jacket in brown cashmere, gleaming white shirt, pink rose in the buttonhole. He sat on a swivel chair behind a mahogany desk, reading a leather-bound ledger under a fluorescent lamp. A charcoal brazier warmed the room. The air was stale like a tomb. The windows had been shut for months. For good reason: the view was the spot along the river where the city's dead were dumped.

"Is that the best you can do?" Soong said.

"I opened at sixty. He bargained it down. Won't budge. He knows they are the only game in town."

"Sit down. You look awful."

Victor eased himself into the chair facing the desk. Like the other chairs in the office, it had a shorter stump than the host's armchair. He had to look up at Soong.

"Something happened when I was talking to Shiozawa. I had a seizure. It was bad."

"Don't get sick until you're done. Did Shiozawa agree to the usual terms?"

"Yes."

"Let's close the deal. I want to get out of here."

"There is one thing. They want the goods in Nanking."

"Good. Save on transportation cost."

"Shouldn't that worry you?"

"Why?"

"It can only mean one thing."

Soong didn't ask what it was.

Victor continued, "I don't think we should go along."

"Why not? Even fifty cents on the dollar will make us a ton of money."

"I am not talking about money."

"What else is there?"

"It's no secret that the Japanese are planning an attack on Nanking. What if they use the arsenal for that purpose?"

"The weapons came from Russia."

"But we're the ones delivering the goods."

"There are at least two dozen big-time dealers in Shanghai, plus a hundred small ones in the shade. Guns are bought and sold every day. Who can prove we brokered the deal?"

"The Japanese can, and will, if and when it suits their purposes. We've done business with them. We've been careful, but it's more than likely that they have collected a few mementos over the years. Shiozawa made a point of saying he knows you're here. This is a lot of firepower and it will do a lot of damage."

Soong made a noncommittal shrug.

"If China's capital is attacked, it will make headlines around the world. Countries might join together and condemn Japan. The Japanese wouldn't like it. They might decide to expose your association with Airsea and let us share the blame. It would diffuse their culpability and shift the attention to you. It would be disastrous if the world finds out the Generalissimo's brother-in-law supplied weapons to the enemy for the attack on the capital."

It was not something Soong wanted to hear and he looked very displeased. "Who would believe that *I* helped to destroy the city where my relatives live? It's too preposterous."

You won't be here when the Japanese open fire, Victor replied in silence. You and your sisters and their husbands will be safely ensconced in Chungking.

"Even if they try, there won't be any evidence to support the claim," Soong went on. "My name is not on anything. Not the books. Not the incorporation papers. There has never been a contract, a receipt, or a single scrap of paper with my name on it. I own the bank in Hong Kong and my people will bury the money so deep even our own auditors won't find it. If the press wants to put the blame on Airsea, well, it would mean you, Victor. You are the manager of the company and you are the one who put the deal together."

Thanks a lot, Victor thought. "What about the Generalissimo? He won't like being dragged into something like this."

"I'll give Kai-shek an extra cut of the profits. That'll make him happy. Always does." An affirmative nod. "As far as my brother-in-law is concerned, there is nothing for you to worry about. Big Sister will make sure you stay on our good side. You know you can count on that."

Big Sister was Ai-ling, oldest daughter of the Soong family and wife to H.H. Kung, Minister of the Treasury. Victor had been her lover briefly after he quit his missionary work. When her husband grew suspicious, she had ended the affair and convinced her brother to give Victor the lucrative job at International Airsea. To ensure his continued discretion.

"Big Sister still speaks fondly of you—only to me, of course. You made quite an impression on her."

"That was a long time ago."

"Women don't forget, especially when they were in love."

"Please, Paul," Victor said uncomfortably, using Soong's English name.

"Hard to miss the twinkle in her eye whenever your name comes up. That was her first affair—the only affair, as far as I know. Big Sister is old-fashioned."

Victor had no doubt that Soong had brought up his sister to soften him. He said blankly, "My relationship with Mrs. Kung was a brief incident that happened years ago. She is a friend. More accurate, an acquaintance. I would prefer to keep her out of what we do."

"My sister would be heartbroken if she heard what you said, but I won't be the one to tell her." The business tone returned. "There is always risk of scandal because of who I am. There are people out there who like nothing better than to see me go down. I can handle them. We can handle them. It's not like we haven't been in similar situations before. Nothing has gone wrong and nothing will."

"It feels different this time. I have a premonition."

"What?"

"When we were about to close the deal, I was looking Death in the face. It was not my imagination. It was a real, physical thing."

"Your seizure," Soong remarked with a frown.

"I am not a novice, Paul. We have cut riskier deals, done business with worse people. But this one is different. I'm not sure if I can go through with it." Victor lifted his eyes to the wall behind the desk, speaking to Soong's shadow. "Something dreadful is going to happen in Nanking. I can feel it in my bones. A deeply evil thing. I don't want to any part of it."

As if underscoring Victor's point, the orchestra brought the music to a crescendo and ended with a bang.

Soong pulled back his chair and regarded Victor firmly. "Dreadful things have been happening in China for the past three hundred years—the Manchus, the Taipings, the Europeans, the Japanese. You've heard the Chinese saying: Turn a risky situation on its head and you score an opportunity." He raised his hands over the ledger on the desk, blessing it. "We are *here*, making money, having the time of our lives. That's what is real. You are exhausted. We get shaky when we are tired. Happens to the best of us."

"But…"

"I'll let you have a holiday after you close the deal. You've earned it. Take your mistress along. Book a suite at the Gloucester in Hong Kong. I am a partner. You'll be my guests and they'll treat you right."

"Thanks. But please let someone else handle this."

"There is no time. I don't care if you had ten seizures. The deal has to close tonight." Soong licked a finger and turned a page. "Your customer is waiting. Go back and shake the Jap's hand."

5

Having had time to think, Henry concluded there was only one explanation for Chiang's decision to leave him and his family behind: his cover had been blown. All along he had anticipated his secret life would catch up with him, but he never expected it to happen at a critical moment when he needed Chiang's help to take his family out of harm's way.

How did Chiang find out? How long had he known? What else would Chiang do to him and his family?

What if he stayed? How much danger would there be? He wouldn't rely on the Chinese Army to protect the city from the Japanese. Chiang would take the best troops to Chungking; the ones left behind wouldn't survive the first attack. He could ask Rabe for help. The German was serious about organizing a Safety Zone. But how long would the Safety Zone remain safe? Even a tenacious foreigner like Rabe couldn't keep bullets from hitting civilians. There was also his new position. Tang wouldn't let him hide in a foreigners' shelter.

Staying was *not* an alternative.

They had to leave. Fast. Canceling his son's birthday banquet would tip Chiang off and spur him to take immediate action. Until he had a plan, he and his family had to carry on as if he was following orders. How to get away? Every train, plane, and boat out of Nanking was fully booked. They could drive. There was the risk of being recognized at checkpoints, but the guards could be bribed. They would get far away from the capital, hide in a village, and see how the situation developed with the Japanese before making the next move. He didn't have friends living in a village. He and his family would have to rely on strangers' discretion. An even greater risk. What about money? Counting on his wife's relatives, he had prepared only for six months' expenses. Most of his assets were in real estate and stocks overseas. It would take time to liquidate them. He had cash in local banks, but making big withdrawals would arouse suspicion. There were jewelry and antiques in the house, but they might not be enough. The exile could last years.

The odds seemed insurmountable.

He had fooled Chiang for twelve years. No reason why he couldn't for two more days. He would find a way out, even if it would mean calling in every favor, selling his wife's jewelry, or taking some of the antiques from National Museum.

He was drafting various escape routes when a servant knocked on the door and reported a delivery from Shansui. It had been expected. A key had arrived in a pouch the day before. He cleared his desk, glad of a distraction.

"Send the man in," he said to the servant.

Alone again, he retrieved the pouch from the drawer.

The servant returned and held the door open for a man dressed in the uniform of Han's couriers. He was wheeling in a trunk on a cart.

"Good day, Professor Li. General Han sends his greetings. Where should I put the trunk?"

"Right here."

He slid the trunk off the cart. It landed with a loud thud. The wood floor vibrated. Han had never sent anything this large or heavy. The man was someone he had never seen.

"You drove all the way from Shansui?" he asked the man.

"Yes, Professor."

"What's your name?"

"Tong."

"Never heard of you."

"I usually handle the westbound routes."

"Westbound——that would be Yunnan, Szechwan, Tibet…" Henry held his gaze. "But you are a native Shanghainese."

"I went to work for General Han recently."

"How recently?"

"About a month ago."

"Who hired you?"

"Someone in General Han's Shanghai office."

"Who?"

"He said I was to call him Mr. Chang. I wasn't sure if it was his real name. After I was hired, he said General Han needed an extra driver in Shansui and sent me there." Tong presented a badge with Han's insignia. "The regular man had a death in the family. I was a last-minute replacement."

"There is no regular man for Nanking."

"That was what I was told, Professor."

Henry glanced at the man's left cuff and located the black button in the row of bronze, the code of Han's convoys to him. He took the key out of the pouch and inserted it into the trunk's lock. Clicked. He left the key there but didn't open the trunk.

"I am to drive back tomorrow morning. I don't know anyone in Nanking. Could I have a bed for the night?" Tong asked, keeping his head down.

Henry said to his servant, "Arrange that."

"Thank you, Professor."

"We are having a party tonight. Mind giving my staff a hand?"

"Not at all."

Alone, Henry locked the door and drew the drapes. He went to the trunk and lifted the lid. The top was the expected layer of coded camouflage: newspapers from exactly one month ago and a copy of *Legend of the Water Margin* with a circle on page 15. Folds of velvet. Something flashed underneath. A piercing brilliance. Reaching down, his fingertips came into contact with cold surfaces. Round and hard. Cannon balls? Marble globes?

He scooped one up.

A gold sphere with a cleft down one side. Sculpture of a peach. He turned on the desk lamp and examined it in the light. Solid gold. Peach is the symbol of longevity. A trunkful of them. They were Han's present for his son's birthday.

There was a letter.

My friend:

Congratulations on this joyful occasion. I would have come to Nanking to deliver my good wishes in person, but our former emperor has accepted my invitation and I have to be here.

Henry, let me get to the point. I want you in Shansui. Not to visit, but to live. The director of the Shansui regional museum will retire and you will succeed him. The position will be your new cover.

My contact in Tsingtao reports things are progressing as planned. A preliminary agreement has been reached with Berlin. The months ahead will be critical as I launch my Grand Strategy. I need you here. I know you are going to Chungking with Peanut Head. Turn it down. If Peanut Head and his cronies suspect, let them, though I'm sure you can come up with a perfect explanation for the change of plans.

Remember those nights when we talked about my vision of a renewed old China? You understood right away what I had in mind, and what it would take to turn my dream into reality. I knew then that I found a soul mate in you. If a man can find one true friend, he will die a happy man. *I, of course, have no intention of dying. But it pleases me that you are my friend.*

Enclosed is a token of my affection. One hundred and thirty-eight peaches — one for each month of our friendship. The appointment letter from the museum will follow.

Give my regards to your beautiful wife. And nine thousand happy returns to your son.

> *General Han Tang-ming*
> *Crescent Moon Villa*
> *Shansui City, Shansui*

Henry read the letter one more time before he slipped it into the brazier. A tiny flame flared up. He watched the paper writhe, blacken, and dissolve into ashes.

All his problems were solved.

To hell with Chiang, the Kuomintang, the order to stay in Nanking. Shansui would be his new home. He and his family would live in Han's secure compound protected by Shansui's superb army. He would have to sever his ties in Nanking: his wife's family, the university, the Party. It would be a small price for their safety, and a huge prize if Han won the country.

"You are my other half," Han had said heartily after Henry's first success as his spymaster. "Between us we make one great man. We are the leadership China has been waiting for."

If Han only knew.

He never shared Han's vision of a resurrected feudal China. The years in Europe had given him a different perspective on history and politics. The Industrial Revolution had changed the world forever. Feudalism had become irrelevant. It might take longer for China to catch on, but no one could stop the tide of progress. But he had seen no pointing in trying to dissuade Han from his fantasy of an imperial utopia. Han had never been outside China and he wouldn't give up his obsession because of anything anyone said. Cautionary advice would be taken as dissent and Han had no tolerance for dissent, however well meant. Henry had gone along, made the appropriate admiring noises, and let Han believe he was an ardent supporter.

As long as his own prosperity was ensured, Henry didn't care who governed the country and with what political system. He was not a man driven by ideology. His convictions were formed from personal experience, not from lofty ideals. When he was recruited to spy on the Kuomintang leadership, he had accepted the job for one reason: money. Money to restore his family estate and the aristocratic life style he had missed. Money to be independent of his wife's powerful family. Money to let him live as he pleased.

To live as he pleased…

Would that be possible in Shansui?

He would be at Han's beck and call. Every day. Round the clock. Han as neighbor, landlord, and boss. Henry was not sure he wanted one person to have that much control over his life. And there were bigger concerns. What if things didn't turn out the way Han planned? Worse, what if Han pulled off his crazy deal with Berlin and blew up the world? How much did he believe in Han? Enough to risk his family's safety and their future?

Henry picked up a gold peach. It sank reassuringly in his palm. The rest shone like treasures out of a fairy tale. But they were not figments of his imagination. Gold. What could be more real?

One hundred and thirty-eight gold peaches. What would be the worth?

Out of the bright yellow haze a wild idea leaped at him.

Noises interrupted his thoughts. He closed the lid of the trunk and listened. Hurried steps, animated voices of a gathering coming in the direction of the front lawn. Excitement, not panic. It sounded like the prelude to a street demonstration. That was odd. The house was in a secluded part of Purple Gold Mountain, the most exclusive residential neighborhood in the city. Not a choice location for public protests. The grand residences attracted an occasional burglar. But in broad daylight?

Don't tell me someone has already found out about the trunk of gold.

He took his pistol out of the drawer, a Luger in an imprinted case with a cleaning brush. It was a birthday present from Han. Flown in from Germany, custom made for his spymaster. Han had become partial to things German after meeting an arms dealer, a native of Bremen living in Tsingtao. The German was an old China hand who had impressed Han with his network of international traders. The two had become friends. In Han's world, no friendship would be complete without conspiracy—the German was involved with Han's secret deal with Berlin. Henry checked the gun's chamber. Full. The last time he fired the weapon, it had been the hunting trip with Van Gilder and members of the Europe Club. Everyone else had brought rifles, but Henry had wanted to try out his new handgun. It had worked beautifully.

He pulled back the curtain. A crowd of neighbors and servants had gathered on the lawn. They talked in hushed voices as they milled around a police car parked in front of the house. One of the car doors was opened; there was no one inside. Its occupants must have already entered the house.

What brought the police here? Could they have been sent by Chiang?

Local police were not involved in apprehending spies, Henry reasoned. But after the meeting yesterday, he couldn't be sure what Chiang might do. What if they searched the house? The secret documents were stored with his academic papers, buried in a complicated filing system only he could decode. His notes were written in English. The police couldn't understand the foreign language; most couldn't even read Chinese. What concerned him were the tools of his subversive trade. They would condemn him on the spot.

Better take care of them now.

He pulled two books from the middle shelf of the bookcase, uncovering a switch. He flipped it. The painting on the opposite wall went upward and revealed a locked chamber the size of a pillow. He made turns with the dial. It clicked open. Inside there were a radio transmitter and a telegraph machine. He removed the plug and the inked ribbons, and then carried the machines to a corner on the floor. He covered them with books and newspapers, arranging them in a careless way.

Best place to hide anything is in plain sight, Sun Tzu or someone had said.

He relocked the safe and tucked the Luger into the back pocket of his trousers. He wouldn't want to fire inside the house, but a weapon might come in handy if he needed to scare off intruders. In the mirror he saw a nervous man with fatigue lines across his forehead. He breathed deeply, willing calm to be restored to his face. Needing something to fortify his composure, he put on gold-rimmed spectacles and a smoking jacket.

He went to meet his visitors.

The living room was in the main wing facing the atrium garden. The space was elegantly appointed with hand-carved furniture, silk cushions, and antiques that had been in the Li family for generations. Henry found his wife and his daughter in the company of two policemen. His wife, Su-chen, stood in the middle of the room like a child who had lost her way. Their daughter, Yunna, was flanked by the policemen. She looked like she had been through a sandstorm, hair tousled, clothes smudged with dirt. Her wrists were handcuffed.

She beamed when she saw her father.

"Good afternoon, officers," Henry said calmly.

"Good afternoon, Professor."

"This is unexpected. What brings you here?"

"Your daughter, sir. She was involved in an incident."

"What kind of incident?"

"A street demonstration."

"You've handcuffed her. Has she broken any law?"

"Miss Li and a group of students were parading in the middle of Chung-shan Road, shouting slogans and waving banners. At an intersection, Miss Li and another student climbed up on wooden boxes and began to make speeches, while their followers distributed leaflets to passersby." He paused to underscore the next point. "Both the speeches and the leaflets contained hostile views on the government."

"It sounds like what usually happens at street demonstrations."

"We can tolerate the demonstrations—if they are orderly," the policeman replied. "We have experience in similar situation, a lot of experience. We can tell when there are unruly elements. This one had all the signs. Emotions were running high. The crowd was swelling by the minute, getting agitated. A riot would be next. We couldn't allow that to happen."

Henry asked his daughter, "Was the demonstration unruly?"

"It was a gathering of concerned citizens. They were eager to show their support. It was uplifting to be there."

The name Yunna meant Maid of Perfection. She was a beautiful girl. Long hair framed an almond-shaped face.

Her cheeks were a rosy flush; her lips a playful curl; the fierce light of intelligence gleamed in her eyes. In the midst of antiques and stark brush paintings, her loveliness radiated like spring sunshine.

Henry said to the policeman. "Even if the crowd was unruly, why did you single out my daughter?"

"She was the leader of the group."

"Were you the leader?" Henry asked Yunna.

She nodded.

"Did you do anything to provoke a disturbance?"

"I tried to provoke people to think. The police must have found that disturbing."

Henry couldn't suppress a smile. "Was this your first demonstration?"

She shook her head.

Su-chen was dabbing her eyes with a handkerchief. "No one in this family or mine has ever been arrested. On the street, in front of strangers. That was so shameful."

"How long has this been going on, Yunna?" Henry asked.

"A while."

"How long?"

"Since the bombings in Shanghai."

"That's four months ago. Why haven't you told us?"

"It's something we do after school. I didn't think you would mind. You're always encouraging me to take part in extracurricular activities."

"This is more serious than rehearsing a play."

"A lot more serious. We should have started sooner and gotten more people involved. Maybe Shanghai wouldn't have become such a sorry mess." She turned to her captors. "You know in your hearts we were doing the right thing.

We took to the streets because it's the only way to get our message across. Remind people they should do something if they care about the future of the country. If you wanted a better life for your children, you would have joined us instead of putting us in handcuffs."

"Keep your opinions to yourself, Yunna. The police have their job to do, same as everyone else."

Su-chen shook her head. "Girls shouldn't have opinions, period."

Yunna mouthed a protest at her mother.

Unexpectedly the policeman came to her defense. "We have no doubt that though these young people are misguided, they mean well. That's why we are willing to give them another chance. We hope they would learn a lesson and grow up to be good citizens."

"That's remarkably progressive of you," Henry said.

"If Miss Li promises not to repeat the offence, we are willing to overlook her involvement this time."

Henry said to his daughter, "Can you do that, Yunna?"

"I promise I will not repeat in the same manner what I did today," she said with a sly smile.

"Good enough for you?" Henry asked the policeman.

"We count on Miss Li to keep her word. There is another concern, Professor Li."

"Let's hear it."

"When students from respectable families take part in a street demonstration, there is an element of added danger. We would be remiss in our duty if we didn't bring it to your attention," he said, a bit too eagerly.

"What kind of danger?"

"They make easy targets for thugs. Last month two young men were kidnapped on Nanchang Road. They were grabbed from behind. No one noticed until it was too late. Easy for criminals to do that when the targets are mixed in with an agitated crowd and people's attention is on someone making a speech. The young men were held for ransom. The families had to pay a tidy sum for their release. When we saw it was your daughter, we kept an eye on her and made sure she was not harmed."

"Thoughtful of you."

"If we'd gone by the book, we would have hauled her in to the police station, taken her fingerprints, and filed a report. But we thought you would prefer to work things out so her future won't be tarnished by a youthful indiscretion. We waited until the crowd dispersed, and then we brought her home, though it was past our shift." The policeman adjusted his cap slightly. "As a gentleman and a respected citizen, we hope you appreciate those extra efforts."

"I do."

Henry took out a wad of cash from inside his jacket and stuffed it into the policeman's hand. The man's fingers curled up around the bills before they disappeared into his trouser pocket. The transaction lasted two seconds, smooth like a conjuror's sleight of hand. At once the scene started to dissolve. Yunna's handcuffs were removed. Su-chen sank into a chair, sighing with relief. Servants peeking from the hallway realized the spectacle was over and scurried back to the kitchen.

Henry saw the policemen out and waited until their car turned the corner. He bolted the door before he returned to the living room.

Yunna had been watching with disapproval.

"Father, I didn't do anything wrong. You shouldn't have paid them off."

"They went out of their way to bring you home. They should be compensated for their trouble."

"The police are as corrupt as the criminals. Those two are going to get the word out that there's money to be made. Every policeman will find an excuse to give me a ride home."

"I'd rather pay them than have you thrown in jail."

"There will *not* be another time, Yunna," Su-chen warned. "And don't try to fool me with your excuses and tricks. You are not to do anything like this again. If you do, I won't let you leave the house."

"You can't lock me up, Mother. I am not a child."

"Then don't behave like one."

Yunna said with disbelief, "You think what we did was childish?"

"It was worse than being childish. You made the family lose face."

"Would you rather lose the country?"

"That's silly. We'll never lose the country."

"The government is handing the country to foreigners, piece by piece. Look at the concessions in Shanghai. Look at what has happened to Shantung and Manchuria. Look at…"

"What the government does is not your concern. You are a girl. Your place is in the home."

"The country is my home too."

"The country is too big for you. Home is right here. After you're married, your husband's home will be your home."

"That's your choice, Mother. It doesn't have to be mine."

"What?"

"Just because you chose to be a housewife doesn't mean I have to follow you."

Su-chen's face darkened. "You don't want to follow me. Whom do you want to follow?"

"Anyone I choose. Or no one. Why should anyone follow anyone?" Yunna said unhurriedly. "We are in the twentieth century. Men and women are equal. I can do the same things as a man."

"What same things?"

"I can make a difference and convince people to do the same."

"What happened just now has gone to your head. You stood in front of a crowd of laborers and coolies, and you made a speech. That's all. It doesn't prove anything and it doesn't mean anything. You are a girl. Girls are not meant to be leaders."

"If we are smart, capable, and determined, we can be leaders."

"Are you saying women would run the government?"

"Why not?"

"I have never heard anything more absurd!" Eyebrows raised, chin up, Su-chen's face looked ten years younger and remarkably like her daughter's. She said to Henry, "I shouldn't have let you send her to an international school and I should have insisted that her feet be bound. She would have learned to behave."

"What Yunna did took courage and conviction. That's something we should be proud of."

"For a boy, yes. For a girl, it's unnatural. Imagine if I abandoned my duties as wife and mother, spent all day shouting slogans in the street. See if you'd be proud."

That wasn't their first argument on the topic. Henry had learned long ago that anything against the grain of tradition was unacceptable to Su-chen, no matter how compelling the circumstances.

"The banquet guests will be arriving soon," he said. "Let's put this behind us. If you want to take part in a demonstration, Yunna, you must ask for permission."

"Henry, you can't let her…"

"Remember, ask first. Can you do that?"

Yunna pressed her palm on her chest. "I hereby promise notice of my patriotic activities will be provided ahead of time."

"Good. Now, go. Do what you have to do and leave us alone."

"Okay," she said in English. She gave her father a smile and left the room.

"Henry, we have to talk about Yunna's future," Su-chen said.

"There is no need to make too much of this incident. You know how young people are. They get worked up about things and spur each other on. Yunna probably went along to keep her friends company."

"It's not about today." Paused. "We have a marriage proposal for Yunna. A very good offer. I think we should consider it."

"Marriage? She's too young."

"The suitor is from an excellent family, almost equal to ours. You know there aren't many like that. He is the only child. His parents left him the family's chain of goldsmiths and two houses in Soochow with three thousand acres of farmland. After the wedding, he plans to take Yunna back to his ancestral home and start a family. From what I heard, it's a beautiful estate. Yunna is a lucky girl."

"What do you know about the man?"

"He is a graduate of Peking University. He has been overseeing the family business since his father died. Quite good at it, apparently. In seven years he has added five new shops and doubled the acreage around his ancestral home. He is also an outstanding philanthropist. He donates to many charities. Last year he was honored by the Buddhist monks and the Christian missionaries."

"Does he believe in both religions?"

"He believes in doing good works. He is not spoiled like most children from wealthy families. He has never stepped inside a gambling house, an opium den, or a brothel. The matchmaker has been a friend of his mother since before he was born. She said she has never known a more honorable and moral man."

"This 'she'—mother or matchmaker?"

"The matchmaker. His mother passed away last year. Yunna won't have to put up with a mother-in-law. With her temperament, that'll be a benefit for everyone concerned. One more thing: he is older than Yunna."

"How much older?"

"Twenty-seven years."

"Why has he waited this long to find a wife?"

"There was one. She died four years ago."

"Are there children?"

"Three. Girls. Understandably he is anxious to have a son. He saw Yunna at the Mid-Autumn Festival parade and he was favorably impressed. Being a cautious man, he had the matchmaker ask for Yunna's astrological signs and compared them to his. They turn out to be a harmonious match. The fortune-teller said they will have a long and prosperous marriage and Yunna will bear him many children."

"He listens to fortune-tellers. I thought you said he was a graduate of Peking University."

"He is an educated man, but that doesn't mean he should dismiss traditional beliefs." She went on, "As soon as he heard from the fortune-teller, he made the proposal through the matchmaker. I told her we are going to Chungking. He said he is willing to put off the wedding until we are back. But he would like to have your consent now."

"Being wife to an older man and stepmother to three children. Yunna won't like it. Neither will I."

"He'll be a stabilizing influence on her. We both know how much she needs it. As to the children, two are married. The youngest is betrothed and will move in with her future family when she turns fifteen. Yunna will only need to take care of her for a little while."

"Yunna can barely take care of herself."

"She has to grow up, Henry."

"She will do that in her own time."

"It's our duty to decide what is good for her."

"Not if it concerns her happiness. She should decide for herself."

"She is too young to decide."

"Then she is too young to marry."

Needing to put distance between himself and his wife, Henry got up and paced the room. On the floor by the table there was a squeezed paper ball. He picked it up and straightened out the page. A mimeographed bulletin on the urgency of making personal sacrifices to save the country. Yunna must have dropped it. The layout was crooked, the ink ran, the printing barely legible. But he was aware of the effort and the risk involved in producing the flimsy publication. Half the students at Nanking University were engaged in patriotic campaigns, abandoning studies and taking chances with the law and their personal safety. So much hope and fervor. And so much waste. In a few years—if the students survived the war—they would look back and laugh at their youthful folly... Maybe not his daughter. Yunna was strong-willed and persistent. Once she set her mind on something, she wouldn't give up.

He folded the paper carefully and put it in his pocket.

Su-chen was watching. "That is another reason for Yunna to marry. She won't be able to keep up this nonsense when she has a husband and a family."

He removed the gold-rimmed glasses and spoke intently. "Have you talked to Yunna about what she wants to do? About whether she wants to marry so soon? If she does, what kind of man does she want for a husband? Is the man you have in mind suitable? Is he who you think he is or is he some fantasy cooked up by the matchmaker? Even if everything you were told is true, will Yunna want to be this man's wife, stepmother to his children? Will they get along? Will she be happy?"

Su-chen was not prepared for the barrage of questions. "Of course I have not discussed with Yunna," she cried. "We are not in America, Henry. If you are not sure about the man, we'll invite him here and you can look him over."

"It won't be necessary. I can't approve the marriage."

"Don't you want Yunna to have a family of her own?"

"She is not ready. To make her marry a stranger will destroy her. When things calm down, she will continue her studies. She will have a university education, here or abroad. She will study a subject that interests her and pursue a career if she wants to. She will choose when and whom she marries. I want my children to have the same opportunities as I."

"But…"

"My mind is made up. I won't talk about Yunna's marriage unless she brings up the subject."

"But I have accepted the betrothal presents. You should see them. He sent only the best: perfect jade pieces, the finest silk…"

"Send them back with an apology."

"You won't at least give the man an interview?"

"I don't see the point."

"So that's it?"

He nodded.

Su-chen was crestfallen. "Yunna might never get an offer as good as this one."

He smiled his first bright smile of the day. "Is that what you think, Su-chen?"

She nodded.

"You underestimate our daughter. Yunna won't have trouble attracting admirers. Wait till she blossoms into a young woman. Our front door will be crowded with suitors ten times more eligible than this man. You will be glad that we didn't accept his offer."

If we survive the Japanese, he added in silence. The precariousness of their situation hit him without warning. Time was running out.

"You are too indulgent of Yunna."

"Am I?"

"It's not good for her."

"Who knows what is good for anyone?" He gave his wife an apologetic grin. "There's something I need to discuss with you. Privately. Wait for me in the bedroom. I'll lock up the library and then I'll join you."

Yunna had stayed in the anteroom to nurse a bruise on her elbow and heard the conversation.

Mother is out to punish me. Because I am her firstborn and not a boy. Her only regret in life, as she keeps saying to my face, like it's my fault. She had to have a son, because the Li family had to have an heir. For years she consulted fortune-tellers, burning incense sticks and feeding herself strange concoctions to get pregnant. Her wish has finally come true with little Sung. Why can't she leave me alone?

There is no way I'll be an old man's housekeeper and domestic pet for the rest of my life.

I'll run away. I'll do the things I want. On my own.

The moment the banquet breaks up, I'll leave. I'll slip out from the side door, follow the footpath to the main road and find a rickshaw to the train station. I'll pawn my last birthday present, a jade bracelet. It should be enough to pay my way out of the country. I'll ride the train to Canton and cross the border to Hong Kong. It would be easy to go abroad from the British colony. Where abroad? It has to be a progressive country where a woman has a chance to prove herself. America.

Then she heard her father's objections: reasonable, firm,. She choked with relief. Father understands me and he cares. This episode should keep Mother off my back. Yunna chuckled as she imagined her mother trotting back to the odious suitor with the jades and the silks, making her apologies, losing great face.

Suddenly famished, she headed for the kitchen. She would have the cook fix a bowl of thick noodles and a dish of her favorite pickled turnips. Then she would leave the house for an hour. Should be easy with everyone busy with the banquet. She would join her friends at the deserted temple by the lake. To plan the march to the mayor's office the day after tomorrow.

I'll miss this house, Henry thought. He was walking along the open corridor to the master suite in the north wing.

One of the grandest in the province, the house was classic Ming Dynasty, a rambling compound built around atrium gardens. Henry had inherited the property from his father in 1919, the year of the May Fourth Movement, the first step China had taken to break away from feudal rule. Over two hundred years old, the house had been in near ruins. An architect had recommended demolition and rebuilding. But Henry had chosen to have it restored, painstakingly refurbishing the ancient frame and replicating architectural details, while adding modern conveniences to the rooms, sparing no expense. The house represented the kind of antiquated grandeur that was vanishing around him. He wanted to preserve his piece of history.

With windows overlooking Hsûen Wu Lake, the master suite had the best view. It consisted of a living room, a bedroom, a study, and a modern bath. When Su-chen found out she was with child, she had had the study converted into a nursery. The room was being furnished when they had learned about Chiang's plan to move to Chungking. Su-chen, like her cousins the Soong sisters, did not believe any outside event could affect their way of life; any disruption would be temporary. She had gone ahead and completed the room.

The door of the nursery was open. For a moment Henry stood and watched.

His wife rested her head on the cradle's edge, her long hair falling to one side, a shiny black cascade of silk over the white lace of the crib. Backlit by the window, she appeared to be shrouded in a halo. She had left anxieties and defenses in the living room. Here, she was a happy mother, rocking the cradle gently and singing to the baby, her face soft with tenderness.

Looking up, she smiled at her husband. "He is having his nap. Isn't he beautiful?"

"He is so small."

"He will grow quickly, and he will look like you."

"Maybe he will look like you."

"Sons always take after their fathers. Sung will be tall and handsome and strong."

"He may not want to be like me."

She caressed the baby's cheek. "Of course he'll want to be like you. He is your son. You want to be like your father, don't you, little Sung?"

"Su-chen, we need to talk."

She tucked the blanket under the infant's chin and kissed his forehead before following Henry out of the nursery. They sat on the sofa in the sitting area. He took the gold peach out of his pocket and put it on the small table.

"What is this?"

"General's Han birthday present for little Sung."

She picked up the peach and weighed it in her hand. "This must be real gold."

"It can't be anything else. It's from Han."

"What a lovely present. How thoughtful of him."

"I think it's more like down payment for my services."

"What do you mean?"

He told her about Han's offer of the position at the Shansui museum, leaving out the true nature of the job. From the first day, Henry had kept his secret career from his wife. She would have been a security risk. Su-chen was first cousin to H.H. Kung, husband of Ai-ling, the oldest of the three Soong sisters. The Kungs were direct descendants of Confucius. Su-chen's childhood had been privileged and insular. She was brought up to live by Confucian codes; she followed them unbendingly. Family was the defining structure of society and individual. Every person was required to think and act according to their place in the hierarchy. Henry had little doubt that despite of her devotion to him, she would object to his stealing secrets from her relatives. He had not wanted to test his wife's loyalty.

"It's a pity we are going to Chungking. You'll have to turn down General Han's offer," Su-chen said.

"Our trip to Chungking has been canceled."

"What do you mean?"

"Yesterday Kai-shek sent for me at the Club. I went to see him. May-ling was there. They told me they are leaving without us."

"That can't be right. When I talked to Ai-ling, she said she'd make sure there's a crib in the plane for little Sung."

"Your cousins are notorious for saying things they don't mean."

"Not Ai-ling."

"She didn't know then. Talk to her now, I'll bet she won't be so helpful."

"You saw Kai-shek yesterday? Why didn't you tell me?"

"I needed time to sort things out."

"Could you have misunderstood?"

"It was an order. Clear as day."

"Let me talk to May-ling."

"It won't do any good." He lifted his gaze to their wedding photo on the wall. It was a black-and-white studio portrait, hand-painted with color. He would have preferred the original photograph, but Su-chen had framed the colored copy after she saw Soong May-ling's wedding portrait. He concluded, "Your family has never considered me one of them."

"We are a big family. It's not possible for everyone to be attentive all the time. And you can be over sensitive, Henry."

"It was an official meeting. Supervisor to subordinate. I was told to stay here and join the new defense team."

"But you are not a military man."

"It makes no difference to him. His mind was made up and that was that. I tried to state my case—our case: I want us to be where it's safest. I thought he would want the same thing, at least for you and the children. That was wishful thinking on my part. Your cousin doesn't care that he is putting our lives in danger. The man is selfish to the core." Henry paused, expecting his wife to defend her cousins. She was gazing at the gold peach. "I am not joining the defense team. I'll submit my resignation after they've moved to Chungking. We'll leave on our own."

"We are going to Shansui."

He was hesitant. "The Shansui Regional Museum is small. Its collection is less than one-tenth of the one in Nanking. There's not much to do there."

"But you'll be working for General Han. Isn't it that what you want?"

"What makes you think that?"

"You are deeply interested in what he does, more than you are in teaching or the work you do for Kai-shek. There is an affinity between you and General Han. I feel it every time I see you two together. It's like you share a special secret." She smiled. "I'm surprised his offer hasn't come sooner."

"Am I that easy to read?"

"Your face and voice change whenever you speak of General Han. The mention of his name is enough to take your mind somewhere else. More than once you've said he would be a force to be reckoned with and the world would be caught off guard by him. You have never said that about anyone else. You also said he was the best thing that ever happened to you."

"I did say those things, didn't I?"

"General Han is a special man. I'm happy that you are close to him."

"That's good."

She looked at him. "You don't think so?"

He wished he could tell her about the real Han, the monster behind the statesman's veneer, the catalog of his crimes and his preposterous Grand Strategy.

"It's one thing to be friends, another to work together, live together. There is also the politics of the situation. Kai-shek will not take kindly to my resigning from the new post. If he finds out I did that to join Han's camp, he will go after me with a vengeance. You know the animosity between those two. The rest of your family would take his side and they would include you in the blame."

"Ai-ling is fond of me. I'll ask her to speak to Kai-shek on our behalf. Let him know we are moving to Shansui for our safety. We'll be back as soon as the Japanese are out of here. That's the truth, isn't it? We wouldn't have considered that option if we've been allowed to go to Chungking."

"Don't involve your cousin. This is something I have to resolve on my own."

He got up and walked the few steps back to the nursery. Sung's face was luminous in the square of sunlight. His chest rose and fell rhythmically. A tiny person in his image. When Sung became a man, he would be old and feeble. He wanted to protect his son now. He wanted him to live in a safe world, safe from the Japanese and the likes of Chiang and Han.

"I have a different plan," Henry said. "We are not going to Shansui. We are going abroad."

"Abroad? Where?"

"Europe."

"Europe," she repeated, stunned.

"I lived there. I know the place. It will be a good life. Peaceful, uncomplicated, safe." Once again he wished he could tell his wife how frustrated he was, taking risks for causes he neither cared for nor believed in, and how much he wanted a fresh start.

"It's the other side of the world. What made you think of something like that all of a sudden?"

"Moving to a safe place—it has been on my mind since the bombings began. A full-scale war will break out. It will be a horrific war and it will start here in Nanking. The city might not survive. The country might not survive. Going abroad may be the only way to ensure our safety."

Thoughtful for a moment, she said, "Look at recent history. We have lived with threats of unrest and we have always made it through."

"The past troubles were home-based. The Manchus and the Mongols were minority races, but they were Chinese. The country remained intact under their rule. The current situation has no precedent. Foreigners are carving up China. Foreigners with better trained soldiers and advanced weapons. Foreigners who are determined to swallow China. We are losing control of our destiny."

"What about the Generalissimo? What about General Han? They won't sit back and let the foreigners take over."

"It's more than a few foreign powers trying to take their piece of China. It's the Japanese and they want the whole country, every province, every city, every village. If Kai-shek and the warlords were united, maybe we'd have a chance. But he doesn't want to share power, and the warlords are fighting among themselves. Divide and fall—that's why China is weak. We are a selfish people."

"If we are in such grave danger, all the more you should stay and help defend the country." She added, "You thought what Yunna did was commendable."

My daughter is an idealist. I'm not.

"On whose side should I fight? Chiang Kai-shek's? General Han's? Mao Tse-tung's? To what end? To support a corrupt government? To help a warlord stage a coup? To turn the country into a socialist state?" His voice softened. "What about our children? Who takes care of them if I join the fighting? My first responsibility is to you and our children."

"What about your responsibility to the country?"

"The country is divided. I have to take a side. There isn't one I want to take."

"Not even the side of my cousins?"

"How can I take the side of people who want to put our lives in danger?"

"They did one thing wrong and you are willing to abandon the country."

"I want us to be safe. If it means we have to leave the country, so be it. We are in a war; self-preservation is the only thing that matters."

Her eyes held his. "You are right, Henry, we *are* a selfish people."

He ambled to the other side of the room. On the wall was a photograph of him on graduation day. He had put it there when Sung was born, a memento from his youth for his son. It had been taken in front of the Auditorium Maximus at Göttingen University in Germany. He remembered the day. Early summer. Cloudless sky. Flowers everywhere: Alpine violets, freesias, geraniums. The young man in the photograph had been filled with lofty ideals. Working for Han had put an end to them.

"Who wouldn't want to make choices like a hero?" he said, feeling very alone. "But, putting our lives at risk is too great a price. I am not someone with nothing to lose, Su-chen. I am a husband and a father. My choices affect you, our children, and our future. I have to make them with your safety and well-being in mind. Please understand."

"Do you need my understanding, Henry?" she said to the sky; her eyelids fluttering with strain. "Your mind is made up."

"Yes, my mind is made up."

"When are we leaving?"

"Soon."

She bit her lips to hold back tears. "How soon?"

"With Sung it'll be more comfortable on a ship. I'm looking for one that leaves from Shanghai, before the Japanese shut down the docks."

"Is it a matter of days, weeks, or months?"

"Days."

Chilled by the finality, she murmured, "I see."

"Once we are out of China, things will be fine."

"Have you picked the destination in Europe?"

"Bern, Switzerland. I have friends there."

"Friends."

"Old friends from my university days. Good friends."

"Will they be enough?"

"We have each other and our children. We'll make new friends."

"How will we live, thousands of miles away, in a foreign country?" Su-chen cried, unable to contain her anxieties. "What about our life here? This house? My family? What about General Han's offer?"

"Europe is a civilized place: modern and efficient. Give it a chance; you'll like it. I'll have someone maintain this house. It'll be our home when we return." He took a deep breath. "Family should support each other in times of need. Your family has shown how little they care about us. Or maybe it's just me they don't care about—not much I can do about that. As for General Han, he'll be disappointed. But he can find someone else to fill the position. I am not indispensable to him."

"He is your best friend."

"I'm going to miss him," he said. Not sure if he would.

Her response came after an age; it was resignation rather than consent. "It will be difficult for Yunna and me. We will be living among strangers, people who look and think differently from us. Sung will grow up a European. He won't share our beliefs and our habits. Your friends might be hospitable to us, but we will never be one of them. It's not a future I would choose." She swallowed the thickness in her throat. "I am your wife. Yunna and Sung are your children. Our lives are with you. We will go where you take us."

He came up behind her and held her waist, feeling her apprehension and resentment. He kissed her hair; she was impassive, cold. He lifted his eyes, and found himself looking at the peak of Purple Gold Mountain. A corner of the Middle Kingdom. A city famous for monuments to dead emperors and dead heroes. He closed his eyes. In the darkness of his mind, he saw a vast mausoleum. Ghosts from past dynasties roaming over the landscape.

He steadied himself.

"I should get some work done before the banquet," he said. "Are our bags packed?"

"For Chungking."

"That'll be fine."

"Won't anything change your mind?"

"No."

"I shouldn't even try, should I?"

"It's going to be all right, Su-chen. I promise."

Before he left the room, he put the gold peach next to his son's pillow.

Happy birthday, my son. This day will be the turning point in our lives.

6

Victor Maurier emptied the last drop of brandy from the flask, and wondered if he would make it to Nanking alive. Since he boarded the train, the four Chinese men across the aisle had not stopped staring at him. Not because he was a *kweiloh*, but someone who had warm clothes. There was no heating in third class; the temperature in the compartment plummeted as the day darkened. His cashmere muffler and fur-lined gloves must look like diamonds to the shivering passengers. He wouldn't be surprised if they leapt across the aisle and went at him with their bare hands. Since Shanghai fell, things had been deteriorating rapidly. Not only were people living with the threat of bombs and gunfire, they had to struggle with constant shortages of essentials. Even when supplies were available, people might not have enough money to purchase them. Inflation was spiraling out of control. With nothing to lose, desperate people turned into savages. Last week he had watched a man being beaten to death in broad daylight, right in front of the Customs House. Bystanders had divvied up the clothes and left the body on the sidewalk. Dogs had pounced on the corpse, ripping it to pieces...

Victor needed to relieve himself. He was hesitant to make the trip to the urinal. A gang of bandits had been robbing people in public lavatories. No reason to assume the ones on trains would be safe. God, no. Not one originating from Shanghai. He would have a smoke instead. As soon as his hand touched his pocket, his watchers' eyes brightened. Forget it. Cigarettes were like hard currency. A pack of Gauloises would buy a night with a virgin. American Bull Durhams would go further, a coolie for a week or ten baby girls. His fingers glided over where his emergency kit— passport, pocketknife, compass, five gold coins—was kept in a crossbody pouch. Still there. Couldn't be too careful. Chinese pickpockets could perform sorcery with their hands.

Had he not been following orders, he would have taken an entire first-class compartment where he could have enjoyed some privacy behind a bolted door and peed into the carpet if he felt like it. But Soong had insisted on third class. Victor would draw less attention in packed cars. Soong seemed to have forgotten a Caucasian would stand out no matter where, or maybe he wanted to punish Victor for protesting the arms deal. Had he not been following orders, he would not have shaken hands with Shiozawa. Not have boarded this train to Nanking. Not have had anything to do with supplying weapons and getting innocent people killed...

Stop. Don't blame someone else. My choices got me where I am. Every step of the way.

He had made the move to seduce Soong's sister. He had not been attracted to her, but he knew she was his ticket to the rich and the powerful. When she had led him to her brother and Soong had offered him the job at International Airsea, he had accepted, fully aware of what it entailed. And he had chosen to stay on, kept adding accomplishments to his gangster resume.

At least a good part of the day was over. In a few hours, he told himself, the job will be done and I will be free to make new choices.

He took out his notebook, opened to a blank page and began to sketch a rendition of the Eiffel Tower as he once again toyed with the idea of going home. The inherent risks of criminal dealings aside, China was becoming dangerous even for a white man protected by Extraterritorial Rights and the almighty political machine of the Soong family. There was also his son's future to consider. Would he want Pierre to grow up not knowing where he came from? What kind of future would his child have in China?

With the money he had earned—if *earned* was the word, Victor thought with a chuckle—life after China would be a dream. An apartment in the sixteenth Arrondissement, furnished like a chateau, with views from every window. A villa in the country—Provence, of course. A fleet of luxury cars. A diplomat's wardrobe, British bespoke suits, Italian hand-sewn shoes, silks from the finest Hangchow mills. Should the good life get to be a trifle monotonous, he would buy himself a political appointment. The years with Soong had imbued him with enough savvy to play the role of a competent public official. A position in the Cultural Ministry would be desirable. The work wouldn't be too taxing, and it would guarantee the best seats in theaters and the best tables in restaurants. And respect. It would be nice to be on the right side of the law for a change.

Assuming life would be normal in Europe…

From what he had read in the newspapers, it might not be. Big trouble had been brewing in the heart of the continent. Germany. Mass murders and a plot to invade surrounding countries. France might be the next target… If France was going to be as dangerous as China, what was the point of returning? Why give up the life here only to find out he couldn't live the way he wanted in Paris? He knew impending war was not the primary cause for his hesitation. The real concern was personal. Going home would mean having to face up to his unresolved marriage.

I'll figure out what to do after I collect the commission for this deal, Victor decided. A fat wad of cash always boosts one's resolve. He squeezed the Eiffel Tower into a ball and stuffed it into the crevice of the window ledge. He got a glare from his watchers. He flipped open his coat, flashed the pistol in his belt and glared back. The men averted their eyes. He grabbed his cigarettes, lit one, and puffed furiously.

If anyone makes a move, I'll shoot.

The train sounded its horn as it entered the city limits of Nanking. Victor smelled the stench of danger that arrived with the dying light. This will be my last run, he assured himself once again. He stubbed out the cigarette, rewrapped the muffler around his neck and buttoned up his coat. A year ago I couldn't wait for the next assignment. Now I'm nervous in the company of unarmed strangers. I have been at this too long. I'm losing my edge.

Time to leave China, the job, Soong.

Five men were waiting at the train station. Two were from Victor's team: his assistant Pao Sheng, who had arrived ahead to get things ready, and a driver dispatched from Soong's Nanking office. Representing the Japanese side were three flat-faced gnomes clad in black. Victor towered over the group like a pale-faced giant. They exchanged codes before climbing into the car. The host team occupied the front seat, the visitors the back. The first stop was International Airsea's safe house on Chung-shan Road. Soong never sold on credit; payment had to be made before delivery. Door bolted and windows shut, the group watched as Victor called the bank in Hong Kong and confirmed that the deposit had been made in the designated account.

It was dark when they were back in the car. Victor directed the driver to the outskirts of the city. Traffic thinned out. Buildings became sparse. Soon they were moving on an empty highway.

Victor noticed trucks following them. A queue of headlights as far as the eye could see.

"Are they yours?" he asked the Japanese who appeared to be in charge.

"Yes."

"They're coming to the warehouse?"

"Yes."

"The agreement stipulates only three people are allowed from each side."

"For the transfer of ownership. It doesn't say we can't bring in more people to handle the goods."

"Handle? How?"

"Do what has to be done."

"Are you moving the weapons out of Nanking?"

No answer.

"Are the people in the trucks armed?"

One of them giggled. "Why would they be armed? Why bring coal to Newcastle, like you Limeys say."

"I am not a Limey."

"Limey, Yankee, same to us. Orders from Tokyo. The goods are to be assembled as soon as we take ownership."

"You mean tonight?"

Again no response.

Victor tried a different tack. "The warehouse is in a remote part of town. You have a lot of men. They'll need accommodation and provisions. We can help."

"We don't need your help. We are prepared."

"Your men may have to be here for days. The warehouse is just a warehouse. No running water. No electricity. In the middle of nowhere."

"As I said, our soldiers are prepared."

"What do you plan to do?"

"We'll put on the biggest fireworks show you Chinamen have ever seen. How about that?" blurted the giggling Japanese.

"In Nanking?"

The question came from Pao, breaking the rule that no one except Victor was to communicate with customers. Pao, a former engineering student from Ching Hwa University, had fought with Sun Yat-sen to end Manchu rule. Sun's death had crushed his hopes. He had grabbed the first job offer that came along. Victor knew Pao wasn't happy working for Soong.

The Japanese ignored Pao.

"I'd also like to know," Victor said.

"You are here to deliver merchandise we paid for. Not to pry into our plans."

"We are worried about our safety," Pao persisted. "Does a fireworks show mean opening fire?"

"It means nothing."

"You've brought an inordinately large number of men to pick up an inordinately large arsenal. It stands to reason that we suspect an attack on the city is imminent. If you have a different purpose for the troops, we'd be glad to hear it," Victor said, a knot in his stomach.

None of the Japanese seemed to have heard.

"Whatever you say, it will stay in this car," Victor continued. "You have my word."

"We have no answers to your questions."

Which was answer enough.

They endured an hour of cheerless silence as the car and its escort of trucks proceeded on the winding mountain road. Cold air streamed through the window cracks. No moon. No stars. Aside from an occasional glimmer on the roadside, the darkness was complete.

The weapons were stored in a defunct slaughterhouse, surrounded by a mountain range. The only access was a narrow road through the pass hidden by bushes taller than a house. Two years ago, when International Airsea was looking for a warehouse near Nanking, the site had been chosen for its natural seclusion. Its drawback had been a thriving community of farmers and their families. To buy them out would be costly. To evict would incite resistance and draw attention to the location. One of Soong's advisers had come up with a plan. Agents were sent to poison the fields. Within a month, half the children had gotten sick and died. They had sent fortune-tellers who made a show of assessing the topography, and then told the terrified community that the strange calamity was the result of a malign astrological convergence. The bad feng shui had brought a curse on the inhabitants. The rest of the villagers had packed and fled. Since then no one had dared to go near the site. The place had been preserved like a shrine. Pleased with the result, Soong had repeated the method with other parcels of real estate.

They arrived at a vast tarmac. Abandoned cottages were scattered on the periphery like crumbled graves. In the center was the slaughterhouse, black and sprawling like an ancient tomb.

The moment Victor's foot touched the ground, a rush of wind blew out from nowhere. In seconds, it escalated into a cyclone. Trees rattled. Dust and debris funneled in whirling spirals. Dead leaves hit their faces. Coats were flapping wildly. They stood there, holding onto hats and scarves; unable to move.

As suddenly as it had started, the wind stopped. The world was calm again. A primeval quiet enveloped the universe.

It's a message from the gods, Victor thought, and I don't need to ask what it's about.

The Japanese looked as stoic as before. Victor's men seemed to share his premonition. They gazed at the sky, searching for answers.

Victor handed a key to the Japanese in charge. "The merchandise is inside the building. It has been arranged according to the order on the inventory list. It should be easy to check. You can do a quick walk-through. We'll wait."

"No need to wait. Go."

"Our agreement specifies that once we leave the site, no claim of discrepancy will be accepted."

"No claims will be made."

"Better to be sure. We don't mind waiting."

"We don't want you here."

"Once we take off, the deal is closed."

"It's closed as of this moment."

Victor, Pao, and the driver watched the three black figures march to the slaughterhouse. On cue, the trucks behind them rolled forward and lined up on the tarmac. Men—some three hundred of them—leaped out from the beds and formed two parallel rows.

They have to be doing more than moving weapons, Victor thought. But there was no point in speculating. Their job was done.

"Let's get out of here."

Glumly they walked back to the car. Behind them, the Japanese were filing into the warehouse. Two long queues of men were moving, but hardly a sound was made.

"They always check everything. They get agitated over the smallest details. Why do they trust us this time?" the driver said when the contour of the warehouse faded from view.

"It has nothing to do trust. Even if there is a discrepancy, they won't make a claim. They expect none of us will be alive tomorrow," Pao summed up quietly.

None of us will be alive, Victor said to himself once, and then again. The words worked on his mind like a spell. Darkness gathered at the edge of his vision. A chill descended from head to toe. A roar filled his ears, mounting, drowning out voices around him. He had had these sensations before. In the Shanghai nightclub.

He closed his eyes until the roaring faded. Still cold. He double-wrapped the scarf around his neck.

"It's freezing," he said, testing his voice.

"It's going to snow."

"We should be back at the safe house in an hour," the driver said.

"An hour."

"Sooner if I step on the gas."

"No need to hurry. Drive carefully," Victor said. He breathed on the windowpane and drew a skull on the glass.

"Mr. Victor, are you all right?" Pao asked.

"Exhausted." I am unraveling from the edges.

"Should we call someone?"

"About what?"

"Isn't that obvious? The Japanese are mounting an attack. We are the only ones who know. We have to do something."

"I suppose we should."

"Please call Mr. Soong. Ask him to tell the Generalissimo."

"I can do that, can I?"

They were driving past the hills below the new Sun Yat-sen Mausoleum. Ahead was the Avenue of Emperors, ancient and mysterious in the spectral illumination of infrequent streetlamps. Purple Gold Mountain loomed. Its name was a reference to imperial colors—the place had been a favorite of royalty through the dynasties. In autumn, Victor remembered, cassia blossoms covered the slopes and valleys. Their perfume filled the city. The same scents and sights had invigorated emperors and poets for thousands of years. Tonight he felt their presence, felt it as part of the landscape.

"I'll do something," Victor murmured, not sure what. "I'll do what I can."

It was past midnight when they returned to the center of Nanking. The streetlamps had been extinguished to save power. The sky was an inky canopy. Wind was whipping up again, cold gusts accompanied by bouts of frigid stillness. Hail began to fall. Large pellets splattered noisily on the roof of the car.

The strange weather is following us, Victor thought.

"Oh no," Pao muttered, staring at the falling hail.

"The mountain pass will be a mess," the driver said. "We need to find another way to get out."

The windows were fogging over. The trace of the skull Victor had drawn reappeared. If we can get out at all, he thought.

"If the hail keeps beating down, the Japanese will be stuck in the warehouse. They won't be able to put on their fireworks show."

"They won't be able to bear the shame. They will commit hara-kiri."

"They will put on clean uniforms, polish their shoes, and queue up in a perfectly straight line before they pull the knives on themselves."

"It will make a great display."

"Maybe China's joss is taking a good turn."

"We'll hire a team of fortune-tellers to put a curse on the Japs."

"A voodoo war. How about that?"

They laughed nervously.

In the safe house, Pao started a coal fire. He and the driver squatted on the floor and gazed at the flames. Victor peered out the window, feeling listless from the day. The light from the house picked out the sheen of falling hail. The rest of the world was invisible. They could be alone in the universe. The only sounds came from the hail beating on the roof. The quiet was getting on everyone's nerves.

"Find us some food," Victor said to the driver. "And wine for me, French labels. Red. You can't find those in a store. Go to the Europe Club and ask for Jacques. Tell him it's for me and he'll sell you a couple of bottles."

"Some girls to keep us company. Would that be all right, Mr. Victor?" the driver asked.

It was against the rules. But this might be their last night alive. "Go ahead."

The driver took off. Pao resumed staring at the fire.

Victor picked up the telephone and dialed Soong's private number.

"I didn't know the Japs had a sense of humor," Soong said when Victor repeated the remarks about the fireworks show.

"The weapons are being assembled as we speak. They have hundreds of men working. They'll be ready in a matter of hours."

Silence on the other end.

"Paul, are you there?"

"Maybe it's standard procedure to assemble weapons before moving them. Maybe they want to give their soldiers something to do. There could be all kinds of reasons."

"I don't think there is any doubt what they plan to do."

"Give it a few days. See what happens. I'll decide then."

"A few days may be too late."

"If there is solid evidence that they are mobilizing their troops, I'll take the matter up with Kai-shek."

"We have all the evidence we need. They *are* mobilizing their troops."

"You could be reading too much into some asinine remark made by some rank-and-file."

"It's not just what that one man said, it's everything else."

"If you are wrong, I'll look like a fool. Better wait and see."

Wait and see. Victor had heard the phrase spoken time after time, by laborers, housewives, politicians. The perennial tenet of Chinese life except where money could be made.

"We've known they plan to use the weapons in Nanking. Shiozawa was quite blatant in his remarks."

"I'll think about it."

"We can't wait, Paul. You need to *do* something. Quickly."

"I'll call Tokyo and get a feel for what they have in mind. If necessary, I'll ask them to hold off for a while. Good enough for you?"

"How long can you ask them to hold off?"

"Enough time for you to get out."

Enough time for *you and your family* to take off in a jet.

"I can't promise Tokyo will do as I ask," Soong continued. "It's a big favor and they are going to make some outrageous demand in return. You'd better get ready to leave first thing tomorrow."

"What about the people here?"

"What about them?"

"They can't defend themselves."

"Everyone knows the Japanese are moving in," Soong said impatiently. "We have soldiers in Nanking."

"There aren't enough soldiers to counter an all-out attack," Victor protested.

"How do you know it will be an all-out attack?"

"With an arsenal like that, what else could it be?"

"Speculation," Soong snapped. "You've worked yourself into a state because some Jap made a joke."

"It was not a joke…"

Soong hung up.

Victor stared at the mouthpiece.

"What did Mr. Soong say?" Pao asked.

"He said he doesn't want to do anything hasty."

"Will he do anything at all?"

"When the time is right."

"They have the men, the weapons. They are in our backyard. What is he waiting for?"

The driver brought back smoked meats, crocks of rice wine, two bottles of French red for Victor, and three girls who had barely reached puberty. They were dressed in padded jackets and soiled petticoats, with lipstick smeared over their cheeks and fingernails, like little girls who'd been playing with their mothers' makeup. Pao and the driver made their selections and took the girls to their rooms. The one left with Victor claimed she was a virgin and demanded an extra fee. He wasn't in a mood to deflower a stranger, though he was sure she was lying. Some young prostitutes planted tiny pouches of blood to simulate virginity. He paid and sent her away.

He opened a bottle of wine to let it breathe, observing with amusement that at a time like this he had not abandoned his bourgeois habits. He leaned back on the sofa and closed his eyes, listening to every sound around him. A crow cawed. The coal in the fire cracked. A mattress squeaked in the next room. A rat scampered in the attic...

He poured himself a glass of wine and went back to the telephone.

"Little Pierre is terrifically fine," Lillie answered in her throaty voice. "He took your place, darling. We just made beautiful love. Are you jealous?"

Victor imagined Lillie in her silk camisole, her slim legs thrown carelessly across the crimson sheets, long black hair like a shawl. He would give anything to be with her. To feel her soft, curvy body. Kiss her as she had kissed him the first time they met, in the Cathay Hotel where he had occasionally played the saxophone with the jazz band. She had come up to the stage during intermission. Number one star of the Paramount Ballroom had wanted to thank him for the beautiful music. She had placed her luscious figure in front of him. An impish smile had announced her intentions. He had smiled back, numb, dazzled. A rainbow of lights had played across her face. There had been nothing in the world except her dark eyes holding his. Her lips had touched his, lingered. When she released him, he had been left with an acute longing.

"Of course I'm jealous."

"I love it when you are jealous." She laughed. He imagined her tilted nose wrinkling prettily. "You finished the job?"

"Finished... Yes, it's finished."

A pause. "Is everything all right?"

"Yes."

"You don't sound all right, Victor."

"I'm a little overwrought. Do keep talking. I need to hear your voice."

"Okay. Know what I did today?"

"Tell me."

"I cleaned house. I went down on my hands and knees, scrubbed floors, washed windows. I nearly broke my back. Maybe your wife was a good missionary worker, darling, but she was not a good housekeeper. The place looked like she had not dusted in years. The filth was a foot deep. Dead bugs, cobwebs. I threw away a lot of junk…"

He took "junk" to mean things left behind by his wife, Celeste, or as Lillie called her, "the nun," on account of her austere wardrobe. A year and a half ago, when Celeste found out he had been spending his afternoons in the boudoir of a Chinese singsong girl, she had screamed and cursed through the night. The next morning, she had packed a suitcase and stormed out of the house, leaving little Pierre behind, Victor had suspected, as a way back. Poor Celeste, he had thought, if only she knew. Adultery was a trivial transgression compared to what he had been doing for Soong. Two weeks later a telegram had arrived from France. Nothing about herself. Nothing for Pierre. The message had been one stern command: Victor was to come home if he wanted God to forgive him.

Victor had laughed until tears filled his eyes. Finally the truth came out: The woman who shared his bed and bore his child didn't know him. Hadn't she noticed he had not paid any attention to God for years? He had dropped the telegram in the trash, relieved that the farce was over. The marriage had never worked. Celeste was a strident moralist who had to function within a prescribed set of rules. Victor regarded rules as barriers to impulse and inspiration. They were to be bent or, better yet, removed. When the heat of physical attraction burned off, they had found they had little in common. Like most men who married young, he had felt trapped. Every evening spent in their small apartment had been a missed opportunity for adventure. Every woman who wasn't his wife had looked alluring. Six months into their marriage, Celeste had brought up the idea of joining the missionary in China. She must have hoped the change would revive their relationship. He had been enticed by the prospect of seeing the other side of the world and agreed.

China had revived his life. Not the marriage.

"Why are you so quiet, Victor? You mind that I threw away your wife's things?"

"No. Of course not."

"I want to redecorate the house. A Swedish family near the French Park is selling their furniture. They are moving back to Europe. I went to take a look. Beautiful pieces, very modern..."

He switched to English. "Listen, Lillie. We are going on a trip."

"What?"

"It'd be good if we got away for a while."

"You mean a holiday?"

"A long holiday."

"Where are we going?"

"My home in France."

A generous settlement should convince Celeste to give him a divorce. If not, he and Lillie would live together in Paris as they did in Shanghai and to hell with laws and morals and what people thought. If war broke out in Europe, they would move to America. Armed with a fortune, they could live anywhere.

"You want to go home? Because you miss your wife?"

"The trip has nothing to do with her. France will be our first stop. We'll travel and take in the sights. Italy, Austria, Spain, England. Wouldn't you like that?"

"A holiday in Europe. Of course I'd like that very much. Actually I don't mind if we make an appointment with your wife. She is Pierre's mother and she should see her son, even though she hasn't shown a sign that she cares. Oh well, that's her business. You can see her too; you'll have to. Pierre can't go by himself; he wouldn't know the way. I'm not worried. I know you love me only. I can go shopping in the department stores in Paris."

"Don't bother with a lot of luggage. We'll only take the valuables. They should fit into one suitcase. Be ready to leave when I'm back."

Silence.

"How long will we be gone?" she finally asked.

"I can't say at this point. It depends... We'll have to see, Lillie."

"See what?"

"I'll tell you when I get there."

The playfulness in Lillie's voice was gone. "What's wrong, Victor?"

"I have been sitting on my backside too long. I feel restless. I could use a break."

She's biting her lips now, he thought, the way she does whenever she tries to restrain herself from asking more questions.

Her voice was calm. "I understand now, Victor. Don't you worry about anything, okay? We'll be ready when you get home."

"I love you."

"I love you more. I know nothing is wrong, but please will you come back right now?"

7

Midnight. The banquet guests had departed. The servants had finished tidying up and retreated to their quarters. The house was quiet once more. Henry waited until Su-chen had fallen asleep before he slipped out of bed. He headed to the library in the main wing.

He locked the door. He needed to be alone. To destroy the evidence of his secret life. To plan their escape. To figure out a way to shake off Chiang's watchers in Nanking and General Han's agents in Shanghai. He knew too much. Han would not want him on the loose. It would require maneuvering, but Henry was confident that he could pull it off. The watchers would likely be focusing on the warehouse; he didn't doubt that Chiang was more concerned with the priceless art pieces than with him. If Chiang had assigned someone to keep an eye on him, he would pay the man off. Chiang's people earned miserable wages. A nice chunk of cash would convince the man to look the other way. He had recruited and trained Han's agents. He knew how and where they operated. He knew the routes, the codes, the safe houses. He just needed to outsmart them.

They will be my last subversive acts, he thought. Once out of China, I will live the life of an upright, law-abiding citizen. I will never lie, never do anything dishonorable, and never inflict harm on anyone.

He found a schedule of ships departing from Shanghai. For the current month the destinations were in Japan. The next would leave in four days for Yokohama. If they missed that one, they would have to wait a week for the next ship. Too long. Tang would have arrived and he would expect Henry to assume his new position. And who knew how much damage the Japanese would have inflicted on the city by then.

Four days. To be exact three—it was past midnight. They would have to leave in two days to get to Shanghai in time to board. He had less than twenty-four hours to secure passage for four on a fully booked ship. There wouldn't be time to tie up all the loose ends and for Su-chen to adjust to a reality she hadn't chosen. They would have to slip away quickly and quietly. The four of them and the trunk of gold. Traveling with the baby would be difficult until they were on board. But he and Yunna would manage. She was strong and independent. He could count on her to cope under pressure. From Yokohama they would sail to Hong Kong. There would be time to rest in the British colony before boarding the next P & O to Liverpool.

He set about retrieving secret documents from drawers and cabinets. Reams had accumulated in a decade—enough intelligence to indict half the Party officials. But the truth would never see the light of day. Not in his lifetime. It would take a brave man to chastise the power that rule. He was not a brave man. Someday I'll write a book, he thought. Everything had been stored in his compendious memory. *Memoirs of a Chinese Gentleman Spy*. He would write it in English and have it published in America. Posthumously. He wouldn't want to be around when his family found out.

He lighted the brazier, expecting to spend a good part of the night in the room. While waiting for the fire to catch, he unlocked the trunk for another look at the means of his family's salvation. The peaches rested neatly in the folds of velvet. Solid gold. Wealth in its rawest form. Only Han could think of a present like this. Correction: Only Han could afford a present like this. Not for the first time, Henry wondered how much gold was there in Han's vault. How much would go to Han's war chest? What was Han buying from Berlin?

He reminded himself that Han's dream of becoming emperor—however it might turn out—was no longer his concern.

He ran his hand over the peaches and noticed that Han's seal had been carved into each one. Damn. How was he going to sell them without leaving a trail for Han to hunt him down? The seal would have to be scraped off and the surfaces refinished. He would have to find a goldsmith who couldn't read Chinese and who had not heard of Han's gold. There might be European goldsmiths in Hong Kong or Macau who could do the work. The trip out of Yokohama would have to be paid by other means. With the baby, they would need to go first class, and he would have to bribe the crew to keep their names off the passenger list. The cash in the house should be enough; if not, he would make the bribes with his collection of expensive watches…

Footsteps. Approaching the library.

He held his breath. Listened. Cautious movements of someone who didn't want to be heard.

He went to the door and pressed his ear to the crack. The footsteps halted. A hushed silence. Whoever was out there must have also become aware of his presence. He and Su-chen had seen every one of the guests to the door. The servants had been trained to stay away from the library. It had to be an intruder. He stepped away quietly, relocked the trunk and slipped the key inside the cloth jacket of a book.

From the desk drawer he took out the Luger.

"Who's there?"

Silence.

"I know someone's there. Speak up."

Silence.

He tapped the barrel of the pistol on the door. "Identify yourself or I'll shoot."

Movement. Hurried steps, fleeing, fading, gone.

Whoever had been there decided not to confront him. Henry was about to open the door when he heard fresh footsteps from a different direction.

What was happening tonight—of all nights?

The footsteps were lighter, quicker, without caution.

"Father, are you there?" Yunna's voice.

He let his daughter in. He stepped outside and looked down the hallway. Nothing.

"Who was outside the door?"

"The man sent by General Han."

"What was he doing?"

"He was poking around like a thief."

Han had never replaced a courier without letting him know in advance. Who was this man? Did he really work for Han or was he an imposter? He spoke the Shanghai dialect and said he'd been recruited there. Even if it were true, it wasn't a helpful clue. The city was a hotbed of insurgent groups. He could have been a member of the leftists, the triads, Japanese infiltrators, Western spooks... He shouldn't have let a stranger stay in the house. The problem with Chiang had distracted him.

Then it dawned on him. Clear as day. Shanghai was headquarters of the Blue Shirt Gang, Chiang's personal army. The man was a Blue Shirt. There is a Blue Shirt inside my house, he thought. Chiang sent the man to kill me. That's why he ordered the packing of the art treasures be done before the banquet. He expected I wouldn't be alive after tonight.

How did the man get his hands on the trunk? And the uniform—it was the one worn by Han's courier. They must have found out about the delivery and abducted the courier en route. This Blue Shirt had killed the courier and assumed his identity. What else had Chiang planned?

"Father."

He nodded distractedly.

"You are frowning."

"Am I?"

"You are worried that the man may be up to no good?"

"He probably just wanted to look around," he assured her. "Why are you up so late?"

"The noise woke me up."

"What noise?"

"Like a line of trucks passing through the hill."

"Trucks don't usually take this route. Are you sure?"

She went to the window and opened it a crack, letting in a draft of icy air. "Listen."

The rumble came from the base of the mountain. Military trucks, Henry could tell without looking. Yunna handed him a pair of binoculars. He adjusted them until he found the line of headlights, moving like a steady stream of fireflies in the dark. He zoomed in. By the silhouette he could tell they were Japanese. An entire army had entered the city.

"Can I see?" Yunna said.

He closed the window. "Not much to see. Just trucks delivering goods to the markets."

"There are dozens of them. There isn't that much stuff going to the markets. And these are moving at precise intervals—commercial trucks don't do that."

"Let's not speculate."

Yunna crossed her arms, eye at the window. "Red Bandits? Daikon Heads? The Blue Shirts? It's past midnight. They picked the time because they don't want to be seen, which means they're carrying out a secret mission... I bet it's the Blue Shirts smuggling the art collection from the National Museum for the Generalissimo. It's the right direction. It's kept in the warehouse by the Yangtze River."

"How did you find out about the art collection?"

"I must have heard you mention it to Soong May-ling."

"Soong May-ling—is that how you refer to your aunt?"

"All right, Auntie May-ling."

"Have you told anyone else what you heard?"

"Only my closest friends." Reading his face, she added, "It's not a secret that Chiang Kai-shek is a thief."

"Yunna, do be careful. You could get into trouble if the wrong people heard what you said."

"Who doesn't know the safe thing is not to speak up? What would happen if everyone kept quiet? The government would feel they can keep selling out. The country would stay backward and weak. There would be repeats of the Opium War, the Boxer Rebellion…"

Henry was not in a mood for a political debate. He said in a light-hearted tone, "I know you have strong convictions. You made your point quite eloquently this afternoon. But it's past midnight. Even revolutionaries need sleep."

"I am not a revolutionary. I am a patriot."

"Even patriots need sleep. Go back to your room. Get some rest. We are taking a trip tomorrow."

"Are we going to Chungking?"

"That trip has been changed. We are going to Shanghai."

"Shanghai? Why?"

"We'll go Christmas shopping," he said without thinking.

Yunna was keen neither on Christmas nor shopping. She eyed him suspiciously. "What made you want to do something like that? Haven't the Japanese bombed all the department stores?"

"They did, some of them. Terrible. I meant to say we'll go to Shanghai, and then…" He wasn't sure this was the time to tell her the itinerary he had planned. "Didn't you say you want to see Shanghai before the war turns it into…? What was the word you used?"

"A graveyard."

"A graveyard. You have a morbid imagination, Yunna."

"I wish it were only my imagination. You are not joking, Father? We're going to Shanghai?"

"Yes."

"I'd like to see the Majestic Hotel where Soong May-ling—I mean, Auntie May-ling—had her preposterous wedding. If only someone had dropped a bomb there that day, we would have a different country... Can you get me into a polo club? I want to see if it's true that foreigners use Chinese coolies as horses."

"We'll do all those things. Now, would you please go?"

"I'm wide-awake. Let me sit here with you for a while. Please."

She was standing in the middle of the room, in her white nightgown, like an angel landed on earth. Her long hair fell to one side of her face. The light of the fire danced in her dark eyes. She was looking at him with her mischievous smile.

"All right. I could use the company."

Yunna sat snugly in the armchair, legs crossed Buddha-like. She watched him feed papers to the blaze.

"Why are you up so late, Father?"

"I ate too much at dinner, couldn't sleep."

"You hardly touched a thing at dinner. I was sitting next to you. Your mind was somewhere else, I could tell."

"Could you?"

"Absolutely."

"Got lots to think about. That's what we bookworms do."

"What are you burning?"

"Old files."

"Why are you burning them tonight?"

"Something to do."

"But this is your work."

"They are out of date. Not relevant anymore."

"How come you never let me read your writings?"

130

"Since when have you been interested in your father's work?"

"I've always been interested, but you said I wasn't ready."

If it be not now, yet it will come: the readiness is all. Would he ever be ready?

"I'm going to write a book, Yunna. I promise I'll let you read the first draft."

"Are you sure you'll have time?"

"There will be plenty of time to do plenty of things."

"Do you plan to retire?"

"I'd like to take a break. A long break."

"How long?"

"A year or two. Maybe more."

"That'll be nice. You've been working too hard. But are you sure you won't miss your work?"

"I will not miss my work."

She noticed the trunk. "I've never seen this before. Where did it come from?"

"You are full of questions tonight."

"No more than usual." She got up, paced around the trunk and ran her hand over the surface. "Looks like something from the Forbidden City. What's in there?"

With a self-mocking grin, he said, "The fruits of my career. The representative body of my work by which future generations will assess the true value of my contribution to the world."

"Can I see?"

"No. Not now."

"When then?"

"Soon. I hope."

She looked at him. "Something wrong?"

"Why do you say that?"

"It's on your face."

"I'm tired and worried. We have been getting ready for the move. It's a big move and we don't know when we're coming back. There are things to put in order before we take off. Lots of things."

"I thought the servants had finished packing."

"There are situations I have to resolve before we go."

"If there are things bothering you, you can tell me."

He nodded.

"Will you tell me?"

"I know I can count on you."

She returned to the chair. "What was bothering Mother?"

"Was she bothered? I didn't notice."

"Of course you did. You told her to try to look relaxed in front of the guests. That was before the smoked goose. You whispered, but I heard you."

"Your mother was worried about your little brother. She thought we were too noisy."

"The dining room is miles from the nursery."

"It has been a while since we had an infant in the house. Understandably, she is more anxious than usual."

Yunna was twisting her hair with her fingers. "Are you and Mother planning to make more babies?"

"That is not something we can plan. It'd be nice if it happens."

"So you do want more children?"

"Who wouldn't like a big family?"

"I wouldn't."

"You'd have brothers and sisters to play with."

"I am not a child. I don't play."

"You can do things together. I was the only child and I was lonely. I wished I had brothers and sisters. It would have been nice to share."

"I don't like to share. I like to do things my way. I like to be the center of attention."

"I didn't know I have raised a little empress. Your mother is right—I do spoil you."

"If I were a boy, she wouldn't have wanted another child."

"She believes a family must have a son to carry on the name."

"A daughter can carry on the family name. In her way."

"I agree. But it'll be a while before the rest of China catches up with us."

"Sung is all Mother cares about now."

"He's a baby. He needs her."

"It won't change when Sung grows up."

"You should be happy for her. For me too. Be more tolerant, Yunna."

"'Tolerant' is another word for complacent. Complacency means being passive…"

"Let's talk about something else. Would you like to see more places after Shanghai?"

"Like where?"

"Countries in Europe."

"Really?"

"It's time you saw the world outside China."

"What would I do in Europe?"

"Meet people. Learn new languages. Experience different cultures."

She beamed. "I'd like that very much. You mean it?"

"I mean it."

"I'd like to travel on my own. Not right away. In a year or two. Can I do that?"

"If a girl can stand up to the police, she can travel on her own. Where will you go?"

"America. I want to study at a prestigious university, graduate with many degrees, and be as learned as you."

"You will be more than me."

"Mother thinks I should be a traditional wife. Take care of the house, nurse babies, be a slave to my husband and mother-in-law." She smiled sweetly at her father. "I'm sure she will give in if you insist."

Henry had finished burning the files. A feeling of freedom buoyed him like glorious music. I am liberated from the prison of secrets. He was pleased he was sharing the moment with his daughter.

"What would *you* like to do, Yunna? Tell me the one thing that would make you happy."

"One thing?"

"We can start with one."

"What if it's a very big thing?"

"I wouldn't expect anything less from you. Tell me what it is. I will do everything I can to make it come true."

She crossed her arms over her chest, hugging herself like an angel in prayer. She spoke solemnly, "I want to be the most powerful, most famous woman in the world. I want to be more powerful and more famous than the three Soong sisters combined."

"That's a very tall order. Are you sure?"

"Yes."

"And you are confident that it can happen?"

"Yes."

"How?"

"I would prefer to make it happen on my own. But since I am a girl and this is China in the year 1937, I'll have to find the man who can help me. When I do, I'll marry him. I'll be his partner."

"What kind of man?"

"He must be a born leader with superior intelligence and qualities appropriate for a head of state. A military genius, because the war is likely to go on for a while. A patriot who wants the best for China. Someone as visionary as Dr. Sun, as politically savvy as Chiang, and as smart as President Roosevelt."

"Is that all?"

"Hopefully he'll also be as lucky as Emperor Shiao Yan of the Liang Dynasty."

"Ah, you've done your homework."

"Under his rule, every person will have enough to eat, a place to live, an education, and a job that will earn enough to support himself and his family. The country will be great again and people will be proud to be Chinese. We have been on the losing side for too long. Time for the tide to turn. I believe the right leader can make it happen."

"How long have you been thinking about this?"

"A very long time."

"What if this world-class leader, this amalgam of Sun Yat-sen, Chiang Kai-shek, Roosevelt, and Emperor Shiao Yan doesn't exist?"

"He may not have the qualities in equal amounts, but I know he is out there somewhere."

"What if you don't love him?"

"I will make myself love him."

"It isn't love if you have to make yourself. You don't choose love. Love chooses you. When it comes, it takes over. The person becomes the center of your life. You love him regardless of who he is and what he does. Love is something you can neither explain nor manage."

"If that is love, I don't want it. I want to choose. I want to be in control."

"What you want now won't matter when you fall in love. All you'll want is to be married in a beautiful wedding, make a home for him, and have his babies. You won't mind if you don't become famous."

Yunna was visibly disappointed. "I thought you were the most enlightened man in China, and you wanted to encourage women to take on more than the traditional role. I thought you believed in me."

"I want you and Sung to go as far and as high as you can. It's the world that I don't believe in. It's a place where few noble intentions are realized. I learned it the hard way, Yunna. I hope you will have better luck with your dreams. If you ever find this man, you have my blessing to marry him and be the person you want to be." He stood up. "It's getting late. Let me walk you back to your room."

"What about you? Are you going to stay up all night?"

"Not all night. Just one more thing I need to do before I turn in."

Tong cursed his luck as he found his way back to the servants' quarters. The moment had been perfect: Li alone in an isolated part of the house and everyone else asleep. If the daughter had not shown up, he would have killed Li. He would be on his way home.

Maybe not. Li was no fool, not the fumbling scholar he had imagined. The man was vigilant like a hawk. Only a pro would sense the presence of an intruder when none was expected. Tong realized he had made the unpardonable mistake of underestimating his target. Just as well that there had been no confrontation. That would have been a comic scene: He threatens Li with a rusty saber while Li has his finger on the trigger of a pistol.

Now he had a new problem. Li's daughter. She had seen him snooping and she must have told her father. Suspicions aroused, Li would contact Han to verify his identity. Li would use the machine that sent invisible messages miles away. His cover could have been blown by now.

Buddha, what's worse? Having Han or the Blue Shirt Gang on his back?

Tong sat on the bed and looked around. The furniture was worn but of fine quality. He guessed they were discards from the master's suite. They would fetch good prices in the secondhand market. The professor lived well. His servants' quarters were better appointed than most people's living room. The man had everything: wealth, connections, beautiful wife and children… Yet he was willing to risk them all by spying for an opium smuggler.

People are such fools.

Himself included. For having become a gangster when all he wanted was a job that paid the rent and put food on the table.

He was stuck. Being stuck was better than being dead. To stay alive he needed to kill Li. There's no way around it.

He stood up and jabbed the saber into his waistband. This time he would also take the pistol. If he fired and the shot woke up the whole house, so be it. The daughter should have left by now. If not, he would kill them both and set fire to the whole damn house. He would get out of Nanking and drive all night back to Shanghai.

He was about to retrieve the pistol from his knapsack when he sensed someone had been watching.

A shadow flitted past the door and materialized into a man in the room.

He was taller than Tong by a head, broad and muscular like a Shantung giant. He wore a black pajama suit and soft-sole shoes.

"Who are you?"

"Professor Li's valet."

"Why are you in my room?"

"You know very well why."

8

Pao Sheng found Victor sleeping on the couch in the office. The wine bottles were empty; and there was a pile of cigarette butts. The Frenchman had been up most of the night. What was he doing by himself? Making morbid drawings? Calling the bitch-goddess Soong Ai-ling for help? That wouldn't have been likely. The liaison had ended a long time ago, and the Frenchman was faithful to his Chinese mistress. More faithful than a Chinese husband. International Airsea was the largest arms dealer in greater Shanghai. As managing director, Victor received a cut of every deal. He was a rich man and could have a different girl every night, but he preferred to go home to his mistress.

Caucasians are a strange lot, Pao thought. They believe that love and carnal pleasure are connected. A man must stay true to the woman he loves. One woman. His whole life. He would be committing a sin if he didn't. Unrealistic, to say the least. We Chinese are more sensible. We see coupling as nothing more than release for our yang. When the urge is strong, the man finds release with his wife, concubine, singsong girl…. Love, well, I wouldn't know. Not the kind between a man and a woman. And no regrets. From what I've seen, it's messy, treacherous, childish…

Pao found an old blanket in the closet and draped it over Victor. It would be a difficult journey home, fraught with physical dangers and political hazards. He wouldn't want the Frenchman to get sick. As a European man he had a far better chance of getting his way with the Japanese, and if they needed to ask for help, he had Soong's ear. Pao took out the cash box. Inside were two stacks of brand-new bills, fresh off the press. The Kuomintang was printing new money faster than the banks could update their books. These bills were probably worth half their face value by now, and shrinking by the minute. No wonder the poor were joining the Communists. Nice to believe that the state would take care of everything for everybody. To Pao it sounded like another bunch of lies.

He needed forty yuan for the two girls. He took six tens; he wanted his girl to have an extra twenty. She had pleased him, made him climax twice though he had been nervous and tired. He put the cash box back and tiptoed out of the room. He slipped two bills under the door of the driver's room. Back in his, he found the girl had not dressed. She wrapped herself in a bed sheet, knees curled up to her chin, huddled on the mattress. Her long hair framed a sweet face with a dimpled chin.

He put the money in her purse.

"I can stay, if you want me to," she said.

"We'll be taking off soon. We're going back to Shanghai."

"I heard Shanghai is a very modern city."

"Parts of it."

"You must live in a posh neighborhood."

"I live in the French Concession."

"I heard only important people live there. Even the Japanese wouldn't dare to drop their bombs on it."

"Who can tell with the Japanese?"

"You are a very strong man, a very terrific lover."

He sat down next to her. "I bet you say that to everyone."

"Sometimes I do mean it."

"I won't ask if this is one of those times."

"It is."

She took his hand and guided it under the sheet. Her small breasts were cold. He could feel the bumps on her skin, the stiff nipples. He was aroused immediately. Without the awful makeup, she looked like a child, younger than his daughter. He was ashamed but he couldn't pull away.

"I hope I pleased you?" she said, sensing his discomfort.

"You did."

"Let me please you again."

He gently removed his hand. "There isn't time. Go home."

"I don't have a home."

"There must be a place where you keep your things."

A nod.

"Go there and get some rest. You couldn't have slept much last night."

"I won't be able to get in."

"Why not?"

"The owner of the restaurant on Willows' End lets me sleep in the kitchen. The space is available at night after the restaurant is closed. At this time it's locked and I don't have the key."

"That's your home?"

She nodded. "From midnight to eight in the morning, I have it to myself. There's room for a cot in the kitchen. The space is warm from the stoves. Sometimes the cook leaves me a bowl of leftovers. All for free."

"You are alone in an empty restaurant every night. You aren't afraid?"

"I'm more afraid when I'm with strangers."

"These are bad times. Try to be careful."

"If bad things happen, there's not much I can do."

"I want you to stay safe."

"You are a kind man. I can tell by the way you touched me. You are not like the others." She fixed her gaze on his chest and said quietly, "Will you take me with you? I'll please you every night. I'll do whatever you want. I'm honest and I work hard. I won't need wages. Give me a bed and two meals. That's all I ask."

The faces might be different, but they all wanted the same thing, Pao thought wearily. They hoped a round of Clouds and Rain would lead to a meal ticket. In the beginning, he had felt sorry for these homeless girls selling themselves to stay alive. The terror in their eyes when they followed him to bed; and, after they overcame fear and inhibition, the effort they put out for an extra tip. He had listened to too many sad stories and witnessed too much despair. His compassion had dried up. He would have sent this one off, as he had done with the others. But after the encounter with the Japanese, he felt a nagging fear for the people in Nanking. This one was so young. As a lover, she was like a butterfly, fragile, weightless...

"I don't ask every customer to take me home," she said, as if reading his thoughts.

"I'd like to help, but I can't. I have a wife and children." He took out his wallet, extracted half the bills and put the money between them on the bed. "This should let you take a break from the streets. I do want you to take a break."

"It doesn't have to be like this. I'll be respectful of your family. I can cook, keep house, take care of your children. I much prefer being a servant to... You can dismiss me when you don't need me, or if I'm not doing my job. I'll go. I won't make trouble."

She found his eyes. He looked away.

An awkward silence.

She slid out of bed. Her movements were brisk and efficient, assuring him that she was neither hurt nor disappointed. With her back to him, she began to dress.

"What are you going to do?" he asked.

"I'll walk to town."

"I don't mean now. I mean in the future."

"I don't dare to think about the future." She gave her hair a quick brush. "The money is nice. Thank you."

Victor and the driver were still asleep. It would be at least an hour before they took off. The morning air would clear his head. He said, "Let me walk with you."

He stepped aside to let her go first. She was confused for a moment, not accustomed to courtesy. They walked the length of the hallway to the front door. He liked looking at her slim back and the way her hair fell on her shoulders. He wished there was a way to let her know he hadn't meant to be heartless.

It was still dark in the street. Beggars were sleeping on the pavement. Pao and the girl picked their way through bundles of tattered rags. The air was permeated with the smell of unwashed bodies. Movements here and there, snoring, coughing, an occasional mumble. Frosted breath rose like steam from tiny kettles. That they can sleep through the freezing night is a miracle, Pao thought. That the country remains intact through decades of famine and war is a bigger miracle.

The girl shivered in her petticoat. Pao took off his jacket and draped it over her shoulders.

"Thanks." She buttoned up his coat. "At least I don't have to sleep on the street."

"Do you have family?"

"Had. There were four of us. Parents and a brother."

"What happened to your parents?"

"Died."

"How?"

"It's not a happy story."

"I wouldn't expect it to be. Tell me."

"My father had a job in the mills. The work was steady and the wages covered the basic necessities. It was a simple life, and a good one. Soon after the war started, his employer shut down the place and sent the workers home. The other factories weren't hiring. My father tried selling dumplings in the street. Mother did laundry for families in the neighborhood. They didn't earn much, but it was something; anything helped. After a while everything dried up. The dumplings didn't sell and the families canceled the laundry service. They couldn't pay the school fees; my brother and I were dismissed. We spent the day going through other people's garbage, looking for food scraps, bits of things we could sell. It was awful, but we got used to it. We turned it into a game. I pretended to be a cockroach, my brother a rat."

"That didn't last long, I hope."

"No."

"Don't go on if it makes you sad."

"I can be sad without saying a word," she said simply. "One morning Father went up to the mountains and returned with a basket of herbs. He had worked for an herbalist when he was a boy; he was trained to identify those used for medicinal purposes. We thought he was finding a new way to make a living. That night he made soup for himself and Mother. It's not for children, he said when we wanted a taste. They went to bed and didn't wake up. The next morning we thought they'd overslept. We didn't realize they were dead until a day had passed. A charity cremated them." She blinked away her tears. "We had no clue they were desperate. They never said a word."

"What happened next?"

"An orphanage took us in. After a month they needed room for younger children. The older ones had to move out. There was nowhere for us to go. We needed a place to live. That's when I started to… As I said, it's not a happy story."

"You have to support your brother?"

"For a short while, and then he was drafted. He was only fourteen. The army took him anyway. He was killed in Manchuria."

"Relatives?"

"A few."

"Can they help?"

"They come to me for money. I am the lucky one."

"How did you learn your Shanghainese?"

"From my customers." With a hint of pride, she said, "I hear a word once and I remember. I've picked up regional dialects, and some English, Russian, German, and Japanese."

"That's remarkable."

She spoke a series of words in different languages.

"What did you say?"

"Same thing in Russian and Japanese. 'Twenty yuan? Too much for a skinny girl with no curves. If you blow my dragon too, we have a deal.' My vocabulary is limited."

They passed a temple, a relic from the Sung Dynasty. The structure was intact, but the doors and window frames had been pillaged for firewood. The hollows stared like a skeleton. A family had moved in. Laundry was drying in the front yard. Chickens were running on the gravel. A rickety altar had been refitted into an ironsmith's workbench. At its foot, a little boy was playing with a rusty frying pan, merrily banging it on the ground. He looked up at the sound of their footsteps. He wiped a dribble of mucus with his hand and let out a gurgling laugh.

Will the child survive when the Japanese open fire? Pao thought. If he does, will be grow up to be a stronger man or will the experience scar him for life?

The girl seemed to have read his thoughts. "He is happy. He doesn't know what's going on. Let's hope when he does, it will be a different world."

"What is your name?"

"Why do you want to know?"

"I might look you up next time."

"Are you coming back soon?"

"Hard to say."

"If it's meant to be, we'll meet again." She added, "I hope it won't be like this."

"It won't be. I'll treat you to dinner at an American restaurant. I know a good one by the lake. They serve thick slabs of beef with gravy and dishes of ice cream."

"I've never had ice cream."

"It's like nothing you've tasted."

He picked up a torn newspaper from the pavement, ripped off a corner and wrote down his name and telephone number. "The number of my office, if you are ever in Shanghai."

She memorized the number before putting it in her purse.

"When the war's over, promise you won't do this anymore."

"I won't do this if I can find another way to make a living."

"What would you like to do?"

"I'd like a job in a factory, like my father. I'd like to be able to support myself."

"Don't work in a factory. Go back to school."

"School?"

"It'll be a waste if you don't."

Something in his face encouraged her. She slipped her hand into the curl of his elbow and rested her head on his arm. The gesture was more intimate than the coupling in bed. It was awkward, but he didn't mind.

"People say Shanghai is the grandest city in China. Tall buildings. Wonderful restaurants. More electric lights than stars in the sky," she said, optimism rising. "I'd like to see it very much. I'll start saving for a train ticket."

"Shanghai isn't what it used to be. The bombings have ruined a good part of the city. Things may get worse."

"How much worse?"

"I wish I knew."

"Maybe our luck will change with the new year."

"The new year is only a few days away. Change won't happen that quickly."

A rumble in the distance, low and massive like an approaching avalanche, punctured the morning calm.

"What's that?" she said.

"Sounds like a crowd."

"A big crowd."

"Heading this way."

"Can't be any good. It has to be the Japanese."

"How do you know?" he asked.

"Who else?"

They have finished assembling the weapons, he thought. They are storming the city.

The rumble grew louder, drawing closer every second, and breaking into distinguishable sounds. Footsteps and horse hooves and wheels, brisk and chaotic. Clanging metal and rattling crockery. Children's cries. The clamor of a frightened mob on the run. More disturbing sounds blared. Gunfire. Thumps. Shrieks of terror.

The killing has begun, he thought.

"I need to go back and wake up my boss and the driver. Do you have somewhere you can go?" Pao said.

"I'll be fine."

He was about to turn around and head back to the house when the mob rounded the corner. In an instant they flooded the street like a tidal wave. Horse-drawn wagons were loaded with children and furniture. Families hurried along donkeys piled with household goods and provisions. In the half light of dawn, they looked like a pack of ghosts let loose from hell.

The beggars staggered up from the pavement. Startled by the crush of people, they scrambled to collect their belongings and dashed off in different directions. Pao and the girl were swept up by the horde. She held on to his arm.

He grabbed a man at the head of the pack. He was dressed in a Western style jacket and woolen trousers. He was carrying two suitcases in his hands and an attaché case squeezed under his arm. He seemed to be on his own.

"Where are the Japanese?" Pao asked.

"Ahead of us. Behind us. Everywhere."

"When did the attack begin?"

"Crack of dawn."

"Do you know where they broke into the city?"

"They crashed through the north gate."

The direction of the warehouse.

Pao said to the girl, "Come with me."

"Are you sure?"

"Yes."

They negotiated the throng like a vehicle going against traffic. The panicked crowd kept pushing forward, confused and chaotic, leaving a trail of broken utensils and single shoes. Another rumble was rising in the distance. A different crowd. There were no screams, no jumbled noises of frenzied refugees. The movement was coordinated and purposeful.

Soldiers.

Pao and the girl raced back to the house. He locked the door as soon as they stepped inside.

"Stay here."

He headed to the driver's room and banged on the door. "Wake up. Get the car ready."

A sleepy voice asked, "What's going on?"

"The fireworks show has begun. We have to leave. Now."

He went to the office and woke Victor.

"My God," Victor said when Pao gave him the news.

"It's an all-out attack."

"I'll call headquarters." Victor got up from the couch. "Then we'll take off."

"The roads may be blocked."

"I can unblock them. I have papers." Victor cranked up the telephone. "Damn. The line is dead."

"Do you mind if the girl rides with us? I just want to drop her off somewhere safe."

"All right."

In the reception room, she was watching the street from the window, arms wrapped around her body. Pao put his hand on her shoulder. She jumped.

"We're leaving. You can come with us. We'll take you as far as the city limits," Pao said, immensely glad that he was able to take her out of harm's way.

"Thank you."

Better secure the place. Soong wouldn't want it vandalized. Pao located the wooden bolt under the stairwell and carried it to the door.

"You are bolting the door?" the girl asked.

"Yes."

"Aren't we leaving?"

"From the back. The car is there. Give me a hand. Hold the other end…"

The door flew open before they could fit the bolt into the slot. They were thrown back, their heads slamming onto the wall.

Japanese soldiers poured in.

Pao pulled himself up and stretched his arms to block the intruders. "Stop. Hold it right there. All of you."

It was a futile effort. One unarmed man against a battalion. The room was filled with moving bodies in drab green. Same build, same flat face and slit eyes, same bland expression. They are just a group of oversize mechanical mannequins, he thought wildly. If I can find the switch, I can stop them in their tracks.

"This is an office of the Chinese government," he shouted. "You have no right to enter. Get out."

Soldiers were surrounding the grounds, their helmets and the tips of their bayonets visible from the window. This many soldiers in one location, Pao thought. They are carrying out an order to occupy. If they're looking for state secrets, they won't find them here. The house was owned by the government, but it had been used by Soong for smuggling and gun-running.

His eyes caught a soldier's. Cold. Executioner's eyes.

The arms deal. The Japanese representatives were here last night. They got the address. They sent their soldiers to eliminate the witnesses.

A riot had broken out in the back. Boots stomping on the floor. Furniture being thrown about. Glass shattering. The driver's prostitute was squealing like an animal being butchered. They were assaulting her. Pao could tell by his girl's face that she was thinking the same thing.

"Ask them what they want. Tell them we are willing to negotiate."

She stepped forward bravely and spoke to the soldier at the head of the pack.

"He said they want the country and they don't need to negotiate with you... Oh, no, please, don't hurt us."

A soldier bounded up to Pao and pressed a gun to his temple. The cold barrel torched his skin. He shut his eyes and waited for the blast. One second, two… Nothing. He opened his eyes and realized the gun was there to hold him in place. He wasn't the target. The girl was. She had been pushed down on the floor. A soldier tied her hands and threw them over her head. Another held her legs down. Her head was the only thing she could move and she shook it wildly. A soldier grabbed her skull and pounded it against the floor until her face was blue. She seemed to be losing consciousness. He pulled down his trousers and mounted on her chin, leapfrog-style. His fist punched down her forehead as he jammed his penis into her mouth. She was struggling to breathe. The motion seemed to enhance his sensations; he kept punching her. Another soldier took over her lower body. He spread her legs, ripped off her panties and thrust into her.

The bastards think she is my daughter and they are keeping me alive to watch.

"She's just a kid from the street. She knows nothing about the deal. Let her go."

It was a hideous scene: two bare buttocks gyrating on the girl's undernourished body. The rest of the battalion formed a ring, cheering like bettors at a cockfight. The soldier who occupied her lower body finished first. He got up and wiped his mouth with his sleeve, grinning as he tucked his penis back into his trousers. The spectators applauded. Another's turn. This one wrapped a handkerchief around his gun barrel, and rammed it up the girl, cleaning her for his occupation. He was rough; the cloth came out bloody.

A loud howl. From the man on her face. He rolled over, grabbing himself between his legs. Blood was gushing. The girl had bitten off half his penis.

The one next in line aimed the gun at her forehead and fired. Her brain was splattered on the floor.

Pao shrieked.

He was next. The whole lot was coming down on him, hitting his head and chest with gun barrels, kicking his crotch with the steel tips of their boots. The monster-gnomes with identical faces were multiplying into one massive cyclone, whirling and circling. He was the center of the spin. Air exploded from his lungs. Hard objects smashed into him. He saw blood on the floor, trails of red, dripping from his face. He had to use his mouth to breathe. His tongue tasted the brine of raw tissue… Someone decided to make a game of it. They lifted him up, bowled his body to the wall, picked him up and threw him again. The crowd hollered and cheered. Mustering all the strength he had, Pao fought back. But he couldn't raise a hand before the next crush into the wall. Every one of his bones was breaking. The pain was blinding.

Then everything stopped. He didn't hear a sound. He didn't feel any pain. He was wrapped inside a cocoon, soft and floating and filled with light.

There was no need to fight any more. Peace had arrived.

From the safe room in the attic, Victor heard the gunshots and Pao's screams. Poor man, got himself trapped because he tried to help a prostitute. Well, he himself wasn't that much wiser. If he hadn't climbed up here to collect Soong's files, he would have been on his way out of the mayhem. A well-intentioned but foolish impulse. More foolish than Pao's chivalry. There was little chance the files would be found. The only way to the attic was by a fold-up ladder tucked inside the bathroom wall. The contraption was concealed behind movable tiles activated by a lever behind the toilet. Only someone who knew where to look would find it. And what if the files were found? What if the world discovered Soong had been diverting American aid to his family's accounts while making huge profits from crime and graft? Why should he protect Soong's reputation when Soong and his brother-in-law the Generalissimo didn't care to protect their own people? Now he had cornered himself in this space the size of a closet, crouched like an animal, with no food, no water, and soon, no air. The only other way out was a dormer window the size of a porthole. A child might be able to crawl through. Not his six-foot frame.

What if the Japanese decided to bomb the house?

He never was comfortable in tight spaces. The veins in his neck throbbed; his throat was parched. He tried to suppress the urge to break out from the ceiling and shoot his way out of the house. He fished in the pockets in his jacket, found half a pack of cigarettes, and lit one. A few puffs, the space was choked in smoke. Bad idea. The smoke might leak through the cracks. If the Japanese noticed, they would blast off the ceiling with machine guns.

He stubbed out the cigarette and closed his eyes.

He tried not to think about the tight space.

He thought about his own bed. About Lillie. About leaving China and starting over.

The noises were thinning out.

He pressed his ear to the floor. The frenzy had dissipated. Footsteps were moving to the front, leaving the house. Unhurried conversations like those of crowds at the end of a sporting event.

Victor waited until all was quiet, then unlocked the trap door and climbed down.

It looked like a tornado had hit the house. Anything that could be broken was smashed up. He called Pao's name, tentatively first, and then loudly. The driver's. No answer. He made his way through the rubble to the reception room.

He saw the girl first. Her body was in the middle of the floor, naked from the waist down. Her legs were apart, her white dress splattered with blood. Not much was left of her head. In a corner he found Pao. His face was locked in a grotesque scream, the rest of him a mass of broken flesh and bones. The bastards had beaten him to death. Victor knelt beside the corpse. He closed his eyes and then removed Pao's watch and the jade pendant around his neck. He would take them to Pao's wife in Shanghai, and he would tell her how Pao had sacrificed himself on duty and how his death had been painless and instantaneous—things officers said to families of soldiers killed in combat. In the driver's room, he found the body of the other prostitute. Three bullet holes in her chest. Her clothes had been torn to shreds.

The car was parked behind the house. The driver was slumped on the hood with his head blown off. Victor dragged the body into the house. Back in the open, he drew in deep breaths of air before his stomach turned over. He retched.

Reeling from the horrors he had witnessed and his incredible good luck, he decided he deserved a memento of the occasion. He climbed back to the safe room and took Soong's files.

He set fire to the house.

The car had half a tank of gasoline. It would get him outside the city and not much further. The Japanese might be waiting around the corner or he might be shot on the way. But somehow Victor knew he would be all right.

9

Su-chen had been aware of Henry leaving the bed during the night. He must have gotten up to make arrangements for the trip to Europe, she thought, staring at the empty pillow. In spite of her promise yesterday, she wished he would change his mind. She couldn't understand why he would choose Europe over Shansui, an uncertain future over a secure one.

Europe. What would they do in a strange place among strangers? They would have to rebuild their life, day by day, piece by piece. Henry might be out of favor with her cousins at the moment, but family was family. She was sure her cousins wouldn't abandon them. If he would just be patient, find out what he'd done wrong and make amends, they would come around. If change was what he wanted, he should accept General Han's offer. They would move to beautiful Shansui and live in Han's palace.

If only Henry would make the right choice.

She got out of bed and pulled the drapes open. A sliver of the morning sun was visible over the lake. Heavy clouds. It would be a dreary day. She looked in on her son. The baby was sleeping soundly. The cradle was festooned with celebratory red brocade, General Han's gold peach next to the pillow as a mascot. She checked his pulse. The morning after an infant's first-month birthday was a precarious time. The gods might be set off by the celebrations and decide to take back the gift of life. Satisfied that Sung was all right, she kissed the tiny cheeks and reminded herself to give thanks to the ancestors and the gods. She washed and dressed, preparing for the day.

As expected, she found Henry in the library. He was sleeping on the sofa. He had moved the brazier to the middle of the room; it was overflowing with ashes. He'd burned papers to keep warm, she thought. I'll have the servants refill the charcoal bin. Make sure there'll be enough fuel to last the winter… What's the point? We'll be leaving.

Days, he had said.

The creases between his eyebrows betrayed his worries. He'd been sleeping fitfully. She stared at the face she knew so intimately. Or did she? It came to her that there might be another reason for him to want to leave China. Some dark secret he had been hiding. Doubts and uneasiness that had been tucked away resurfaced. She searched her memory for clues. The days and nights he had spent in the library—door locked and drapes drawn. Mysterious parcels arriving from mysterious places. Unexplained wires and telephone calls. The frequent trips. To Shanghai, Chengdu, Macau, everywhere, too numerous to keep track. The trips were necessary to maintain contact with regional institutions; nothing could take the place of meeting people face-to-face—he had given the same explanation whenever she asked. Of the trips he had shared only the trivia: how slow the trains were, how dreadful the weather, and always, how glad he was to be home...

What had he done to alienate her cousins? Why did he want to run to the other side of the world?

Their future had been a prescribed course following generations before them. Overnight, it had turned into a maze of uncertainties. She didn't know what to think any more. She needed reassurance.

She left the library and returned to the north wing. The door of Yunna's room had been left ajar, probably had been through the night. My daughter has no sense of decorum, Su-chen thought. Next she'll be camping on the street with her wild friends and wearing skirts indecently cut to expose her legs. A pity that Henry turned down the marriage offer. It would put some discipline in Yunna. Force her to learn obedience and proper etiquette, as she had done when she was her daughter's age. As every Chinese girl should. She entered the room and closed the door behind her. She picked her way through shoes, stray clothing, piles of newspapers, misplaced furniture. The bedside light was still on, shining on a stack of books. A translation of *Pride and Prejudice*, a book titled *Famous Women in World History*; magazines in English.

"Get up, Yunna." No response. Su-chen repeated, louder. "Get up, get up."

Small movements under the blanket.

"It's past six. The sun is halfway up the sky."

"I went to bed late. I want to sleep in." Yunna pulled the blanket over her eyes.

"How many times do I have to tell you? You must get into the habit of rising early. All well-bred girls do."

"Tomorrow. I'll be a well-bred girl tomorrow."

"That's all you ever say."

Su-chen lifted the blanket, reached inside her daughter's nightgown and ran her hand down her spine.

"That's cruel, Mother. Your hand is cold."

"Keep up your lazy habits and you'll have a worse time with your mother-in-law."

"Soon it will be a different world. Uncivil mothers-in-laws will be exiled to Mongolia."

"You always answer back."

"What should I do? Not answer?"

Grudgingly Yunna got out of bed. Bare-footed, she padded to the sideboard and splashed water from the basin on her face. In the faint morning light, the contour of her body was visible underneath the nightgown. It seemed only yesterday that my first child was running around in rompers. Su-chen mused. Now she is on the threshold of womanhood. How much of her is me? What is the rest? Su-chen never knew how to handle her; Henry's progressive ways didn't help. Yunna was too confident, too curious, too outspoken for a girl. Things came easy for her. She did well in her studies without applying much effort. She was popular in school, particularly with the boys. They worshipped her like she was a goddess from the moon and she used them shamelessly. Whatever uproar she was in, a school play or a street demonstration, Yunna was always the lead, claiming the spotlight like she owned it. Su-chen was sure yesterday's run-in with the police had not been her only transgression.

"Put on proper clothes," Su-chen said.

"Why?"

"We are going out."

"Where?"

"To the temple."

"What for?"

"You'll find out when we get there. The temple is a sacred place. Try to behave."

Yunna made an emphatic bow. "Yes, Mother. I will pay respects to the monks like they were our dead ancestors."

Su-chen checked her daughter's appearance before they left the room. An amah was in the kitchen, making porridge for the staff. Su-chen left word that if Henry asked for them, just tell him they would be back soon. She and Yunna went out by the back door.

The air was freezing; a thin frost covered the ground. A faint sign of the sun peeped through the trees. Su-chen walked briskly. She planned to be home before Henry woke up. No point in having him find out she had consulted with the monks. He was not a believer and he would dismiss their advice as superstitious nonsense. Yunna was two steps behind, eye on the sky, humming a tune. They walked the short distance to the temple without exchanging a word.

The temple had been built in the Tang Dynasty when Buddhism was the dominant religion in China. Renovations through the centuries had added ornate rooflines and modern features like glass windowpanes and indoor toilets. The grounds were landscaped with rock gardens and fruit trees. Inside the main hall, a fifty-foot statue of the Buddha presided over an altar twenty feet long. Incense sticks burned in rows of clay pots. A gray light rose from the hard cement floor and filled the room with metallic cold. The congregation had finished morning prayers. Robed men filed past through shafts of sunlight, disappearing behind the altar one by one. Su-chen and Yunna waited in the back of the hall.

An acolyte recognized Su-chen from previous visits and came forward. "Can I help you, Patron Li?"

"Please ask your master if he would grant us an audience."

"Do you have an appointment?"

"I'm afraid not. Please tell him it's urgent."

He led them to the back. They walked along a corridor that had one side open to the lawn. He unlocked the door of the third room. "Wait here. I'll see if the master is free."

The room had two windows with views blocked by a hedge, no furniture except a shelf lined with hand-sewn volumes of Buddhist texts, cushions on the floor, and a life-size statue of Kuan-yin, the goddess of mercy.

Yunna repeated her earlier question. "Why are we here, Mother?"

"To have our fortunes read."

"Didn't you do that before little brother was born?"

"This is for something else."

"You mean there are things you haven't found out about the future?"

"Of course there are things I haven't found out about the future. How could I possibly…"

"Look, I am taller than Kuan-yin," Yunna cried. She poked her head behind the statue. "'Made in Chiu Chow'. I thought all the gods descended from heaven."

A white-haired monk in a flowing saffron robe entered. Su-chen bowed hastily. She caught Yunna's hand and gestured her to do the same. Yunna dipped her head and then looked straight at the monk.

"Good morning, Venerable Teacher," Su-chen said. "So sorry to come without an appointment. There has been an unexpected turn of events. We need your guidance."

"The gods are merciful to those who are truly humble."

They sat down on the floor cushions, the monk occupying the apex of the triangle.

"Do tell me what's on your mind."

"My family is faced with the prospect of moving to a distant place. It will happen soon—too soon. I want to know if it will be the right thing to do. If it is, I hope to ask the gods to guide us safely to our destination and help us adjust to this new phase in our lives. If it isn't the right thing, we will pray for mercy so that our allotted misfortunes may be lessened."

"Where is this distant place?"

"The continent of Europe."

"That's indeed quite far away."

"You can understand why I am anxious."

"So it's really going to happen," Yunna cried, elated.

"Do be quiet."

Yunna crossed her arms and scowled.

"I need to see the dates and times of your births," the monk said.

Su-chen handed him a piece of paper with the year, month, date, and hour of four birth dates written on it. He pulled an astrological almanac from the shelf, licked a finger, located the pages, and cross-checked the dates with the information in the book. He made calculations with his fingers.

"You were born in the Year of the Ram, the Month of the Rabbit, the Day of the Tiger, and the Hour of the Snake. Wood is your dominant element," the monk said to Su-chen. "This is the Year of the Boar, your perennial adversary. Every one of your four signs is in opposition to the current constellation. It's an unusual convergence. As I told you before, you've entered a phase of endings and beginnings, as marked by the conception of your son." He took her palm and held it up to read the lines. "A line crosses the life line and heads upward to your marriage line, indicating an interruption will take place." He tilted her chin and examined her face in the light. "There is cloudiness at the inner corners of your eyes. It must have appeared recently; I don't remember having seen it last time. Eyes tell one's destiny from the age of thirty-one to thirty-nine. You are in the middle of the range. The cloudiness indicates you are about to face tremendous upheaval."

"It has to be the move to Europe."

"You will separate from your husband."

"Do you mean he and I will travel to different destinations?"

"Your lives will part. Remember, no fortune or misfortune is absolute. This separation, though difficult, will let you escape a calamity."

Worry filled her face. "Will there be a way to avoid the separation?"

"Your life will go through a complete change. Someone from far away will take you to a place you have never been before. You will enjoy a period of prosperity."

"What about my husband and my son? Will they escape this calamity? Will they come with me to this place?"

"Every life must realize its course as it is meant to be."

"Venerable Teacher, the Li family is prepared to do whatever is necessary to ensure the well-being of their descendants."

"I can't answer your questions because I don't have the whole picture. There are unclear elements. For a full reading, I need to see your husband."

"My husband, as you know, has been swayed by Western thinking. I hope he will change; I really do. Until then, we have to do without him. I've brought my daughter along. Perhaps she can fill in the gaps."

"A daughter's joss is tied with that of her future husband."

"I understand the gods show special mercy on young girls who are untouched by men and motherhood."

He turned to Yunna. "Let me see your hand."

Yunna pulled down her mouth in a shrug and let the monk take her hand. He read the lines and felt the center of her palm. His face became intent, intrigued by what he saw.

"Your daughter, too, has come to a juncture in her life." He lifted the left palm up to the light, gasped. "Extraordinary. I don't think I have seen joss like this."

"Will I marry a great man and be famous?"

"Don't be impertinent, Yunna."

"You do have uncommon joss, little girl."

"How uncommon?"

He was hesitant.

"Please tell me. I want to know."

"Keep in mind that a person's joss comes from the gods. They can take back what they give, without forewarning or reason."

"I'll remember."

"This is what I see. One day you will rise above the world. You will live the life of an empress. You will reside in palaces and be waited on by servants. You will have more wealth and power than a person can enjoy in a hundred lifetimes."

"Venerable Teacher, there is no need for excessive assurance," Su-chen cried. "My daughter is capable of fanciful thoughts on her own."

"The words are not mine. They come from the gods. I am only an instrument of delivery."

Bright-eyed and happy, Yunna said, "Will I marry a great man?"

"Your marriage will take place within two years. To an important man."

Two years. It meant her daughter would marry in Europe and likely to a Caucasian, Su-chen thought. She would have a foreigner for a son-in-law and cross-bred children for grandchildren.

Su-chen asked, "If we stayed in Nanking, would the marriage of my daughter not take place so soon?"

"We may think we have some ability in steering the course of our lives. This ability is but an illusion." To Yunna: "Like all life's occurrences, there is a dark side to your fortune. A price will have to be paid."

"What is the price?"

"Loneliness. Power and wealth will set you apart. You will find it difficult to trust anyone, including those who are close to you. Some of your suspicions will not be unfounded."

"The man I'll marry. Won't I have his companionship? Won't I be able to trust him?"

The monk was thoughtful.

"Won't I?"

"Life is a complex process which, given your youth, may not be fully comprehensible."

"My youth is temporary. If I don't understand now, I will later."

"Yes, youth is temporary. As is everything else."

"Please."

"All right, I shall allow myself to speak freely." He lifted his gaze to Kuan-yin with a new wistfulness. "Love is the most elusive of good fortunes, yet the most vital of life's forces. Not everyone is blessed with its true incarnation, yet people yearn for it, pursue it, young and old, rich and poor." To Yunna: "Little girl, love will come to you easily. Men will be enchanted by your beauty and offer themselves to you. Many men. But only three will be of significance."

"Three?"

"One you will marry but you will not be wife to him. One you will be wife to, though he will not be husband to you. One will stay with you every day of your life but you and he will never marry."

"You've given me a riddle!"

"Life is a riddle to those who seek the answers."

"Of course I seek the answers. It's my life. I want to know everything."

"Knowledge, you must be aware, is not wisdom."

"Wisdom doesn't come from ignorance."

"You are an intelligent girl—that in itself is a mixed blessing," the monk remarked kindly. "You must understand that even if the answers are given to you now, they will not be meaningful until the events come to pass."

"I don't care; I want to know."

"That's enough, Yunna. No more questions," Su-chen said firmly. "Thank you for your advice, Venerable Teacher."

"Mother, I am not done."

"Yes, you are. Aren't you always saying you can figure things out on your own? That's what you will do." To the monk, "We appreciate your attention to our undeserved concerns. We should be heading home."

"One moment, Patron Li."

The monk retrieved two objects from a box on the bookshelf: a small scroll and a piece of jade in the shape of a new moon suspended on a red silken cord.

"The scroll contains passages from sacred texts and it will ward off evil. The jade moon will enhance your spiritual strength in times of travail as well as those of prosperity. Keep these with you at all times."

Su-chen stared. "Such weighty precautions. What is going to happen to me?"

"Questions will only cause untimely anxiety. Accept these as no more than reminders of Kuan-yin's infinite mercy."

"But..."

"I'd like to end our session today with some advice."

"Please do."

"Bear in mind that our will is weakest when our corporeal needs are satisfied to their fullest extent, and our soul is most vulnerable when our lives are free from the burden of responsibilities. Simply put, when times are good, it would be wise to refrain from carrying out excessive enterprises in gratifying your desires."

"But my desires are only for the good of my family."

"Our self-understanding may not always be accurate and complete."

Somewhat subdued, Su-chen slipped the red cord around her neck and put the scroll in the pocket of her skirt.

"You must keep faith, Patron Li."

"I will. Thank you."

"And you too, Miss Li."

Yunna nodded.

"We'd like to thank the Buddha now," Su-chen said.

Back in the main hall, an acolyte came forward with the donation bag. Su-chen filled it with cash. Another acolyte lit incense sticks. The head monk knelt down. Su-chen and Yunna took their places behind him. He recited the prayer of benediction. Two rows of acolytes chanted the chorus. Su-chen touched her head reverently to the floor. Yunna stared at a shaft of sunlight, lost in thought.

A gong tolled. The sound rolled through the temple, louder with each bang. The chanting trailed off. The monks looked at each other, not sure what to make of it. An expectant silence enveloped the hall. The head monk was about to order prayers to resume when a young monk rushed in, face pale.

"Master, Master, we are under attack. The whole city is under attack..."

"You are interrupting our prayers. Slow down and speak clearly."

"Sorry, Master. The Japanese are here. There must be thousands of them. They are marching to the town center, killing people and burning houses. Nobody is stopping them."

"Where did you get this information?"

"From two families. They came to us for help and told us what they saw. The Japanese set fire to their homes. They got out with their lives; but they lost everything. They asked if we could let them stay until they find somewhere else to go."

"Where are they?"

"In the guest quarters."

"Bring them here after they've had some rest. I want to speak to them."

"Can they stay?"

"We will accommodate them, at least for a few days."

"We may not have a few days, Master. Parts of the mountain are burning. Someone set fire to the houses in the neighborhood."

"This mountain?"

"Right below us."

The monk hurried to the edge of the terrace, followed by Su-chen, Yunna, and the monks. They formed a ring by the railing. Black smoke rose from the foothills, passing tree lines and rising to the sky. A film of ash permeated the air.

"The burning houses seem to be close to the main road, but the fire will spread," the head monk observed. "Get someone to run down the hill and notify Public Works. Let's hope they would put them out before the fires reach us."

"Second Master wants to know what to do if more people come for help," the young monk asked.

"Go to the storeroom and calculate how long our supplies will last. Get a count of mattresses and blankets. We'll take in as many as there is space to accommodate and as long as we are able. Tell everyone to stay calm and get on with normal duties."

"Yes, Master."

"So those were Japanese trucks,"Yunna muttered.

"What did you say?" Su-chen asked.

"Last night Father and I heard a rumbling down the hill. It was dark, but we could tell it was a large number of vehicles. Father looked with his binoculars and then said they were trucks transporting goods to the market. I thought he knew they were something else."

"What else did he say?"

"Nothing more about the trucks. He had things on his mind."

"But you think your father knew something."

"Something was worrying him. Something he didn't want us to know." Suddenly Yunna cried, "Look! That's our house! It's on fire!"

Su-chen bent over the railing, searching the rooftops. "Where?"

"See that single plume of smoke between those two trees?"

"Are you sure, Yunna?"

"It's our roof!"

Another monk rushed into the terrace. "Master, a foreigner has driven his car through our gates."

"What kind of foreigner?"

"Caucasian. He must be a missionary worker or a diplomat. He speaks our language."

"What does he want?"

"He has been shot in the arm. He needs a safe place to tend to his wounds. He said he would stay only a short while and wouldn't bother us."

"Let him stay. No harm helping a foreigner in need."

Su-chen was ashen-faced. "Venerable Teacher, please excuse us. We need to find out what has happened to our home."

"If the gods have extended their mercy, come back with Professor Li and your son."

"'Extended their mercy'—what do you mean?"

"No more than the words." The monk made a gesture of blessing. "Go in peace."

In the courtyard, Su-chen and Yunna found a tall blond man sitting on the running board of a motor-car. One side of the car was pocked with bullet holes. The man's sleeve was stained with blood. He was trying to bandage the wound with his good hand, but couldn't keep the strip of white gauze in place.

Yunna went up to him. "Can I help?"

"Yes, please."

She held down the gauze. He tore off the end with his teeth and made a knot.

"Thank you."

"Which way did you come?"

"Southeast."

"What did you see?"

He retrieved a flask of brandy from the car and swallowed a gulp. "Dead bodies everywhere. Piles of rubble. Fires. Armed Japanese blocking the roads. I couldn't get out of the city—that's why I took the road up Purple Gold Mountain."

"Did you drive past a gray house with a blue tiled roof?" Yunna asked. "It's about two-thirds of the way up the mountain. The biggest house on the block, with a view of the lake."

"A Fokker tri-motor parked in front?"

"Yes."

"It's the only house on fire. On that street."

"How bad?"

"The flames were on one side of the house. The fire must have just started."

"Which side?"

"North."

"The bedroom," Su-chen cried. "Henry and Sung. Oh no!"

"We need to go home, Mother."

"If someone set the fire to the house, they might still be there," the foreigner said. "You shouldn't go alone. Get help."

"We can't wait for help. Would it possible to borrow your car?"

"Do you know how to drive?"

"My father has given me lessons."

He took another look at Yunna. "Let me come with you. I'll drive."

"What about your arm?"

He stood up. "It's a flesh wound. I'll manage."

A third of the house was in flames.

The car had barely reached the curb when Su-chen opened the door and flung herself out. The foreigner stepped on the brakes and pulled the car to a halt. Yunna jumped out after her mother. The gate was wide open. Su-chen and Yunna rushed up to the house.

"Oh, Buddha, Kuan-yin… Our home, everything…"

"Father! Where are you?"

The heat scorched their skin. They fanned away fumes as they negotiated the heaps of smoldering debris. Without warning, a body in flames staggered out of the smoke bank and collapsed in front of them. Mother and daughter shrieked, jumping back. It was the cook. Hair singed, face charred, blood oozing out of cracked flesh. The body writhed like a trapped animal, jerked violently, and then became inert.

Su-chen and Yunna stared at the corpse, too terrified to utter a sound.

The foreigner caught up with them. "You know him?"

"He's our cook."

"No much you do for him now. Let's move on."

"Where is everyone? Where are the neighbors? Where are the police?" Yunna cried.

He glanced back. "The motor-car is gone."

"None of the servants know how to drive. Who took it?"

Su-chen jolted into motion. "Henry. He took the car. He got out with Sung."

"Father wouldn't have left without us."

"He didn't know where we were. He must be looking for us. It's my fault. I should have let him know."

"If he is safe, he will come back for us."

"Yes. We'll wait for him here."

"We should try to put out the fire," Yunna said.

"We won't be able put out it on our own," the foreigner said. "We should call Public Works. Is there a telephone in the house?"

"It's in the library." Yunna pointed at the south end, the only part of the house not touched by the blaze.

"Let's hope it still works."

"If it doesn't, we can drive to Public Works and report the fire."

They followed the lane circling the house to the library, through a drizzle of ash, sidestepping charred wood and debris. The door of the library was open. Su-chen screamed the moment she stepped inside.

Henry sat upright on the floor against the side of the desk. A bullet wound dead center in the chest. His eyes were open, the face locked in an expression of disbelief. His left hand clutched a book; the other hand rested on the infant in his lap. The baby's clothes were covered with his father's blood. The room had been turned upside down, chairs flipped over with cushions torn out of covers. Books had been swept off the shelves, paintings unhooked from the walls. Drawers had been pulled open, the contents dumped on the floor. The telephone had been yanked off the wall.

Su-chen picked up the baby from Henry's lap and cradled him with her arms. She pressed a finger at his nostrils. The baby trembled.

"Sung is alive. Sung is alive," she cried, hugging him, sobbing. "Buddha, Kuan-yin, thank you. My son is alive."

Yunna knelt down beside her father's body. She felt his pulse, first with one hand, then with both. Not getting any response, she turned frantic. She kept switching hands and pressing down on his skin.

Abruptly, she stopped.

"How is he?" the foreigner asked.

Yunna couldn't speak.

Su-chen handed the baby to the foreigner. She went down on her knees by her daughter's side and picked up her husband's hand.

"Henry. We were at the temple. We rushed back as soon as we saw the fire. Sung's hurt but he's going to live." She squeezed his hand, willing him to respond. "Do you hear me? Please say something, Henry."

Her thumb found the inside of his wrist, pressing gentle at first, then harder.

The foreigner checked Henry's neck. "He is your husband?"

A nod.

"I am sorry. It looks like only the baby survived."

"What?"

"Only the baby survived."

A blank stare.

"Your husband was shot at point-blank range. He suffered a fatal wound," he said. He looked around and found a bullet on the floor behind the desk.

"We will take him to a hospital."

"It's too late."

"It can't be too late."

"He cannot be saved. I'm sorry."

The information sank in. Su-chen shrieked. "Noooooo!"

"The killers might still be around. We'd better get out," the foreigner said.

Su-chen and Yunna didn't seem to have heard.

"We might be in danger. We have to go," he repeated.

"Go? Where?"

"Back to the temple. The baby needs to be in a safe place."

"The baby."

"Your son is running a fever. You want to save him, don't you?"

She nodded, tears spilling down her cheeks, yet her crying produced no sound. "What about Henry?"

"We have to leave him here. For now."

She picked up her husband's hand and brushed it on the baby's face, and then hers. "I have to take care of Sung now, Henry, but I'll be back soon." A new wave of sorrow hit her; she burrowed her head into his inert shoulder.

The foreigner grasped her arms and raised her gently. "Go to the car, and watch out for the smoke."

Su-chen staggered out of the room, Sung clasped in her arms.

Yunna remained by her father's side. Immobile.

The foreigner turned to her. "We must leave."

"My father is dead. Someone killed my father," she mumbled.

"Yes, someone did that."

"Why?"

"We are in a war. People get killed in wars," the foreigner said.

"This couldn't have been random. Every house on the block is intact, except ours. And this room wasn't just ransacked; it was searched."

"If you are right, it could be that your father had something the intruders wanted. Maybe they couldn't find what they were looking for. That's why they shot him," he said hoarsely, his throat seared by the smoke.

"I want to find these people."

A crackling in the next room. A big bang followed. Something heavy fell and sent off clouds of dust. The floor shook.

"You'll have to do that later. We need to go."

"I don't want to leave my father."

More crackling, followed by another thundering thud.

The foreigner grabbed her arm as she extricated the book from her father's grip. They hurried out of the library. Two pillars in the hallway had collapsed, pulling part of the roof with them and exposing the sky. The opening thinned out the smoke; they could see all the way to the front lawn. The charred body in the foyer had shriveled into a blackened log. The contours remained hideously human.

Su-chen was in the back seat of the car, wiping the blood off the baby with a handkerchief. Sung's tiny nostrils were drawing in air, fingers quivering.

The foreigner took off his jacket and handed it to Su-chen. "Keep the baby warm."

Yunna stood by the car like a block of stone.

"Get in." She didn't respond. He pushed her into the passenger seat and went to the other side. "Hold tight."

He drove at top speed back to the temple.

Sung had been hit in the thigh. A bullet had grazed the flesh. Blood seeped from the laceration. The monks took out a medical chest. They found herbal ointments, rolls of bandages and a thermometer.

"Do you have antiseptic?" the foreigner asked. "We need to disinfect the wound."

The monks looked perplexed. "We don't have anything like that."

"Alcohol?"

"No alcohol here."

They cleaned the wound with warm water and wiped down the skin with the brandy in the foreigner's flask and then bandaged the leg. The monk took the baby's temperature. Sung was running a fever of 102, drifting in and out of consciousness.

"He needs a doctor."

"Our family doctor has left Nanking."

"There must be a clinic or a hospital close by."

"Someone please, please get a doctor," Su-chen cried, kneeling by Sung's side, hand stroking his forehead.

"The closest clinic is in the central district," the monk said.

"How far away?"

"Twenty minutes by car, if the Japanese haven't blocked the roads."

"What are we going to do?"

"I'll go," the foreigner volunteered. "It may be easier for me to get past the Japanese."

"Let me come with you," Yunna said.

"I don't know what would have happened if we didn't have you to help us," Yunna said when they were back in the car. "Please accept our thanks."

"No need to thank me. We are in this together. I'm Victor Maurier."

"I'm Yunna. Family name Li."

"Your father. Was he Professor Henry Li of Nanking University?"

She nodded. "You knew him?"

"I've heard of him. Your father was highly regarded in the international community." He added, "I'm from Shanghai."

"Are you going back?"

"Yes."

"Can we go with you?"

"Wouldn't you want to talk it over with your mother?"

"She isn't in a state to make decisions. If the people who killed my father didn't get what they wanted, they will come after us. We have to get away."

"I agree. What happened at your house wasn't random. Will you be all right in Shanghai?"

"Once we're there, we'll be all right. We have relatives. We won't be a burden to you."

It came to Victor that this was what the Chinese called joss. The gods had arranged the chain of incredible events in the past few hours for him to rescue Henry Li's widow and children.

"I'll check with my boss and see if he can help us with better transportation to get out of here."

"There's one more thing, Mr. Maurier."

"Yes?"

"I'm afraid it'll inconvenience you further."

"Let me decide," he said kindly.

"There is a trunk in my father's library. It contains the best of his work—he told me last night. I want to keep it in memory of him. Can you help me get it out of the house?"

The best of Henry Li's work had to be top intelligence material. It would be invaluable to the Kuomintang, Soong, anyone.

Victor started the engine and rammed the car into gear. "We'll stop at the house first."

The wind had changed direction. The force of the fire had dissipated before reaching the southern end, miraculously leaving the library intact. A tangle of charred beams surrounded blackened remnants of furniture. The flames were dwindling to embers. Large gaping holes in the ceiling let in bars of the late morning sun. Ash floated in the air like gray snowflakes. The stench of burning stung their eyes.

They stepped into the library and noticed fresh signs of disturbance. The configuration of the debris had shifted. A path had been cleared through the rubble from the doorway to the bookshelves. Above the credenza, a wall safe gaped open; bullet holes dotted the metal door. The contents were gone.

Henry's body had been turned over. It lay face down on the floor.

"They came back," Yunna said.

Victor stepped over the debris to the safe and examined the bullet holes. "It could have been a different group of people. The bullets that hit the safe were different from the bullet that killed your father. You have any idea what they were looking for?"

She shook her head.

"I wonder if they found it this time. Did your father keep his valuables here?"

"The valuables were kept in the bedroom."

"What was in the safe?"

"A radio transmitter and a machine for typing. Father ordered them from Germany. He called them his toys—he was fond of mechanical devices. I never saw him use them, or maybe he only used them when he was alone."

Tools of the spy trade. No wonder they were seized.

She pointed at the cabinet. "The locks are broken and the drawers have been cleared out. They weren't just now."

"What was inside?"

"Decoys."

"Decoys?"

"That's how my father described them. I asked him what he meant. He said decoys were handy to have around because they provided easy protection."

Fake evidence to satisfy searchers.

"Can you think of anything that happened recently that might explain this?"

"It's been an unsettling couple of weeks. First we were packing up to leave for Chungking with our relatives, and then out of the blue, my father said we were moving to Europe. In the last two days, he was worried and nervous, like he knew something bad was about to happen."

"Anything specific related to this room?"

"I wouldn't know. This was father's private space. He did his work here, always with the door closed. No one was allowed to come in without his permission. When he was out of town, he locked the door. He was the only one who had the key."

"This room was the target of the break-in. The burglary has to be related to your father's work."

"He was a scholar. Why would anyone want to take this much trouble to steal his work?"

"Didn't he also work for the Generalissimo?"

"For that position, he had an office in the government building. I've been there. There was hardly anything in the room. His files were kept by the secretary."

"You said there was a trunk?"

"It's about the size of this desk and made of dark wood. It looks like an antique."

She made her way through the mess, searching under broken furniture and scattered piles of books. She found it under the blanket and cushions.

He joined her. "It's locked. Where is the key?"

"I don't know."

He tried to move it. "It's very heavy."

"It's probably packed with books and papers."

He handed his pistol to Yunna. "Take this and look out for intruders."

"Let me help you."

"I can manage." Then he winced. "My arm. Damn."

He used both hands to push the trunk, a few inches at a time. Yunna moved ahead to clear a path through the debris. At the door, he let her help him lift the trunk over the step.

"Feels like it's filled with bricks," Victor remarked.

"It rattles—"

"Hold it right there. Don't move another inch."

Three men were blocking the corridor. Two had their guns out. The third was dressed in the uniform of a Japanese officer. He stepped forward.

"This house has been confiscated by the Japanese Imperial Army. No one is allowed to remove anything from the premises," he announced in Chinese.

"Who are you?" Yunna asked.

He tapped the medals on his chest. "Official representatives of the Japanese Imperial Army."

"You don't look Japanese to me."

"I'm acting on orders from General Matsui Iwane."

"This is China. Go to Japan and follow your orders there."

"China is losing. General Iwane is taking over Nanking and I am helping him to do it."

"Traitor."

"Call me whatever you like. I am on the winning side."

Yunna raised Victor's pistol.

The man was amused. "Weapons are not for young ladies. Hand it over."

"Get out or I'll shoot."

He swaggered up to her and tapped his fingers on her cheek. "You are one nice-looking girl. How old are you?"

"Get your hands off me."

"Fifteen? Sixteen? Never made Clouds and Rain, I bet." He licked his lips, eyes running down the length of her body. "Must be dying to find out how it feels. Me too. Been a while since I broke in a girl."

He grabbed his crotch and shook obscenely.

"Stop!"

"A temper to boot. I like that."

She gripped the gun with both hands, aiming at his face. "This is my house. I want you to get out."

"*Your* house? You think we can be scared away by a little gun, Miss Li?"

"How do you know my name?"

"Your father was a well-known criminal."

"My father was a decent and honorable man."

The man snorted. "I don't give a damn what kind of man your father was. He could have been Confucius for all I care. We are here to do a job."

"What job?"

"Treasure hunting."

"What treasure?"

"The collection of the National Museum. Your father has been hiding it for the Generalissimo. My boss in Tokyo is a connoisseur of fine art. He has a better place for it. If you tell us where it is, I may let you go."

"It isn't here."

"We know it isn't here. We want to know where."

She didn't reply.

"Where?"

"In a warehouse."

"Where is the warehouse?"

No answer.

"Where is the damn warehouse?"

"Did you kill my father?"

"We'd have loved to, but someone else got to him first."

"Who?"

"Who knows? Your father made himself a nuisance to many people."

"I want their names."

"You are not getting them from me. If you want to find out, ask your Generalissimo."

"Generalissimo? Why?"

The man shrugged.

"Why?"

"Why, why, why… Who are you to ask questions? You are getting on my nerves. Tell us where your father kept the stuff. Now."

Victor said, "She's just a child. She doesn't know. Leave her alone."

The man turned around to check out Victor. "I'll be damned. This barbarian can speak our civilized language…"

Gunshots exploded.

The men in the back collapsed first. Two loud thumps as they dropped on the floor. The last shot hit the uniformed man in the leg. Clutching his wound, he struggled to pull the gun from his waist band.

"You filthy bitch, I'll get you…"

One shot.

The bullet entered his abdomen and exited through his back in a spray of blood, skin, and tissue. He slammed backward and landed on top of his companions. The body was rigid for a moment and then became limp. Blood was flowing out in a web of red tributaries.

Victor went to the bodies and checked their pulses.

"Are they dead?" she asked.

"Yes."

"All of them?"

"Yes."

"Good."

"You just killed three men."

She was still aiming the gun at where the men had stood. Eyes blazing.

"Put the gun away. It's all right now."

"It will never, never be all right."

She tightened her grip, wouldn't let the gun go. He had to force it out of her hand. Her fingers were stiff and icy. When she gave in, she surrendered herself with it, hands dropping to her sides. He wrapped his arms around her. She felt like stone.

"You picked the right moment to pull the trigger. Took them by surprise."

"They invaded my home. I couldn't let them live."

She let herself out of his grasp and returned to the trunk. Without a word they hauled it out of the house to the car.

The clinic was a free-standing building in a busy section of the city. Today it was a ghost town. Abandoned possessions of refugees scattered on the pavement. The air was thick with the tang of gunpowder. An eerie calm settled in the emptiness. The flood of refugees seemed to have dried up.

Those who could leave have left, Victor thought.

They pushed open the wooden gate and stepped into a battlefield after combat. The clinic could not accommodate all the wounded and the bodies had spilled onto the lawn. People lay on the grass, issuing murmurs of pain. In the sunlight, blood-soaked garments glared like signposts of danger. Victor and Yunna picked their way through injured bodies. Near the front door, they almost stepped on a baby. A newborn, like Sung. A bullet had pierced his tiny skull. The mother, covered in blood, slumped by the infant's side. Both could be dead. Behind them, a man was holding his own hand, half shot off, gazing in a hypnotic stare.

Yunna turned white. She sagged forward, heaved and retched.

"Let me handle this," Victor said. "Wait in the car."

"All these people need help. How can they spare a doctor for Sung?"

"I'll find a way."

The reception room was like the front lawn, crowded with the wounded and the dying. Some of the bodies have to be corpses, Victor thought, his eye picking out inert lumps on the floor. This is just a tiny fraction of the casualties. There must be hundred times more dead bodies out there. The warehouse in the village came to mind. You are making big strides, Mr. Soong. From poisoning a village to butchering a city. Nausea welled in his stomach. He forced himself on, waving his Kuomintang Party badge like a fool.

In the hallway he stopped a nurse.

"Excuse me, I must speak with you," he said in English. Most Chinese wouldn't ignore requests from Caucasians.

"Yes?"

She had clipped hair and rimless glasses; a surgical mask was pushed up on her forehead. Her white gown, like everything else in the room, was stained with blood.

He switched to Chinese. "I need a doctor to come with me. It's an emergency."

"The whole city is in an emergency."

"It's for the child of a government official."

"Haven't they all left town?" she snapped.

"The child is one month old. He has been shot and he is running a high fever. I have a car. I'll take the doctor there and bring him right back."

"There are only two doctors on the premises. We can't spare them."

"Is there another clinic close by?"

"It wouldn't be any different. Why can't you bring your patient in like everyone else? Do you think we give a damn about those government officials after they abandoned us?"

He took out his gun. "Sorry, I don't have a choice. Take me to the physician."

She shook her head wearily, as if saying she wouldn't expect him to pull the trigger but she didn't care enough to resist. She led him through a pair of swing doors into the operating room. Moments later, Victor was marching a doctor out of the clinic.

In the car Victor apologized, "We should have waited our turn, but the baby is fighting to stay alive."

"We'll bring you back as soon as we can," Yunna said.

The doctor had a stethoscope around his neck and a line of sweat under his hairline. He leaned back in the seat, grateful for a respite.

"The wounded keep pouring in," he said wearily. "There's only so much we can do. Even if we did manage to treat them, they'll be shot as soon as they are out of here. The Japanese are spraying the streets with bullets. We're running out of supplies, out of time, out of everything. I don't see how we can keep up. What difference does it make where I am?"

"It will make a difference to us," Yunna said.

"Can't you get help?" Victor asked.

"From whom?"

"Neighboring towns."

"The telephone lines are jammed. There's no way to send telegrams. The communication equipment has been moved to Chungking. Our government has left us to die."

"My relatives," Yunna said dryly.

"How come you didn't get out?" the doctor asked.

"We didn't expect things to fall apart so quickly."

"The Generalissimo did. He was out of here faster than anyone."

The doctor leaned back into the seat and fell asleep almost immediately. Victor woke him when they arrived at the temple. Groggy from the short nap, the doctor walked stiffly behind the monks to the guest cottage.

"Please save my son," Su-chen said. "We'll be grateful for the rest of our lives."

"I'll do what I can."

While the doctor tended to Sung, Su-chen stepped away from the bed and knelt down. She clasped her hands in front of her body, like a prisoner waiting for the judge to hand down the sentence.

No flames in sight now, though the air was choked in smoke. The afternoon sun shone through the grayness like a searchlight. The rays felt cold and indifferent. It can't be the same sun that shone on her way to the temple, Yunna thought, looking out from where they had first noticed the fire in the morning.

A different world. A different me.

"Your mother is heartbroken over your brother." Victor had brought a coat and draped it on her shoulders. "Go comfort her. She needs you."

"She needs her son. She wants Sung brought back to life."

"That's not possible."

"Why would that stop her? That was what we thought when my mother wanted a son. Women her age don't bear children. She didn't give up. It became her sole purpose in life. A son to carry on the family name. Didn't matter that she had me. She'd made up her mind a daughter couldn't make her life complete." She managed a smile. "You see, my mother has never accepted the impossible."

"Your mother needs time to heal. So do you."

"We have had more than sixteen years together. When Sung was born, I became nothing. Now he's gone, I'm still nothing. If she had a choice, she'd prefer I was the one who died."

Her bitterness was jarring. Victor sensed it wasn't part of her normal catalog of emotions. He wished he had known her before today. He wished there had not been today.

"It's been a horrific shock. Give yourselves time. Your mother will come around."

"Not if she finds out I was responsible for Sung's death."

"You are not responsible. He was too fragile to survive the gunshot wound."

"If I had not made you stop by the house for the trunk, the doctor could have arrived in time to save Sung." She fixed her eyes on the sun, taking in the glare like punishment. "All I had on my mind was preserving my father's work. I didn't think of my brother."

"We are in an impossible situation. Your father and your brother are victims of this colossal tragedy. That is the reality. Nothing you did could have changed that."

"'Nothing I did could have changed that.'"

"No."

"Why couldn't I have?" she demanded, voice cracking under strain. "Why did these things have to happen? It's not supposed to be this way. Last night my father promised I was going to have the future I wanted. My father always kept his word."

"It's still possible to have the future you want."

"How?"

"I've contacted General Han's people. They will meet you in Shanghai and escort you to Shansui. It's far away from the war zones. You and your mother will be safe."

"Why General Han?"

"Your mother said he was your father's best friend, and he'd be willing to help."

In silence they looked ahead. Beyond the haze, Hsûen Wu Lake was calm and gray as on any day. In any winter. Any dynasty. Soon today's catastrophe would be remembered as no more than an incident in five thousand years of changes and upheaval, Victor thought. Five thousand years. Staggering. Unimaginable. How many lifetimes? How much experience, absurd, wise, and everything in between? What do I know about China? What does anyone?

"It has been a long day," he said.

"The longest in my life."

"Mine too. It's coming to an end."

"Is it?"

"The worst is over."

To his relief there were tears in her eyes.

Victor set about planning the trip back to Shanghai. It would be a hazardous journey. The roads would be congested. The Japanese would be everywhere, along with thousands of refugees. His arm was hurting. There were Su-chen and Yunna, the trunk, and Soong's papers from the safe house. He had one car and one gun, no bodyguard, no fuel, and no provisions.

He called T. V. Soong.

"Please arrange a plane at the South Gate airfield tomorrow morning," Victor said. "There will be two more passengers."

"Who are you bringing back? You said everyone was dead."

"Henry Li's wife and daughter."

"My cousins?"

"Yes."

"Are you sure?"

"Yes."

"How did you meet up with them?"

"By chance. I'll explain when I see you."

"Did you tell them you work for me?"

"Not a word."

"Keep it that way. Su-chen is harmless, but she can be too righteous for her own good. What about Li? Was he there with his family?" Soong asked.

You must know that Henry Li was killed. Your brother-in-law ordered the execution. "Li's dead. I have something better. I have his papers. The whole archive."

"Are you sure?"

"They were right there in his house. In one big trunk. His daughter told me."

"Well done. Let's hope there is a map of Han's gold mine," Soong said. "My sister asked about you. She wanted me to see to it that you will be all right."

"How kind. Please thank her."

"She expects to see you when you are back."

"I will thank her in person."

"She may want you to do more than say thanks."

"I have done more. I don't think a repeat performance is what she has in mind."

"Who knows what my sister has in mind? Just so you know, her husband is in Hong Kong setting up a new chain of pawnshops. He'll be gone for another week. She's lonely."

"I am spoken for."

"But it's Big Sister."

"Sorry."

"Oh well. Even Big Sister can't have everything she wants. I must say your loyalty to your mistress is commendable." Soong added, "I hope your loyalty extends beyond your Paramount star."

"Of course it does."

Loyalty. That was implied in the relationship. But Victor knew the bond between Soong and him was a tenuous one. If he had been alone, he knew Soong wouldn't have hesitated to leave him in Nanking. And he had no intention of letting Soong know he had taken his financial records out of the Nanking house. The inquiry from his former paramour had been a surprise. He hadn't expected she would be concerned for his safety. Maybe it had been love for her. The woman had been a volcano. She had gone after him like she had not made love in decades. No surprise there. Her husband was a walking abacus; the man didn't seem to possess an ounce of libido. Wonder what she had in mind.

10

The scion of China's last imperial dynasty emerged from a silver Rolls-Royce. Barely over five feet tall, Pu-yi had spindly arms and legs, a narrow head that sloped down to a pursed mouth. He was dressed like an Englishman at the races, in a brown striped suit with a white carnation boutonnière, sunglasses, saddle shoes, and an ivory-tipped walking stick. Taking a long look at the facade of Crescent Moon Villa, he seemed perplexed, blinking to make sure it was real.

"Welcome to Shansui, Your Majesty," Han said, extending his hand. By traditional protocol, he should kneel down and bow to the Emperor. But to do so would acknowledge sovereignty of Japanese-controlled Manchukuo. Han remained standing.

Pu-yi didn't seem to mind. They shook hands.

"Kind of you to invite me."

"How was the journey?"

"Uneventful. Glad it was so." He pulled at his earlobe. "Is it always so warm here?"

"We are fortunate to be blessed with mild weather all year round. How is the Empress?"

"Fine. She sends her regrets. She likes winter in Manchukuo. For the snow games."

"Perhaps she would visit us on another occasion."

"Perhaps."

It was rumored that the royal marriage had never been consummated. After the wedding night the Empress had let the word out that the royal yang was flaccid, the Son of Heaven was likely sterile; therefore no imperial heir should be expected of her. To save face, the Emperor had recruited a troupe of concubines and had them take turns sharing his bed. After being exiled to Manchukuo, the royal couple had reconciled and become friends.

"Meet my chief of staff, Lin Jong," Han said.

Jong stepped forward and greeted the Emperor with a military salute.

"You were the one who spoke to me on the phone?"

"Yes, Your Majesty."

Pu-yi took off his sunglasses. "How splendid you look. Like a prince in a storybook. Where did you find him, General? In the foreign concessions? Abroad?"

"In downtown Shanghai. Many years ago."

"Shanghai. Nothing that lucky has ever happened to me."

The Shansui military band launched into a medley of Pu-yi's favorite American jazz tunes. Han had decided it would be a suitable substitute for Manchukuo's national anthem. It had to be one of the more bizarre tableaus in history, Jong observed. A ceremony for a Manchu emperor dressed up as an English aristocrat accompanied by

American Negro music played in front of a Chinese warlord's palace.

"Nice music," Pu-yi mumbled, putting his sunglasses back on. "Played a lot of it in Tientsin."

"Shall we, Your Majesty?"

Mindful of the Emperor's penchant for things foreign, Jong had staged a Western welcoming ceremony. It opened with the inspection of troops. Han and Pu-yi led the way, followed by Jong and the small Manchukuo entourage. A brigade with gleaming swords queued up like rows of life-size toy soldiers. The audience was a select group of local citizens, a gathering of three hundred, well dressed and attentive. It was a scene familiar to Pu-yi and he found it reassuring. Head up and back straight, he walked along the carpet to the stage. Pu-yi and Han took their seats under a yellow canopy. Han delivered the welcoming address, thanking the Emperor for the honor of his presence, thereby making history by bestowing on Shansui the honor of being the only city in the southwest having been visited by a bona fide emperor. Pu-yi responded with an all-purpose speech he recited flatly, pressing his small body against the lectern for support. Midway he stopped to wipe sweat off his brow. His face flushed deeply as if he was about to faint. The pause was long enough to cause the audience discomfort. When he resumed, he galloped through the remaining script like a nervous student.

It has been a long time since the Emperor faced an audience, Jong thought.

"How did this happen?" Pu-yi's eyes darted around the guest chamber, his hand busily caressing the furniture. "Did you clean out my old room in the Forbidden City?"

"We don't have access to the Forbidden City. We did the next best thing and had the furnishings replicated, Your Majesty," Jong replied.

"You got all the details right."

"General Han wants you to feel at home."

"I do. Sort of." Pu-yi stopped at the "Longevity" calligraphy. "Do you know this was my grandmother's favorite word?"

"Yes, we heard."

"She decreed that the word be displayed in every room, every corridor. We were tired of looking it, but she had to have longevity in her sight. Didn't matter that it was just ink and rice paper. She thought if she saw it often enough, it would happen. She was one obsessive woman. Did you ever meet my grandmother?"

"I didn't have the honor."

"You didn't miss much. Take away the costumes and the jewelry, she would have been no different from any one of the old ladies in Chang An Park with nothing to do except sit around and watch the day go by. She was lucky. Very lucky." A chuckle. "Same goes for me. For a few years, anyway."

Couldn't think of a suitable response, Jong kept quiet.

"She did everything to extend her years. Couldn't blame her. In her position, who wouldn't want to live forever? In the end, nothing worked. She got old and sick, passed away, and that was that. Death is democratic."

"It is."

"If Elizabeth saw this, she would think Old Buddha had risen from the grave," Pu-yi said with a chuckle. Elizabeth was the Empress's English name. Old Buddha had been the Empress Dowager's preferred alias—the Buddha was believed to have lived eight hundred years.

"If it pleases you, we can ship the calligraphy to Manchukuo."

"I'll put it in my wife's room. Give her nightmares."

Jong pointed at the adjoining alcove. "Something else you might like to see, Your Majesty."

On elaborately constructed beaverboard was the latest model of a Lionel and American Flyer electric toy train set flown in from Chicago. Jong pressed a button. A whistle blew. The engine of the diminutive express fired up and started to move, gathering speed as it rolled through a make-believe American countryside, passing a church with a Sunday crowd on the front lawn, a farm with windmills and grazing cows. Pu-yi's eye followed the freight meandering up and down the miniature landscape, mesmerized. Toy trains had been his passion since childhood. Without warning, a section of the beaverboard opened up. The train ducked and disappeared. A rolling sound was heard under the board, followed by a long splattering, like marbles hitting wood. The train resurfaced, with the twelve container cars filled with black pearls the size of grapes. They made a full circle before they stopped in front of the Emperor.

"You recognize these, Your Majesty?"

"Should I?"

"They were among the treasures buried with your grandmother in the Eastern Tombs."

"You are not joking?"

"No."

"How did they get here?"

"The General bought them from black market jewelers in Peking. Ten catties of pearls have been located. The other forty are believed to be in the hands of Kuomintang officials."

Pu-yi grabbed a handful, held them up to his face, and squinted as if the pearls hurt his eyes. "These were buried with Grandmother?"

"General Han was outraged by the desecration of the royal tomb. On this point, he is ashamed of his association with the Generalissimo. He has taken it upon himself to salvage as much of the imperial treasure as he can. These pearls serve as a reminder of the injustice inflicted upon your family. They are yours, Your Majesty."

"Mine?"

"And rightfully so."

Pu-yi rubbed them on his cheek. Tears filled his eyes.

"Your Majesty must see that though there is no question this is a worthwhile undertaking, the process involves a great deal of expense and risk."

He nodded. "You have to do business with nasty people."

"And our resources are not unlimited."

"Whose are?"

"Nonetheless, it is our intention to keep up the efforts as long as they please you."

"Of course they please me." Pu-yi's eyes were fixed on a spot beyond the pearls. "But there is a catch. You didn't invite me here because General Han wants a friend. We met only once before and we hardly said a word to each other. And you didn't give me these pearls because you liked my grandmother."

"It's our honor and our pleasure to have you here, Your Majesty. We also hope we can convince you to lend your support in a matter of vital importance to the future of the nation."

"What kind of support?"

"An arrangement where you can play an important role."

"A political arrangement?"

"Yes."

"With the Kuomintang?"

"With General Han."

"Only him?"

"Yes."

"I see. Will the role be public?"

"Yes."

Pu-yi was thoughtful. "I am the head of Manchukuo. It's a young country; much in its administration has to be improved. My Japanese sponsors have their own ideas about how the country should be run; inevitably, some of those ideas do not agree with mine. We are trying to work out our differences. This is an uncertain time. I cannot promise anything until I know what General Han has in mind."

"He will discuss with you, but only after you've had a chance to enjoy his hospitality. He wants you to know that regardless of your participation in this arrangement, these pearls are a gift from him."

"No strings attached?"

"No strings attached."

"It'll be for Christmas then," Pu-yi said with a wink, somberness gone. "I've heard all kinds of wild stories about General Han. His palace. His women. His gold. I thought people were making them up. Now I get to see for myself. I must say he has done very well for a regional official. Tell him I like my present. I'll put it under the tree when I get home."

The first step of conspiracy has been completed, Jong noted as he put the pearls in a velvet bag. The Emperor accepts a bribe offered by a warlord, implicitly agreeing to a proposed rebellion. Han had planned it perfectly. Convince Pu-yi he was taking back something rightfully his and he wouldn't turn it down. Jong hoped the value of the gift was not lost on the Emperor. The contents of the bag could easily match half Manchukuo's annual budget.

"Shall I have them stored during your stay? Or would you like to keep them with you?"

With a fluttering of eyelashes, Pu-yi said, "Take care of them for me."

"They will be kept in a portable safe. I will personally hand you the key when you leave Shansui."

"Personally. Your hand to mine. Wonderful. Anything else you want to show me, you, lovely man? This is turning out to be so much fun."

"Would you like me to go over your itinerary? Perhaps there are things you'd like to do that we overlooked."

"Itinerary. Sounds so official. I'll do whatever I feel like doing whenever I feel like it."

"Of course, Your Majesty."

"Tell me, what do you do as General Han's chief of staff?"

"I do whatever the General wants done."

"Anything he wants?"

"Yes."

"I don't suppose you want to live in Manchukuo?"

"Not at the moment."

"I have no doubt that you'll be good at whatever you'll do. How about I let you pick a position in my government? You don't have to give me an answer now. Think about it."

"Thank you, Your Majesty. But I have made my commitment to General Han."

"Commitment. So serious. Oh well... Come anyway. For a holiday. Don't think Manchukuo is all sand and snow. It has lovely pastures and blue skies. Premium horse country. You like horses? Sure you do. Who wouldn't? I keep a stable of thoroughbreds. When the weather is fine, we can play polo. I'll bet you look stunning on horseback." He gazed dreamily at the picture in his mind. "I'll show you my collection of Arabian etchings. You'll see how much you look like one of the princes."

"I am honored to be invited, Your Majesty."

"Will you be the one who handle our communication?"

"It will be up to General Han."

"Tell him I want you."

Pu-yi was ready to render a gesture of affection, but Jong had already moved out of his range. He gave a signal. Servants appeared with bath salts and towels. The Emperor was to enjoy a hot bath and massage before the evening banquet.

Han believed how a man performed Clouds and Rain revealed much about his character and political acumen. Over aggressiveness indicated low confidence and impatience for results. Someone who took his time to draw out maximum pleasure valued strategy over firepower, but might not be prepared for the unexpected. The man who identified the point of attack at first try and went on to tame a crew of seasoned singsong girls without straining himself—he would be the one to look out for. Rivals and allies had been invited to the Villa for Han to observe this aspect of them.

Tonight it was Pu-yi's turn.

In a room adjoining the new imperial suite, Han and Jong watched behind a two-way mirror. Pu-yi and two eunuchs were engaging in half-hearted foreplay. Three pairs of arms and legs entwined, twirling like one giant octopus. On the other side of the bed, a pretty-faced boy, stark naked except for a silk scarf around his neck, was wrestling with pillows between his legs. Two girls in camisoles waited beside the bed, holding trays of food and wine. Under the Longevity calligraphy, Gin-lin curled up on the chaise, fully clothed and snoring noisily.

Pu-yi was the center of the trio, legs apart, staring vacuously at the ceiling. He mumbled a command. The eunuchs began a fresh round of motions. They licked his face, sucked his nipples, and stroked his genitals. Pu-yi seemed to enjoy the simple ministrations, giggling and writhing like a child being tickled by nannies. The boy, not to be left out, climbed on top of the Emperor. Pu-yi brushed the eunuchs away, pulled the boy's face down, and kissed him on the lips in small, repetitive smooches.

"The royal yang is pitiful," Han observed, stroking his chin. "It's too weak to penetrate a woman's Jade Well. It might manage a little girl's, but I doubt there's enough power to break the shield. He is a born sodomite, and a miserable one at that. The man is thirty-one years old. No reason to believe his yang will improve."

"He was brought up by eunuchs. It's inevitable that they shaped his habits," Jong said.

"He has turned into a eunuch himself, intact yang notwithstanding. Pathetic. China's last emperor is a twit and a pederast. Better for the country that he was evicted from the dragon throne. He wouldn't have been man enough to rule." Han crossed his arms. "Where are the rest of the girls?"

"He sent them away as soon as they showed up. All ten of them. He didn't give them a look. Gin-lin made an excuse to stay, but he didn't let her come to his bed."

"We have to find another way to incapacitate him."

"It may take time. Sodomites' habits are not well studied."

"Too bad we can't just shoot the idiot and put him out of his misery." Han had seen enough. He got up from the armchair. "Send Gin-lin to Manchukuo. If any woman can rouse a weak yang, it's her. Tell Pu-yi she is a gift from me."

"Gin-lin?"

"She wants to be a royal concubine. This is her chance."

"Yes, General."

They left the anteroom and walked along an open corridor surrounding a garden. Light from a half moon filtered through the treetops. Scents of night blossoms saturated the air.

"A Caucasian man flew Henry's widow and daughter out of Nanking in Soong's plane," Han said. "He tracked down our people in Shanghai—the ones not in the books—and asked me to help them. When you are there, check out who this Caucasian is."

"I will, General."

"You must be glad to be done with Pu-yi."

"It was no trouble."

"He has his lecherous eye on you. It couldn't have been comfortable."

"I am sure by now he knows his attention was misplaced."

"Pederasts are a peculiar bunch. What makes a man want to make Clouds and Rain with another man?"

Han regarded Jong's profile. "But easy to see why he finds you attractive. Most people do. I've noticed how women look at you. They can't wait to climb into your bed. I know you are saving yourself for the great love of your life, but why not have fun before she shows up?"

"I am not deprived, General. I only appear so in your company."

Han laughed heartily. "Hard for any man to compare himself with me."

"No one should try."

"Tell me, has there been a woman who came close to your heart?"

"Close, but it wasn't my heart."

More laughter. "That's how it should be. Women are necessary distractions. An indispensable source of pleasure. We let them enjoy our yang; our head and our heart are off limits."

"What about you, General? Have you loved a woman?"

"Never. And I don't intend to. The stuff about falling in love and how that would make a man do crazy things—I don't buy any of it." He added, "I'm sure your Western half would disagree."

"There isn't a Western half in me."

"There is, Jong. No question there. Don't ask me to explain. Certain things one just knows."

The Villa was dark except for the sentry lights along the wall. Darkness eliminated the superfluous. Only the outline of the architecture was visible. Without the garishness, it looked like a palace in a dream. Was it the same with people? Jong wondered. Could it be that he meant this much to Han because he kept a part of himself out of sight? How long could he go on being partly invisible?

His thoughts were going to a murky place. He pulled himself back to the task at hand. "Will Mrs. Li and her daughter be staying with us?"

"Henry died on the first day of the Japanese invasion. Their house was burned down. They lost everything. His wife and daughter will need a home."

"We can put them up in an apartment in the east wing."

"That's what I had in mind."

"I'll have the staff get the place ready."

"I am certain Henry was killed because of what he did for me. Chiang found out and sent his Blue Shirts. That's what he does to anyone who gets on his wrong side. The man is a thug. And a gutless bastard. If he wants to go after me, why not do so in the open like a real commander-in-chief? Murdering my spymaster won't bring me in line."

"The Generalissimo had his cousin killed?"

"Henry was a cousin by marriage. Not real family. But Chiang would have his own son killed if it suited his purpose."

"Could it have been the Japanese? Henry fought back and got himself killed?"

"At that time in the day, the Japanese had just reached the town center. Even if some of them had gotten to Purple Gold Mountain, they would have destroyed the entire neighborhood. Nothing happened to the other houses on his street. Henry was singled out."

"Does Henry's wife have a clue that her cousin murdered her husband?"

"She wouldn't believe it. She is devoted to her family; she thinks her cousins are beyond reproach." His voice softened, "She has suffered enough. No point in telling her the truth. But do tell her that I am heartbroken. Tell her I'll do what I can to make things right for her."

"I will, General."

"You haven't met Su-chen, have you?"

"No, I have not met Henry's family."

"She grew up with the Soong sisters, attended fancy schools, moved in the best circles. Impeccable pedigree. Quite a woman." He breathed. "She doesn't know about what Henry did for me. She thinks we were just good friends."

"I'll be discreet."

"Tell her I will find out who killed Henry—she will have no need to ask her relatives for help. I don't want her talking to the Soongs until she's here and we can monitor the communication." He paused. "Between us, let me be clear about this. I don't want anything done about Henry's murder. No inquiry. No investigation. I'm disassociating myself from what happened."

"Publicly?"

"And privately."

"For how long?"

"As long as it takes. I don't want to give even a hint that Henry's death meant more than the loss of a friend. Any extra effort on my part would be an admission of what he did for me." Han frowned at the next thought. "We need to know whether the Blue Shirts found Henry's files. It'll be disastrous if Chiang gets his hands on them."

"When I telephoned the office in Shanghai, I was told a trunk was salvaged from the library. It was believed that it contained Henry's work."

"Well, then," Han said, relieved.

Noon, the next day. Pu-yi was having breakfast in the courtyard of his suite. He wore a white silk robe over a pair of loose pantaloons. By the sculptured fountain, a buffet table displayed an array of delicacies: sausages, caviar, breads, pastries. Three maids were waiting on the Emperor. One stirred coffee. One held a plate of food. The third massaged his feet. Pu-yi was lounging in a cushioned chair, munching on a buttered croissant.

Han entered without announcement. A guard placed a chair across from Pu-yi. He registered Han's presence but offered no greeting. Han sat down. A maid brought his customary cup of hot ginseng tea.

"A fine morning, Your Majesty." Han held up his cup in a symbolic toast. Pu-yi gave a nod and went on with his breakfast. "I hope you had a good night's rest."

"I'm not used to the air. Too humid."

"Air. That's an interesting subject."

"How so?"

"The air in Peking, for instance. You must have noticed how much the air has changed since they took away the trees inside the Forbidden City."

"Why would I? I don't live there anymore," Pu-yi said blithely and licked off a dab of butter from the croissant.

"The trees were over two hundred years old; they'd witnessed the history of a dynasty. Overnight they were chopped down and moved to a cold lumberyard miles away. Such a waste, don't you think?"

Pu-yi frowned at the obvious allusion to the Ching Dynasty's demise and his own exile. "Not waste. Change. The world is changing. I am not sentimental about the past."

"I can see how tempting it would be for the young to dismiss the past," Han replied amicably. "They are not burdened by memory or experience. But I'm from the old school. I belong to the unfashionable minority who revere the past."

"The past is the past. Gone. Done with." With that, Pu-yi tossed the half-eaten croissant into the bushes.

"The past defines the present, and the present launches the future. For thousands of years, China was an orderly place. Rules were obeyed. People were respectful of one another. Society functioned on principles molded by centuries of practice. Tradition. That's what makes our country great. Not motorcars. Not radios. Not anything foreigners can offer us."

It was a reference to Pu-yi's recent efforts to enlist Japanese and Russian help to regain his throne in Peking. He sulked in his chair with his arms folded.

"Never mind foreigners," Han went on. "If we ourselves cannot be respectful of our ancestors and our tradition, why blame people outside our culture?"

"Why indeed?"

"It is unfortunate that the current leadership sets a poor example. What the Generalissimo did to your grandmother's tomb was unforgivable. His wife swiped the imperial jewels to decorate her shoes and paraded in front of the foreign press. The jades worn by your grandmother are now on the bosoms of concubines and courtesans." Han took a sip of the tea. "I was told that you are pleased with the recovery we made."

Pu-yi's look was wary, his tone blunt. "Your chief of staff said you want something from me. What is it?"

"As the Sage said: 'Extreme situations inevitably bring forth their own demise.' Since the Ching Dynasty came to its tragic end, unscrupulous people have been in power.

210

They are ruining the country with their ineptitude and corruption. China is on the verge of collapse. These people should not be allowed to go on governing. I consider it my mission to make sure the Sage's words will come to pass."

"How are you going to do that?"

"I have a plan. I can't tell you the details, but I can tell you what it will accomplish. It will keep the foreigners out, stop the war, restore peace and order to the country."

"Peace," Pu-yi repeated and closed his eyes. "It has existed only in empty talk and dreams. I am not sure I'll experience peace in my lifetime."

"You will."

"How can you be sure of something like that?"

"Because it will be up to us."

Pu-yi opened his eyes. "You and I?"

"We are both dissatisfied with the state of affairs. And we are in unique positions to effect change."

"Speak for yourself. I like where I am."

"Of course you like where you are. A home, however temporary and unsatisfactory, is home. But it could be better. *It has been better.* You must remember the years in the Forbidden City. You were just a child, but you knew how special it was. You knew what an extraordinary joss the gods had bestowed on you."

"I was the Emperor and the Forbidden City was my home. It will be in the history books. No one can take that away. But I am the head of Manchukuo now."

"You are with a friend. So, let's speak frankly. We know what Manchukuo is. A Japanese colony. A transitional state. They set you up in the old Salt Palace and dress you up as emperor with the title 'Chief Executive.' But it's a far cry from what you were accustomed."

"What I was accustomed to is unmatchable."

"No question. But it might be less painful to accept the reduced circumstances if your hosts were mindful of your feelings. They aren't. They treat you like the help. Worse, they let the world know you are there for their use. You are their puppet king. They've turned you into an object of ridicule in China and abroad."

Pu-yi's face flushed over the cheekbones. He spat out the coffee and wiped his mouth with his sleeve, leaving a huge brown stain on the white silk. "Who are you to judge me? A renegade warlord. An opium smuggler. Don't think I don't know what you've been up to."

"I am sure you know a lot, Your Majesty, including the truth of what I've said. I am sympathetic to your reaction. The truth can be unpleasant."

"You are an impertinent man."

Han was unruffled. "And a renegade warlord, as you said. I don't abide by other people's rules. I don't want what the Kuomintang wants. They want to worship the West. I want to restore China to its former glory. The China you miss, Your Majesty. All the grandeur and pride and privilege of being the emperor of the most advanced, most esteemed civilization in the world. You as its supreme ruler sitting on the splendid dragon throne in the Forbidden City, with the country at your feet. It wasn't so long ago you were there. You must remember the feeling."

Pu-yi seemed to have given up resisting. His eyes misted over, filled with irrepressible longing.

"I can bring it all back, Your Majesty," Han said in a whisper. "I can bring back the past. A better past. Custom-made for you."

"Can you?" Pu-yi said weakly.

"With your help."

"*My* help?" A nervous laugh. "I am just a 'puppet king.' What can I do?"

"You don't need to do anything. You stay where you are and keep playing the role of Manchukuo's chief executive. When I make my plan known to the world, that's when I want to count on your cooperation." A pause. "You will join me in declaring the restoration of the monarchy in China."

A startled silence.

"I can be emperor again?"

"A new kind of emperor in a new kind of government."

"What do you mean?"

"The undignified demise of the Ching Dynasty taught us an important lesson. Your forebears' way of governing has become irrelevant. A different approach is needed if we want our dynasty to last."

"How different?"

"Move forward *and* preserve the past. That will be our goal. I have given this matter much thought—over twenty years—and have come to the conclusion that we should borrow from the British."

"You and the Brits go way back, don't you?"

"This isn't based on my family's association with them, but strictly on their record of success. The speed with which they expanded their empire attests to the effectiveness of their method."

"What are you borrowing from the British?"

"Their form of government. China will have a constitutional monarchy. It will begin with you. You will move back to Peking and sit on your former throne. You will have the privileges of being emperor, but none of the burdens of governing."

"I see."

"You will still be called the Son of Heaven."

"What makes you think it'll work for China? We and the British have little in common, well, except the habit of drinking tea." Pu-yi pointed at the teapot and chuckled.

"Set against the standards of the Middle Kingdom, the British could be a tribe from the Netherworld. But the two countries do have something in common: feudalism. The British Empire works because they enforce feudal rule—in their colonies. They wouldn't admit it of course, but it's feudal rule any way you look at it. Class divisions, landed gentry, restricted social mobility."

"China has thrived on feudalism for four thousand years," Pu-yi said with a nod.

"It is to this magnificent core we shall return. Never mind it's the twentieth century and there are these fads for democracy, socialism, fascism, and the various brands of fashionable ideologies. None is relevant to China. We cannot have court officials negotiating and cutting deals among themselves, peasants and coolies deciding who rules the country. What absurd notions. Leave it to the Westerners to come up with such foolishness. Thank Buddha, Confucius, and our ancestors that we are not like them."

Pu-yi was staring into the distance.

"Every Chinese believes in one thing: perpetuation and preservation of the family. There is no better framework to support the institution of family than our feudal tradition. The lord rules the vassals. The patriarch rules the family. And the emperor is the patriarch of the country. That will be your role." Looking at Pu-yi's elfin face, what he just said seemed comic. Han concluded,

"Feudalism is in our blood. The Chinese will always want and need an emperor."

"What will you be?"

"Prime minister."

"How long will you hold the position?"

"It will be a lifetime appointment to serve the country."

"What happens when you die? Who chooses the next prime minister?"

"To ensure the integrity of rule, I will choose my successor."

A long pause. "What is the difference between what you are offering and what I have now?"

The ninny isn't as stupid as he looks. Not missing a beat, Han replied, "Manchukuo cannot be compared with China. It is small, remote, and insignificant. The Japanese may call it a country, but it's barely a province. They will dismantle its government after they've secured a firm hold in China. Sooner if it serves their purpose. No telling what they have in mind. The Japanese are capricious, totally untrustworthy. After three years in their company, you must know that better than anyone."

Pu-yi didn't say a word.

"You must have been worried when they mobilized their troops around Nanking," Han went on. "My invitation gave you an excuse to get out of their line of fire, didn't it? You must realize that you cannot go on living like this. Not knowing when you wake up whether you would be alive the next day. And if you were, whether you would still have a place to live. I can put an end to these uncertainties. Once you return to being emperor, the throne will be yours and your children's. Forever."

"A permanent rice bowl."

"A permanent *golden* rice bowl."

Pu-yi stared at the sky. Han sipped his ginseng tea.

Jerking his body around, Pu-yi fixed his eyes on Han. "How can you, a warlord in a remote province, take over the country? Tell me your plan. I need to know every-thing—if you want me to believe you."

"We are potential allies, but at the moment you are not part of my world. I cannot tell you my plan. To whet your appetite, I am willing to say this much: I have in my posses-sion the means to terminate a large number of political and military careers. As well as the power to inflict irreparable damage on a vast territory."

"You are talking about your spies and saboteurs? Everybody knows about them."

"That is only a part of my plan. The rest is secret. But you won't have to wait long. In a matter of months you will see startling developments."

Pu-yi rolled his eyes.

"All I need is your word. No contract, no signature, no announcement. Sit back and wait for the throne to be handed back to you."

"Just like that?"

Han nodded. "Meanwhile, I don't mind if you hedge your bets in other places. As a matter of fact, I encourage you to continue what you've been doing with the Russians and the Japanese."

"Why?"

"It'll camouflage my plan."

"You've thought of everything, haven't you?" Pu-yi said unhappily. "What if the Russians or the Japanese come through for me? I won't need you then."

"We'll have to see, won't we?" A smile of absolute confidence. "Let me give you a piece of advice, as a prospective political partner. You shouldn't put your trust in foreigners—any foreigner. Just remind yourself what they have done in the last hundred years since they forced China to open its ports to their mercenaries. They will make you pay a hefty price for their help."

"How can I be sure you will deliver on your promise—if and when you win?"

"Because," Han replied, somewhat wearily, "currently, there is only one emperor alive in China."

Pu-yi brightened instantly. "That's right. I am the *only* emperor in China. There is no one else. You need me to play your constitutional monarchy game."

Putting the man in his place, Han said, "It's true you are the only qualified candidate for the position. But until I act, there is no position. The reality is, you have become irrelevant. The commoners may remember you, but they are too busy trying stay alive. A few diehard royalists might include your portrait in their ancestral shrines. But these fans of yours have no soldiers, no money, and no influence. They are not going to stage a rebellion with farm tools so you can reclaim your birthright. You are quite alone, Your Majesty."

"I'm used to being alone. That's the nature of being emperor."

"You sat on the dragon throne alone, but you had the whole country at your feet. Now you have nothing."

"I have the Mandate of Heaven."

"Do you? The Mandate of Heaven doesn't drop from the sky. It is fought for and won by men. Men with might and vision and incomparable joss. I don't need to deliberate on my vast wealth, my superior power base, the reach of my foresight—without which no dynasty can be brought back to life. So, let us burn incense sticks to the gods and pray that our future alliance will be a successful one."

11

A summons from Soong was waiting for Victor at the airport in Shanghai. Coded extremely urgent. He was to report to Party headquarters immediately, no reason given. He arranged for Su-chen and Yunna to wait in the flight crew's room, then went to the office near the airfield to telephone Lillie. He told her about the guests from Nanking.

"*The* Li family?"

"Yes. Someone killed Henry Li and set their house on fire. I happened to be there and gave the wife and daughter a hand. They're on their way to Shansui. We'll put them up for a day or two. They've been through hell."

"Everyone is talking about Nanking. You knew something was going to happen when you called, didn't you?"

"Yes."

"You are not hurt?"

"No."

"Thank the Buddha. I've been worried sick. Our trip— is it still on?"

"Yes."

"But..."

"Don't say anything to anyone. Not a word. Have to run. I'll be home as soon as I can."

After he put Su-chen and Yunna in pedicabs and told the coolies where to go, he climbed into the Party car and headed for T. V. Soong's house. Streets widened as they entered the French Concession. He was glad to see the cobbled streets, stately churches, and well-kept gardens. At least this part of his world was intact. Around Soong's Georgian mansion on Rue Molière, cars and jeeps were parked two and three deep. Half the Party top brass must have been summoned. Glum-faced chauffeurs waited by vehicles like attendees at a funeral procession. Gone were the usual smoking and chatting. The windows of the house were shut, the drapes drawn. Armed guards patrolled the grounds. In the foyer two soldiers frisked Victor—something that had never happened before. His questions were met with blank stares. He was directed to the conference room on the top floor. Mounting the steps, he noticed the furniture had been covered with dustsheets and valuable antiques removed.

A meeting had just broken up in the conference room, which had been at full capacity judging by the number of teacups and ashtrays on the table. A thick cigarette haze lingered below the hanging lights. Victor had been here twice: when he had been offered the job to run Soong's arms-dealing outfit and when he and Soong had finalized the Nanking deal. Soong used the room only for private meetings with his top aides, seldom for a gathering this large.

Victor waited.

To his surprise, the next person who walked into the room was Soong Ai-ling. His former paramour.

Her face lit up at the sight of him.

"Good day, Madame."

"Well, good day to you too," she said warmly, moving up to him. "Such a nice surprise. I didn't expect to find you here."

She wore a pine-colored silk cheongsam and matching jacket trimmed in black fur. Her hair was pulled back with a pearl clip the size of a mothball. Her lips were painted pink, her face thickly powdered, her cheeks tinted with a fresh layer of rouge. Her eyes were filled with anticipation and they held his like a vise. He sensed purpose in her and suspected the encounter wasn't accidental.

"I am here to see Mr. Soong," he said politely.

"He had to meet with Kai-shek's staff. He should be back soon." A half smile. "But I am here."

"It must be a busy day for him."

"It's a busy day for everyone. His aides were here earlier. You are late."

"It wasn't possible for me to be here sooner. I arrived only an hour ago. From Nanking."

"We were there just two days ago. I helped my sister close down their house; we left as soon as we could. Never cared for the city. It's dull and old. Looks like you got out all right."

"I nearly didn't."

"I'm very glad that you are safe," she said and moved a step closer.

"I was lucky. The situation was worse than what happened here in August. I've never seen anything like it. The city was a living hell. The carnage, the destruction, the barbarity. If the Japanese are not stopped, the entire population may be wiped out."

"We know all that," she cut in. "That's why you are here. To deal with the future, not the past. When you see my brother, make sure the report you give is current. He doesn't have time to reminisce." She added ruefully, "It should be natural for you, Victor. You don't dwell on the past. You are not a sentimental man."

What just happened in Nanking could hardly be described as the past, but there was no point in arguing with her. "I'll give an eyewitness account."

"Only to my brother. You are not to tell anyone else what you saw. We don't want the news to spread."

"It's already in the newspapers, and on the radio."

"Never mind them. They tell their story; we tell ours. Your job is to do as you are told. Don't make things worse than they are."

"Things couldn't be worse…"

"They could be if the news reports get out of control. The foreign press likes to sensationalize everything, even ordinary events."

"This is a horrific event. Thousands of people have been and are being slaughtered."

"It's what happens in wars. People die."

"It's an all-out massacre."

"That's what the foreign press call it. This kind of labeling is not helping us. Easy to get stuck in people's minds."

"It's what happened…"

"What happened is not as important as how it's perceived. This is how politics works," she said pointedly. "You must know that. You are not a stupid man. Not the Victor I used to know."

The resentment in her tone was personal. Something was setting her off. He doubted it was the massacre in Nanking or the foreign press—more likely his lukewarm reaction to her presence. He had seen it before. A sexual liaison turned sour in retrospect because one party was still smarting from the breakup. Since their affair ended, he had not maintained contact. On the few occasions they'd met, he had been polite and detached. Given what her brother had said, she must have been expecting more from him.

"I'm not thinking clearly. The journey has tired me out. I'm not as resilient as I used to be."

"Who is? Bad times for China these days. One thing after another. Can't even stay put in one place. I haven't had a good night's sleep since I don't remember when." She touched her cheek. "I must look awful."

"You look wonderful, Madame."

"Do I?"

"You haven't aged a day."

"I don't believe you."

"I speak my mind."

"That you do."

"I've always admired how well you manage your responsibilities: Party, Treasury, family. And still have time to appreciate the finer things in life."

"That's what you said. A long time ago," she said with a pout.

He had indeed, the first time she invited him to tea at her house after they had met at Wing On department store. He had been the sales manager in the women's wear department, his first job after leaving the missionary. He had had no experience in retail or fashion, but the store owner had been eager to have a Caucasian on staff. Victor had been hired on the spot. When an important customer like the wife of the Treasury Minister came to shop, the manager had been the one to wait on her. After she signed her bill, she had told him she would like his opinion on her new summer wardrobe. He had guessed then that she had something else in mind. The light in her eyes and the way her body insistently brushed his had conveyed her intentions better than words. Next day he had showed up at the Kung mansion. She had greeted him alone, all dolled up in a pink cheongsam, with enough perfume to infuse a village. The servants are busy with errands, she explained, and, as usual, Minister Kung is out of town. After viewing the wardrobe in her bedroom, he had deftly fulfilled her expectations. As later she had fulfilled his, when she brought him to her brother and asked that Victor be given a position in Soong's empire.

"I meant it then and I mean it now," he said. "The passing of time has only confirmed my... observations."

"How time flies. So much time has gone by so fast."

"Yes."

"We are not getting younger."

"No."

"Don't you wish we could relive the past?"

"Sure."

"Which part would you like to relive?"

He said what she wanted him to say. "Meeting you. That was the brightest moment in my life."

"No!"

"You changed my life. You made my dreams come true." He didn't have to lie about this. She had been the break he needed. Working for Soong had transformed him from wage earner to wealthy player.

"You haven't lost your touch, Victor. Ten minutes in your company and I feel like a girl on her first date." A coquettish laugh. "Frenchmen are good at this sort of thing. And you are incomparable."

"Am I?"

"You know you are. You have the Paramount's number one girl to prove it. She is your official concubine now, I hear."

"I don't deny I have a soft spot for beautiful Chinese women. Since I couldn't have the moon, I've learned to settle for less."

His words sounded phony, but she was taken in. If being phony would help him get through the day, why not? As long as he was in China, no one would fault him for buttering up a Soong matriarch. Lillie would be the first to agree.

"You always know the right thing to say."

"Only to the right person."

She beamed. "I've never regretted bringing you into the family."

"I am relieved to know that I have not been a disappointment."

"Disappointment? No. That's not what comes to my mind when I think of you."

He didn't want to know what was on her mind and he hoped he would never find out. He was leaning against the wall. She planted herself in front of him; her rump pressed the edge of an armchair. There were only inches between them. He could see the down of tiny gray hairs on her forehead and the crow's feet at the corners of her eyes. She must be at least forty-five.

"It's been too long, Victor."

"Sure."

"Unbearable."

"Indeed."

"I have never stopped thinking about us. I have tried, but I couldn't." She closed her eyes. "Do you know why you are so special, Victor?"

"No."

"With you I could be a real woman, do the things I wouldn't do with my husband. Explore new feelings, and I could count on you not to judge. You made me complete." She opened her eyes. "I promise it'll be private in Chungking."

"Private—that's always good," he said automatically. What did Chungking have to do with me?

"I want you to see the new villa in Kunming."

Now it's Kunming. What was she up to? "Never been to Kunming."

"It's gorgeous. You'll love it. From Kunming we'll go to Kweilin, and then to Hainan Island. We have a house on the beach. I'll get a plane. The two of us alone in a tropical paradise. Would you like that?"

"Marvelous, Madame." Don't tell me she's planning to take me on a grand tour of China.

"Skip the 'Madame' when no one's around. You had a special name for me when we were alone, remember?"

Chèrie. Oh God, I was an ass.

"Of course I remember," he said.

"Will you say that again?"

"If it pleases you."

"Have I told you that you were the best by far?"

You did. Five seconds ago. How long would this go on? Holding his smile, he said, "I'd love hearing it again."

"You were the absolute best, Victor Maurier. And I don't make a habit of handing out first prizes."

"Thank you."

"I don't want you to thank me. I want you to... Oh, Victor, I've missed you. We didn't have to part. I was worried and scared. I had never ever done anything like that. I am a good wife and a moral person. But you took me by storm. Yes, you did. I was so happy. We were so happy. We should have found a way to stay together." She cradled his face with her palms, her thumbs rubbing his cheeks. "I have a plan. Come to Chungking. I'll make it worth your while. You know I keep my word. It'll be like old times. Better..."

Her face tilted upward, eyes closed, the fur collar of her jacket touching his coat. The Generalissimo's sister-in-law was waiting to be kissed. Should he oblige? If he did, what would she have him to do next? He had neither the desire to go to Chungking nor to renew the relationship. But she was who she was and she was holding his face in her hands, demanding love...

A shrill female voice shot from the open door. "Anyone here? Where are the servants? Where is everybody?"

It was the youngest of the Soong sisters, May-ling, the indomitable Madame Chiang Kai-shek herself, looking like Mother Christmas in a white ankle-length fur coat, with a heavy green jade necklace encircling her neck. Her signature red open-toed pumps were topped with an outrageous bow. She swaggered across the room, coat flapping to reveal her legs all the way to the top of her thighs. She didn't seem to have anything else on.

"Good day, Madame Chiang," Victor said gratefully, stepping away from Soong Ai-ling.

"Who are you? What are you doing in my brother's house?"

"Victor Maurier. I work for Mr. Soong."

"Maurier. Oh yes, I remember. You are Paul's linguist. He said you speak all the languages in Europe."

"That's most complimentary, Madame. I'm afraid my abilities are by no means that extensive."

"Does Little Brother know you are waiting for him?" she asked, eyeing her sister.

"He should be here any minute," Soong Ai-ling said. "Victor just returned from Nanking."

Soong May-ling made a face. "Ghastly business, wasn't it?"

"Horrific."

"I didn't see anything. Paul got us out of there in time. Don't ask me how he knew."

"Maybe he had a premonition," Victor said dryly.

"Whatever it was, I'm glad we left. The Japanese are certifiably insane. You must tell me what happened. Later. I'm not in the mood for horror stories today."

"Yes, Madame."

"Stay for tea. Just us girls and you." She winked. "It'll be a cozy party."

Victor wondered how much she had heard or seen. Like him, Soong Ai-ling had resumed her formal demeanor.

"Thank you, Madame. Another day perhaps. I'd better wait for Mr. Soong. How is the Generalissimo?"

"Fine, fine, fine. Kai-shek has flown to Chungking with his lieutenants. He's getting the place ready." Turning to her sister, she said, "I don't feel like going to Szechwan. I can't take the inland weather this time of the year. It's absolutely horrid. I'm going to Canton."

"You know better than anyone that Kai-shek shouldn't be left alone."

"If he wants to hook up with the Yao woman again, let him. He can sleep with the whore every night for all I care."

"This is not the time to risk a scandal. What about the people from *Time* magazine? Didn't you invite them to travel with us? You can't take off on your own."

"I'll retract the invitation. The Luces are like family; they won't mind."

"You are the first couple of China. It won't look good if you and Kai-shek live apart."

"If you're so keen on managing Kai-shek, you should have married him. He might have held your attention better than that ferret-faced husband of yours."

Stunned, Soong Ai-ling mumbled, "You can be so rude."

"Speaking of husbands, will Daddy Kung be joining you in Chungking? Or do you have another prospect in mind?" Soong May-ling went up to Victor and playfully tapped the tip of his nose. "Mmm... An alluring prospect? A handsome prospect? Are you going to keep this gorgeous man all to yourself or will you share?"

In one swift motion, she pulled Victor toward her and kissed him on the mouth.

Soong Ai-ling watched with mouth agape.

Another kiss.

"May-ling, that's enough," Soong Ai-ling cried.

The sisters were staring each other down. Looks like neither is getting what she needs from her husband, Victor thought. Maybe I should go to Chungking and bed both of them. The two most powerful women in China. It would be something for his memoirs.

Soong May-ling stepped back and regarded him from head to toe. "I like you, Maurier; you have class. Why don't you work for me? Claire needs staff and you would fit right in. Is your English as good as your Shanghainese?"

Claire was Claire Chennault, a retired American brigadier general Chiang had recruited to modernize the Chinese air force. Chennault was putting together a team of pilots called Flying Tigers.

"I'd like to think my English is slightly better. My knowledge of planes may not be good enough for Mr. Chennault though."

"You can join his administrative staff."

"Victor already has a job," Soong Ai-ling objected. "He works for Tse-ven."

"And Tse-ven works for my husband. So does your husband. So does the rest of China." To Victor, "I'll tell Claire about you. You two can meet and work something out. *Deal*?" She said the word in English.

"*Deal*."

"I'm trying out a new pastry chef from Vienna. If he's any good, I'll send him to the house on Long Island. I want to spend Easter there. And summer too, if the Japanese are still here. I can't wait to go back to the States. New York, here I come." Blithely she turned and pirouetted to the door, heels clicking like a pair of castanets. "God, I'm absolutely positively famished."

Chungking, Victor thought when he was alone. A city built on hilly terrain in backward Szechwan province, choked in coal soot ten months of the year. How long would Chiang's entourage stay? Where would they go if the Japanese chased them down? Chengdu? Lhasa? He couldn't see himself following them, anywhere, for any reason. He looked at the blank walls. Even the Kuomintang flag and Chiang's portrait had been taken down. The move had to be imminent. If Soong Ai-ling went ahead, set up a love nest and he refused, the consequences could be dire. He was also bothered by what Soong May-ling had said about having him work for Chennault. The last thing he wanted was to join the Chinese air force under the command of an American cowboy.

He should get out now. Leave before more offers came his way.

Too late.

T.V. Soong walked in. Face taut and pale, overcoat dusty, hair disheveled, he looked like he had been through a windstorm. Taking the seat at the head of the table, he signaled Victor to close the door.

Soong slipped off his fur-lined gloves and slapped them down. "Did you come straight from the airport?"

"Yes."

"Talk to anyone?"

"Lillie. Your staff at the airport. Your sisters."

"No one else?"

"No."

"Keep it that way. Don't say a word to anyone about what you did in Nanking."

"Yes, Paul."

"Destroy all the evidence related to International Airsea. Everything—correspondence, financial records, contracts, address books, leftover stationery. The company never existed. Is that clear?"

"Perfectly."

"You never went to Nanking. Never sold anything to anyone. Never worked for me. We never had this conversation. Understood?"

"Understood."

"Leave China immediately. Take your woman and your child. Travel inconspicuously. Pick somewhere far away and stay there. Promise you will not set foot on Chinese soil without my permission. You know how far I go to enforce my orders."

Victor nodded.

"Your compliance must be absolute."

"It will be."

"Good."

Victor asked softly, "May I ask what has prompted these measures?"

Soong's voice dropped an octave. "Let's just say I should have paid more attention to what Shiozawa said to you."

The Japanese must have leaked the deal and implicated Soong. "How bad is it?"

"Bad enough. Fortunately Kai-shek is sympathetic, having been through similar situations himself. I have to come up with a plausible story for the foreign press. They are such a nuisance. I should find a way to avoid them altogether." Soong pushed back his chair, ready to go. "For this unforeseen development I will pay you ten times your last commission. You will get the money in Hong Kong. American currency. Okay?"

Victor bit his lip to suppress his elation. "Okay."

"Don't forget what I said."

"I won't, Paul."

Victor followed him to the door.

"The scene in Nanking. Was it as bad as they say?"

"Yes."

"Anything left of the safe house?"

"Shouldn't be. I set fire to it."

Soong was relieved. "No one will be able to get their hands on my papers. Some of them were pretty dicey."

"Were they the only copies?"

"Never keep anything I don't need. Except money, of course." A smile at the thought of his greatest love. "You'd better go. Get out before the Japs seal up the airport."

They shook hands. Victor felt a pang of nostalgia. Right or wrong, Soong had given him the most exciting years of his life.

"Will you be going to Chungking?" Victor asked.

"Only for the opening ceremony. It's not my kind of place. I prefer Shanghai."

"I hope we'll meet again."

"We will. When things settle down, Laura and I will have a tour of Europe. She's crazy about Paris."

"Good-bye, Paul. And thanks."

On his way home, Victor realized that Soong, preoccupied with the fallout from the Japanese assault on Nanking, had forgotten to ask for Li's trunk.

Another trump card, along with Soong's papers. To be used when the opportunity presented itself—when or how, there had to be a way to profit from them.

It had been a very good day indeed.

Lillie had had her eye on the trunk the moment the coolie carried it into the house. She had heard about the Li family in Nanking: superbly connected, wealthy, lived like aristocrats. The trunk was the only thing the professor's wife had taken out of their ravaged home. It had to contain valuable possessions.

It would be the solution to her predicament.

Lillie had no doubt that Victor's feelings for her were true, and she was fond of him. A lot more than fond. Hard to believe that after two years, this world-weary, sexually jaded pair would still be excited by each other, not only in bed but in the most mundane situations. More astounding was the sweetness that turned them into wild young things when they were alone. She had never regretted giving up her job as top hostess at the Paramount Ballroom; the trouble she had taken to plant clues for Victor's wife to discover their liaison; and then, after the wife, to Lillie's immense delight, had walked out on her family, the responsibilities she had taken upon herself, acting as wife and mother, managing the house. The year as Victor's live-in mistress had been the best in her life. She was happy and content.

Out of the blue, he had announced the plan to leave China.

Mr. Soong was concerned for their safety and he wanted them to get out quickly, Victor had told her after meeting with his boss. But since when did someone like Soong care about anyone's safety? Victor had to have made it up. He was homesick and didn't want to admit it to her.

"Imagine, darling, next week we'll be in Europe. You'll see where I grew up. You'll meet my old friends."

"So soon?"

"I've made the arrangements. We'll sail first, and then we'll fly. We'll find an apartment in the center of Paris. We won't have to worry about bombs and the Japanese."

"We are moving to Europe?"

"Yes."

"So it's not just a holiday?"

"It can be a holiday. A long holiday."

What kind of place was Europe? She had only seen pictures in magazines. Snow-capped peaks, mountain goats, a tower like an elongated iron cone. It could have been the moon.

It was not the future she wanted, she had told Victor.

"Europe isn't the moon. I lived there; I know."

"I don't speak a word of French. What am I going to do?"

"You won't have to do anything. I'll take care of you."

"I don't want you to take care of me. I'm not an invalid."

"You're having reservations because it's a big move and you feel rushed. I understand. I'd have liked to take our time, but we want to be out of here before things get worse." He had planted a kiss on her forehead, an adult pacifying a child. "I know my darling Lillie is brave and she is not afraid of adventure."

"I am worried."

"About what?"

"What if people there don't like someone from China? You'll lose face because of me. I'll be lonely and miserable."

"The French love beautiful women. They'll love you."

"I don't want strangers to love me. I want to live the same way we live now."

"We'll live the way we live now. In a different location."

"What if your wife wants you back?"

"What she wants has nothing to do with us."

"What if I don't want to leave China?"

"We can come back when the war's over. Trust me. You'll feel differently once you get used to living there. It'll be a good life."

"Would you go on your own?"

"Without you?"

"Without me."

He had hesitated. "Do you want me to go without you?"

"Don't turn the question around. I'm asking you."

"Of course I don't want to go without you, Lillie, you know that."

The way he wouldn't look her in the eye had convinced her that he was prepared to leave, with or without her.

What was she to do, without Victor?

She couldn't go back to the ballroom—that much was certain. The months of domestic bliss had sapped her will to work. Love had tamed her. She balked at the prospect of ingratiating herself with strangers again. She would rather die than be with another man. But how else would she make a living? She had no training. She was barely literate. The cook at the Paramount had taught her a few words so she could read newspaper headlines. The limited vocabulary wouldn't get her a job. Even if she had the qualifications, there weren't no jobs to be found. Half the city's businesses were closing down; the rest were run by hoodlums. Her savings would last a couple of years, and then what? She knew Victor had put away a substantial stash and there were valuables around the house. But she didn't want to steal from him.

The Lis were different.

They couldn't have escaped from Nanking without Victor's help. The way she saw it, the trunk would be the price of their rescue. They owed their lives to Victor and she would collect the payment on his behalf. It's not as if she would be taking away their livelihood. With Gold Fox Han offering to take care of them, they would be well provided for. The Lis had had their share of the good life, while she had only begun to experience hers.

It would also teach them a lesson. They might have been royalty in Nanking, but they were refugees in her house. The least they could do was to treat their hostess with respect. But no. The moment they set eyes on her, they saw the neon sign of the Paramount Ballroom. They turned up their noses and pointedly avoided contact as though she had the clap.

While preparing dinner, Lillie added a dose of sleeping powder to the soup. The drug would keep everyone sound asleep until mid-morning. Excited by the company of the guests, little Pierre was distracted. He hardly touched his food, but the child usually slept like a log.

Midnight. Lillie slipped out of bed. Victor was grinning in his sleep. Probably dreaming about France, she thought; he is more homesick than he is willing to admit. She waited until her eyes grew accustomed to the dark before she retrieved the black down-filled pajama suit and black canvas shoes she had hidden under the bed. She put them on, tiptoed out of the room, and closed the door behind her.

The door to the guest bedroom had no lock. She pushed it open and stepped in. The moon cast a plank of silver on the ceiling, illuminating the space. Mother and daughter were sleeping on two bunk beds, their belongings in a heap on a chair. Lillie gathered them up and carried them to the hallway. Under a window, she examined her finds: jackets, skirts, woolen vests, and a drawstring purse. She went through the pockets and linings of the clothes. The material was expensive, the tailoring top quality. In the pocket of the mother's skirt she found a tiny scroll filled with weird scribblings; in the pocket of the daughter's jacket a book with a tattered cover. Inside the drawstring purse, 800 yuan in cash and a red envelope containing another 500, someone's birthday present.

She went through everything again. No key.

It might have been attached to the jewelry they were wearing, as she sometimes did with her own keys. She returned to the guest room. She approached the mother's bed first. Gingerly she turned down the blanket. For a second Lillie thought she was seeing her own ghost until she remembered she had lent them her pajamas. The woman was breathing heavily, head to one side, cheeks pale, tear-streaked skin translucent in the faint light. Wisps of hair hung loosely around her face. Quite a face, Lillie admitted grudgingly. Classy. If the woman had not been born into the Kung family, she would be a hit on the ballroom circuit. Lillie found a cheap jade pendant around her neck. No key attached.

The daughter was next. As soon as Lillie's hand touched the blanket, the girl moved. Lillie retreated and stepped on a pair of slippers, staggered, barely suppressing a cry. She straightened up. How would she explain herself if the girl woke up? The professor's daughter unnerved her. She had her mother's good looks. And something else. It made Lillie feel she was in the presence of an empress. She held her breath. The girl didn't wake. Lillie edged forward and looked her over. No jewelry on the girl. No key either.

She left the room, feeling like a fool.

The trunk was under the stairwell. She examined the lock. A steel contraption, formidable like a lock on a bank's safe. There was no way she could force it open with the tools in the house. She couldn't even move the damn thing. Not an inch.

What to do?

"Auntie Lillie, what are you doing?"

She swung back. "Oh, Pierre."

"I need to pee."

"The toilet is in the other side of the house."

"I saw you so I came," he said, rubbing his eyes.

She put her arms around the child and led him to the bathroom, a cubicle next to the kitchen with newly installed plumbing. She untied the strings of his pajama pants. Pierre relieved himself.

"Now go back to bed," she said.

"So cold."

"I can't do anything about that."

"I don't want to sleep alone."

"What's the matter? You always sleep alone."

"I feel different tonight."

"You want Aunt Lillie to keep you company?"

The child nodded.

"All right, only for a little while."

In his room, Pierre climbed into bed and backed his body up against the wall to make room for her. Lillie took off the pajama suit and shoes. In camisole and panties, she squeezed herself in beside the boy.

"You're right, it is cold."

"Why are you up, Auntie Lillie?"

"I got up early to do housework."

"Why?"

"I want to clean the house before the guests wake up."

"Is that why you wore those ugly clothes?"

"They are my work clothes."

"I like Yunna. She is so pretty. How old do you think she is?"

"Never mind, she's too old for you," Lillie said, hugging the child. He was warm like a hot water bottle. "Are you thinking about another girl? I thought Auntie Lillie was the only one for you."

He nestled his head in the hollow between her breasts. "But you're Papa's."

"When your Papa's not home, I'm yours. You know that." She kissed his eyelids. "Promise Auntie Lillie she will always be your best girl."

"I promise."

"And you will always be her darling boy. Don't ever forget that."

"I won't. Are we saying good-bye?"

"Why do you say that?"

"You sound like you are going away."

"Oh, Pierre."

"Are you?"

"You are a silly boy. Now, do you want to keep talking or do you want to make Auntie Lillie happy?"

"Make you happy."

She pulled up her camisole and slipped her nipple into his mouth. He sucked contentedly. She began to massage his buttocks.

"Do you do this with Papa?" he asked, briefly taking his mouth off the nipple.

"Not exactly."

"What do you do with Papa?"

"You'll find out when you're older."

"Why can't I find out now?"

She slipped a hand inside his pants and patted his penis. "Wait till your yang grows up."

"How long do I have to wait?"

"I'd say five, six years. Sooner if you are a good boy."

"That's an awfully long time," he said, arms circling her waist. "I don't want to wait."

"The years will go by fast, believe me. You'll be a gorgeous man, like your father."

"I want you to do that thing with me."

"What thing?"

"Remember last time when Papa was away and we pretended…"

"Oh, you bad boy."

"Please."

"Try to sleep."

"I can't. Too many thoughts in my head."

"We'll do that only if you close your eyes. All the way… No more thoughts about anything. Now, there… Feel good?"

"I love you, Auntie Lillie. A whole bunch. I think I love you more than I love Mother…"

"I love you too."

"Don't stop."

"How about this? Doesn't this feel nice?"

"Mmmm."

"Now pay some attention to Auntie Lillie."

Obediently Pierre took a nipple. As before, the combined sensations produced an intensely relaxing effect. His breathing became even. A tiny snore issued from his nostrils. With a sigh of relief, she eased herself out of the bed and put the clothes back on. My Pierre will grow up to be an expert amorist, she thought, looking fondly at the child. It tickled her to imagine what he might do with the real thing. In the beginning she had let the boy sleep with her when Victor was away, hoping physical closeness would break barriers. Along the way innocent caresses had progressed into titillating fondlings that Lillie could no longer be sure that they were in themselves a form of Clouds and Rain. She never had any intention of seducing Pierre. Having no experience in child rearing, she resorted to techniques she had learned in pacifying men.

A faint light in the east. She should get going.

She took a bottle of whiskey from the sideboard, matches and an iron poker from the kitchen. She filled a pail with water and brought it with the rest to the trunk. She poured whiskey over the lid, in careful trickles to minimize spills on the floor. When the surface was soaked with alcohol, she threw a match onto it. The wood caught fire like paper. Thank the Buddha Victor could afford a house built of concrete and bricks. She couldn't do this if they were living in one of the tenements in greater Shanghai. And lucky that the coolie had put the trunk under the stairwell, away from a window. People passing by the house wouldn't see the small bonfire.

She watched to make sure no sparks went astray. As soon as a good part of the cover was burned off, she doused the flames with the pail of water, setting off a sizzling vapor and a cloud of white smoke. With the iron poker, she brushed away the remnants of burned wood and the layer of ash.

She gasped.

In a hundred years she never would have guessed.

Dear Buddha. Dear Christian God of the bearded man on the cross. Dear venerable ancestors and the dead emperors of the Middle Kingdom. Thank you.

Gold peaches. Every one perfectly shaped. Bigger than the real fruit and stamped with a personal seal. *Han Tangming. Shansui.*

General Han.

Why did the Lis have the warlord's gold?

Gold is gold. Who cared where the peaches came from? They were hers now.

Light seeped through the windows, growing brighter by the second. She collected suitcases and bags and filled them with the treasure, going about the task with a wild surge of energy. She figured one peach weighed about a catty. One catty was made up of sixteen taels. A necklace of regular length weighed about one and a half taels. One peach would equal ten necklaces. She had bought a gold necklace when she left the Paramount. What she had paid would have bought food for three months. That was two years ago; the war must have driven up the price of gold. She could live off the trunk of gold for the rest of her life.

When the transfer was complete, she pushed the emptied trunk to the back of the house, through the door and all the way to the end of the alley. There was a spot where neighbors discarded decrepit furniture and unwanted items too big to fit into garbage bins. Every morning, junk dealers and scavengers came by looking for things they could sell. They would discover the camphor chest and haul it away. Even without a lid, the fine wood would fetch a good price. It would be impossible to trace it to her.

Back in the house, she returned to the bedroom. She found the car key in the pocket of Victor's overcoat and the spare pistol he kept in the nightstand. The pistol was too large to fit into the pocket of her pajama suit. She grabbed one of Victor's jackets.

It took her five minutes to lug the gold-filled luggage from the house to the car. There was no one on the street as far as she could see. Even if neighbors noticed her, they would think she was running away from her Caucasian lover, and that the luggage contained her belongings.

The suitcases and bags covered the floor and the seat on the passenger side.

Without saying good-bye to her lover, Lillie drove away as the sun rose over the silted water of the Huangpo.

12

Jong never knew his parents. Never found out who they were, or why, when he was a few days old, they had left him on the street a stone's throw from the Forbidden City, in a district off limits to foreigners. As his fame rose, the mystery of his birth became a popular topic in Shansui where he lived, and in Shanghai where he had spent most of his childhood.

One story cast his father in the role of an English baron, a knight of the empire who believed conquest of the world was his birthright. On a trip from India to China, he decided to appropriate a piece of the Middle Kingdom. One night he climbed over the wall of the Forbidden City and broke into a satellite palace. The daughter of a mandarin was sleeping in a curtained bed. Moonlight revealed a pretty face on the pillow, smooth ivory skin, her mouth a ripe cherry to be plucked. He climbed into bed and made love to her. She responded like someone in an erotic dream, naturally, feverishly. The young man deposited his seed before she woke up.

Another tale traced Jong's non-Chinese half to the Volga River. A young Cossack on his first trip to the Middle Kingdom. Tall and muscular with the features of a god, he had a yang that was perpetually resolute—so the story went. After weeks on the road, he ravished the first woman he encountered. She was a concubine of the Manchu court, part of an entourage traveling to Peking. He stopped the caravan and climbed inside her palanquin. After he had his way with her, he jumped back on his horse and fled, so swiftly that no one saw the face. How he knew it was a woman inside that palanquin, why she didn't scream for help, and why others in the entourage had been willing to stop for the lone marauder, no one could explain.

One story prevailed. A young missionary from Massachusetts named John Linden arrived in Peking after the Boxer Rebellion. He was employed by a wealthy Manchu family to tutor their children in English and world history. They were to be groomed for careers in diplomacy. Linden fell in love with the oldest daughter. She was equally smitten. Appalled by the prospect of a Caucasian son-in-law, the parents discharged Linden and locked the girl inside her room. For days, he waited outside the house, writing reams of letters to plead their case. The parents didn't budge. When enough time had passed, the girl's condition became obvious. By then Linden had returned home, heartbroken. The girl gave birth to a boy, a handsome thing with his father's blue eyes. She swore when her child was old enough, she would join his father in America, never to return. Her parents took pre-emptive action. One night, they removed the baby from her bed, carried him to other end of the city, and left him by the roadside.

Jong had searched court records for his mother's identity. There were few to work with. The Ching Dynasty had ended two decades ago. Official archives had either been removed or lost. Most royals had fled back to Manchuria. Those who stayed behind lived on the fringes of society; they preferred to keep out of the public eye. Even in normal times, an illegitimate half-breed child was not something a Manchu woman would readily admit. The flimsy traces had led to dead ends. Jong had published announcements, inviting those who had known his parents to come forward. Pranksters had showed up with claims that didn't withstand scrutiny. Years of efforts had produced nothing.

Jong's first memories were of a brothel. A prostitute called Nan-fei had found him on the street. She took him back to where she lived and worked. The brothel was a converted residence off Wang Fu Jing Road in the center of Peking. The rooms were built around a courtyard. Those in the front were used for receiving customers. The space was subdivided into closet-size units where disheveled men stumbled in and out at odd hours of the day. The women lived in the rear. Nan-fei paid extra for space enough to accommodate two cots. She kept Jong out of the front, warning him away with stories of ghosts and monsters. The little boy spent most of the day in the backyard with old toys and picture books Nan-fei had found in secondhand stores. She checked on him when she had a break. He only saw the other women in the kitchen when they had their meals.

Sullen and bedraggled, they reeked of a peculiar odor, a mixture of stale fish and dead flowers that stayed with him long after they left Peking. The women laughed the way crazy people did, savage and unprovoked. He sensed it was their way of letting off sadness, and there was a lot of it. Beneath the hysteria were fountains of unused maternal affection; they lavished it on him. Jong loved them back, as a child loved indulgent aunts, without guile or reserve.

When Yuan Shih-kai died in 1916, ending his five-month imperial rule, riots broke out in the streets of the capital. The unemployed joined the gangsters, banding into mobs and plundering the city. The brothel was ransacked. Robbers ripped off fixtures from the walls and made off with the cash box. The women grabbed their belongings and fled. With Jong on her hip, Nan-fei fell behind the group. She kept walking through the night. At daybreak, the lone pair trotting along the side of the highway got the notice of a sympathetic driver. He let them ride in the back of his truck.

In Shanghai, Nan-fei rented a room in a boardinghouse off Rainbow Bridge Road. She took care of Jong during the day and worked the streets at night. Times were not any better. There was little money left after paying rent and buying food. She saved what she could, knowing that with a child there would always be situations where extra cash would come in handy. When Jong was old enough to go to school, she took him to the missionaries, one by one, begging each in turn, until she convinced a Baptist minister on Rue Joffe to waive the fees.

It had been there that Jong discovered his gift for the English language. After he finished primary school, he had mastered an extensive vocabulary and was able to conduct simple conversations in English. The skill landed him an apprenticeship at Charlie Soong's Bible shop. Most of the customers were missionaries and expatriates; it was handy to have someone bilingual on staff. Nan-fei negotiated a lighter workload for Jong so he could continue school. He studied hard, read every book in the library, and practiced his English with the foreigners he met at the shop.

The month after Jong turned fifteen, he met General Han.

It was at the wedding of Charlie Soong's youngest daughter, May-ling and Chiang Kai-shek, rising star of the Kuomintang. Jong was called to help at the reception. The whole town had gathered in the Majestic Hotel. The ballroom overflowed with guests, press, and onlookers eager to catch a glimpse of the new first couple. Han arrived at the end of the ceremony, alone. He didn't offer congratulations to the hosts, didn't mingle. He found a corner where he sipped his tea and assessed the scene with the detached amusement Jong would come to know well. Jong was going around the room, refilling tea for the guests. Han noticed his Eurasian features and asked the usual questions. Jong's answers were polite and well phrased. Han sensed the boy's keen intelligence. He asked him to sit with him. They talked like friends.

Before Han left Shanghai, he went to see Nan-fei. He told her his wife had passed away and he didn't have children. He would take the boy with him and would treat him like his own. He promised her that Jong would have a better future than anything the Bible shop could offer. Nan-fei couldn't say no to the warlord, and she believed he was sincere. Jong accompanied Han to the province in southwest China and lived in his palace.

Han kept his promise. He taught Jong the ways of politics and warfare. When he was ready, Han made him his chief of staff.

Arriving in Shanghai, Jong did what he would always do when he was here. He went to see Nan-fei. She lived in Putung, a settlement for the poor on the eastern side of town. Her home was a tiny apartment above a noodle shop next to an open market. Jong had the driver park at the far end of the street. He would make the rest of the trip on foot. Once he had pulled the car up to the noodle shop; word quickly got out. A crowd had gathered to greet the city's favorite son. Nan-fei had been appalled.

Jong mounted the rickety stairs to the top landing and knocked. "Na-na, it's me."

The door opened instantly. In a frayed woolen jacket and ankle-length cheongsam, Nan-fei seemed to have aged years since he had seen her in the summer. Her hair had thinned; her face was brown and wrinkled like a coolie's, her hands mottled with liver spots and threaded with visible capillaries. She had lost weight, looking frail.

"Why, it's you. What are you doing here?" she said curtly as she did whenever Jong showed up unannounced, but her pleasure in seeing him was irrepressible.

He took her in his arms. "Na-na, I'm here to see you."

"Oh, you big-nosed *kweiloh*, you are embarrassing me," she said, half pushing him away.

There was only one room, eight paces from the door to the bed and twelve paces the other way. A window looked out to the wall of a warehouse; she liked that she didn't have anyone peering into her apartment. The kitchen was a counter with a stove and a basin. There was no toilet. She shared the one in with the noodle shop downstairs.

"How have you been?"

She shrugged.

"You look well, Na-na."

"I look awful."

"You look well to me."

"Don't bother with your smooth talk. Save it for the birds."

He spread the presents on the narrow bed: dried shark's fins, smoked hams, Korean ginseng roots, and a cashmere shawl. He draped the shawl over her shoulders. She winced but let him.

"You keep bringing me things. I haven't finished what you gave me last time. This place is turning into a rich man's pantry. People can smell the stuff from the street," she complained while she carefully collected the presents and locked them in a storage bin behind the door. "Thugs are going to break in."

Not wanting to cause her discomfort, he hadn't told her that he paid the owner of the noodle shop a monthly stipend to keep an eye on her.

"If you don't feel safe, move to Shansui and let me take care of you."

Her face screwed up in disgust. "I don't want to be anywhere near that man."

"You always say that, but you only met General Han once. You don't know him."

She sat down next to him. "I know enough."

"Those are just rumors," Jong said as he slipped an envelope filled with cash under the pillow.

"When you hear it once, it may be rumor. When you hear the second and the third time, it could still be rumor. When you hear the same thing fifty times, it has to be true."

"I have never seen him abduct young girls."

"Of course you've never seen him doing that. He doesn't do the dirty work himself; he has his guards do it for him. They snatch the girl from the parents and then lock her in his bedroom. The next morning she is dismissed with a crumb from his gold mine. Her whole life ruined." She added, "It's hard for you to believe someone you care about could do such terrible things."

"General Han is a complicated man."

"Don't assume for a minute you can figure him out."

"There is no need for me to figure him out. I trust him and he trusts me."

"If that's true, you are the only person he trusts."

Not for the first time, he wondered if there was more between her and Han than they had told him.

"The Villa is like a small city. There is plenty of space," he said. "I can set you up in an apartment far away from the Grand Hall. You would be miles out of his way. You wouldn't see General Han if you didn't want to."

"You are blessed with strong joss, Jong. I felt it the first time I held you in my arms. My joss is feeble. Look at my life. It wouldn't be able to withstand the man's powers."

"Joss is an excuse when one doesn't want to reason."

"Joss is destiny. The gods' plans for mortals. Everyone is given an allowance of good fortune. Mine is pitiful. I wouldn't try to push the limits. I know you think a person can make his own destiny. Fine, Jong. That's the Caucasian in you and I accept it." She sighed. "I want to live the rest of my years in peace. There won't be many left. That I know without checking with the gods."

"There will be many if you let me take care of you."

"You are smart and capable and strong, but even you can't change my joss. And you have more important things to do than fussing over me." She got up. "Let me make you a cup of tea."

She lighted twigs in the woodstove and fanned up a small fire. Smoke filled the space. She opened the window and let in a waft of unpleasant odors from the market. The hawkers' chatter was as loud as if they had joined them in the room. Jong had urged her to find more comfortable living quarters. But Nan-fei would not move. Comfortable living quarters would mean a posh neighborhood. An old woman living alone in a posh neighborhood would invite attention. Here she could keep to herself; no one bothered her. What better place to hide in a city than its slums?

"I worry about you," she said, measuring tea leaves into a cup. "You are in the man's company every day. Whether you know it or not, he is having an influence…"

Seized by a violent cough, she nearly dropped everything. Jong held her, patted her back until the coughing stopped. She pulled a handkerchief from a pocket and wiped her mouth. Mindful of Jong's habits, she washed her hands before she picked up the cup again.

"Keep out of his harem. Nothing corrupts a man faster than debauchery. I don't know much else. That I do know." She poured boiling water into the cup and handed it to him. "If you'd told me you were coming, I would have cooked you a decent meal. You could use one."

"I am well fed, Na-na."

"Too well fed. Too much of a good thing can be bad. You should get yourself a wife, Jong. Find a good woman. Let her take care of you. Have children. A family will keep you out of trouble. I know men your age. Your head follows your yang."

"With all the unrest and uncertainty, it would be immoral to bring new lives into the world." He sipped the tea. It was his favorite: narcissus and jasmine, fragrant like a bouquet.

"Nonsense. How could having children be immoral? It's more important to have children when people are being killed. War or no war, it's a man's duty to have a family." She filled her cup, warming her hands with it. "Pity you are a soldier. These days, girls from good families wouldn't want to marry soldiers."

"Girls from good families wouldn't want to marry a half-breed orphan."

"Too bad it was me who found you, Jong. Someone else would have given you a real home. And a good name."

"Someone else might have sold me to the slave traders."

"No one could have given you away once they held you in their arms. You were the most beautiful baby. A child of the gods."

"Are you sure you are not my mother? You sound biased enough."

"If I were your mother, why wouldn't I have told you?"

"You want to protect me. You don't want people to know my mother is..."

"A prostitute," Nan-fei said plainly. "Would you be ashamed if your mother was a prostitute?"

"Of course not."

"An association like that would tarnish your accomplishments. People are small-minded; they like to find ways to belittle somebody else's good fortune. You are a special man and you will do great things. I wouldn't want anything to get in your way."

"If people have less regard for me because of what my mother did, let them."

A nod. "You can ignore them because you are in a position to do so. Nothing people say can affect you. As much as I hate to admit it, going with General Han was the best thing that could have happened to you. In spite of the man."

"The best thing. I suppose it was."

She looked at him. "Something wrong?"

"Nothing is wrong. Things are going well, as a matter of fact."

"Things are going well with Han?"

"Yes."

"What about you?"

"I'm fine."

"You are not fine. I can tell something is bothering you. It's in your eyes."

"I need a new perspective, that's all."

"On what?" she asked.

"The future. The country."

"What's bothering you—does it have to do with Han?"

"Everything in my life has to do with him."

"He is making trouble, isn't he?"

"He is ready to break from the Party. He wants to take over the country. He's going to do something big. Something destructive and irreversible. I don't know how to stop him."

"You shouldn't try. Because you can't."

"I won't know unless I try."

"Han is not someone you should offend."

"If I don't intervene, no one will."

"Han is richer than an emperor and more ruthless than the Shanghai Triad. He is not going to do things differently because of anything you say."

"Not say. Do."

Silence.

"Will you put yourself in danger?"

"I want him to see that it's possible to win by fighting fairly."

"Will you put yourself in danger?" she insisted.

"He won't harm me."

"Don't count on that. Don't get in his way. Don't let him know what's on your mind. If he wants to start a war, let him. Let joss decide. What you should do is leave before that happens, Jong."

"Leave."

"Leave Shansui. Leave China. Go somewhere far away. Out of Han's reach."

"What will he do without me?"

"He was fine without you and he will be fine without you. He has his gold."

Nan-fei climbed onto the bed, stacked the pillows, and knelt on them so she could have a full view of the street. She watched Jong leave the noodle shop and move down the crowded sidewalk. Tears filled her eyes. Would this be the last time she saw him? She knew how fast her health was deteriorating. The numbness in her arm had spread to her chest and neck. The sores on her chest had turned from pink to red to black. Sometimes her heart beat so fiercely that she expected it to pop out of her mouth. She dutifully fed herself the medicinal soups prescribed by the herbalist. They made her feel better for a while, and then things would go wrong again. She knew a real doctor, preferably a Western-trained one, was needed. And fast. It could be arranged in a matter of hours if she told Jong.

What was the point of prolonging a life like hers in a world like this? If her ailments didn't kill her, the thugs or the Japanese would. She had no desire to fight any of them. She was very, very tired. Death would be a reprieve. For her next life, if she could choose, she would return as a bird or a fish. Enjoy a brief and carefree existence. Not as a person. Definitely *not* as a woman. Ever again. Most of her life had been spent on her back with her legs apart, taking in the yangs of faceless men.

If it had not been for Jong, she would have taken her own life at the first sign of war. War would have made her miserable existence unbearable. But Jong had been a child, helpless and dependent. She had been all he had. He had needed her. She had bit her lips and braved the ferocious journey from Peking to Shanghai. She had wanted Jong to live. And herself with him. He was the only good thing in her wretched life. A half-breed child, he didn't belong to anyone or anywhere—in that way he was like her. But there was so much more: intelligence, kindness, integrity, qualities she had not experienced in men.

Nan-fei wiped away her tears and climbed down from the bed. Enough rumination for the day. Time to prepare for the inevitable. Time to bring closure to the secret she had been guarding since Jong was born.

She bent her pain-ridden body, reached under the bed, and pulled out a rusty metal chest. Pushing it aside, she removed the loose tiles where the chest had been. In the recess cut into the tarlike surface lay a man's leather pouch. Last time she had examined the contents, Jong had been an infant.

A photograph was on top of the thin sheaf of documents. Holding it to the light, she squinted to study the portrait. She was once again awed by the miracle. The resemblance was there; no mistaking from whom the boy had inherited his good looks. But a magical transformation had taken place. The boy had left the crassness and the spite with the father and emerged a splendid human being. The papers were promissory notes signed by the man in the photograph. She had been present at some of the transactions. One piece of paper was different. Official-looking, printed with seals and signatures. The birth certificate.

Jong would make sense of them.

She put everything back in the pouch and slipped it under the pillow. Should death claim her, Jong would have no trouble finding it. He would find out about the two people who were his parents. And then he would understand why she had hidden the truth from him.

The Frenchman's house was located in the less affluent part of the French Concession, a flat, leafy enclave favored by middle-class Europeans and well-to-do Chinese families seeking a safer neighborhood. Jong posted guards around the premises before he approached the door. The front lawn was well kept, flowerpots, a fishpond. The water in the pond was clear enough to see five beautiful goldfish swimming around a sprawling plant. By the pond's rim, a yellow wooden duck lay on its side. Clothespins dotted on the empty laundry lines. It's a mother's house.

A shadow moved behind a window, stopped, disappeared. Jong rang the doorbell. He heard the sound of unlatching. A slit revealed a child's eye, glittering with curiosity.

"I am Jong Lin from Shansui. General Han sent me."

The door opened. A blond boy in a Chinese pajama suit examined Jong from head to toe. "You must be here for Mrs. Li and Yunna."

"Yes."

"We are expecting you. Come in, please."

"Thank you."

"I am Pierre. My father is Victor Maurier. He met Mrs. Li and Yunna in Nanking and brought them back. They are staying with us."

"Your Chinese is excellent."

"I was born here."

The living room was middle-class fashionable: lace curtains, armchairs topped with white crocheted doilies, a coffee table displaying a crescent of Chinese movie magazines, in the corner a Grundig record player with a trumpet speaker. The afternoon sun filtered through the curtains and settled on the furniture like a film of dust. A trace of wood smoke hung in the air.

"Please let your father know I'm here," Jong said.

"My father is not home."

"What about your mother?"

Pierre shook his head. "She went home."

"Went home?"

"To France. It's on the continent of Europe, very far from China. My mother went back because she didn't like living here anymore. My parents are French. Me too." Head tilted up, he regarded Jong. "You are tall like my father. Your eyes are like his, bluer. Your nose is also high. Are you French?"

"I am half American, I think."

"You mean you are not sure who you are?"

"I know when I am in China, I am Chinese."

The child beamed. "It's the same for me."

"Only you and your father live here?"

"There's Auntie Lillie. But she's gone too."

Pierre gave an account of how they discovered Lillie had left in the middle of the night with the trunk. Jong noted the woman had taken off the day after the Lis' arrival and wondered if there was a connection.

"Did she say why she left?"

"Not a word. Auntie Lillie broke her promise. She said we were not to have secrets from each other, and then she did that."

"Is your Auntie Lillie also from Europe?"

"No, she is Chinese."

"Her name is Lillie."

"She picked the name after she read about an actress in Britain who was the emperor's best friend. She wants to be like her."

"What does she do?"

"She cooks, shops, and takes care of Papa and me."

"What about before she came to live with you?"

"She worked in a dancing hall. But she likes being a housewife. She said she wouldn't want to dance again. Auntie Lillie is very pretty."

"A dancing hall?"

"The biggest one in Shanghai."

"How long has your father known her?"

"Two years. Maybe longer. She moved in with us after Mother went back to France."

"Would your father know why Lillie left?" Jong asked, as he puzzled out the relationships in the Maurier household.

"He said the trunk belongs to Mrs. Li and Yunna. Auntie Lillie shouldn't have taken it. It was wrong. That's why she ran away."

"What was in this trunk?"

"Stuff that belonged to Yunna's father. She got it out before the fire burned down their house. My father was there and he helped them."

"Did your father know Mrs. Li and Yunna before they met in Nanking?"

"I don't think so."

"When do you expect your father home?"

"I wish I knew. When he found out Auntie Lillie had run away, he dropped everything and went out to look for her." Pierre lifted his eyes. "Is my father all right?"

"There is no reason to believe he is not."

"What if he can't find Auntie Lillie? So many bad things are happening everywhere."

"Shanghai is a big city. It's not easy to find someone. It will take time. I'm sure your father knows what to do." He patted the boy's head. "Can I see Mrs. Li and her daughter?"

"Mrs. Li is in bed. She isn't feeling well. She's been crying a lot. I'll tell Yunna you are here."

How did a Frenchman and a Chinese ballroom hostess get tangled up with Soong's cousins? Jong looked around when he was alone, more carefully this time. Crucifixes and ink calligraphy hung side by side on the walls. The furniture was European imports from Shanghai's upscale department stores. A rosewood cabinet housed a collection of pre-Ching Dynasty antiques, choice pieces worth a tidy fortune. Had the Frenchman gotten rich working for T. V. Soong? Doing what? What brought him to Henry Li's family in Nanking? What had been in the trunk? Why did the Frenchman's mistress run away with it? Who was she?

"We are so glad you are here."

Jong turned.

There she was. Standing still, graceful and beautiful, in a square of sunlight. He couldn't breathe or move or think. The background receded and the world dissolved. He was in a place filled with light and sweetness and warm air. Alone with the girl. He had the curious sensation of never having seen her, yet feeling he had known her in his previous lives.

She was regarding him with her dark eyes.

"I am Yunna. Henry Li was my father."

"I am Jong Lin."

"Jong Lin," she repeated, eyes intent.

"General Han sent me."

"Pierre told me."

"How is your mother?"

"Not well, I'm afraid."

"And you—are you well?"

She gave a small nod. They sat down on the sofa.

"Your father was a dear friend. General Han was crushed by the news. He hopes you will come to Shansui—if you don't have other plans."

"We don't have any plans."

"A plane is waiting at the airport. We can leave when you are ready." The questions concerning the Frenchman and his mistress were not important now. Only the girl's safety mattered.

"How long can we stay in Shansui?"

"As long as you wish. It will be your new home."

"That's very kind of General Han."

"He is glad to be able to help."

"Where will we live in Shansui?"

"Inside his compound. You and your mother will have your own apartment, servants, anything you need. General Han is anxious to make things right for you."

She smiled politely with a shake of her head, indicating she understood Han's intentions were well meant, but they were not achievable.

"We lost something valuable. It belonged to my father. I hope we can recover it before we leave Shanghai. Can you help?"

"I'll do what I can."

She described the trunk and what her father had told her about the contents.

"'The fruits of his career.' Is that what he said?" he asked.

"Those were his words. I remember thinking he should be proud, but he wasn't. He seemed sad when he said that, out of sorts."

It was the trunk with the gold peaches, Jong decided. It answered the questions: why the Frenchman had taken the trouble of escorting them out of Nanking and why his mistress had stolen the trunk.

"If the Frenchman's mistress is acting alone, she couldn't have gotten far. I'll have our men search in and around Shanghai."

"Why would she want my father's work?"

"She might think it's holding something valuable. Did you save anything else from the house?"

"No, there wasn't time."

He didn't want to remind her how her father had died, but he had to ask the questions. "Your father was found in the library. Was the room searched?"

"More than once. The place was turned upside down."

"Was anything taken?"

"The machines in the safe. Some stuff in the cabinet. There could be other things missing, I can't be sure. Father never told anyone what he kept in the library."

"What about your father's files?"

"He burned them."

"When?"

"The night before he was killed."

"Do you know why?"

"I asked him. He said they weren't useful anymore."

"What kind of files?"

"They weren't the usual academic writings. There were all kinds of scribbling and drawings on the pages: notes, graphs, numbers, handwriting of different individuals. There were also photographs and a stack of telegrams. They could have been materials for his research. He wouldn't need them after he wrote the essays. That's what I thought."

"But you are not convinced?"

"The contents didn't seem academic, not what one would associate with European Art History. And he made a point of turning the pages face-down when he slipped them into the fire—why bother when they would be destroyed anyway. There were stacks. He must have cleaned out the whole cabinet." A pause. "Why are people asking about my father's files?"

"Who else has asked?"

"Mr. Maurier. He thought that's what was in the trunk. He couldn't understand why his mistress would want my father's files."

Jong registered the information. The Frenchman took the trunk to Shanghai because he thought it contained Henry's files. He had an interest in what Henry did as Chiang Kai-shek's cabinet member. And possibly what he did for General Han.

"Did your father burn everything?"

"There didn't seem to be anything left—except what was in the trunk. And he seemed relieved."

"How?"

"As if he was set free. Like a child let out of school." She looked at him. "Did General Han have anything to do with what happened to my father?"

"What makes you think General Han is involved?"

"I can't explain. Just a feeling that he was always in the background."

"He and your father were friends. Good friends."

"There wasn't anything more than friendship?"

"They were interested in each other's work."

"What do you mean?"

"Things going on in the Party, the country, the international scene. General Han valued your father's opinion. He liked to run things by him."

"He was General Han's advisor."

"You could say that."

"Anything else you can tell me?"

"I only know the generalities. They liked to talk alone."

For a moment each was lost in thought.

"Tell me about Shansui," she said.

He described the spectacular scenery, the strangely shaped mountains rising from the rice fields, the legends intertwined with the landscape, the kindness of the people and their simple way of life, and Han's magnificent palace.

"Shansui. Home. I never would have dreamed," she said.

"Neither had I."

"You are not a native?"

"I was born in Peking. My foster mother took me to Shanghai when the riots broke out. I was fifteen when I met General Han. He brought me to Shansui and I've been living there since."

"What about your parents?"

"I don't know them. They left me soon after I was born. I looked for them, but they couldn't be found."

"They just vanished?"

"It seems so."

"Hard to believe."

He nodded. "Parents wouldn't abandon their child unless there was a compelling reason. I wanted to know the reason. And people didn't just disappear from the face of the earth. They had to have left something behind, people who had known them, places they had lived. With mine, there wasn't a trace that they had existed. It took a long time before I realized it could be that they didn't want to be found."

"Maybe they were forced to let you go, and not leaving any trace was their way of protecting you."

"That's entirely possible, given the situation in and around Peking at the time. I may never find the answer, and that's something I have to live with."

"It must be hard."

"It could have been harder. I was lucky to have my foster mother and General Han." He added, "With or without parents, life goes on. We live our own lives."

"Men can do that. A girl isn't so free."

"No. At least for now."

"Do you believe things will change?" she asked.

"They will. It's inevitable. China is in transition. It may be a long and messy transition, but the time will come when the new order replaces the old."

"What kind of new order?"

"The people, not one person, will rule."

"Like the Western democracies."

"Like what the May Fourth Movement championed."

"I've read about it. Such an extraordinary time." Her eyes stayed on a shaft of sunlight as if it were a tunnel to the past. "I wish I could have been there. I would have joined them—thinkers, writers, students. They weren't afraid to stand up for what they believed in. They were willing to sacrifice for the greater good. Where can we find people like them now?"

"Hard to be concerned with the greater good when people can barely stay alive."

"The people I know are well fed. They have bodyguards and they live in fortresses, yet they are selfish and corrupt."

"And some of them want to bring back feudal China. Start a dynasty and rule with absolute power."

"The Mandate of Heaven."

He thought of the emperors through the dynasties, living in supreme luxury, having total control over the country, yet they were no different than the people they ruled, flawed and weak and vulnerable. Their subjects hadn't questioned their authority because they believed the emperors had the Mandate of Heaven. Such grand words. Fooled generations. Millenniums.

He got up and ambled to the other side of the room. On the wall was a crucifix. The cross was made of walnut; the body of Jesus had been carved out of ivory. There had been identical ones for sale in Charlie Soong's Bible shop. The Frenchman might have bought it there. A spider had woven a web between the tip of the cross and a nailed hand.

"I don't believe in the Mandate of Heaven," he said, eye on the tiny web, thinking once again about Pu-yi and the dead emperors before him. "One man controlling the lives of millions, governing at whim, squandering resources as he pleases. Not accountable to anyone. Privileges exclusive to one family and one family alone, passing from generation to generation. Such a system of government shouldn't have a place in the modern world."

What if Han heard what he said? How would it change their relationship? He always played his role of faithful cupbearer. Never challenged Han's scheme of restoring imperial China, though in his heart he knew Han was dead wrong. He didn't speak up because it would hurt Han and he loved the man. But at this moment, in the company of the girl to whom he knew his life would be bound, he saw the truth about himself. He was a coward. He didn't have the courage to risk Han's trust.

"My father must have liked you," she said. "He liked people who think and act independently."

"Your father was an open-minded man."

Probably Henry had been like him: pledging allegiance to Han while harboring his own set of convictions.

"He said he had learned more from having lived in different countries than from books," Yunna said. "He believed China's leaders should get out of their imperial cocoons. See the world beyond the Middle Kingdom."

Imperial cocoon. Han's world. Mine too, if I don't get out.

"The night before he died, he was planning a trip."

"Where was he planning to go?" he asked.

"Europe."

"To visit?"

"To live."

"For how long?"

"He didn't say, but I had the impression he planned to settle there."

An alarm went off. Jong asked, "Was this the first time he talked about such a trip?"

"In a serious way. We were going to take off before Christmas."

"That wouldn't have given him much time to arrange such a big move."

"He was spurred by something. As if he knew a disaster was about to happen. Which it did."

More likely the gold was what had spurred Henry. One hundred thirty-eight catties of the precious metal would fund any junket.

"I keep thinking if my father had made the travel plans sooner, we would have left before the Japanese came. He and my brother would still be alive."

But Henry didn't have the gold before that day, Jong thought. And he doubted that they would have made it all the way to Europe. Even if they'd managed to get out of China, Han would have had Henry captured. He knew too much about Han's operation. The punishment for his betrayal wouldn't have been different from what happened in Nanking.

He didn't want to tell her. He felt her loss. He wished he could make up for it. But he couldn't even find the words to comfort her.

"Let me see if Mother is awake. She would be glad to meet you." Yunna got up. "Perhaps it was joss how things turned out."

"Joss."

"Do you believe in joss, Mr. Lin?"

"I didn't. But I do now."

Because he'd found her.

They waited for the Frenchman to come home. Pierre kept running up to the street corner, looking for his father. The afternoon light was fading fast; the day was turning cold. Jong reminded them that they must get to at the airfield before nightfall. With the worsening situation in Nanking, things were volatile. The airfield might be closed without notice. They shouldn't take a chance. Not wanting Pierre to be left alone in the house, Yunna packed some clothes for him; he would accompany them. Jong wrote down the place and the time of their departure and left the note in the living room for the Frenchman.

At the airfield, they waited another hour. When it was time to take off, Pierre boarded the plane with them.

The child would be safe. The Frenchman would have to show up in Shansui to claim his son, Jong thought. And he would have to confess what his connection to Soong was all about.

13

Lillie made sure she had gone a distance from the French Concession before she slowed down. The sky was brightening, gray with streaks of pink haze. Occasionally a truck or a car sped by; mostly she had pedicabs and bicycles to keep her company. She was approaching the town south of the city where she had grown up. Nameless alleys crisscrossed like a maze. Mud huts mingled with clapboard houses. The air was saturated with the stench of rotting fruit and human waste. Few foreigners ever set foot in the neighborhood; Victor wouldn't find his way here. Passing rows of defunct shops and a zigzag bridge, a street market came into view. The stalls were opening for the day. Coolies were unloading wheelbarrows piled with cabbages and daikon roots. Hawkers were arranging tangerines and melons on the stands.

Time for a break. Get something to eat and then figure out what to do.

273

She pulled up to the clearing in the center of the market and got out of the car.

The hawker at the closest stall was glad to have a customer. "Today's special is fried onion pancakes. Steamed buns are six cents apiece, sixty a dozen."

"You have soy milk?"

"Fresh and hot."

"Can you fill a jar? I want to take it on the road."

"Fancy wheels you got there. Drove all the way from the Bund?"

"Do you have a jar or not?"

He bent down and looked through his supplies. "Don't have anything like that. You can buy one from the shop on the next street."

"How far away?"

"Just around the corner. With your car you can be back in seconds."

A buzz was going through the market. She felt eyes were on her. All the eyes.

A quick glance around. Three new customers had arrived. An old couple balancing themselves with canes. A woman carrying a bamboo tote. Under a tree, coolies were gesturing and talking in hushed voices. Everyone seemed to be looking in her direction. She was buying soy milk. Why should she become the center of attention? And since when did coolies behave like gossiping housewives? What if they weren't coolies? What if they were undercover police? She stiffened. She had left the house almost an hour ago. The Li women could have awakened from their drugged sleep, discovered the trunk was missing, and contacted the police. Fear flared in her like a match. What was the punishment for a theft of this magnitude?

Fingers chopped off? The whole hand? Beheading in the street?

The hawker tapped a pair of chopsticks on the rim of the wok. "What about onion pancakes? Dumplings? They are good with soy milk."

"What?"

"Onion pancakes. Dumplings. I thought you wanted breakfast."

"I've changed my mind. I don't want anything. I have to go."

As she climbed back into the car, she heard the hawker say to his neighbor that he thought only *kweiloh* women were allowed to operate a vehicle. Who was this Chinese woman driving her own car?

Was that it?

Think. Even if the Li women had called the police, they couldn't have put together an undercover team this fast. Victor might have some pull through his connection with Soong; on his own, he wouldn't get much cooperation from Chinese law enforcement. In downtown Shanghai, a female Chinese driver would be a rare sight, and here she was in a neighborhood so poor a donkey cart was luxury. Of course she stood out. She should have parked the car at a distance and walked to the market. She had done a foolish thing by drawing attention in a public place. If word got out about the gold, everyone in Shanghai would be looking for her. People here could give a detailed description of the car and her.

A fly battered the window of the car, buzzing like it was sniffing out the gold. The damn insect is freer than I am, she thought, staring at the bags on the passenger seat. They could be a pile of explosives.

Taps on the window.

She swung around. A toothless beggar was pressing his contorted face against the glass. She waved him away. He took the gesture as encouragement, pulled back a few inches so as to present himself properly. He wetted his lips and offered his tongue, dirty fingernails pecking on the window.

She rammed the car into gear and stepped on the gas pedal. The car roared off. The beggar stumbled backward.

Gripping the steering wheel, she kept her eye on the rear view mirror, checking if she was being followed. A boy on a bicycle. A peasant on foot balancing baskets from a shoulder-pole. More peasants. They fell behind as she sped on. The sky was threaded with low clouds. What if it rained? Could she handle the slippery roads? The gasoline gauge read half full. How far could she go on the remaining fuel? Should she make a stop to fill up the tank? How could she do that without being noticed?

Which would happen sooner, running out of gasoline or being caught by the police?

She was sweating in spite of the cold.

I couldn't be the first thief in Shanghai to make off in a car. Stay calm.

She couldn't drive aimlessly. She was using up precious fuel; worse, the longer she stayed on the road, the more people would notice her. The license plate would link her to Victor and the address in the French Concession. Where to go? She had no family, no relatives. The few friends she had were from the ballroom, and since moving in with Victor, she had not maintained contact. They were part of the past she preferred to forget. She could cross the river, go beyond the city limits, rent a room in a village. It might be possible to lie low and wait until Victor left China. But could she? A village was a tight community. Peasants could pass information faster than a wireless machine. It wouldn't take long for neighbors to figure out the woman from Shanghai was on the run. Once she became the object of their curiosity, there would be no peace. God forbid if they found out she had bags of gold with her.

She'd lived in Shanghai all her life. It was a vast metropolis. Hiding in plain sight wouldn't be hard as long as she had a place to keep the car. She needed to be with people who wouldn't ask questions.

There was only one such place.

She made a sharp turn and headed back the way she came.

"Absolutely not. You can't stay here. This is not a hostel for vagrant women," said the man in the manager's office. Twenties, slick hair, tea-stained teeth, black jacket over a wrinkled shirt. In her days, someone who dressed like this wouldn't have been allowed in the front office. The Paramount had fallen on hard times.

"Let me speak to the manager," Lillie said.

"I am the manager."

"What happened to Mr. Liu?"

"Left town. I replaced him."

"Since when?"

"Eight, nine months ago."

"You are new to Shanghai?"

"Maybe."

"You would make an exception if you knew who I am."

"I don't care if you are the Empress Dowager's reincarnation. We don't rent out rooms."

"I was one of your top performers. My picture was on the playbill. Every night."

He took a longer look at her. "You do look familiar. Were you fired?"

"I left on my own. Look, I need a room for a few days. I'll pay."

"You are not a bad-looking woman—if you fixed up your face and got into some decent clothes. Tell you what. We have some big parties coming up. I don't have enough girls. I'll give you a job, at the going rate for freelance. You can stay while you work."

"I don't want a job. I need a place to sleep."

"Go to a hotel."

Lillie counted a hundred yuan. "Would this do?"

"For the ballroom or for me?"

"Your call."

His eye went to the thick stack in her purse. She added another hundred.

He stuffed the money into his pocket. "You can have the shack by the rear exit."

"I also need space to park my car."

"A car—is it yours?"

"My husband's."

"Who is your husband?"

"An important man."

He scrutinized her. "Are you Big Ear Tu's concubine? Don't tell me you're one of Chiang Kai-shek's mistresses? Are you in trouble with his Dragon Lady?"

"Can we stick to reality? We are talking about a parking space."

"There is always space on the street."

"I want a more private location."

"Why do you need to hide the car?"

"I wouldn't want to know too much if I were you."

"How private?"

"Where the car can't be seen from the street, and close enough if I need to get to it quickly."

"That is not a simple request."

Another hundred yuan facilitated his thinking. The man had earned a month's pay in ten minutes. At this rate she would have to start liquidating the gold tomorrow.

"They are repairing the building behind us, the one owned by the Jewish tycoon, Sassoon," he said unhurriedly. "Don't know why he bothers; the bombs can hit again. Maybe he made a deal with the Japs. The Jews can make a deal with the devil and come out ahead. The supervisor of the construction crew is a friend of mine. I'll tell him to keep an eye on the car. Your personal security guard. How about that?"

"Fine."

"It won't be cheap."

"Fine."

"I take it if anyone asks, I keep my mouth shut."

"Right."

"Will I be compensated for my trouble?"

"When I leave, and if nothing happens to me or my car."

"You want to tell me who you are?"

"You guessed right the first time. I am the Empress Dowager's reincarnation."

"Whatever. Here's the key to the imperial suite."

The shack smelled like an outhouse. Lillie remembered an old Korean maid had died here. It looked like the cooks had been using it as a garbage dump. At least the door had a lock. A tip for the tea boy got her a bowl of noodles, a basin of warm water, and a hand towel. She locked the door after he delivered the amenities. Famished, she slurped down the noodles, then gave herself a sponge bath. Somewhat refreshed, she examined the dreary surroundings. A dust-laden window looked out on a heap of broken shingles. The walls were blackened with grease. The beaverboard ceiling was marked with scorched spots. Jumble of charred wood and chipped crockery was piled high in the corners. The only furniture were a wooden bed with a frayed bamboo mat and a decrepit closet. Half a day on her own, already the quality of her life had deteriorated beyond belief.

How much worse would it get?

If she had not run away, she would be in bed, safe and warm in the sweet cocoon of half-sleep, Victor caressing her naked body with a flurry of soft kisses... No more mornings like that from now on. No more Victor. No more love. Just herself and the gold. She shook off tears. I am in a temporary shelter with a creep in the front office who would sell me for a tip. This is not the time to feel sorry for myself.

Better take care of the gold.

The closet had one side of a double door; the other side had been ripped off. The shelves were rickety. Even if they were useable, she wouldn't want to put the gold there for everyone to see. She'd have to improvise. She went through the pile of scraps and found a short-handled hoe with a pick on the backside of the blade. The shack had been a hurried addition to the main structure. The owner had never bothered to finish the floor. She tested the hoe on the ground.

The surface crumbled after a few thumps. She pushed the bed aside and began to hack.

An hour of labor produced a shallow pool and sent a family of rats scurrying for cover. By nightfall it was big enough to accommodate one suitcase.

She went back to the kitchen. A bigger tip got her a bowl of cabbage soup, two pork buns, and an oil lamp. The cook was another unfamiliar face. He was making a stew in an earthen pot, busily feeding the blaze with broken charcoal. He didn't give her another look. The old cook had been her friend, her only real friend in this awful place. After the guests had left and she had been too frazzled to sleep, he would fix her favorite fried dumplings. They had sat around the brazier. He had taught her how to read by using the burnt ends of firewood sticks to write on the floor, stroke by stroke, radical by radical. He had also taught her simple arithmetic and how to work an abacus. He had told her she had a quick mind; she was smarter than the managers. The compliment had changed how she looked at herself. She wanted to ask the new cook what had happened to his predecessor; but she didn't dare invite more attention. She returned to the shack and ate her dinner. The soup was stale and the buns dry. She was too hungry to complain.

The level of chatter in the ballroom was rising. She could see the scene in her mind. Painted women in tight cheongsams. Men gripping them, mumbling lewd things as they blew cigarette smoke into their faces. In an hour the lights would dim and the ballroom would charge the guests prime rates for the ease of groping the women in the dark. Seventy-five percent went to the house, ten to the staff, and fifteen to the girls; a more favorable split if the girl could push quick turnovers. The real money was to be made later, away from the premises, in the back of a pedicab or in a hotel room. For nine years it had been her life. A different man every hour, every night. Constantly worrying about infections, abuse, physical safety...

She lit the oil lamp and resumed digging. When the noises in the ballroom died down, she had a grave for the gold. Its perimeter was a few inches narrower than the bed, deep enough to accommodate the bags. She arranged them in the pit and pulled the bed over it.

It was done. The gold was safe. She was so relieved she could have sung.

Someday she would tell Victor about this.

When that day would be, she could only dream.

She was filthy. Her body ached. Too tired for another sponge bath, she fell asleep with Victor's pistol by her side.

She woke with a start. Boots stomping, furniture smashing into walls, men shouting. The girls would have turned in. The place should be quiet. It must be a party of drunks staying through the night, she thought sleepily. Caucasians, probably Russian. They were the rowdiest and the meanest. Few of the girls liked to serve them... She couldn't go back to sleep. Something was not right. This uproar had a different tone. Where were the sounds of clinking glasses, music, laughter? Why was the air filled with firecracker fumes?

The building was on fire.

A blade of panic sliced through her.

The air was still cold. It couldn't be a fire.

Wide-awake, she turned to the line of illumination under the door. She was relieved to see the faint blue glow of dawn, not orange light from open flames. She held her breath and listened. Men's voices. Women pleading. Heavy boots on the wooden floor.

Boots.

She sat bolt upright, grabbed Victor's pistol, and jumped out of bed. Having little space to move, she stood stock-still. They have come for me. Where I worked—of course it would be the first place they checked. It was foolish to have thought the Paramount would be safe. The cadence of noises was escalating, the thumping of boots drowning out other sounds. The place must be swarming with police. One pistol wouldn't be enough.

She had to think of something else. Fast.

Screams. A blizzard of footsteps. More screams. She put her ear to the wall. The commotion came from the part of the building where the girls slept. The manager also had a room there. If the police were looking for her, she had no doubt he would have led them straight to the shack.

Maybe she wasn't the target.

Who were these people out there making a ruckus?

The police didn't wear boots. Chinese soldiers didn't have boots—the government wouldn't pay for them. Boots were worn by soldiers from a country that could afford them.

Japanese soldiers.

There was only one thing they wanted from a place like this. A tingling terror spread from her chest to her feet.

Buddha. I have walked straight into hell.

The boots were heading to the kitchen. In seconds they would see the door to the shack and they would think it was the supply room. They would raid it. There was no time to run. She tightened her grip on the pistol, but she couldn't control her trembling. *Lose your nerve and you'll lose your life*. A defiant courage swelled in her, along with the will to survive.

There was no way she could defend herself with a gun against a troop of soldiers. She needed to use her wits. Trick them. Get them to leave her alone.

In her Paramount days, she had learned the Japanese had a mania for hygiene. They would pay extra for the woman to take a bath before they let her into their bed. She scraped grease off the walls and smeared it on her face, teeth, and neck, with an extra rub on the fingernails. Would filth be enough? Better go all the way. Turn herself into an Untouchable. She remembered seeing a trash can outside the shack. She opened the door gingerly and pulled the can inside. She rummaged until she found the bag of soiled menstrual napkins. Japanese men believed anything tainted by a woman's cycle would blemish the male soul. Suppressing the urge to throw up, she scattered the bloodied bundles around the bed. Then she dumped the rest of the trash over herself. She shrugged into Victor's jacket, buttoned it up crookedly, and left the sleeves hanging. Then she lay down on the mat, hands over her head, knees to her chin.

The door burst open.

The boots stomped on the soft earth and sent up a dust storm. Buddha and Jesus, she prayed, don't let them see the pit. If they found the gold, she would be dead. The men were shining flashlights around. At the sight of the soiled napkins, they winced. One light halted on the bed. A circle of glare framed her body. She crushed her fingers on her scalp, holding down the shaking. One soldier stepped forward and poked her back with the barrel of his gun. She bit her lips. Do it now before they pull the trigger. She jerked her body around and looked at them full in the face, grateful that the glare from the flashlight blurred her vision. She made a bold grimace, let out imbecilic giggles, and started to writhe like an octopus.

"Madwoman."

"Could be a man—look at the clothes."

"Got tits."

"Such filth. Only the Chinese can live like this."

"This thing probably has enough clap to infect all the men in the province."

"We could make her our present to the jackass Tsujita. She would foul up the whole camp."

"How many have we rounded up?"

"About thirty."

"Should be enough for the district. We don't need this garbage heap."

They turned and walked out, slamming the door shut.

Lillie gripped the edge of the bed to control her shaking, then she eased out of bed. Her legs were wobbly. She blinked to clear her eyes, breathed deeply, and straightened her back. She went to the door and opened an inch.

The soldiers were gone.

She stepped outside. The kitchen was deserted. Dusty footprints in the long hallway. The flurry of activity had moved to the front end of the building. The noises seemed to be coming from the office. They must be looting the safe. The ballroom took in large amounts of cash every night. The owner had bought an imported safe used by Swiss banks. It had been built into the wall with a set of complicated locks. Cracking the safe would keep them occupied.

The back door was a few feet away.

Grabbing the car key, she broke out of the shack and raced through the alley. Her foot caught a tin can. She staggered and then crashed into a pole, righted herself, and pulled away. Coming to the end of the alley, she crossed the street and dashed to the construction site. The building was a skeleton of concrete beams, empty like a bombed-out city. She scampered over raw dirt, weeds, and broken stones. The sight of Victor's car brought immeasurable relief. She unlocked the door and ducked in. She leaned back on the seat, clutching the steering wheel as though it were a lifeline to safe haven in a world gone mad, and wept. For her unbelievable luck. For the thirty women whose terrible fate she wouldn't have to share, living out their life in a "comfort house," a sex prison where women were locked up in cells and raped by Japanese soldiers around the clock.

A swell of sounds issued from the direction of the ball-room. She looked up. Japanese soldiers were leaving the premises. She was out of their sight, but she didn't want to take a chance. She slouched down, banging one knee against the steering wheel. Gingerly she eased up and peered over the dashboard.

Through two columns of unfinished concrete, she watched a queue of women move out of the front rotunda. Japanese soldiers lined up alongside, guns raised, pointing at them. The women had been dragged out of bed, hair disheveled, movements uncertain. Lillie recognized an occasional face, aged more than the time since her own departure. The unpainted complexion could have been any overworked housewife's, but only in their next life would they experience the joys of being wife and mother.

The queue was heading to a truck in the middle of the road. The vehicle was constructed like a giant cage with bars around the bed and chains over the frame. A wooden board was hoisted up the rear. One by one, like condemned prisoners to the guillotine, the women mounted the gangplank.

The moment the truck drove away, Lillie fired up the car and headed back to the alley. Keeping the engine on, she dashed to the shack. With more strength than she thought she had, she unearthed the bags and hauled them to the car.

She drove where there was open road, not caring where she was going. Her mind was a blank while the rest of her tried to recover from the shock. People and vehicles were filling up the streets. Another day was beginning.

She had made no more progress than when she first drove away from home. Exactly twenty-four hours ago.

Swallow your pride, Lillie said to herself as she stared at the gasoline gauge trembling in the red. She was a complete fool, to think she could begin a new life on her own. Time to accept that she had failed. Miserably. There was only one thing to do. Go back and beg for Victor's forgiveness. Tell him it had been a fit of craziness. The killings in Nanking had scared her, and the sight of the gold had taken away her reason. She had had a day to clear her head. There wasn't any doubt now. No matter what happened, they would be together for the rest of their lives. If Victor wanted to live in Europe, it would be fine with her.

On Rue Lafayette, she located the church where she had once attended a wedding. There was one vehicle in the small parking lot, a black sedan with a rosary over the dashboard. The priest's car. She pulled up next to it, got out, and walked up the steps. Chill whipped across her face; it might snow tonight. Bad weather wouldn't bother her now, she thought with anticipated relief. Soon she would be home and she would be warm and safe. She gazed up at the campanile of the church and made a promise to Victor's God.

I will never leave him again.

The entrance was decorated with Christmas ornaments. The double doors opened at a push. Quiet. At the far end, a stained glass window depicted a dove against a backdrop of blue skies. On the altar, two vases filled with full-bloomed lilies stood on both sides of the crucifix. Lilies. She smiled. A good omen. A Caucasian man in a black robe sat in the front pew, reading a Bible on his lap. At the marble basin by the entrance, she took out a handkerchief and dipped it in the water. She leaned forward and gave her face a vigorous scrub. The man was absorbed in his reading. He didn't pay attention to the small washing noises in the back. Must be wonderful to have found peace in this chaotic world. She rinsed the handkerchief and rubbed her face again. The grease was coming off. The basin of holy water turned into a tiny swamp. She mumbled a silent apology and put a wad of cash in the donation box. She hoped she looked reasonably clean. She didn't want Victor to welcome a charwoman.

She drove at top speed, heading home. Approaching the house, she saw there was no light in any of the rooms. Maybe the power was out. Maybe Victor and Pierre had gone somewhere. Feeling less certain than a moment ago, she parked behind the house.

She walked to the front and unlocked the door.

"Victor, are you home?" she cried, flipping light switches as she moved from room to room. "I'm back. Please don't be mad at me. Pierre, it's Auntie Lillie."

No answer.

The Li women's things were gone from the guest room. They must have left with Han's people. Good riddance. They wouldn't be present to testify against her. She noted with some irritation that the beds hadn't been made and her pajamas had been left in a heap. On second thought, she couldn't blame them for not tidying up when she had made off with their gold.

Victor's down-filled jacket was absent from the rack, as were Pierre's boots. Father and son must have gone out together, probably to have a meal at a hotel where they served French food. She returned to the car and carried the luggage back into the house, happy to perform the same task at a leisurely pace.

Taking a respite from the day, she went to the sideboard and poured a whiskey. A note was lying near the bottle. She picked it up. The handwriting was a stranger's.

Mr. Maurier:

General Han received your request and he thanks you for taking care of Mrs. Li and her daughter through what must have been a hazardous and difficult journey. I am his chief of staff and have come to escort them to Shansui.

The situation in and around Shanghai, as you are aware, is becoming urgent. No telling where the Japanese may attack after Nanking. To ensure our safety, we must leave before nightfall. Since we do not know where you are and have no means of contacting you, this note will have to do.

Miss Li thinks we shouldn't leave your child alone; I agree. We are taking him with us to the airfield. We hope you will see this message and meet us there. If not, please contact me in Shansui. We will arrange for your son to come home.

Jong Lin

Lillie took a careful look at the note. A faint thumb print on a corner. She sniffed it. A whiff of whiskey. Victor must have read it while having a drink.

He had come home and then joined them at the airfield.

Victor and Pierre were gone.

She's all alone in Shanghai.

She needed to know how much danger she was in. She began with the scene of her crime. The spot where she had burned the lid off the trunk. It had not been touched; traces of ash were visible on the floor. In the bedroom, her things were where she had left them. There was no sign the space had been searched. It should be safe to assume the police hadn't been called.

General Han's chief of staff had to know what was in the trunk; that someone in Victor's house had stolen Han's gold would have caused alarm. But the tone of the letter was helpful and friendly; not a word about the theft. There couldn't have been little doubt she was the one who took the trunk, yet she was allowed to come home.

Maybe this was a trap.

Suppressing a new wave of panic, she bolted the door and turned out the lights. Moving cautiously along walls and darkened areas, she chose a window that had a full view of the street. Beggars huddled around an open stove of smoldering coal lumps. A festering dog was sniffing around a porthole. The retired writer who lived across the street was smoking his water pipe on the verandah; he was ninety years old and half blind. An occasional bicycle sped by; otherwise no traffic. The street was not a bus route and only three families in the neighborhood had cars. The two vehicles parked along the curb were owned by the other two families. It's the same scene as any other night. She had been in the house almost an hour. If pursuers had been waiting, they should have pounded on the door by now.

The havoc this morning might have been her lucky break. If anyone had traced her to the ballroom, they would have witnessed the raid and assumed she had been abducted with the other women. General Han has a gold mine in Shansui. As large as Shih Huang-ti's tomb. Losing one trunk's worth wouldn't be a big deal.

She hoped.

What she had to do was to find Victor. Having stolen Han's gold, she couldn't show up in Shansui. She would have to meet him at his next stop. She knew he had an important appointment at Soong's bank in Hong Kong. If she missed him there, she would go to France.

Two things she must have: the permit to leave China and the address of Victor's wife. In Pierre's dresser, she found a wad of letters sent from France. She kept the one with the most recent postmark. With the spare key Victor had hidden in a vase, she unlocked the bottom drawer of his desk where he kept important documents. There were surprisingly few items: an address book, extra bullets for his handgun, stacks of foreign currencies, an old Bible.

Something inside the Bible. She opened it. Cached inside were three exit permits.

Three exit permits. Why hadn't Victor taken his and Pierre's if they were going to leave China from Shansui?

Could it be that Victor had not gone to the airport and was still in Shanghai, looking for her?

Wishful thinking. In times like this, who wouldn't take advantage of passage in General Han's private plane? It would be safer than public transportation. Shansui was not far from Hong Kong. Victor and Pierre could easily make a quick transfer to the British colony. The warlord made his own rules. The permits might not be necessary with Han's staff chaperoning them out of China.

Something else was inside the Bible. An envelope had been slipped next to the back cover. She opened it. A ticket for a first-class suite on a British-registered oceanliner. A sheet of paper outlined the itinerary: one-way, Shanghai to Yokohama to Hong Kong. The ticket had been purchased the day Victor returned from Nanking. He must have gone to the shipping office after the meeting with Soong. He hadn't taken it with him—confirming her guess that he decided to go to Hong Kong by way of Shansui...

She noticed he had penciled the word "Chiu" next to Hong Kong on the itinerary. Chiu must be his contact in the bank there. She made a note of the name.

The ship was scheduled to depart for Yokohama at noon, tomorrow. She had sixteen hours.

She wrapped the peaches with undergarments and arranged them under a layer of clothing in the suitcases, hoping the customs officers wouldn't look too closely. The exit permit had been handled by Soong's staff; it would give the traveler special privileges. With luck, she might be able to skip that part of the procedure.

Once out of Shanghai I'll be safe, she thought with renewed hope. The gold will be mine to keep. No, *ours* to keep. Victor won't have to risk his life for Soong anymore.

Having eaten nothing since the paltry meals yester-day, she decided to treat herself to a nice dinner. In the pantry she found a slab of ham, half a loaf of bread, a block of moldy white cheese Victor had bought from the international market. After a year, she was learning to savor this delicacy that looked like soap and smelled like the Huangpo. She scraped the mold off and sliced the cheese. She browned the ham along with the bread in oil and garlic in the heated wok. To go with the sandwich, she opened a bottle of Victor's favorite burgundy.

Not bad, she thought, feeling mellow as the wine warmed her. I should give Europe a chance.

After a long soak in the bathtub, she went to sleep with Victor's pistol on the nightstand. If anyone broke into the house, she would shoot. She's spending her last night in her home no matter what.

14

It could have been a room in the Summer Palace in Peking. The furniture had been chiseled out of a single slab of marble, trimmed in rosewood polished to a gleam. A beige wool carpet had been woven with a pattern to fit the room. The silk cover on the bed was trimmed in fur white as new snow. On the nightstand a cup of jasmine tea issued a whiff of fragrance; the delicate porcelain had a Tang poem in fluid script etched on the surface. Outside, lush green trees frothed with blossoms. Bright yellow trumpets, pink cones, lavender stars. Butterflies whirled like oversize confetti.

Su-chen blinked in the sunlight streaming through the window. When the glare subsided, she saw the woman waiting at the door.

"Good morning, Mrs. Li."

"Where am I?"

"You are in the east wing of General Han's Crescent Moon Villa, in Shansui."

"I took a pill to calm my nerves before we took off. I must have slept through the trip. And you are..."

The woman stepped forward. "My name is Ah Ching. I have been assigned to serve you."

"When did we arrive?"

"Last evening."

"I have been sleeping since?"

"Soundly. You were exhausted. General Han ordered us not to wake you."

"What time is it?"

"Noon."

Ah Ching went to the bathroom and came out with a towel and a basin filled with warm water. She wetted the towel and patted down Su-chen's face.

"Have you seen my daughter?"

"Yes, Mrs. Li. She has been up since daybreak. Mr. Lin is giving her and the Caucasian boy a tour of the Villa. They are having a picnic lunch by the river. Would you like to join them?"

"Not right now."

"Your daughter is lovely. She looks like you. Mr. Lin is very taken with Miss Li."

"Mr. Lin is very kind."

"He is," Ah Ching said with a smile.

She padded away with the basin. When she returned, she picked up the teapot and filled the cup on the nightstand.

"This is the east wing?" Su-chen looked around, sipping her tea.

"One of four buildings in the Inner Court."

"Who else lives here?"

"The Inner Court is reserved for General Han's special guests. At the moment, you, Miss Li, and the Caucasian boy are the only occupants. I was told that you and Miss Li will be staying in Shansui. This is your home now."

"Home."

"This is the best address in China. The Villa is more luxurious and better appointed than the Forbidden City."

"That's what I've heard."

"It's true. But there will be plenty of time to find out for yourself. For now, let me show you what we have here." Ah Ching pointed to a door. "Through there is the hallway to the living room. Miss Li's room is on the other end; the Caucasian boy's is next to hers. There are two additional rooms for your guests. Each room has its own bath and toilet—General Han prefers Western-style facilities. There is a kitchen but you wouldn't need to use it. The meals are prepared in the central kitchen and delivered at the hour of your choice. We have a team of chefs who are trained in all the regional and international cuisines."

"I should pay my respects to General Han and thank him. Would it be possible to see him?"

"He has given word that you can have an audience."

Su-chen got out of bed. Her legs felt weak. Steadied, she smoothed down her nightgown. "We left Nanking in a hurry. I don't have proper clothes with me. I can't see the General like this."

"It has been taken care of." Ah Ching pointed at the tall wardrobe. The front was made of four panels, carved with portraits of the four Great Beauties of China. She pulled a lever. The panels folded back like a stage curtain. "Take a look, Mrs. Li."

There were dresses, skirts, cheongsams, evening gowns of different colors and lengths. All new.

"Can I borrow one?"

"They are yours, Mrs. Li."

"Mine?"

"Our tailors worked round the clock as soon as we knew you were coming. The General said if you don't like the clothes, I am to send for the tailors and they will make a new wardrobe."

"I'm sure that won't be necessary."

Su-chen chose a black jacket and a long black skirt, an outfit suitable for a widow in mourning. She went behind the screen and tried them on. The jacket was made of brocade, cut in the traditional style, stand-up collar, three-quarter length sleeves trimmed in satin, a fitted bodice. The skirt was silk chiffon with gathers at the waist. They fit perfectly.

Ah Ching pulled out a drawer at the base of the wardrobe. Rows of silk slippers and leather pumps were lined up as in a department store display case. Su-chen selected a pair of black slippers.

"I also need..."

"It's been prepared."

Ah Ching went to the dresser and retrieved a white woolen flower the shape of a chrysanthemum bud; loops of wool threads curled to form a ball of petals, a hairpin attached to its base. Su-chen held it in her palm, gazing at the woolen flower, tearing up. The emblem of my widowhood, she thought. I'll wear it for the next one hundred days. To remind the world of my loss. To tell people to keep their distance because a widow is expected to bear her sorrow alone.

Alone. Thousands of miles from home.

Home. The house on Purple Gold Mountain. Life as she had known it. Gone.

"Like a moment of quiet, Mrs. Li?"

She blinked away her tears. "I shouldn't keep General Han waiting."

"He wouldn't mind."

"Everything happened so fast. I never thought my husband would leave us so soon..."

"It's joss, Mrs. Li."

"I suppose it was."

"We all have to live with joss. Even the great General Han," Ah Ching said, pinning the woolen flower behind Su-chen's ear. "After his wife passed away, he didn't let his loss affect him. Not that the General was without feeling, but he put public responsibilities before personal concerns. He carried on. In time he was able to enjoy life again. It'll be the same for you, Mrs. Li. The heart is resilient. Given a chance, it will revive."

Su-chen stared at the sky outside the window. "Will it?"

"You are in Shansui, the most scenic place under heaven. The air and the water make everything bloom. A month will bring back the flush in your cheeks. In the meantime, these would be useful."

Ah Ching lifted the hinged cover of the dressing table to reveal an array of rouge, powder, perfumes, and tubes of imported lipstick.

"I am in mourning. It isn't appropriate to wear makeup," Su-chen said.

"Just a touch here and there to highlight your beautiful face."

She draped a shawl over Su-chen's shoulders and adjusted the mirror, then picked up a lacquer box from the dressing table, removed the lid, and dipped the puff into the face powder. She glided the puff expertly over

Su-chen's forehead and face, back and forth, till the layer of powder evened out. With her fingertips, she applied rouge sparingly on her cheek bones. To finish, she brushed a charcoal pencil over her eyebrows.

"A few strokes and you look ravishing." She removed the shawl carefully to keep the loose powder from falling on Su-chen's jacket. "Ready to see the General?"

She nodded.

"Let me call a sedan chair."

"Let's walk. I'd like to see the Villa."

They followed a covered corridor, passing ponds and flower beds. The corridor emptied onto a winding footpath shaded by camellia bushes. They were walking next to a man-made brook, carps swimming alongside. At every turn there was a new vista. A cul-de-sac opened to an exquisite garden. A stone path led to a satellite palace. It seemed to go on forever. Henry had been here countless times, Su-chen thought. Why hadn't he said anything about this incredible place? And hardly a word about what he did with Han, for Han. For more than a decade the two men had been close friends, yet she knew next to nothing about what they did together. Had friendship been the only bond, or had they shared something else? Had she not been paying enough attention, or had it been Henry's design to keep this part of his life secret? But he wouldn't let her have any secrets from him. He had always been keen to find out what was going on with her side of the family: the Kungs, the Soongs. Casual descriptions had never been enough. Tell me more, he had always insisted, it's the details I enjoy. She had shared everything she knew first hand along with what she'd overheard, including things that had been intimate and embarrassing. She had believed he was interested because he wanted to be part of her family. Was he?

"Your first visit, Mrs. Li?"

She nodded. "I had no idea it was so grand.

"Few do. General Han keeps the Villa private. Wise of him. People are easily jealous of others' good fortune."

"Is that why he called it simply 'villa'?"

The maid nodded. "It should be called the new Forbidden City. His grandfather, who built what are now the Central and Inner Courts, had named it Yuan Ming Palace of the South, after the one in Peking. In the following year, foreign barbarians destroyed the Peking palace. He didn't want the association and changed the name."

"My husband was a regular guest, wasn't he?"

"Professor Li had his own apartment in the Central Court, close to the General's."

"His own apartment?"

"Like the one you have."

"All to himself?"

"Yes."

"That's very spacious."

"He didn't use all the rooms."

Su-chen hesitated. "I've heard the General enjoys the company of attractive women."

"He certainly does."

"What about when my husband was here? Were there female guests to keep them company?"

"I wouldn't know. I didn't have the privilege of serving Professor Li."

"You must have heard from those who did."

"I'm afraid not. We have strict rules: Servants are not to share what they see or hear when they serve the General and his guests." Ah Ching hurried on. "Here we are. This is the Grand Hall."

It was a building of perfect symmetry resting on a base of silver marble. A scroll above the doorway announced: Peace and Justice in Heaven and Earth. Two bronze dragons guarded the entrance. Su-chen and Ah Ching mounted the steps and entered a large foyer, empty except for a lifesize statue of Han, and two sentries posted at the corners.

Su-chen waited while Ah Ching went in to announce her arrival.

A few moments later Han appeared, striding towards her with open arms.

"Good day, General." Su-chen bowed. "Thank you for seeing me and for giving us a home."

He raised her by her elbows. "You had enough rest? Are you comfortable? Is everything to your satisfaction?"

"I am comfortable and everything is perfect."

"That can't be right," he said with mock alarm. "My staff did everything in a hurry. There must be things they haven't thought of. I'll have to ask you again."

"You are too kind, General."

"Come."

Han led the way, through a reception hall, a conference room, chambers, to a spacious sunroom with a veranda overlooking a lotus pond framed by weeping willows. A dining table and two chairs had been placed on the veranda. A feast for ten was spread out on the brocade-covered surface: shark's fin, marinated goose, scallops and prawns, rare mushrooms from the Sea of Japan, exotic fruits from

Southeast Asia. The food was arrayed on golden plates and bowls; the chopsticks were also gold.

"I would like to host a banquet to welcome you. Under the circumstances, this will have to do," Han said.

"I'm afraid I shouldn't be enjoying…"

"I know there are customs you have to observe for the next hundred days. The chef wasn't aware and prepared my favorite dishes. There must be a few things you can eat."

"This is a splendid feast."

"I didn't invite anyone. I assumed you wouldn't be in a mood to socialize. I also like us to spend some time together, alone. It's been a while since we talked and a lot has happened."

"Yes."

"Do sit down."

She waited until Han took his seat before she did.

He held her in his gaze. "Well, well, finally." He lifted his wine cup. "Welcome to Shansui."

"Thank you."

"How do you like my place?"

"It's very beautiful, very grand."

"It is."

"It's like the Forbidden City."

"The rooms are bigger and there are more amenities."

"And so much more elegant."

"I have better taste than the Manchu royals."

"Henry must have enjoyed his visits."

"He did. And I enjoyed his company." Han selected the largest prawn and put it on her plate.

"You were good to Henry. It's his misfortune that he cannot be here to serve you."

"Misfortune. Indeed it is."

"He was happy to receive your offer of the position in the museum. He told my cousins we weren't going to Chungking and he gave the university notice that he wouldn't be returning for the next term. He was looking forward to coming here." The truth wasn't relevant any more. Why not please Han with a harmless lie?

"Was he? I wasn't sure I'd convinced him. You are close to your family and you would want to be where they are. And Shansui's museum cannot be compared with Nanking University."

"It was more than a position; it was the privilege of being close to you."

A thoughtful pause. "I wish I'd asked him sooner. He would have left Nanking and escaped the tragedy."

"You couldn't have known." She swallowed the thickness in her throat. "No one could."

"Maybe so. But I can't stop thinking about what else I could have done."

"He wouldn't like to be the cause of your anguish. Your friendship meant the world to him."

"Henry was devoted to me, and I to him. He had everything a man wants in a friend and he was marvelous company—you must know that better than anyone. The way he knew how to put people at ease, with the right amount of attention and deference. And what a raconteur. I could listen to his stories all day long. He had style, eloquence, and polish. A perfect mix of East and West." Fondness filled his voice. "There will never be another Henry. His passing has left an irreplaceable void in my life… What's the matter? Have I upset you?"

She was sobbing.

"Henry was in his prime. We were blessed with our first son. It was the best time in our lives." She pulled out a handkerchief and dabbed her eyes. "And little Sung. You should have seen him. A perfect little Buddha. What did we do to offend the gods?"

"It wasn't anything you did. Like you said, it's joss."

"Henry was making a contribution to the country. Sung was the family heir. Why them? Why not someone else? Why not me?"

"I forbid you to talk like this, Su-chen. What happened was most shocking and tragic. It happened; there was nothing anyone could have done. Well, maybe our government could have made a real effort to defend the capital... The important thing is you are alive. Alive. It means you can go on doing things that give you pleasure; being with people you like." His voice softened with self-remonstrance. "I shouldn't have rattled on like that. Henry was my friend and I miss him. But he is gone and we must accept his absence. What we must do is help each other, cope with the loss. And look to the future."

"Future? I don't even know what will happen tomorrow."

"Tomorrow will be better than today."

She looked up uncertainly.

"You don't believe me?"

"I believe you, General, but I've learned that life is unpredictable."

"It won't be anymore. I'm in charge. You will be safe."

She seemed lost.

"Do you trust me, Su-chen?"

She nodded.

"It would please me to hear you say it."

"I trust you, General."

"You do believe me when I said tomorrow will be better than today?"

She nodded.

"How about we let the future begin now?"

At his signal, a maid came forward with a tray holding a chest and a gilded mirror. She bowed to Han before placing them in front of Su-chen. The chest was polished wood inlaid with mother-of-pearl carvings, the size of a shoebox.

"Don't you want to see what's inside?" He gave her an encouraging nod.

Su-chen lifted the lid. A glimpse of the contents took her breath away. The chest was filled to the brim with precious gems and jewelry. Necklaces, rings, bracelets, brooches, earrings.

"Pick something you like."

Not knowing where to begin, she picked from the top of the heap. A necklace. The chain was white gold; the pendant encrusted with diamonds with a huge ruby in the center.

"Put it on."

She obeyed.

"Like it?"

She glanced at the mirror and nodded.

He selected a bracelet of lavender jade, picked up her hand and slid it onto her wrist. He adjusted the mirror. "See how well it goes with your lovely face."

She held the bracelet against her cheek, feeling the jade's cool smooth surface.

He watched her with satisfaction. "That's what these things are for. To make a beautiful woman smile." He selected a pair of diamond earrings and an emerald ring.

"These were designed by European jewelers. A German friend brought them back from Switzerland."

She put on the earrings, shifted her profile for a different angle. Light reflected from the mirror and caught the facets of the stones, the earrings turning into two points of fire.

"They are my welcome present to you."

"Thank you," she said shyly and closed the lid.

"Everything in the chest is yours, Su-chen."

"Everything?"

"There will be more."

"Such magnificent gifts. How can I thank you?"

He held her hand and slid the emerald ring onto her middle finger. "Turn my house into a home. Let me enjoy your company. That's how you can thank me."

15

"Have you seen her?" Victor shouted over the music.

The maitre d' held up the photograph, brow furrowed to show he was thinking hard. "Very pretty. I'm sure I'd remember the face."

The nightclub on Bubbling Well Road was called Le Vieux Carré. It catered to wealthy merchants and the expatriate crowd. Business was slow. Two couples moved languidly on the dance floor. The bar was empty; the bartender was having a smoke, chatting with a busboy. The band had turned up its volume to enliven the atmosphere. Music was blasting through the roof.

"Her name is Lillie. In case you run into her, will you contact me?" Victor gave the man his address with twenty yuan.

"No problem," the man said blithely and tucked the money inside his jacket. "Come back tomorrow. If I can't find her, I'll find you someone just as pretty. No shortage of beauties in Shanghai."

"I don't want another woman. I want her."

"Sure you do, sir. Good night."

The man flashed tea-stained teeth as he patted Victor on the back. The gesture seemed familiar. Victor took another look at the green and orange neon sign. Have I been here before? Last week? The day before yesterday? One out of twelve businesses in the city was a brothel, the majority disguised as nightclubs. He must have visited every one and talked to every pimp, waitress, bartender in the city. The days were becoming a blur.

No one had seen Lillie.

Where had she gone? What had he done to make her leave him?

The clock on top of Big World Center merged its hands. Midnight. Another day gone, wasted. He stood on the pavement, tired to the bone. His feet hurt and his head ached. The dreams would be bad tonight—if he could sleep. He would put them off. He would put off his whole stinking life if he could. The night was freezing. Home would be warm, but he didn't want to be there. Home hadn't been home since Lillie left. There's another thing. In the deserted house, he would be reminded of his other responsibility: Pierre.

He hadn't been home when Pierre and his guests from Nanking left for the airfield. After roaming the neighborhood, he had gone back to his old office at Airsea to use the telephone. He could talk freely there without his guests from Nanking overhearing the conversations. He had called people he and Lillie knew and asked if any of them had seen Lillie. Getting no helpful answers, he had rummaged the drawers, found half a bottle of brandy, emptied it and fallen sleep on the sofa. When he woke up, it had been morning the next day. He had returned home and found the note on the sideboard. After the initial shock, he had consoled himself it was a good thing that Pierre had gone to Shansui. The child would be safer there and he could concentrate on finding Lillie. Not wanting to stay in the empty house, he had dashed off to see a small-time arms dealer who owed him a favor. He had asked the man to let him borrow his car. For three days, Victor had driven around the city, hoping to spot his own car with Lillie in it. But there had been no sight of her anywhere. He had even gone to the Paramount, though he knew she detested the place. She had told him she would make a detour whenever she was in the vicinity. She couldn't stand even a glimpse; she didn't want to be reminded of the awful times she had spent there. But he had had to make sure. He had found the ballroom boarded up and deserted. Neighbors told him the Japanese had raided the place and taken the girls. The rest of the staff had been disbanded.

He had run out of places to look.

Time to put the search on hold. Time to go to Shansui and take his son home.

For the night he would get a drink and then find a room in the city. It would be better than lying alone in the double bed. He turned on Tibet Road and entered the YMCA, a favorite watering hole from his missionary days. He had come for the company of fellow Europeans when he felt homesick. He had stopped feeling homesick after Lillie moved in with him.

He walked through the swinging doors and was instantly enveloped by the babble of an international

311

gathering. The lobby was like a railway station, the air warmed by the crowd. Foreigners in overcoats with suitcases at their feet queued up at the check-in counter. A ship must have docked. He placed the new guests in two groups: journalists arriving to cover the war, missionaries seeking lost souls.

Men with noble intentions. Until they discovered the addictive power of fast money.

As I did.

He moved through the throng, picking up conversations in English, German, French, Russian. The atmosphere was festive. Anticipation shone in the travelers' eyes. For most of them, it must be their first trip to the Far East. He remembered how his spirits had soared when the ship glided into the Huangpo harbor. Shanghai on the Bund had been a fantastic metropolis with a European skyline, rickshaws, motorcars, pretty women in silk gowns with parasols.

At the bar he took the only empty seat at the counter and ordered a brandy. To his right, two Germans were drinking beer and talking in a Bavarian dialect. One of them cast a long glance at Victor before resuming conversation. On his left, a priest and a bespectacled Chinese man shared an English newspaper. The brandy came; he drank gratefully. The din was rising. A group of newcomers entered and took the largest table. Leather bomber jackets, well-pressed khaki trousers, speaking American English. They could be Claire Chennault's pilots.

Flying Tigers. What an asinine name.

The bartender refilled his glass. He downed half in one gulp. Standing up to stretch his legs, he heard French voices talking about Marseilles. He looked for the source.

Two sailors were sharing a bottle of French red at a table in the corner. He grabbed his glass and got off the barstool. He had not eaten all day; the brandy was making him light-headed.

"Good evening, my friends. Just arrived?" he said in French, pressing against the table to hold his body steady.

"Two hours ago. What about you?"

"Been here for years."

"How marvelous. Like it here?"

"Love it."

"Do sit down."

The three men shook hands and made introductions. Victor grabbed an alias for himself out of nowhere and forgot it immediately. The sailors were in their twenties, with wavy hair and scrubbed clean faces.

"First time in China?" Victor said.

"First time in Asia."

"That's something to celebrate." Victor stopped a waiter and ordered food in rapid Chinese.

"Chinese is an impossible language. How do you manage?" one of the sailors asked.

"Dedication and a Chinese mistress."

"You have a Chinese mistress?"

"I *had* a Chinese mistress."

"What happened?"

"She ran away." With emphatic nonchalance, "She likes to do that. Sometimes I do the same. It's a game we play. Keeps the relationship fresh."

They wanted to confirm a rumor about a certain anatomical part unique to Asian women. Victor obliged and got a round of chuckles.

The waiter delivered a platter of dim sum and hot canapés.

"You are an old China hand," the sailor remarked.

Victor dipped an egg roll in a black vinegar sauce and devoured it in one bite. "You could say that."

"What do you do?"

"Buying, selling. This and that."

"We heard one can get rich fast in Shanghai. Any truth to that?"

Victor nodded. "It's a wild place."

"How wild?"

"The police act like gangsters and the gangsters control the city. The value of money fluctuates from hour to hour, as does the price of things. The black market is where real business is done. Crime pays; hard work doesn't," Victor said, cupping the glass with his hands, swirling the brandy. "It can be scary, but you get to make your own rules."

"What are your rules?"

"My rules change with each occasion."

"In other words, no rules."

"That's right."

"To no rules." They toasted. "What advice would you give to a couple of novices who want to make a lot of money fast?"

"How fast you make your fortune depends on what you are willing to do and who you know."

"We are willing to do anything, but we don't know anyone."

"You'll meet people. All kinds of people. But if you want to get rich quick, you need to know the right kind of people."

"Where can we find them?"

"They are everywhere. You know when you meet them."

"Can you point us to the right direction?"

Victor shook his head. "It's luck. Just be on your toes all the time."

"You look like you have done well for yourself. Tell us how you made your fortune."

"It's a long story."

"We have the whole night."

In a fog of alcohol and fatigue, Victor began. How from a penniless missionary he became an underworld entrepreneur with more money than he knew what to do with. The existence on the edge, the lucrative payoffs, the glorious life of excess... Much of what he did for Soong had to be kept secret; the experiences had been bottled up inside. Once he let go, words gushed like water from a broken floodgate.

"All because you screwed one woman?" one sailor remarked, eyebrows arched in the Gallic acknowledgment of the inexplicable.

"This wasn't any woman. Her husband controls China's purse strings." Victor pulled an invisible string and winked. "And she controls him. But for all her clout and savvy, she is over a barrel in the bedroom. You know why? Because in this country a man can go whoring night after night and no one bats an eye. The bastard is just releasing his yang energy, good for his health, like doing *tai chi*. A woman takes a lover, she is hanged before she pulls up her skirt." People at the next table burst into loud laughter. Victor leaned forward to make himself heard. "My benefactress was from a highly respectable family. As high as you can imagine. Life at the top can be very lonely. She had no outlet for her passions. Until she met me. I am a foreign barbarian. I don't give a damn about feudal morals. I have no scruples about bedding another man's wife. If passionate love was what she wanted, passionate love was what I gave." A nod. "A concentrated dose she could coast off for years."

His audience was thrilled. "Bring us to her. Name your price."

"Too late. She left Shanghai."

"She got a sister?"

"Two. One is the empress of China."

"You are making this up!"

Victor shrugged.

"How about let us work for you?"

"I've retired."

"You can't retire. You are too young."

"Seen enough, done enough and earned enough for ten lifetimes."

The sailors pressed for more stories. The conversation led to Nanking and the arms deal with the Japanese.

"Half the Kremlin's arsenal was in the warehouse. It must have been like Christmas for the Japanese. Couldn't blame my Chinese friends for thinking it was the end of the world." Victor emptied his glass with a sigh. "As it turned out, it was."

"For a day of work, you made enough to retire?"

"Two days. There was some cleaning up afterwards."

"What was there to clean up? You unloaded the whole arsenal."

"I had to make sure no one got their hands on my boss's secrets. He has many, many secrets. Bad, nasty secrets. I set fire to the whole mother-fucking building. Two stories. One matchstick. Made it look like the Japs did it. Got an extra bonus for my thoroughness."

"Incredible."

"You'd better believe it happened. I almost got killed."

"Of course we believe. We just didn't expect we would meet a master saboteur on our first night in China."

"I am not a saboteur."

"Master deal maker—you like that better?"

An alarm went off inside Victor's head. He had said too much. He tried to push back the alcoholic clouds in his head as he looked around the room. No one he recognized. Speaking French might have saved his life. But one could never be sure in Shanghai.

His carousing mood was gone.

He shoved back his chair, pushed himself to his feet, and dropped a wad of bills on the table. "Getting late. Got to go. Wouldn't want my old lady making a fuss."

"You said your mistress left you."

"I have another one. I have lots of mistresses and concubines. I go to bed with half the women in Shanghai."

"Where can we find you?"

"You can't. I'm a phantom. I don't exist. Good-bye."

Outside, the temperature had dropped ten degrees. Flakes of frost stung his face. He tightened his coat and walked briskly. The cold air cleared his head. That was a mistake. He shouldn't have opened up to strangers. At the corner of Chang An Road he turned and headed to the Bund, where there would be rickshaws. Two ribbons of yellow gaslight led the way. The darkness hid the squalor of this overcrowded urban slum. Past two in the morning, the city was hosting its own festival of life. Twinkle of neon signs. Streaming headlights of automobiles. Brothels, all-night eateries, other nameless businesses that thrived in the small hours were opening their doors. Feeling exposed on the boulevard, Victor veered off to an alley. Cooking fires and smoking pipes flickered in the rows of ramshackle tenement houses. The stench of death and excrement was overwhelming. He moved with caution. He wouldn't want to stumble into the open gutters filled with sewage, or the wooden crates where the poor dumped infant corpses for a charity outfit to collect in the morning.

At an intersection, the houses parted to let in the sky. Moonlight filled the clearing like luminous fog. He lit a cigarette.

No sound of footsteps. No moving shadows. A quick motion in the air.

A man stood in front of him. It was the bespectacled Chinese from the YMCA bar.

Victor threw away the cigarette. "You've been follow-ing me?"

"All the way, and you didn't even notice."

"What do you want?"

"You, naturally, Monsieur Maurier," the man switched to French. His face was flat like a mask. "I heard a most interesting conversation, full of delectable details."

"Who are you?"

"We used to work for the same man. I still do; you don't any more. It will displease him to know his former employee has been discussing his business affairs in public."

"I spoke French. No one would have understood."

"I did. As a matter of fact, you had an international audi-ence. At this moment your drinking mates are spreading your amazing stories. You know how Mr. Soong hates indiscretion."

"I didn't mention any names."

"Names were not relevant. You told them about our operation and the deal in Nanking."

"I admit I was careless. It has been a bad week and I had too much to drink."

"We all have bad weeks and we all have too much to drink. We don't share our secrets with strangers anytime we feel like it."

"Give me a break. I'll make it worth your while. Here's my wallet. You hit the jackpot. I made a withdrawal at the bank this morning."

Victor tossed the wallet to the man. He caught it, extracted the money, and threw the wallet over his back. An extra motion with his hand. Something flashed. An ice pick.

"You took my money. Let me go."

"You know I can't."

"Let me talk to Mr. Soong. I'll make my apologies to him."

"Mr. Soong is not available."

"That's right. He's in Chungking. He won't know if you let me go."

"He will know. He always knows. You did a very bad thing, Maurier."

His field man's instinct returned; Victor made a quick assessment of the situation. He was in half shadow. Movement below his chest wouldn't be visible. The man appeared to be alone. The priest he had been with at the bar might have been genuine, not an accomplice in disguise. An experienced operator wouldn't have bothered with the conversation; he would have crept up from behind, knifed him, and walked away. This man probably had a desk job, didn't have much experience in street fights.

"I was heading to my car. It's parked at the other end of the alley. Take the car. Here's the key." Victor tossed a key to a spot a few feet from where the man was standing. With minimal movement, he inserted his hand into his trouser pocket and gripped the pistol. He positioned his finger on the trigger and pointed the gun at the man, counting on him not seeing the bulk underneath the fabric. He kept talking. "There is more cash in the car. American dollars. Twenty thousand. Look under the driver's seat. I was going to buy my way out of China. You can have the money if you let me go."

The man stepped over, bent down and picked up the key.

Victor fired as he straightened up. The bullet hit the man's throat. In the moonlight, the blood sprouted like a squirt of ink over the collar of his shirt. He stared at Victor, shocked. His mouth moved, couldn't make a sound. He staggered and fell.

Victor checked. No pulse. He took back his key and his money. He ripped the man's wallet from the inside pocket, took the cash, and dropped the wallet by the corpse. Whoever found him would assume it was one of the hundreds of robberies that happened everyday. No one would bother to call the police. Vagrants would strip the man's clothes. The body would be hauled away with other debris from the streets.

He looked around one more time to make sure the man had not brought a partner. The night was as calm as before. A light in an upstairs window dimmed. An invisible hand drew the drapes; a silhouette evaporated into the darkness. Someone had been watching but didn't want to be a witness. Victor sidled into a doorway and caught his breath. He should be safe.

But not from T.V. Soong.

He must leave Shanghai. At once. Get Pierre. Go to Hong Kong. Take the money before Soong finds out his breach of promise.

He raced to the main road until he caught up with an empty rickshaw. He told the coolie to drive to the Cathay Hotel on the waterfront. There would be taxis for the nightclub crowd.

He boarded the last one and told the driver to take him home. He had him wait while he dashed into the house. He knew exactly what to grab: change of clothes, the box from the safe house in Nanking, money, travel papers and Jong Lin's note.

He found the note pinned under the whisky bottle, folded in half. He didn't remember having done that. How odd.

He went to the bedroom and unlocked the drawer to get his passport. One of the exit permits and the ship ticket were missing.

Lillie. It had to be her. She was the only one who knew there's where he kept his papers. She must have come home when he had been driving around the city. Finding the house empty and Jong Lin's note, she must have assumed that both he and Pierre had gone to Shansui.

She's now on the ship sailing to Hong Kong.

He should have guessed when his car was recovered at the garage of the Palace Hotel, the only hotel with taxi service to the wharf. He had assumed she stayed there. After interrogating the staff and finding no trace of her, he had moved on.

Why did she steal the trunk? Henry Li's papers wouldn't have meant anything to her, but it was the only thing she had taken from the house. He couldn't imagine her running away with another man. She had to be alone. How did she manage to move the heavy trunk from the house without help? She knew Hong Kong was the first stop on their itinerary and he had an appointment at Soong's bank there. Had she gone there in anticipation of meeting him? But if she planned to join him, why had she run off in the middle of the night?

Nothing made sense.

He would find out when he saw her in Hong Kong.

Victor returned to the waiting taxi and told the driver to take him to the airfield. There might be a plane going in the direction of Shansui. If not, he would buy one and fly it himself. He was determined to be out of China in two days. To arrive in Hong Kong in three.

The pilot was a White Russian who had transported arms for the Blue Shirt Gang; he had a fox face and cracked fingernails like a coolie. Victor found him sleeping inside the only plane at the airfield. The flight log indicated it was scheduled to take off for Macau in the morning. Victor woke him up and offered one thousand American dollars if he would make the detour to Shansui. An additional five hundred convinced him to leave immediately. The plane was a compact Fiat fighter. The rear seats had been removed to make room for stacks of gunnysacks.

"What are these?" Victor asked as he handed the cash to the pilot.

"Stuff. What do you have there in the box?"

"Papers."

"Nothing that would get me in trouble?"

"Family records. Do you still work for the Blue Shirts?"

The man stowed the box on the floor behind his seat. "Nope. I run my own business now."

"Same here. Got tired of kowtowing to people I didn't respect. Nothing like being your own man." He climbed into the seat. "The Blue Shirts let you go? No trouble?"

"Nope."

"Nice not have to watch your back."

The pilot slammed the door of the plane shut. "Nothing personal. I don't like to talk when I fly."

"One last thing and I'll shut up. Can I have your word that you won't tell anyone about this flight, or me?"

"As I said, I don't talk."

The man flipped the switches. The panels lit up like a toy city. He revved the engine and checked the instruments, taxing the plane onto the empty runway. As he pushed up the power, the plane started to roll. They were enclosed in a vast darkness as it thundered upward. Victor held on to the edge of the seat. The Russian made adjustments in the throttle and the controls. Gradually the plane leveled. They were afloat in a black sky. Below, Shanghai was a basin of smoldering embers. Victor wrapped himself in his overcoat, huddled in the seat and dozed off.

Turbulence woke him up. The plane was bouncing like a sampan on a rough sea. The Russian didn't seem concerned, eyes half closed as he blew smoke rings from a hand-made cigarette. Victor went back to sleep.

When he woke up again, his body was slouched forward. The plane was descending. Outside was a slanted view of blue sky and pointed mountain peaks. Shansui. He had a crick in his neck and his back; otherwise he felt refreshed. It was the most rest he had had since Lillie disappeared.

The plane had barely touched the ground, but the pilot was getting ready to take off again. "I got you here, pay up."

Victor handed over the remainder of the fee.

"Hurry. I need to get out fast," the pilot said. "Han's people shoot anything they can't identify."

Victor stumbled out of the plane with the box of files. The tarmac was a big stretch of gravel with a surrounding hedge marking the perimeter. No observation tower. No hangar. If Han's people were watching, they had made themselves invisible. He headed to the only building in sight, a shack at the end of the runway. The interior was about ten feet square. An empty electrical socket dropped from the ceiling. A table with an ashtray, no chairs. He couldn't figure out the purpose of the room; he assumed he could wait there. The day was getting warm. December in southern China felt like early summer. He took off his coat and sat on the floor. If nothing happened by noon, he would find his way to Han's palace on foot.

To pass the time, he started to read Soong's files. There were deeds, contracts, facsimiles of checks, records of bank transactions, ledgers, correspondence with Soong's lawyers and managers, memos to personnel in charge of various business entities. Victor even found some old documents with Soong's signature. Soong owned everything: oilfields in the Middle East, forests in South America, real estate galore in the States, and banks everywhere. The zeroes were going off the pages. Yet Soong stole from his country. Obsessively.

American foreign aid was transferred to his private accounts as soon as it reached the Kuomintang treasury.

What could one man do with so much money? What would so much money do to a man?

Noises. A vehicle engine coming to a halt. Then footsteps. A lot of footsteps.

Victor climbed up and peered through the window. A truck was parked on the other end of the tarmac. A line of soldiers was marching in his direction. Fifteen men. Their movements were synchronized like those of a team practicing a drill. He put the papers back into the box and took out Jong's note. He waited until the men were about twenty yards from the shack before he stepped out, waving a white handkerchief and using his posture to convey his lack of aggression in case the handkerchief meant nothing to them. Chinese soldiers were notorious for their disregard of international protocols.

Two soldiers in front raised their guns. "Who are you?"

He raised his hands in a gesture of surrender. "Victor Maurier. I came from Shanghai to see General Han Tangming. I am alone and I am not armed."

Not taking him at his word, they frisked him.

"How did you get here?"

"A private plane flew me in this morning."

"Why do you want to see the General?"

Victor handed over the note he had found in his house.

"My son came with Mrs. Li. I am here to bring him home. Mr. Lin is expecting me."

The leader read the note and showed it to the soldier next to him. They spoke in the southern dialect. Victor could make out only a few words: the letter seemed genuine but extra caution was necessary. Handcuffs were brought out. Victor extended his hands, a supplicant's smile on his face.

They noticed the box containing Soong's files.

"What do you have there?"

Victor decided to take a chance. "Books and ledgers. Feel free to take a look."

They shuffled through the papers without registering the explosive content. At the leader's signal, the troops marched back to the truck. Victor mounted the bed, huddling with the soldiers. A soothing breeze brushed his face. He heard the words "Crescent Moon Villa" and knew he was on his way.

A lifesize Chinese brush painting rolled out before him. Soaring limestone hills and a sinewy river, its serene surface an elongated mirror holding the hills' reflection. A rural town of stone paths and thatched huts preserved through centuries, quaint and lovely and timeless. A simple way of life untouched by the ravages of urban progress.

Pity I can't stay.

The truck drove through a forest. The trees were planted at precise intervals; the trunks were identical in size. A man-made forest. The foliage was thick enough to block the sky. The truck went on for minutes before it was back in the open. Victor blinked in the glare of the noonday sun. Ahead was an immense square. At its far end stood the spectacular façade of a twin of the Forbidden City. Newer. A massive fortress of crimson bricks dominated by two watchtowers on both ends. Sentries lined up along the portico. The truck crossed the length of the square and stopped in front of the gate. The soldiers jumped off and filed through the entrance.

Victor's handcuffs were removed before he was guided through the side entrance to a footpath. It led to a row of bungalows built like stables. He was shown into one. As soon as he entered, the door was clicked shut. It would be unrealistic to expect an audience with the warlord on the day of his arrival, he thought. At least it's safe here. The room was like one in the YMCA, clean and simply furnished, with its own bath. He showered and then napped on the bunk bed. It was evening when he woke up. Dinner was delivered by an elderly guard. A native of Shanghai, he was intrigued by Victor's command of the dialect and stayed to chat. They reminisced about racetracks and jazz clubs.

"Have you seen my son?" Victor asked.

"He has a room in the Inner Court. Only special guards are allowed there; I'm not one."

"If you can find out how he is, I'd appreciate it."

"I'll ask around."

The food was prepared in the classic tradition of southern cooking, fresh ingredients served with warm rice wine and fragrant tea. It cheered him up considerably. He was a houseguest, not a prisoner.

Night fell. Victor mounted a chair and peered out the narrow window below the ceiling. An empty courtyard, floodlit, four guards marching back and forth. He watched for a while, then went to bed. He dreamed of playing soccer with Pierre in a forest.

He woke up to the sound of morning drill. He climbed back on the chair. A troop was in the courtyard, their uniforms vivid in the clean air. Han's men looked well fed and in excellent shape. It would require a lot of men to guard a place this size. How big was Han's army? Did he also keep three thousand concubines like the emperors did? Where did he keep his gold?

Breakfast was delivered by a different guard.

"Have you seen my boy? Blond, blue eyes, speaks Shanghainese like a native."

"He is staying with Mrs. Li and her daughter," the guard replied.

"You saw him?"

"In passing."

"Is he all right?"

"Of course he is all right. He has the best accommodations in China."

"Could you bring him here?"

"You are not allowed to have visitors."

"Will you tell him his father has come to take him home?"

"You have many requests."

Victor handed the guard a wad of cash. "Please get word to my son."

"I'll see what I can do, but I can't promise anything."

At least Pierre is well, he thought and reconciled himself to his vigil.

∽

More than a week before Victor heard from his host. By then his nerves were at the breaking point.

The summons came at midday without warning. Two guards escorted him through a myriad of footpaths to a sprawling building. They mounted marble steps and passed a foyer, empty except for a bronze statue of Han. The guards gripped Victor's elbows and steered him through a double door. He stepped into what could have been Kublai Khan's throne room, a hundred feet deep and two hundred feet wide with a high ceiling. Guards were lined up on both sides. A dais stood in the center.

In a gilded chair was the famed warlord in the flesh. A young man sat by his side, writing tablet in hand. Han's chief of staff. The Eurasian.

Victor bowed. "Allow me to pay my respects, General Han. My name is Victor Maurier, resident of Shanghai…"

"We know who you are," Jong said, taking over the interrogation.

"I came here at your request, Mr. Lin. To take my son home."

"You may see your son after you answer our questions."

"I am at your service."

"The questions are of a confidential nature. You are to answer them honestly and completely."

"I will do my best to be truthful."

"We expect the truth whether or not it's your best effort."

"I will speak only the truth."

"Let's begin. Before you came here, did you abandon your son because you were looking for a singsong girl?"

"It was not my intention to neglect my son. It was the culmination of a series of unexpected events. The woman is my fiancée."

"These unexpected events. Did they include your numerous dealings in illegal arms with subversive groups, criminals, and foreign aggressors? Your collusion with representatives of the Japanese Imperial Army to undermine the national security of China? Your role in instigating the mass murder of innocent civilians in Nanking? And the destruction by arson of a government building?"

Victor was stunned. He hadn't expected to face a trial.

"Mr. Lin, I can explain my involvement in these incidents. It was by no means…"

"There is also the question of whether you were an accomplice in the theft committed by your fiancée. She has stolen one hundred and thirty-eight catties of gold. They were a gift from General Han to the Li family."

"Was that what was in the trunk?"

"Yes."

"I did not know there was gold in the trunk and I did not help my fiancée. I was as shocked as anyone when we found that she and the trunk were gone. Please ask my son. He can tell you what happened." How did Lillie know there was gold in the trunk?

"Theft of Professor Li's gold is a grave offense, but insignificant in the full spectrum of your crimes." Jong leafed through the sheaf of notes. "Prior to the invasion of Nanking, you were employed by Soong Tse-ven. You carried out a variety of illegal activities under a commercial entity called International Airsea. Those activities were in direct conflict with the law as well as the interests of the Chinese people."

Soong outranked Han. Shanghai and Nanking were outside Han's territory. What Victor did for Soong was simply none of Han's business. And why would a warlord like Han be interested in dispensing justice? Victor's arms smuggling was child's play compared to Han's opium cartel.

"Did you not engage in an adulterous liaison with Soong Ai-ling, wife of Kung Hsiang-hsi?" Jong asked unexpectedly.

This was interesting—from capital crimes to an extramarital affair. What were they after?

"I did. It was a brief relationship."

"It went on for a period of three and a half months. The relationship began while Mr. Kung was on his first trip to the United States. After he returned, you and Mrs. Kung took advantage of her husband's habit of leaving early for his office. You began your workday in Mrs. Kung's bedroom. A month into the liaison, you and Mrs. Kung spent a full day and night at a resort on Snake Mountain. You registered under a false name and had meals delivered to your room. At the end of the tryst, you made separate departures to avoid being seen as a pair."

"I was Mrs. Kung's employee. I did what I was told."

"Were you hired for that purpose?"

"I wouldn't know. Mrs. Kung can answer the question better than I."

"Were there other duties besides providing carnal pleasure?"

Red-faced, Victor said, "I assembled the Kung family wine cellar, designed menus for important dinners, trained the staff in European-style service. I also took care of Mrs. Kung's correspondence when European languages were required."

"Did you think you were uniquely qualified for the job?"

"I am sure there were others who could do the work."

"Who put an end to the affair?"

"Mrs. Kung did."

"Why?"

Victor didn't doubt that they knew, but if they wanted his version, he would oblige.

"Mrs. Kung thought her husband smelled a rat. I couldn't tell. Not with Kung. The man has a real poker face. But I had no reason to doubt her. She said after weighing priorities, she decided to let me go. I was to collect my pay and not to show up for work anymore. She seemed agitated; her relatives might have been putting pressure on her. I didn't like to be treated like short-term help and told her so. She said she would see me right if I didn't make a fuss. A week later she took me to see Mr. Soong. He gave me a job; you know the rest."

"She made you a rich man," Jong said.

"Yes."

"Sexual favors in exchange for money. You are not ashamed?"

"I didn't think it would be wise to turn down Mrs. Kung. Ninety-nine percent of the men in China would have done what I did."

"What you did was wrong, and justice must be served," Jong concluded. "As these are unusual times, we are willing to make unusual allowances. In lieu of a jail term, you are to disclose the circumstances of each criminal act, and details of International Airsea operations: names of partners and conspirators, agents and customers; money routes; accounts; safe houses. *And* everything you know about your employer."

Soong's secrets. That's what they're after. If he complied, he would be a dead man the minute Soong found out. If he refused, he was sure Han would have him shot on the spot.

"We will use the information any way we see fit. No promise will be made as to how our actions may affect your personal safety, and that of your son."

"I only request safe passage out of China."

"Your request will be granted." Jong slapped the writing tablet shut. "You will stay with your son in comfortable quarters while you make your confession. When you are done, we will provide you with the papers and the means to leave China."

"Thank you."

"I was told that you have Soong's papers in your possession."

"Yes."

"You will not be taking them out of Shansui."

Victor nodded. "I have another request."

"Speak."

"It is necessary for me to travel to Hong Kong as soon as possible. One day in the city is all I need. Will you let me make the trip before the confession?"

"Purpose?"

"Money in a bank. Quite a large sum. I wish to withdraw it before…"

"Before Soong changes his mind."

"Yes."

"Must you go in person?"

"Yes."

"I'll save you the trip," Han spoke unexpectedly. "Tell me how much you have in the bank and I will give you the equivalent in gold."

"Gold?"

"Yes."

"Soong might suspect if I don't show up."

"He would be glad to save the cash."

"But…"

"You will not leave Shansui until we are done with you."

16

The invitation had arrived yesterday. It was handwritten on General Han's personal stationery.

Su-chen:

I'm glad it is coming to an end. Tomorrow will be a special day. You mustn't spend it alone. Come to my chambers at sundown. I'll be waiting.

Tang-ming

For a hundred days Su-chen had followed the customs: wore black and no jewelry; ate no meat or fish; saw no one except her daughter and Ah Ching; confined herself inside the east wing. Today she returned to normal life. Coming from her host and family friend, Han's message was a thoughtful gesture, not entirely unexpected. Yet it unsettled her. She kept tossing his words around in her head.

"Glad"—was it a polite word or a way of saying he had been looking forward to seeing her? How special would the day be? Sundown would mean dining together. A banquet with guests, or just the two of them?

Ah Ching was watching from the side. "Find anything you like, Mrs. Li?"

Su-chen was in front of the wardrobe, trying to decide what to wear. "I can't make up my mind."

"May I offer a suggestion?"

"Please."

Ah Ching picked an ankle-length cheongsam in deep purple. "You've been wearing black; you want the change to be too noticeable. A dark color would be appropriate. Dark, not dull." She held the dress over Su-chen. "The cut accentuates your waist; the side slits show off your shapely legs. You have such beautiful legs, Mrs. Li. Slim and perfectly shaped. Take it from someone who has seen more than her share of attractive women. Legs are the mark of true beauty. Other imperfections you can hide with clever tailoring or cosmetics. Not legs." She turned her attention to Su-chen's face. "We won't put on too much makeup. A hint of rouge, lipstick in a soft tone, and a dab of perfume. Excited about tonight?"

A small nod.

"Please forgive me for asking a bold question," Ah Ching said with a glint in her eyes. "Have you done this before?"

"What do you mean?"

"Been alone with another man who is not your husband."

"Of course. I've been alone with uncles, cousins, sharing a cup of tea..."

336

"Ah, we are not talking about relatives and we are not talking about sharing a cup of tea."

"General Han is a friend of the family."

"He is a man, Mrs. Li."

"What are you saying?"

"Should I speak my mind?"

"You always do."

"Let me put it plainly: Pleasure is important to the General when it comes to his friendships with women."

"Pleasure can be derived many ways."

"Many, many ways, but to some men, only a certain way will do," the servant replied. "I'm sure I'm not saying anything that hasn't crossed your mind." A smile. "The General is a formidable leader, but at heart, a child. Children must have their needs satisfied or there won't be peace."

"Should I have declined his invitation?"

"Why would you want to do that? You want to go and he wants to see you."

"But…"

"No one has ever turned the General down. You would be the first and you would put yourself on his wrong side. It would be very bad."

"What should I do?"

"Have a pleasant time. Enjoy yourself. Nothing wrong with that."

"'Wrong'—what could be wrong?"

"Nothing. But you are from a different world, a world that values appearance. Honestly, we know how people act in public has little to do with how they behave when no one is looking. Behind closed doors, people return to being who they are. General Han is wise. He knows the force of yin and yang cannot be curbed. What nature wants, nature gets. He does what pleases him when it pleases him."

Su-chen was quiet.

"Too much thinking won't do any good." Ah Ching shrugged. "How about a bath?"

Su-chen followed her to the bathroom. The tub was filled with a white creamy liquid. Su-chen dipped her fingertips in it. "Milk?"

"Fresh from the farms. This is a tradition at the Villa. General Han's female guests are offered this treat. The milk can do wonders for your skin, Mrs. Li. One of Soong May-ling's beauty tricks. You must know already."

"My cousin can be indulgent in her ways."

"With that awful complexion, the woman needs all the help she can get. The milk could feed a hundred babies, but why should she care?"

Su-chen undressed and stepped into the tub. "Is this for any woman who shares a meal with the General?"

"Only the special ones."

"Does he find many women special?"

Ah Ching dipped a sponge into the milk and squeezed it over Su-chen's back. "The General believes a powerful man must be nourished by juice of the yin. Constantly."

"What about when he was married?"

"The marriage. That was a sad story."

The milk was warm and soothing, like waves of gentle caresses. Su-chen slid down and closed her eyes. "Tell me about the late Han Fu-jen."

"She was from a prominent family in Peking. Her father was a Court Mandarin, a trusted adviser to the Emperor Kuang-hsü. She was his only child."

"How did she come all the way to Shansui?"

338

"The Emperor had ordained the marriage before she was born. He wanted to honor an esteemed regional official, General Han's father. The General was his only son. When she was of age she married him."

"Was she beautiful?"

"She was a Manchu, but yes, she was beautiful. It was said that after the Emperor's nephew saw her, he asked his uncle to rescind the betrothal. He wanted her for himself. The attraction wasn't one-sided. She had tender feelings for the prince, and she didn't want to leave Peking and her family. She considered Shansui a backward province and the Hans political upstarts. She was prejudiced from the beginning. That could have been the cause of the later troubles. Who knows?"

"Many things can go wrong in an unhappy marriage," Su-chen remarked. "I've seen that in my own family."

"Marriage is a bad deal for women. A wife is Number One Whore and Number One Housekeeper. I don't regret never having been married."

"Do go on. What happened to the prince's request?"

"It was denied—the Emperor could not break a promise. She was sent here. On the ordained date, she married the General. Grudgingly. She was sobbing through the ceremony; her bridal veil was stained with tears."

"That must have been unpleasant for everyone."

"Next morning we could tell by the look on the General's face that the making of Clouds and Rain hadn't been satisfactory. Things got worse. Much worse... Pity she had such a narrow view of the Han family. Being the first lady of Shansui was no less than being royalty—General Han is richer than royalty. As it turned out, she didn't deserve her good fortune. She passed away two years after she became Han Fu-jen."

"How did she die?"

"Suicide."

"That's awful. Many women stay in unhappy marriages. She didn't need to kill herself."

"We didn't know what went on in her head. I can only tell you what happened."

"Please do."

"The real trouble began when Han Fu-jen became pregnant. Good joss, you'd think. But she gave birth to girls. Twice. Bad enough. Worse they were stillborn. Naturally the General was upset. Any man would be when his wife humiliated him by producing dead babies. He looked for comfort in other women. That tells you the kind of man he is. He chose to take his mind off his disappointing wife rather than punishes her. She should have been grateful; instead she protested, even tried to block women from entering his chamber. Never mind they no longer shared the bed, she insisted her husband was not to be intimate with another woman."

"Why would she have cared about his liaisons? She hadn't even wanted to be married to him." Su-chen asked, "Did her efforts stop him?"

"Of course not. He is a man of healthy appetites. If he wasn't satisfied by his wife, what else was he supposed to do? It was about this time that he acquired a fondness for young girls. We thought he was troubled by the loss of the female infants. Or maybe he simply likes his bed mates young. Who wouldn't?"

"Does the General only like young girls?"

"For a while he would have only girls in his bed. Virgins. A new one very night. We were worried we would run out of girls in Shansui. We would have to recruit in the neighboring provinces. It wouldn't have been easy if he wanted companionship at a whim. We were relieved when he got tired of young girls."

"So it was a phase."

Ah Ching nodded. "He was back to his old self in no time. He took any girl or woman as long as she was attractive."

"There must have been many."

"You bet."

"Where are they now?"

"We don't keep track. Poor things. One night and their future ruined. Damaged goods, that's what they became. Decent men wouldn't marry them. They could work in brothels, or sell themselves as maids. That's their joss. Who are we to say? A few of them came back with big bellies and demanded money, but there was no way to tell if the child was the General's. They were sent away and warned never to show up again."

"Some of these claims could have been true."

"They were common girls from common families. The truth was not for them to decide."

"What happened to the marriage?"

Ah Ching rested her elbow on the tub's edge. "Young and used to having her way, Han Fu-jen was not willing to be cast aside. The General, of course, ignored her demands. The more he ignored her, the harder she tried. She began to act in ways inappropriate for someone in her position. Some things she did, I must say, were downright embarrassing. Well, no point in going over details. Though the late Han Fu-jen didn't treat me with the regard I deserved, I have no wish to speak ill of her. I am a discreet person: that's why the General trusts me." She dipped the sponge in the milk. "We tried to warn her. Be sensible—it's China and she's a woman. It's not a wife's place to tell her husband how to behave."

"Did she take your advice?"

"Nothing we said did any good. She became more obsessed. Every female who crossed the General's path was a rival. Even poor me. I admit I was not unattractive those days, and sure, the General occasionally paid me more attention than I deserved. Why shouldn't he? And why shouldn't I accept?" Her tone turned matter-of-fact. "He had to move her to the summer house a hundred miles away, just so he could have some peace. She was quiet for a while. Then—who knows what prompted her to do something like that—she went to a doctor to find out why the pregnancies failed. The quack put it into her head that a child's gender was determined by the father. She took it to mean that the General was to be blamed for the stillbirths."

"What did the gender of the babies have to do with their being stillborn?"

"Nothing. That was when we saw how deranged she had become. She took her case to Peking and submitted a complaint to the Emperor. She requested the marriage be annulled." Her mouth settled into a hard line. "That was most foolish. A woman should never make her man lose face. A week after she returned home, she was found dead in the summer house."

"How did she die?"

"She took cyanide with her sleeping medicine."

"Did she leave a note?"

"She left nothing. There was no need. It was clear that she was ashamed of what she had done. She couldn't find a way out; that's why she ended her life."

"Quite a story."

"Not something the General wants to be reminded of."

"No."

"That's why the General hasn't remarried. It was a very bad experience."

"But General Han must have an heir," Su-chen said.

"There is Mr. Lin."

"Jong. Is the relationship official?"

"Mr. Lin was never officially adopted, but the General has brought him up like a son."

"The General doesn't mind that he is not pure Chinese?"

"He seems to like that Mr. Lin is different."

Su-chen was not surprised that Jong had such promising prospects. The young man was wise and astute; he would make a fine commander-in-chief. And he was in love with Yunna. Deeply. Su-chen could feel his longing whenever Yunna left his sight, felt it like her own for Henry after their wedding. The first throes of love. The world had existed for them and they for each other. Months of absolute bliss. Then Yunna had come. There had been less time alone, more chores, more problems. Imperceptibly, passions had waned. Married life had settled into predictable routine and love into domestic comfort… What was she thinking? Jong. A fine man. Too bad his eyes were blue and his arms hairy. Yunna didn't seem to mind, or maybe she did but wouldn't want to pass up the advantages of being linked to the General's heir apparent. She wouldn't be surprised if her daughter had planned her moves when she sensed Jong was attracted to her. If he married her, Yunna would be the Villa's next mistress. Yunna as mistress of General Han's Villa. Not sure if she'd like that. Wait. It wouldn't be happening soon. It couldn't happen soon. The General was in his prime. It would be years before he relinquished power. Meanwhile, a lot could happen.

Two guards pulled open the double door.

"Go in and take a look," Han said, nudging Su-chen forward.

The dining room in Grand Hall had been transformed. Drapes of heavy brocade blocked views of the Shansui hills. Oil paintings of scantily clad Caucasian women and brooding landscapes hung side by side. A mahogany dining table polished to a gleam was ringed by armchairs in floral brocade; a dripping chandelier glimmered over the center. Maids in pastel bodices were poised rigidly like statues below moldings of alabaster cherubs. In a corner, a musician dressed in French court uniform was strumming a mandolin.

"What a gorgeous, lovely room."

"I like experiencing different cultures, but I don't like to put up with the hassles of travel. So I bring the world here—why not? From time to time I commission designers from foreign countries to redo a room. This one was done by a team from Indochina. It's modeled after a palace favored by a French monarch in the eighteenth century."

"I'm afraid I'm rather ignorant when it comes to western culture, General. I have never been outside China."

"Neither have I."

They sat down at one end of the long table, Han at the head, Su-chen by his side. A maid brought aperitifs in gilded goblets.

"Let's drink to today. A new future begins for you."

344

"Thank you, General."

A queue of servers marched forward with gleaming trays. They lined them up on the table and removed the silver domes one by one, pausing between each revelation like magicians performing a series of tricks. Su-chen had had European meals in Shanghai, but none compared to the array of dishes before her. Enticing sauces, cleverly shaped garnishes, aromatic meats.

"The French claim their cuisine is the best in the world. I regard it a distant second." Han was offered a plate of vegetables stuffed with goose pâté. He waved it away. "France did produce a leader whom, up to a point, I consider a soul mate. Napoleon Bonaparte."

"He built an empire. I've read about him."

"He set out to conquer the world. The breadth of the man's vision was remarkable. It's a pity his strategy didn't measure up. The march to Moscow—the move was doomed. Why bother with Russia when he could go for the Ottoman Empire and the continent of Africa? Bonaparte wanted to conquer Russia because no one had done it before. He did it to prove himself—that was the cause for his downfall. Great leaders take the world on their own terms. They don't need to prove anything." Han picked up a lobster tail coated with mustard sauce and took a bite. "Not bad. Has a Szechuan flavor."

Su-chen accepted a serving.

"What Bonaparte lacked in wisdom and judgment, he made up for with gall and drive. The man wasn't afraid to take chances. He stuck to his goals, ignored opposing voices, and never compromised. He was a courageous man with a big plan. Our Party chiefs could learn from him." He finished the lobster. "They are a bunch of cowards and mercenaries who can't see beyond their belly-lines. How they got to be where they are is beyond me."

Taken aback by Han's unabashed criticism of her relatives, Su-chen lowered her head.

"Hope you are not offended. I speak my mind."

"I am aware of my cousins' faults." She lifted her gaze. "I know you are critical because you care about the state of affairs in China. So do I."

"I have yet to meet a woman who does. The problems are too big for their pretty heads."

"There are exceptions in my gender."

"I'm sure there are, but none has come my way."

"May I speak boldly?"

"Of course you may."

"Perhaps it's the type of women you've allowed in your company."

"What have you heard about me in this regard?"

"That you are liberal in your choice of companions."

"I admit I haven't been a model of discretion." He smiled. "Why exercise discretion when they don't deserve more than my fleeting interest?"

"Perhaps the feeling of fulfillment is also fleeting."

"True. Every word you said. Physical pleasure can make a man lonesome afterwards. But one always hopes next time will be different."

"It would be different with the right woman."

"Oh. Indeed?"

She nodded.

A maid brought a tray of cheeses and fruit, and placed it in front of them. Han plucked a bunch of grapes and tossed them into his mouth one by one.

"You think she can be found."

"I have no doubt, General."

"If I found her, could I trust her not to disappoint me?"

"Any woman lucky enough to be chosen would do her best to please you."

After dinner, Han dismissed the attendants. He led Su-chen to the anteroom, a sitting area furnished like the rest of the suite, with red chintz walls and gilded furniture. Fresh bouquets infused the air with a heavy sweetness. He gestured for her to sit on the velvet chaise in front of the fireplace where a blaze was burning.

From a cart, he picked up a carafe filled with a pale gold liquid. He held it up like an oil lamp. The liquid caught the reflection of the fire. Glistening like crystal.

"It happened fifteen years ago," he began like a storyteller. "A hermit in the Indochina hills developed the formula. He served the drink only to his small circle of friends. Soon word got out about its enticing qualities. Its unavailability made it more alluring. The colonial rule of the French was coming to an end. People's lives were turned upside down. Many sought escape in artificial stimulants, not unlike the time when the Manchu Dynasty collapsed and people turned to opium. A friend in the British Army was looking for a present for me, something special; he was eager to make an impression. He tracked down the hermit and offered to buy the formula at an attractive price. The hermit didn't want to sell. My friend returned with a truck of opium and walked away with the formula." Han handed the glass to her. "Try it."

It was fragrant like the nectar of flowers, tartly sweet with a complex aftertaste.

"Like it?"

"Very much, General."

He refilled her glass. "This time drink it in one gulp. It'll give you a different sensation."

She obeyed.

"Feel it?"

She blinked her eyes. "It's like fire and ice."

"Fire and ice. Heaven and earth. Yin and yang." He sat down next to her. "Do you know why I invited you here tonight?"

"You wanted me to have a pleasant evening after the wake."

"I wanted to find out what your heart desires. Speak to me from your heart. Whatever your heart desires, I will make it happen."

She was not sure what to say.

"You don't think there's anything I can't do, do you?"

"No, General."

"But you are wondering why I'm making such a promise to you."

A small nod.

"It's a big promise. One that I rarely give. Not that I am reluctant, but so few are deserving." His voice took on a hint of wistfulness. "For all my power and my wealth, I am a lonely man. There are people around me. Many people. They say the things I want to hear, do what I tell them, because their livelihood depends on me. They use me as I use them. I can rely on them to be loyal as long as I am their source of support. There's no real trust. There are exceptions. Henry was one; Jong is the other. Henry is gone. Jong is young. We are a generation apart. He doesn't experience life the way I do. Though our trust in each other is absolute, our understanding of each other is not." A moment of quiet reflection. "There is much empty space in my life. Not something people would think of the man who seems to have everything."

"No," she said softly.

"When I found out you were coming, I thought, Su-chen is an exceptional woman. She is not like the others. It can be different." He removed her shawl and let it slide down the chaise. His hands remained on her shoulders. "Getting warm?"

She nodded.

"It has always been my intention for you to live here. That was one of the reasons I offered Henry the position."

"I am deeply honored, General."

"Honored?"

"And grateful."

"Are there other feelings?"

She nodded.

"Tell me."

She blushed. "I'm not sure if I can find the words."

Even if she could find the words, she could hardly articulate them. A weight was descending from her head to her legs, pinning her down, yet she felt weightless, floating. The room was swaying like a sampan. She was riding on the rhythmic thrusts of the waves. The heat from the fire, she thought, it's so warm, like being in a feverish dream filled with heat and red chintz. She managed a smile, hoping it would communicate her feelings. Han seemed to have read her mind. He guided her to lie down. The chaise held her snugly like a cradle. He loosened the collar of her cheong-gsam and removed her shoes.

I am the luckiest woman on earth. To be waited on by the great General Han.

"Comfortable?"

She nodded. "Thank you."

"You have been thanking me all night."

"So sorry."

"I don't want you to be apologizing either."

"What should I do?"

"What would you like to do?"

"I'd like to stay here. For a while. I feel sleepy."

"Do you want me to keep you company?"

"Yes."

"What would we do here?"

Her blush deepened.

"Do you want to please me?"

"Very much."

"Will you do anything to please me?"

She nodded.

"Say it."

"I'll do anything to please you," she said obediently.

Han stood up and started to undress. The medals and epaulets on the jacket jingled as it landed on the floor. The metal caught the glint of the fire and left blotches of light on her retina. The world around her became a blur. Except him. He removed the belt and the trousers with the ease of someone who didn't mind being watched. Naked, he sat down on the chaise to take off his boots, his buttocks touching her arm. His yang was inches from her, illuminated by the fire. He turned so it faced her.

"My yang," he said affably.

He took her hand and put it on his yang. It felt tender, like a baby's limb.

"Keep it there. Don't be shy. Want to know how sing-song girls make men happy?"

She nodded, dazed.

"This is how."

He tucked his penis into her mouth.

"Think of it as a piece of fruit, sweet and juicy you've been longing to taste."

She was staring at his navel, her head swimming. The yang was hardening, filling her mouth and plunging down her throat. She wanted to breathe, couldn't; she was going to choke. She wished she could ask him to take it out, but there was no way for her to make a sound. A part of her was very alarmed. How could she be doing this? It was bizarre, immoral, humiliating. Another part reminded her that it was General Han's yang and she mustn't disappoint him.

"Taste me."

Maybe it'd be enough if he saw she was putting out her best effort. She sucked with all her strength.

Abruptly it was taken out of her mouth.

"Not like that."

She looked up at him.

"You are trying too hard. I should have known. You've lived a sheltered life."

"What... should I do?"

With two pulls he ripped off her cheongsam and petti-coat; another to tear away the camisole and underpants. He groaned at the sight of her naked body. He mounted her, his compact body fitting neatly on hers. His hands cupped her breasts, held them down like a pair of recalcitrant animals as he sucked the nipples, sending startled shivers down her spine. From her breasts his hands glided downward, his fingers playing on her Jade Well like a drummer. The sensations were unbearable. She moaned with pleasure, writhing. He moved inward, deeper, probing, exploring... She couldn't bear it any longer. Her arms slid around his neck, locking him, pulling him to her. He entered her.

"Oh, General."

This was what she had been yearning for, since the first day in Shansui, since the first time she had met him in Nanking. To receive the yang of this great man, to be part of his body, to offer the juice of her yin to him. Every part of her body seemed to be waking up. So many beautiful, irrepressible, and terrifying sensations. Familiar yet more exciting, hungrier, fiercer than the times before. She was a child snuggling up to the soft, flushed bosom of her wet nurse. She was a girl being touched by a boy for the first time, both so shy that they closed their eyes while they explored each other. She and Henry were swimming in Hsûen Wu Lake on a hot summer afternoon, rising and sinking in the cool water. *Let's pretend we're a pair of illicit lovers, stealing an afternoon to be together...* Henry was gentle, mindful of her feelings. Henry was never this impatient, this rough.

Henry.

Han let out a loud shout and collapsed on her.

"Haven't worked this hard since my wedding night," he said, catching his breath. "The damn liquor. It put you to sleep, didn't it? Next time you won't need it."

Su-chen was sobbing.

"What's the matter?"

"We shouldn't have done this. I am Henry's widow."

"What?"

"Henry. He was your friend."

"Henry's dead."

"It's too soon…"

He removed himself from the chaise. "How long did you plan to wait?"

Her sobbing intensified. "It's wrong…"

He sat on the armchair, taking a respite. "Too late for remorse now, Su-chen."

Left alone on the chaise, she felt exposed. She wrapped her arms around her body, in a futile attempt to cover herself.

"You must have known this was what we were going to do."

She turned away.

"So you did. That's good," he said.

She is beautiful, he thought, no question there, but unimaginative and naïve like a village girl. Endearing qualities, up to a point, but unsatisfactory if this were to go on. She needed to overcome her inhibitions and enlarge her repertoire of techniques. A month, that's how long he would give her, to learn to make Clouds and Rain like a Shanghai courtesan; if not, he would have her trained by a professional.

"You did what you wanted to do. You shouldn't feel bad about it," he said.

Easing herself up, she said awkwardly, "Will we see each other again?"

"Of course."

"Like this?"

"Definitely."

"You wouldn't think less of me?"

"Why would I do that?"

"It wouldn't change things between us?"

"No."

"You would always think of me as someone special?"

"Sure."

"When you are tired of me, you won't order me out, like you do with your concubines?"

He joined her on the chaise. "Now, Su-chen, you're being silly." He removed her hands to uncover her breasts, caressing them, pleased to see how quickly the nipples stiffened at his touch. "This is our first night. There will be many more nights. You are so beautiful. How can I be tired of you? You are not a concubine, you're…"

She held off her sobbing for the announcement of her new role.

"You are the woman I've been waiting for," Han said, and regretted it immediately.

A smile rippled from her lips to the rest of her face, fresh, sweet and little-girl, washing away the fretfulness.

"I should have been more trusting. It's just that this is new to me. I didn't know how to behave. I was worried and afraid." She nestled her head on his chest. "Please forgive me."

"There is nothing to forgive."

Her smile deepened. "I have always known."

"Known what?"

"That you wanted me. It was the way you looked at me. The first moment we met, I knew you had special feelings for me."

"I did."

"You couldn't show them then?"

"No."

"You've kept me on your mind. All these years. Even when we were thousands of miles apart."

Both hands holding his chin, she kissed him, working her way downward, earnestly, caringly, sensually. Nice she's taking the initiative, he thought, enjoying the tingling sensation roused by her tongue on his yang. I was right; there is a passionate woman under the reserve.

"You are happy that we are together?" she murmured, returning to his lips.

"Didn't I tell you so?"

"There is no other woman in your life?"

"No."

"You have no desire for another?"

"No."

"Not ever again?"

"No," Han repeated automatically, wondering when her questions would end.

"That will be my promise to you too. I will never desire another man."

"Good."

"It's our joss to be together for the rest of our lives."

Quite a leap she was making. He wasn't sure he wanted to encourage this line of thinking. And then he saw something in her eye. The fire of a woman in love.

He climbed back on her.

17

It's over.

From dawn until dusk, confined in a windowless room, Victor had faced Han's inquisitors. The questions had ranged from Soong's covert operations to his private life. The focus had been on the details: background of supporting players, third-level contacts, fallback modes of communication. He had suspected there was little he revealed would be new to them and they were only using him to verify findings. He had obliged.

A note from Han had arrived, inviting him to late-night supper. To thank Victor for his cooperation and to settle his Hong Kong account. Victor hadn't expected that Han would want to spend an evening with him.

The warlord wants to hand him the gold personally, he thought. He doesn't trust anyone to do it for him.

Early tomorrow morning he and Pierre would be on their way out of China; the most exciting chapter of his life would be closing, likely for good. He felt neither anticipation for the life ahead, nor regret for the one he was leaving. Only a nebulous, persistent anxiety.

Pierre was asleep, a golden-haired boy in a pool of moonlight. Victor gazed at the milky cheeks, soft curls framing the face that could be his at the same age. His son had been born in China. His mother had talked to him about France and had taught him French, but the country wouldn't have meant much to the boy. He was a Chinese child. How would his son adjust to living in Europe?

How would he?

Was going home the cause for his anxiety? The prospect of facing Celeste? Not knowing where Lillie was? Or that he had given away Soong's secrets? His mind was a jumble of doubts and worries and fears. He breathed deeply, trying to dispel the hollowness in his stomach.

"Whatever happens, my son, we are going to be all right," he said softly, assuring himself.

He kissed the boy's forehead and left the room.

He was early. He decided to treat himself to a tour of the Villa. Eschewing the daily route between his room and the investigation chamber, he headed the other way. Grand Hall was the center of the Villa; its tower was visible anywhere inside the compound. He couldn't get lost. The air was heavy with scents of jasmine and gardenia. He took in the sweetness gratefully. In the distance, limestone hills rose like giant fingers pointing upward. The sky was empty except for the moon, a half circle of shadowed light, fuzzy at the edges. Imperfect illumination for an imperfect world. The place was shrouded in a haze. He felt he was moving in a dreamy landscape, and he would wake up to a bustling Shanghai morning. Back to his old life in the

French Concession. Nanking hadn't happened. Shansui returned to being a name on the map.

As he approached Grand Hall, his sense of unreality deepened. The structure looked like an oversize contraption made of colorful cardboard. A Chinese toy palace. A monument to one man's fantasy. Was it fantasy? Foreign powers dismissed Han as an Oriental eccentric who hoarded gold in his cellar and collected virgins for his amusement. The Chinese grouped him with other warlords, rogues who amassed power after the collapse of the Ching Dynasty, local bullies heading fly-by-night armies that wouldn't survive a typhoon. Brief though his stay had been, Victor discerned a different picture. Han's soldiers were superbly trained and armed with state-of-the-art weapons. They were well paid; morale was high. Judging from the interrogation, Han's intelligence apparatus was first rate. Not to forget the immense purchasing power of the warlord's personal wealth.

Han's gold.

Would he see it tonight?

"I'm Victor Maurier," he said to the sentry at the foot of the steps. "I'm here at General Han's invitation."

"He is expecting you."

"Where will I find him?"

He pointed to the back. "Enter the door and keep going: you'll see."

Victor mounted the steps and passed through the double door. Another guard ushered him to an entrance to a corridor. Victor walked alongside an atrium garden, heading to the only lit area in the back. This part of Grand Hall was a different place from the imperial court where he had had his first audience. This was a rich man's residence, spacious, exquisitely furnished and quiet. Only the soothing sounds of an artificial waterfall provided a rhythm for the night.

A door opened when he reached the end of the corridor. Two guards stepped aside. Han came forward.

Victor bowed. "Good evening, General."

"Come in."

"Thanks for inviting me."

"My pleasure. You've been invaluable to us. Ready to take off?"

"Ready, but reluctant, General."

"I hope it's because you love China." Han smiled at Victor's nod. "Well then, you deserve a nice send-off."

They walked side by side like friends, through a beaded screen to the dining room. The table had been set: porcelain plates on gold chargers, white linen napkins, a gold candelabrum with tall candles, fresh flowers. To Victor's surprise, the menu was French. The courses were laid out like a Chinese banquet: custards of foie gras and oysters, Beef Wellington, chocolate marquise with pistachio cream, crêpes ambrosia, plus an unbelievable assortment of cheeses. To his immense delight, there were bottles of rare vintage Bordeaux.

"Have a seat."

"Thank you."

"Your cuisine is remarkable for a Western culture," Han began after a guard served the wine. "Certainly more tolerable than English food, which must have been prepared with horses in mind. The Germans may be the smartest people in Europe, but they have negligible culinary sense. I heard you grew up in France but you speak many languages."

"A few of those around the Mediterranean Sea."

Han picked up an oyster with a pair of ivory chopsticks. "Some old countries there. None as old as China."

Egypt and the countries in the Middle East were older than China, but no point in correcting Han. Victor said, "The Chinese culture is one of the greatest in the world."

"The greatest."

"It's a pity the rest of the world doesn't understand China as well as they should."

"The Middle Kingdom has never been interested in opening up to the rest of the world," Han said, picking up a round of Beef Wellington and eating it in two bites, dropping a cascade of pastry flakes. He emptied his glass in a gulp.

Someone should teach the warlord the subtleties of fine wine, Victor thought.

"You've spent many years here. Do you think you understand us?"

"Can't say that I do, General. It would require lifetimes to comprehend this rich and complex civilization," Victor replied, biting into the freshest oyster he had tasted in years.

"Being aware of one's inadequacies is the first step to wisdom."

"*Confucius's Analects*, Book three."

"Excellent."

"It was one of the first books I read after I learned Chinese. I memorized passages that resonated with my understanding of the world. They've helped me to be a wiser man."

Han seemed to have a new regard for Victor. "Few foreigners are willing to learn our culture; even fewer are interested in the work of the Sage. You grasp the meaning of the Sage's words and apply them to situations. That's remarkable. I want to hear your views on what's happening in China. Do you think the war will end soon?"

"It'll crest before things calm down. We haven't seen the worst yet."

"Will we beat the Japanese?"

"Eventually."

"Not soon?"

"Unless something unexpected happens."

"Like what?"

"If the Americans intervene."

"Do you think they will?"

"My understanding of American politics is limited. My guess is that they won't get involved in this part of the world unless they have to."

"I don't like to depend on foreigners' whims. I want China to be in control of its own destiny."

"It could happen if there were a change in the Chinese leadership," Victor said as he took an appreciative sip of the excellent wine.

"You don't think much of the current regime?"

"I wouldn't dare to judge, General."

"You can speak freely. You might know I am not a fan of them."

"China is a big country. Under normal circumstances it requires a strong central government to keep things in order. Right now, it's in a complicated, drawn-out conflict involving enemies inside and outside China. The government is weak, incompetent and corrupt. The disarray at the top has had a cascading effect on the rest of the country. To turn things around, China needs a strong leader. Someone who can unite the country, and then he can solve the problems."

"Good point. What kind of man would this leader be?"

"Someone tough, competent and incorruptible—the opposite of the current leadership."

"What about Mao?"

"Mao's ideas are too radical. China is an ancient country. People don't change their habits and their values overnight. It would be more effective if the new leader built on what's already here."

"Tradition."

"Yes. Tradition makes people feel safe. When people feel safe, they are more willing to trust. With trust, the leader can rally the country."

Han nodded.

"Having said that, we are in the twentieth century," Victor continued. "It's a different world with new inventions and new ideas happening every day and everywhere. Machines, factories, faster ways to travel. The leader cannot be a blind follower of the past. He needs to be a man of his time. Pragmatic and open-minded. Find new ways to make old principles work—otherwise he wouldn't be any different from past emperors. His reign would be short-lived."

"That was Yuan Shih-kai's mistake. Go on."

"Once the situation stabilizes, the leader has to re-galvanize the country, socially, economically, technically. He must be willing to learn from the West, use their machines and apply their methods to rebuild the country's infrastructure. You can't run a country without good roads and communication tools. Not a country the size of China. That's why, above all else, he must know how to find and grow capital. A lot of capital is needed because China is poor."

"I see."

"Under the right leadership, China could become a world power."

"You are saying we are not?"

"In cultural matters, China has been and will always be superior."

"The rest?"

"The Western powers are ahead."

"How far ahead?"

"A century, give or take," Victor replied.

Silence.

Victor wondered if he had spoken too frankly. The Chinese were fiercely proud. China was *Chung Kuo*. The Middle Kingdom. Center of the world.

"You are not hesitant to speak the truth," Han said. "That takes courage. Courage is rare these days. Too bad you are leaving."

"I wouldn't leave if it was up to me. This is where I feel most comfortable and where my talents are put to their best use."

"You want to stay? Seriously?"

"Seriously."

"For how long?"

"For as long as China wants me."

"You are not homesick?"

"This is my home."

"You are willing to be subjugated to an alien culture indefinitely?"

"I wouldn't put it quite like that, General, but the answer is yes."

"When I hear such sentiments expressed by a foreigner, I assume either he is lying or he wants something from me."

"Some of us are sincere."

"The white race has an inordinately high regard of itself. Arrogant people are not capable of accepting superiority in others."

"On the whole it's true, given this particular moment in time. But there are exceptions."

"Westerners see themselves as masters of the universe. The world should adapt to their standards, think like them, do what they do. The epitome of this attitude is America. They consider themselves *the* superpower. I would quarrel less if their culture was superior, but it's not. It's immature and rudimentary. What can they teach Europe? What can they teach China? The nation is less than two hundred years old. We have spittoons that are older than their capital."

If it had been someone else, Victor would have suggested a more considered view. But at the moment, he and his son were at the warlord's mercy. So Victor nodded along, ate the food and drank the wine. Both were superb. They could have been prepared by chefs in the finest restaurants in Saint-Germain. The warlord must have French chefs on the premises. I could get used to living like this. Easily. Lillie could too.

Across the table, Han was on a roll. When he's done admonishing America, he turned to other Asian countries. Japanese were freaks capable of committing mass murder and mass suicide on the same day. Koreans were the doormats of the Far East, not an iota of ingenuity in their heads, stubborn like mules and should be treated as such. Malays, Filipinos, and Indonesians were half savages who sleep on the beach and pick their meals from trees. Indian culture was a farcical mess. How could anyone take seriously people who worship cows?

"I heard you have a sound knowledge of military equipment, particularly the hand-held variety," Han said, changing the topic abruptly.

"I learned about them at International Airsea. We handled merchandise from suppliers all over the world."

"You liked the job?"

"It was better than the job I had before."

"You were a missionary worker?"

"Yes."

"Quite a career switch you made."

"The change was easier than I thought."

"There's more money running guns."

"A lot more."

"Tell me what you know about guns."

"Now?"

"Why not?"

Victor kept the descriptions concise, but included enough jargon and data to show off his expertise. As he read approval on Han's face, he became convinced that the dinner meeting was an undeclared job interview. Had to be. That's why Han wanted to hear his opinions on the war and the country's future. A position in the Han camp—he liked that. Life in Shansui would be pleasant. More so if he had an apartment inside the compound and a French chef at his disposal. The work couldn't be more hazardous than the job at Airsea. He would be able to stay in China and be protected from Soong. For a well-paid position, he would be willing to renegotiate Han's offer. Let Han keep his gold. He would make a quick trip to Hong Kong and withdraw the money from Soong's bank. He was going to do that anyway. No one in his right mind would leave behind all those American dollars... If Han won the country, Victor would be the first European to take part in the founding of a new Chinese dynasty. His legacy would be greater than that of the dubious envoy to Kublai Khan's court, Marco Polo.

"I could put together a comprehensive list with descriptions, functions and applications, suppliers and prices," Victor proposed. "You'd have the information at your fingertips when you needed them."

"Excellent. Drop it off at my courier service in Hong Kong."

"I can deliver it in person."

"That would be even better. You'll come back as my guest. I enjoy your company."

"The feeling is mutual, General."

Abruptly Han stood up. "Time to make good on my promise."

Victor would have liked to try the Muscadet, and the cakes, but no one tells Han to wait. He emptied his glass and got up. The warlord had left the table. Victor hurried after him. Through a different door from the one he had entered, they headed to what appeared to be the innermost chamber in the building. Reaching the end, Han unlocked a door and relocked it as soon as Victor joined him. Without a word he performed a series of maneuvers with a vase and objects on the desk. Before Victor could register their meaning, part of the wall opened.

"You are about to see the center of my power, where the new China will be born."

They stepped behind the moveable wall. Victor was aware that he was going to see Han's gold, that it was a privilege few had enjoyed. There wasn't any doubt now: his new career would begin in Shansui.

Han showed the way with a flashlight. They descended a stairway three stories deep.

"Holy Jesus. Mother of God," Victor said, breathless.

It was the largest bullion depository he had ever seen. Rows of concrete shelves stacked with gold bars. Han ran the light around the space. The beam caught the precious metal and flared up like arcs of fire. It seemed all the gold in the world was here. Victor had thought the size of the Han fortune might have been exaggerated; now he discovered the legend had not done justice to the reality. This was power. Power to destroy enemies. Power to save China. Power to rule the world.

"How much to make up for the bank deposit in Hong Kong?" Han asked.

Victor pulled a gold bar from the shelf, weighing it in his palm. "Five catties?"

"Exactly."

"That'll be one hundred and five ounces."

"One hundred and six."

"Sixty bars will equal the sum in the bank account."

"Make it a hundred."

Victor swallowed. "That's most generous, General."

"My present to you. For your love of China."

"Thank you."

"My seal is on each one. Hope you don't mind."

"Of course not."

"Go ahead. Help yourself."

Victor looked around. "Should I start from the end?"

"No need. Pick any hundred."

"A hundred," Victor repeated in a daze.

"There is nothing like it in the world, is there?"

"No."

Han made an arc with the flashlight, imprinting a yellow rainbow on the dark ceiling. "The gold will be turned into the new Han dynasty. The place will be empty."

"I can't imagine."

Han's eyes were a luminous black. "Neither can I."

Victor pulled a bar and put it by his feet. Another. The gold was cold, yet intense heat seemed to issue from the hard surface, scorching his hands. Like touching the sun.

"You need something to carry them. I'll go and see what I can find."

Han walked away and disappeared around a corner. Victor heard his footsteps on the stairwell, fading as they went up. A bang. The secret door was slammed shut. The air became still. Absolute stark silence. He picked up the flashlight from the shelf and shone it around. A golden universe, more fantastic than a fairytale. The sensation of being in a dream returned. He blinked. Still here. Better get on with it, before the midnight clock strikes and the gold vanishes. He kept pulling. One hundred bars won't make a dent. How many were here? A hundred thousand? A million? How could one man own this much gold? Where did it come from? Did Han have a team of suppliers, or did he own gold mines around the world? How were the gold bars transported to the vault? Han couldn't have carried them himself. There must have been coolies. Had Han killed them, like the Emperor Shih who had had his tomb builders buried alive in the mausoleum in Sian? Would Han, like Shih, kill anyone who had seen the gold?

What am I thinking?

There was no reason for Han to kill him. He had been cooperative, told his interrogators everything he knew and surrendered Soong's papers. Dead or alive, he wouldn't make any difference to Han. And the rapport they had shared at dinner—it had to mean something.

I should have let him know I am willing to trade the gold for a position. There would have been no need for him to bring me here. Was it too late? Should I put the gold bars back on the shelves?

The gold was making his head swim.

Where was Han?

Thuds, like footsteps marching toward him. Closer. Louder. Han was coming back. Victor was about to run to the stairwell when he realized the sound was internal. Blood was pounding in his ears; his heart was throbbing in his throat. He felt light and heavy at once. Could he be having one of those seizures?

He had left his watch in his room. He couldn't tell how much time had passed. Maybe Han had only been gone for a few minutes. Maybe something unexpected was detaining him. He picked up the flashlight again; the icy metal tube stung his skin. Shining it through the aisles, he found his way back to the stairwell. He climbed the steps to the top. The door was a steel slab like the underside of a grave. He reached his hands upward, searched until he located the outline of the opening.

He pushed the narrow ceiling, blindly, furiously. It might as well have been the Great Wall he was up against. Maybe Han was close by. Maybe a guard was close by. He shouted as loud as he could. His voice echoed in the cavernous vault that was fast shrinking into a locked closet. A coffin. His coffin. He shrieked until his lungs and his throat hurt. His hands were bleeding. He kept on pushing the slab while repeating to himself, Han has no reason to kill me. No reason at all.

Moonlight flooded the pavilion. Han took a pull of warm sorghum, rolled it in his mouth before he swallowed. The liquid fire flowed down his body like a heat wave. Very nice. The best sorghum in China, therefore the best in the world. The French wine had cost two hundred times more and tasted dreadful. The same could be said about most things foreign. Too bad not all the foreigners could be put away as easily as he had done with the Frenchman. The fool must have thought he was on his way to paradise when he was led down the stairwell. It hadn't occurred to him that he wouldn't have been allowed to see the gold unless it was to be his last sight on earth.

It wouldn't be his last sight—if he found the tunnel.

It connected the vault to the north corner of the compound near the river. The subterranean corridor had been built for the coolies to move the gold bars from boats to the Villa. Later Han had changed the delivery method, but the tunnel had never been sealed. To locate it, the Frenchman would have to identify the only shelf in the vault that was not cemented to the wall. And he would have to figure out that he shouldn't follow his instinct and push the eight-inch slab of concrete, but instead pull it towards himself—so the bricks wouldn't tumble out of the ceiling and rain on him. Then he would dig himself out of half a mile of debris that had been piled up inside the corridor. All the while he would need to stay alive without food and water. If he managed to reach the other end of the tunnel, he would look up and see a row of seven coffins. He would notice the middle one didn't have a bottom and it was empty. If he climbed up and lifted himself out of the grave, he would find himself in the small cemetery Han had reserved for old soldiers—old soldiers who had had no family left to visit their graves, guaranteeing the cemetery would be deserted. And then he would see the river was just steps away. If he could find a boat, he would be on his way to the myriad of waterways flowing southward to the border of the province. From there he would make the rest of the journey on land to Indochina. It would be a tough feat for one man to accomplish. But not impossible.

If the Frenchman beat the odds, it would be his joss to live. Han never quarreled with joss.

He wouldn't be upset if the Frenchman made it out alive. The man was likeable and his affection for China seemed genuine. A pity that he had worked for Soong. If the man had had a different résumé, Han would have recruited him. The files he had brought were pure treasure, a gift from the gods to help Han to dislodge the Kuomintang leadership. And that little boy of his. Quick and clever like a Chinese child. In a few years he would be like Jong when he had found him in Shanghai. If his mother didn't claim him, he would keep him, mold him like he had molded Jong. A companion who would never be a rival. No matter how capable, he would always be an outsider.

Han emptied the cup. Heat was rising inside him. A round of Clouds and Rain would complete the evening nicely, followed by a night of dreamless sleep before he prepared for his first meeting with Mao Tse-tung. After weeks with Su-chen, Han wanted someone young. A pubescent beauty unblemished by cycles of womanhood. A pristine Jade Well for his yang to explore. To deposit his seed without concern about the chance of producing an offspring.

Not for the first time he wondered if there were children of his out there. There had to be. Many. Some of them bound to be male. He would claim them if he could be certain they were his. But how? He wouldn't even recognize the women if he saw them again.

He reminded himself that fatherhood is a matter of the heart, not the loins. But it pleased him that his seed was widespread and flourishing.

It shouldn't be a problem to find a girl even at this hour. Hundreds would compete for the honor of offering their first night to the great General Han. If a volunteer couldn't be found, a few gold nuggets would buy one.

He tossed the wine cup over his shoulder and beckoned an attendant.

18

It was late afternoon when the ship arrived in Hong Kong. A light rain was falling. The moisture raised the smells of brine, petrol, sweat. Lillie had spent most of the trip inside the cabin. She hadn't wanted to call attention to her being alone, and there was the gold-filled luggage she had needed to keep an eye on. After days of looking at the sky through a porthole, she was glad to be back in the open and on solid ground. Premium class was first to disembark. Her fellow passengers were rich families relocating to the safety of the British colony, patriarchs with entourages of concubines, children, and mountains of luggage. She joined the queue, keeping herself inconspicuous behind a couple with two screaming toddlers. At the immigration counter, the visa Victor had obtained worked like a diplomatic pass. A glance at her papers and she was waved on. Customs was next. She opened the suitcases, one by one, without hesitation, smiling politely, suppressing a yawn—nothing to hide, just exhausted by the journey. The customs officer was a young man who couldn't speak a word of Shanghainese. After a look at the layers of silk camisoles and brassieres, he pulled down the lids and let her pass.

Most passengers were greeted by family and friends who had arranged transportation. Lillie didn't have to wait long for a taxi. She told the driver to take her to the Gloucester Hotel. Victor had mentioned the name before the Nanking trip. Soong owned the place and he was giving them a complimentary suite. The cab drove through streets that reminded her of Shanghai twenty years ago, European architecture and Chinese pedestrians. The hotel was in Central District, an enclave of tree-lined streets and buildings with Union Jacks hoisted on pinnacles. Hong Kong's Bund. The Gloucester looked like an English club. Wedgwood porticos, striped awnings, two Indians dressed like palace guards at the entrance. Clubs abounded in Shanghai; the English ones were notorious for their snobbishness. Without Victor, Lillie knew she would not be welcome. She told the driver to find her a hotel for Chinese tourists.

The car returned to the waterfront and headed east. She was back in middle-class China. Clattered storefronts, crowded apartment blocks, hawkers selling small goods on the pavement. The taxi pulled up to a green neon sign blinking "Luk Kwok Inn." The lobby had tiled floors and armchairs topped with white doilies. Ceiling fans spun lazily. Two girls in cotton cheongsams manned the reception desk.

Lillie asked for the largest suite. "My family will be joining me."

"How long would you like to stay?"

"No more than a week."

The girl waved. A bellboy stepped forward and picked up the suitcases. "Heavy."

"Books. My husband is a scholar."

The suite was on the top floor, three rooms and a bath tiled in black and white. The balcony looked out on a typhoon shelter; junks and yachts huddled in the bay. A distance away, ferries flitted across the harbor. A light drizzle diffused the glare of streetlamps. An orange dusk streaked across the sky. There's something magical about harbor lights and ships at sunset, she thought, watching cars streaming along the waterfront.

Tomorrow I'll see Victor and we'll have our life back.

She searched for a place to hide the gold peaches. The closets had no locks; the bureaus were too small. She decided to leave the suitcases on the floor next to the bed. Let them sit in plain sight and it would invite less attention. After a bath, she called room service for hot tea and fried noodles. The food arrived quickly. She carried the tray to the balcony, ate and dozed off.

Next morning, she looked up Soong's bank in the telephone directory and copied the address. The bellboy found a rickshaw for her. The coolie was illiterate and spoke only Cantonese. Using hand signals and enunciating slowly, she repeated the name of the bank until he nodded. Haze lingered over the hillside of Victoria Peak. Another humid day. The rickshaw maneuvered like a fish through busy morning traffic. She was back in the neighborhood of the Gloucester Hotel. The rickshaw pulled up to a replica of the Customs House in Shanghai, shrunk down to a third the size. A pair of bronze lions guarded the bank. The lobby was high-ceilinged and spacious like a railway station. Marble columns, potted palms, leather chairs with spittoons tucked in between. An iron grille separated the staff from the public. Uniformed clerks were clicking abacuses, counting currencies and coins. The place was humming.

Lillie chose the Special Inquiries window. A girl was slipping documents into folders.

"Good morning. I'd like to see Mr. Chiu?"

She glanced up at Lillie. "You want to see the managing director of the bank?"

"If his name is Chiu."

"Mr. Chiu doesn't see customers."

"He'll make an exception for me."

"What is your business?"

"I'd like to ask him about a friend of mine. He has an important appointment..."

"I don't think he can help."

"Wouldn't that be something for Mr. Chiu to decide?"

"Mr. Chiu doesn't see customers," she repeated sullenly.

"He will when he finds out who my friend is."

"Who is your friend?"

"He works for Mr. Soong Tse-ven. He was told by Mr. Soong to see Mr. Chiu..."

The phone rang. After saying hello, the girl turned away and spoke softly into the mouthpiece. Her hand was playing with a paperweight, a slab of crystal engraved with the Kuomintang seal. It was Soong's bank. Of course it was connected to the Party, and Han was a member. What was I thinking? Marching in here after stealing a Kuomintang general's gold?

"I may have the wrong name. No need to bother Mr. Chiu," Lillie said as soon as the girl put down the phone.

She found a chair facing the entrance where a column shielded her from the Special Inquiries window. She picked a magazine from the rack. Holding it up to eye level, she watched the door over the top of the page. Customers streamed in. Chinese refugees with bulging envelopes of cash. Office workers with attaché cases. Well-dressed women who could be wives of Shanghai tycoons. She recognized a banker's young concubine from the ship, and a millionaire whose picture she had seen in newspapers. The majority of the bank's clients seemed to be expatriates from Shanghai. What if someone recognized her? An old customer from the Paramount? A neighbor from the French Concession?

Her face must have betrayed her uneasiness. The guard walked up to her and asked if he could help.

"I'm expecting a friend who might be late. No problem if I wait here?"

"Of course not," he said politely and returned to his post.

The crowd swelled through noon, tapered off after lunch, and picked up again around three. She had to use the restroom. When she came back, she looked carefully around to see the new faces. When the clocks struck five, her body was stiff and her back ached. The clerks were tallying up accounts and clearing their desks. The guard was checking doors, preparing to close for the day. Passing Lillie, he dipped his head in a nod of sympathy.

She was last to leave the bank. The streets were packed with people on their way home. Chinese workers in shirtsleeves; Caucasians in suits. She stared at passing faces. Where was Victor? There was no way she could have missed him if he had shown up. Maybe he would arrive after everyone was gone. Soong's people were secretive about their comings and goings.

She waited by the bronze lions and hoped there was only one entrance to the bank.

At half-past five, a black Vauxhall with a Kuomintang crest on the license plate pulled up. The driver got out and waited by the car. Two minutes later, the doors of the bank were unlocked from inside. A man dressed like a model banker emerged: trilby hat, dark pinstripe suit, wingtip shoes, newspaper under his arm.

The driver opened the door of the car. "Good afternoon, Mr. Chiu."

Chiu slid into the back seat. The driver returned to the front. The car drove off.

Victor had missed his appointment.

Back at the hotel, Lillie asked the front desk for a list of travel agencies and hotels. The local European community was small and predominantly British. If Victor and Pierre had been here, someone would have noticed. There were eight travel agencies in the colony. She was able to call on all of them in one day. The list of hotels was longer. It took two and a half days to complete the inquiries. There were guests from France, but no record of a single male guest accompanied by a boy. No one by the name of Maurier. At the immigration bureau, a gold tie clip convinced the supervising clerk to check the Arrivals and Departures lists for the past month. No passengers matched their names and description.

Either Victor had decided not to come to Hong Kong or he and Pierre were still in Shansui. There was only one way to find out. She sent a telegram to Shansui, using the name of Celesté Maurier.

Having learned about the recent unrest in Shanghai, she wrote, she was concerned for her family's safety and had traveled from France to bring them home. She hoped the receiver of this message would tell her husband and her son that she was waiting for them in Hong Kong.

A reply came the next day.

Dear Madame Maurier:

We are pleased to hear from you. Pierre is well. We are delighted to have his company, but as the only child here he is lonely and homesick. It would be best for him to be with his mother.

Arrangements have been made for him to travel to Hong Kong. Please come to Kai Tak Airport this coming Friday. The plane will arrive at 8:30 a.m. You will meet your son in Room 104-F.

Jong Lin

The man who had left the note in Shanghai.

Careless staff General Han had, Lillie thought. The real Mrs. Maurier couldn't have known her husband and son had been detoured to Shansui. And in their rush to rid themselves of their guests, they had forgotten to mention Victor.

Room 104-F was next to the airfield. Lillie watched behind plate glass windows laden with grime. Faint rays of morning sun were pushing through the overcast. Punctually at 8:30, a small plane with a British crest descended and rolled forward on the runway. It taxied into an area marked

"Authorized Aircraft Only." The ground crew pushed a portable staircase to the side of the plane.

The door opened. A stewardess stepped aside. Pierre was the first to deplane. A blond boy in a crumpled new suit. A miniature Victor. He looked around the airfield, lost. The stewardess nudged him on. He stepped gingerly on the ladder, holding the railing as he descended. He was followed by two dozen uniformed men, members of the Royal Air Force, heading to a satellite building designated for military personnel.

A stewardess on the tarmac was holding Pierre's bag. She guided him to the waiting room.

"Auntie Lillie!"

She hugged him. "My dear sweet little Pierre."

"I thought Mother would be here."

"Am I not your mother too?"

He buried his head in her chest. "But you said you didn't want me to confuse you with the woman in France."

"Never mind what I said. Aren't you glad to see me?" He nodded. "Where is your father? Didn't he come with you?"

"Papa has gone away."

"What?"

"He left on his own."

"Are you sure?"

He nodded.

"Where did he go?"

"No one knew. I asked. Many times. They said I'd find out in Hong Kong. So I came."

They paused as the rumble of an incoming plane filled the room.

"Who are 'they'?" she resumed.

"People in General Han's palace."

"Are you sure they were telling the truth?"

"They said they were. All I know is one morning I woke up and Papa was gone."

"When was that?"

"It was the day when we were to leave Shansui."

"Your father didn't tell you he was leaving?"

He shook his head.

"Maybe he made his own plan to leave and he didn't want General Han to know," Lillie said.

"But he would have wanted *me* to know."

Steps away, the stewardess who had escorted Pierre on the tarmac was checking her makeup with a compact mirror. In a corner, a man in a black coat was breathing on his glasses, cleaning them with a handkerchief while he surveyed the room.

"Did anyone come with you, Pierre?"

"A driver took me to the airport. He brought me to the stewardess and then he left."

"You came here by yourself?"

"No, the plane was full. The stewardess had me sit next to her and she brought me chocolate milk and an egg sandwich. Why are you so nervous, Auntie Lillie?"

"Let's go."

By now the stewardess was nowhere to be seen. The man in the black coat was walking behind them, hands in pockets. Lillie slowed down until he passed them. At the exit she watched him leave in a car before she and Pierre boarded a taxi.

Lillie locked the door of the suite and threw the Do Not Disturb sign over the knob.

"Tell me what happened since that morning in Shanghai. The day I left," she said after they had seated themselves side by side on the sofa. "Everything."

It had been the most chaotic day. Victor woke up with a headache and therefore in a bad mood. He coaxed Pierre out of bed and asked him if he knew where Lillie was. When he found out Pierre had made her go to his bed in the middle of the night, he lost his temper. He said he was no longer a baby and shouldn't behave like one. Pierre pointed out it was not his fault that he needed to pee and Auntie Lillie was there to help him—what was he supposed to do? Victor paced the room, the way he did when he had a big problem to solve. Pierre went to the kitchen and made himself toast and a hard-boiled egg; he hadn't had breakfast and his stomach was making noises. After a while, Victor calmed down. He was gentle with him again. By then Yunna and Mrs. Li had come out from their room. They noticed the trunk was missing.

"They must have been very upset," Lillie said.

"Yunna was. They had taken a lot of trouble to get it out of the house in Nanking and carry it all the way to Shanghai. Papa said you couldn't have moved the trunk on your own. Maybe it was a coincidence that you and the trunk were missing at the same time. Yunna and her mother didn't think so."

"What did Yunna say about the trunk?"

"She said she didn't understand why you wanted her father's papers."

"Papers."

"Yunna's father told her he kept his best work in the trunk. He was a scholar. He had to mean his writings."

"Her father never showed her what's inside?"

"I don't know."

"You are one hundred percent sure that she thought there were his writings in the trunk?"

"Yes. That's why Yunna wanted to bring it along. Something to remember him by. Why do you look so strange, Auntie Lillie?"

She held his face with both hands and kissed him, loud smacks on his forehead and cheeks. "Your Auntie Lillie was a fool. The biggest fool in the universe. You can't imagine."

"Why did you leave us? I thought you loved Papa and me, and we were happy together."

"I am crazy about your father and you, and we were happy together. Very happy. You don't know how sorry I am for what I have done. I will do everything to make it up to you." She wiped away her tears. "What happened next?"

"Papa noticed the car and his gun were missing too. He got upset again, more so this time. He put on his coat and left the house."

"Where did he go?"

"He didn't tell me. Yunna said he must have gone to look for you. Mrs. Li went back to bed. Yunna turned on the radio. She wanted to find out what was happening in Nanking. I sat with her. It was nice to have her company. I could tell there were things on her mind, so I kept quiet and practiced my calligraphy."

"You are a good boy, you really are." Lillie squeezed his hand. "How long did you have to wait before your Papa showed up?"

"He didn't."

"Your father didn't come home at all?"

"No."

"But someone came to the house?"

"Jong."

"Who is he?"

"General Han's son. Wait. I'm not sure. Jong doesn't look like General Han. His eyes are blue. He told me he is half American and half Chinese."

"Now I remember. He grew up in Shanghai, studied with the missionaries, and worked for Charlie Soong. I heard of his story. He is General Han's chief of staff."

"Jong is in charge of everything. Yunna liked him and of course he liked her back. She's so pretty. I'm sure one day they are going to marry. Their children would be... Let me think, three-quarters Chinese and one-quarter American." He beamed. "If you and Papa had a child, he'd be like Jong, wouldn't he?"

Whatever jubilation Lillie had felt about the trunk, the child had wiped away with this innocent speculation. She swallowed the lump in her throat. "Did Jong say anything about the trunk?"

"He said they would look for it later. The most important thing was to get us to a safe place."

"That's it?"

Pierre nodded.

"What made you go with the Lis to Shansui?"

"We waited for Papa, but there was no sight of him. Jong said we had to leave. The plane had to take off; it didn't have permission to stay overnight. Yunna didn't want me alone in the house, so she took me along. It was cold at the airport but Jong put us in a room with heaters. After an hour, Jong said it looked like Papa needed more time to look for you. It would be better if I boarded the plane. He would arrange to send me home as soon as Papa made contact. The plane flew for hours. We saw clouds float by, like cotton balls in the sky. So fantastic, Auntie Lillie. The houses were tiny like matchboxes; the rivers were like snakes…"

She had drawn the wrong conclusion when she read the note, Lillie realized with a sinking heart. She should have stayed in the house in Shanghai and waited for Victor.

"What's the matter, Auntie Lillie?"

She forced a smile. "After you landed, how long before your father joined you?"

"Days went by. I was beginning to think maybe something bad had happened. Yunna told me not to worry; she would take care of me no matter what. But I missed Papa, and you, and our house in Shanghai. One afternoon a guard knocked on the door and said there's someone I should see. I opened it and there was Papa."

"Did he tell you where he had been?"

"He was looking for you, and then he had to leave Shanghai because someone was trying to kill him."

"Did he say who?"

"Mr. Soong."

"Did he say why Mr. Soong wanted to kill him?"

"Because he promised to leave China and he didn't."

"Did anyone talk about looking for me?"

"Papa. All the time."

"Just him?"

"Yes."

"How long was your father in Shansui?"

Pierre thought. "I don't know when he arrived. He said he had to wait days before General Han gave him permission to see me."

"So he only spent a few days with you?"

He nodded. "I only saw him in the morning and at night. He was busy in the day."

"What did he do?

"He talked to General Han's people."

"What about?"

"Secrets."

"What made you think they were secrets?"

"They were in a small room. It wasn't cold in Shansui but they kept the door and windows closed. Papa said no one was allowed to go in; he didn't want me poking around. I wouldn't have anyway; there were many soldiers in the Villa and they all had guns. I asked him what they talked about and why it was taking so long. He said he was telling them stories. I didn't think he was in a mood to tell stories."

"How did you find out your father had disappeared?"

"I woke up early the morning we were going to leave. I was looking forward to riding on a plane again. Papa wasn't there and his bed looked like it hadn't been slept in. Maybe he had to tell more stories. A guard came and told me to unpack. He said Papa had stolen General Han's gold and had run away. I didn't believe it. I went to see Jong. He told me to go back to my room and wait."

"For what?"

"He would find out where Papa had gone."

"Did he?"

"He found out what the guard had said was true: Papa had left the Villa. But no one knew where he had gone."

"What about your father stealing General Han's gold? Was it true?"

"Jong didn't say. I asked him why Papa didn't say good-bye. He said he had to get out of a bad situation in a hurry. There wasn't time."

"What kind of situation?"

"I don't know."

"Did you believe Jong?"

"I think he told me what he knew, but he didn't sound very sure." Pierre added, "He was as surprised as I was that Papa had gone off like that."

"What do you think happened?"

"I don't know what to think, Auntie Lillie. Papa said we would come here first. He would try to find you and then we would go to Europe. He wouldn't have left me alone in Shansui. And he didn't take any luggage. Everything was there, even his gun and his money."

"How were you treated by General Han?"

"Very well. Our rooms were comfortable and the food was delicious."

"Did they lock the door of your room?"

"No."

"You were free to come and go?"

"More or less. I was told the Villa was very big and I might get lost on my own. Better if I stayed close to the apartment, that's what I did."

"How was your father's mood?"

"He had a good appetite and slept all right. Sometimes he was sad."

"Why was he sad?"

"He missed you."

Tears welled in her eyes; she tried to blink them away. "Did your father tell you why he wanted to stop in Hong Kong?"

"To close an account in a bank."

"What kind of account?"

"A big one. Father said we would have enough money for the rest of our lives. He also said he had to do it quickly because Mr. Soong might change his mind."

Which meant Victor wouldn't have missed the appointment, unless he had been detained against his will. Where had he gone?

"Will we see Papa soon?"

"Soon, yes. I hope so."

"But you are not sure?"

"I'm sure we will see him."

"Why aren't you happy?"

"I am. I am very happy you are here."

Not sure she could handle more questions from the boy, she got up. "Let's go out for dinner. They have all kinds of restaurants here, like Shanghai. Well, not as nice. The city is small and they speak Cantonese—there's really no place like Shanghai. Tomorrow we'll go shopping. We'll buy lots of new clothes. Next week we'll find a nice apartment in Happy Valley. I'll hire an amah to cook for us. You'll go to the best school and learn to speak many languages. Like your father."

"How will Papa know where to find us?"

"You'll write to your mother and give her our address. When your father contacts her, she'll tell him where to find us."

"But Papa doesn't write to mother."

"One way or another, he will find us. He has never let us down and he won't this time," she said, not believing her own words.

It had to be T.V. Soong, Lillie concluded after thinking about what she had learned from Pierre. Word must have reached Soong that Victor had gone to Shansui. Soong sent his men there and found out Victor had double-crossed him. If he had tried to kill Victor for staying in China longer than he should have, what would he do to punish him for giving away his secrets?

The chance of Victor being alive was almost nil.

19

The coolie didn't see the pool of muddy slush. He slipped and bent a knee to the ground. The sedan chair lurched and dropped with a thud. Su-chen was thrown halfway out of the seat.

She lifted the curtain and cried, "What happened?"

The coolie righted himself. "Just a slip, Mrs. Li. Sorry."

"Hurry up."

Picking up speed, the sedan chair bounced like a dinghy on a raging river. Su-chen gripped the ridge on both sides of the cabin to keep from slipping off the seat. Craning around in the tiny space, she tried to get her bearing. A trace of moon filtered through the tiny window and revealed the dark silhouette of rolling hills. She could see the scattered lights of cottages in the distance. There shouldn't be far to go.

Two hours had passed since the message arrived at the Villa. The placenta had to be consumed within three hours after the birth or it would lose its potency. The herbalist had said twenty-eight placentas were required for the procedure to work, and a majority had to be from male newborns if her goal was a son. Not taking any chance, she had restricted the selection to male infants. In three weeks she had consumed twenty-five placentas. Seven more births were pending in the Shansui City area. She should meet her target.

She prayed she wouldn't be late. A motor-car would have taken a quarter of the time, but she would have to make the request through Ah Ching and explain the purpose of a trip to the slums. Ah Ching would promise to be discreet, but as soon as she was out of sight, the maid would make a beeline to Grand Hall and reveal everything to Han. She did not want Han to know about this. Not yet. And the commotion of a car arriving at the apartment would have woken Yunna. She would want to know why her mother needed transportation in the middle of the night. Su-chen sensed her daughter suspected something. Yunna was shrewd in sizing up people and situations. If she hadn't made the connection to Han yet, Su-chen had the design of her apartment to thank. Her bedroom had its own door to the garden. She could leave without anyone in the suite noticing she was gone. The narrow path was steps away from the main walkway and shielded by tall hedges. It led straight to Han's apartment in Grand Hall. Sometimes she wondered if she was the only one who took advantage of the secret conduit, if there were similar conduits in other parts of the Villa. So difficult being the mistress of a powerful man. More so since she had to hide the liaison, not only from the public, but from everyone in her vicinity. She had been careful to make sure Yunna never saw her and Han together. A few moments in their company, and her daughter would figure out this was more than a friendship. Yunna was fiercely devoted to her father. She would resent her mother's attachment to another man. A resentful Yunna would be trouble incarnate. Better keep things under wraps until Han's feelings were clear.

Going uphill, the sedan chair moved sluggishly. She peered out again. A slope littered with squatter huts. Their tumbling roofs formed a jagged skyline in the moonlight. Midway up the hill, one cottage shone like a lighthouse in the dark. Lights were blazing from every window.

The sedan chair stopped.

"Now what?" Su-chen said.

"Sorry, Mrs. Li, I'm afraid we'll have to finish on foot. The rest of the path is not wide enough for the sedan chair."

"You go on ahead. Find out if the newborn is a boy."

The man took off with the lantern. The flickering light cast dancing shadows on the landscape. Needing a respite, Su-chen eased herself out of the sedan chair. The air stank of boiled vegetables and excrement. Two steps in the mud, and her silk slippers were ruined. When I am Han Fu-jen, I will have roomfuls of slippers and dresses and silks and furs. I will surround myself with beautiful things. It will be my turn to claim the spotlight. I will carry it off with more finesse, more style than my cousin. Soong May-ling's husband may be the man of the hour, but the bastard of a low-class concubine and a hawker could never be the true Son of Heaven. General Han descended from one of the great families of the south and he was the richest man China. And I come from the most prestigious bloodline of all, the family of Confucius. We will be China's perfect first couple...

The moon receded behind a thick cloud. The darkness seemed to accentuate the foul smells. Unbearable. She held a handkerchief to her nose while she strained to catch sight of the messenger. The lantern was bouncing light off the hillside. He was on his way back.

This child had better be male.

She wasn't sure how long she could go on in this limbo of a life. In the beginning she had been grateful that Han insisted their liaisons be kept secret—she was a widow and he her husband's friend. Decorum aside, the furtiveness had been an aphrodisiac. His veiled summonses had read like messages of longing, the trips to his apartment at midnight the enactment of an erotic fantasy. As the weeks passed, and the trysts grew more infrequent, a day without a signal from him turned into endless hours filled with self-doubt and fretfulness. Was he tired of her? Was another woman sharing his bed? Why wouldn't he make their attachment public? Why wouldn't he marry her? She was at sea in the unfamiliar role of mistress. She yearned for certainty and, more than anything, recognition that they were a couple. To be part of his life beyond the bedroom. To be admired and envied and worshipped. By everyone. She had dropped hints. Han had ignored them. On one occasion she had persisted, and the cold glint of steel in his eyes had chilled her. She had not dared to bring up the subject again.

She would go out of her mind if this were to continue indefinitely. She had to take the matters into her own hands. There was only one way to secure her proper place in Han's life. The age-old method well tested by wives and concubines since the first dynasty. Su-chen had consulted with an herbalist and confirmed a procedure she had heard of in Nanking before she became pregnant with Sung.

Three weeks ago, she had begun the hunt for fresh placentas.

The attendant shone the lantern on his face. He was nodding vigorously. Su-chen began the climb, negotiating her way carefully on the muddy path. Her footfalls joined the other sounds of the night: the foraging of dogs and the burping of frogs. Far to the west, the moon reappeared and hung above the hilltop. Its light was guiding her.

A man in a peasant's smock waited at the door of the hut. Gray-haired, a furrowed forehead, skin browned by the sun. He was older than Su-chen had expected.

"Are you the father?" she asked, catching her breath.

"I am the child's grandfather. It is our honor to welcome you, venerable madam." He bowed.

"Is it a boy?"

"Yes. My daughter gave birth to a healthy little boy."

"Let me see him."

The cottage was made up of two rooms. The unpainted walls reeked of mildew. An oil lamp cast a yellow hue on the meager furnishings: a wooden table and two chairs. A kettle sat over glowing coals; by its side was a rusty tub filled with water. Earthenware jars, bunches of medicinal herbs, and a sack of rice were lined up on the counter. In the next room, a bed with a bamboo mattress took up most of the space.

A girl peered from behind a frayed blanket. Hollow sockets set on a face that had been pretty, now gaunt and exhausted. Her skin was flushed from the childbirth. She looked bewildered, as if she was confused by the reality of motherhood. She was about Yunna's age.

At the foot of her bed, the midwife was wiping the infant with a towel. Su-chen went to the baby and lifted up the tiny cotton tunic to confirm the gender.

"Your first child?"

"My daughter's first child," the man said and took his place by the bedside. "The pregnancy was not expected."

"Firstborn a boy. You are lucky." Su-chen took out a red envelope and handed it to the man. "Your fee. Be sure the midwife gets her commission."

"Thank you."

"Where is the father?"

The man hesitated. "He is nearby."

"Why isn't he here?"

"He is in hell, that's why," the girl blurted.

"Something happened to him?"

"We have no doubt he is well," the man said in a sober voice. "Other than that, knowledge of his whereabouts is not available to us."

"Does he know he has a son?"

The man shook his head.

"But he must be told," Su-chen said.

"Why should he be told?" the girl snapped. "He doesn't care."

"The child's father made it clear that he doesn't wish to have anything to do with my daughter."

"I told the missus here," the midwife chimed in. "She shouldn't give up so easily. You know how men are. Give them a son and everything changes. He would be happy. He would come home every night. But the young lady wouldn't listen."

"He isn't anyone. He isn't natural."

"What do you mean?"

"He is a monster. Only a monster would do that to another human being."

"What did he do to you?"

The girl's face was white with bottled-up anger. "He had me locked up for hours. Like a prisoner. It was night when he let me out. He took me to this big room. It was dark, no light, just candles. Red candles. Like a wedding chamber. I told him I wanted to go home. He said, 'Little girl, come to my bed. Make me happy and then I'll let you go home.' He didn't care that I didn't want to be there and I had never been touched. He only cared about what he wanted. I cried and cried. I fought back, but it only made him hurt me more. When I realized he liked that I was in pain, I kept quiet. I pretended to be dead. It wasn't hard; I felt I was dying. When he finished, he handed me a wad of cash like I was a whore. 'Go buy something nice for yourself,' he said. I asked him, 'What's going to happen to me? What am I going to do?' He just waved me away. He didn't even ask my name. I was nobody to him."

She seemed to be seeing the man in the flesh. Her eyes burned. She was gasping for breath, her fingers gripping the edge of the bed sheet.

It was uncomfortable to watch. Su-chen mumbled, "That sounds dreadful." To her father: "I take it your daughter isn't married."

"No, and now she never will be."

"If she is willing to be a concubine, she might be able to find a man who would take her," the midwife said. "It'd be better than being single."

"My daughter will spend the next twenty years bringing up the child."

"That's a lot of responsibility for a young girl," Su-chen said. "She should try to reunite with the man who fathered the child."

"He can rot in hell."

"Even a bastard should know his father," said the midwife.

"We should not wish for the impossible," the man said quietly.

"Why would it be impossible?"

"I'm afraid we can't say."

"You gave the man a son. He will be proud when he finds out."

"I don't want to have anything to do with him," the girl insisted. "This is *my* son."

"After we found out she was with child, our hopes were that she would survive the delivery," the man said. "If the baby was a boy, there might be a family who would adopt him. We are poor. We can't feed an extra mouth. Then your offer came. The money will let us provide for the child. When he is old enough, he will help in the fields. My daughter will have someone to take care of her when she is old. We are indebted to you, madam."

"Good to know the money will be well spent."

"We will be honored if you choose a name for the child."

"Better that you choose the name for your grandson. I prefer not to be involved."

Su-chen was tired of their stories and outpourings of gratitude. Every family had a tragedy. This girl was raped. Another woman's husband was drowned before his son was born. One was too poor to feed her children and wanted to sell the infant for an additional sum. Why did they think she would be interested in their problems? Why couldn't they just take the money and shut up? Sympathy was not part of the arrangement. It was a simple business transaction: the sum of 900 yuan for the timely delivery of a fresh placenta and the sellers' discretion.

She turned to the midwife. "Is it ready?"

"Yes, madam."

Handing the baby to the grandfather, the midwife bent down and pulled a lidded pot from under the bed. She lifted the cover for Su-chen to check the contents. Su-chen nodded. The pot was transferred to the attendant.

"Have you been told the conditions of my offer?" Su-chen asked.

"Yes, madam," the grandfather said.

She repeated them nonetheless. "You will never speak about my visit here to anyone. Not a word. In the future, if by chance you find out who I am, you might be tempted to talk about what happened. If you do, I will see to it that you are punished. Most severely. All of you."

"We will remember a kind lady from a respectable family helped us in a time of need, but we will have no recollection of her face or the words she said."

"Keep your promise."

"We will. We wish you long life and the best of joss."

"Let's go."

Back in the cocoon of the sedan chair, Su-chen let out a sigh of relief as she took the pot from the attendant. Two more births and the ordeal would be over. She couldn't wait for it to end. Consuming a placenta freshly extracted from another woman's womb was the most irksome and humiliating experience she had ever endured. It had taken every ounce of willpower to keep herself from throwing up just at the sight of raw human tissues, before she put them in her mouth, chewed and swallowed them.

Wary of mishap on the way, she circled her hands around the pot that held the promise of her future as Han Fu-jen. She closed her eyes, relieved and exhausted. Someday I'll tell my son the trouble I put myself through for his sake. She said a prayer to Kuan-yin that the someday would be soon.

20

Yunna listened in the dark. A door opened and closed, swiftly and cautiously. Footsteps on the wooden corridor, and then the stone-paved garden path. Hurrying, fading. Quiet again. She counted to a hundred before she switched on the light and checked the clock. Fifteen minutes past eleven, the same time as the night before last and the other nights in the past month. A pattern was emerging in her mother's nightly excursions.

She stepped out to the veranda, trying to get a glimpse of her mother, knowing that she had long gone. Surrounding her were the sounds of the night. Rustling trees, a gurgling brook, chirping cicadas. The air was cool and dewy, saturated with the scents of summer blossoms. The winds had swept away the clouds. A new moon was coming out. There had been a new moon the night before her father died. A sickle shape of light above the black silhouette of Purple Gold Mountain. It had emitted a faint glow as she and her father watched the line of trucks moving along the foothills. He had said she could have anything she wanted and she had gone to bed with dreams of a perfect future. Hours later, the world had exploded, taking her past and her future with it.

The memory hurt like an open wound. She wiped away her tears.

She went back into the room and took a book out of a desk drawer. It was a collection of Sung verses bound in silk, the Li family seal stamped on the spine. She hadn't looked at it since she put it in the drawer on her first day in Shansui. It reminded her of that dreadful day and she couldn't bear the sight of it. She pressed her palm on the soft cover, touching where her father's hand had touched. A whiff of his tobacco issued from the fabric. More than six months since his passing, time had crystallized perceptions. She felt she knew him better now than when he was alive. He had been a conflicted man. A thinker who had needed the reassurance of material possessions. A family man who had preferred life on the road. An idealist who had been reluctant to put faith in ideology, any ideology. How much had he wrestled with his contradictions? Had they hindered his career? She knew from observing her mother's relatives that absolute power demands absolute ruthlessness. The higher the goal, the more insistent the drive to win at any cost. Her father hadn't had it in him. He wouldn't have reached the top.

She decided to take a careful look at the book. Nothing unusual about the edition. No inscription. She flipped the pages, no inserts, no scribblings. But it had been the only thing her father saved when the intruders showed up. Why? She felt something hard inside the cover. She reached in and pulled it out. A key. It had been inserted into the lining. This must have been what he wanted to save. What would the key open? The trunk? Something else? What secret was it guarding? Could it be the clue to solving his murder?

Would it ever be solved?

The investigation was progressing, Jong had told her. Evidence was being gathered, witnesses interviewed, movements of suspects tracked. That it had happened on the first day of the Nanking Massacre added unprecedented complications. And there were mitigating circumstances associated with her father's position: the General's relationship with the Party, her father's role as a Kuomintang cabinet member, her mother's connection to the Soong sisters. Politics, family, friendship, all mixed in with jousting for power and protecting self interest. It would take time to sort them.

The truth would emerge, he had assured her. It always did.

She didn't only want the truth. She wanted vengeance. She wanted her dreams to come true, as her father had promised they would. What happened that morning in Nanking had opened her eyes. Everything dear to her had been snatched away in a matter of hours. There had been nothing, absolutely nothing, she could have done.

I will never be helpless again. Never be passive. Never be a victim. Principles are phantoms, captivating but hollow. Power is real. Power can keep me safe. Power can make things right. Power can change the world.

She hadn't told Jong any of these thoughts. He had a different image of her. An image she might or might not live up to. She was content for the image to stay intact, that he would not get to know her as well as she knew herself, that he would stay in love with the perfect woman he fashioned in his mind... Thinking about Jong made her question things about herself she would rather not. She wished she could just have his love, complete and trusting and forever. It would be there for her when and where she needed it.

She left the room.

She headed to her mother's suite on the other side of the hallway. She stepped into the sitting room and turned on the light. The five crates from Nanking had been left along the wall. They had arrived last week. The coolies had removed the hinges of the lids but hadn't taken out the contents. They remained untouched. Her mother hadn't bothered to look through the belongings salvaged from their home. Her indifference was something Yunna could neither comprehend nor accept.

They'd never had much in common, Yunna thought, never got along. What glued them together had died in Nanking.

She drew the drapes to keep out the light and left the door half open, so that if her mother returned early she would have warning. She knelt down by the crates. They were things from the library, the only room not damaged by the fire. Three were filled with books. The rest contained odds and ends retrieved from her father's desk, stationery, maps, a typewriter, a set of fountain pens, a gramophone, recordings of orchestral music—cherished detritus of an orderly life cut short.

The door to her mother's bedroom was ajar. Might as well take a look in there. Two steps into the room, she nearly stumbled on a pile of clothing. Her mother must have been agonizing over what to wear and ended up pulling out half her wardrobe. Dresses, skirts, shawls, shoes were strewn on the floor and on the bed. She wouldn't have put herself through the trouble for an evening walk—if it was an evening walk. The dressing table was worse. Yunna stared at the tubes of uncapped lipsticks, spilled face powder, the mirror smudged with rouge and fingerprints. Her mother had always been neat and she had used cosmetics only on special occasions. What made her change her habits? Why did she doll herself up like a courtesan? Who was she meeting in the middle of the night?

Yunna noticed a wooden chest sitting on the dresser. The size of a shoebox made of fine wood with carving all around. A place for precious keepsakes. She didn't remember having seen it in the Nanking house.

The chest wasn't locked. She lifted the lid.

The glare was unexpected and intense. She blinked. When her eyes regained focus, she picked up the pieces of jewelry one by one. They were expertly crafted, the designs lavish and intricate. The stones were bright and clear and flawless. Her aunt Soong May-ling had more than a few similar pieces in her jewelry collection. She had bought them at luxury shops on her trips abroad. Her mother couldn't have purchased them in Shansui. The few goldsmiths in the town center catered to the simple indulgences of peasants; they couldn't produce pieces of such quality and sophistication. They must cost a fortune; her mother wouldn't have that kind of cash on her own. Her father's assets were tied up overseas.

Someone had bought them in a city and given them to her mother. It couldn't have been the Soongs. Their relatives had cut off contact when they found out they had moved to Shansui.

The giver had access to world-class jewelers. And was very rich.

Yunna knew.

There was one light in the foyer and another in the middle of the building. Two sentries guarded the front. The closest Yunna had been to this part of the compound was Jong's apartment. She had never been inside Grand Hall; the guards would not recognize her. Even if they did, it would be difficult to explain her presence there at this hour. *I want to ask General Han if there's anything going between him and my mother.* They would think she was mad.

She had to bypass the guards.

She backtracked from the front and re-approached from the side. She chose a semi-circular route, heading to the middle of the building where the light was, moving behind trees and hedges. Her skirt brushed the grass; it rustled like running water. She pulled it up a few inches. The ground was moist; her shoes were soaked. A breeze was blowing, shifting shadows. Capriciously. She looked around.

Nothing.

I am jumpy because I am nervous. I have only seen General Han from a distance since we moved here. He never acknowledged my presence. Maybe he did to Mother and she didn't tell me. Maybe he wouldn't mind seeing me. But what if he minds?

Stop wondering. Go on. Do what you must.

Reaching a gap in the hedge across from the lighted window, she saw the surrounding veranda was elevated about three feet above the ground. Keeping low, she made the crossing. The guards were a distance away; she was out of their field of vision. She pressed her hands on the edge of the wooden planks, pushed, and lifted herself up. A splinter caught her sleeve and ripped the piping. She squeezed her body through the balusters and landed on the veranda with a soft thud. She skirted the wash of light and moved to the wall. Half crouching, she tried to peer through the silk partition. A blur of a lamp and little else. She put her ear to the fabric: labored breathing punctuated by moans. Strange sounds. Titillating sounds.

She edged up. With her fingernail, she drilled a hole through the silk partition and peeked.

Han was naked. As was her mother. They were lying on the bed, their bodies pressed together. His mouth was sucking hers. Her hands were clutching Han's buttocks, frantically, like she were about to fall off the bed. She was moaning, from pleasure, pain, or both. Yunna's eye went to the lower part of the bodies. Glued. Thrusting. Gyrating. An obscene sight. Yet she couldn't look away. Couldn't move or breathe. Her mouth was dry. Her hands were shaking.

A groan. The General collapsed on her mother. Her eyes were closed, forehead glistening, a proud smile hung on her lips, like that of a runner who had made it to the finish line. He stayed on her, panting. After collecting his breath, he raised his head and wiped his brow with the back of his hand. He pushed one hand on the side to lift himself up. Mortified by the sight of the General's genitals, Yunna shut her eyes. When she looked again, he had left the bed. Her mother was gazing in his wake, drawing her body in, as if she needed to summon courage for what she was about to do next. He was standing not far from the partition, pouring water from a carafe. Mercifully the corner of the sideboard blocked his lower body.

Su-chen raised herself and left the bed, marching across the room without a stitch of clothing. Yunna had never seen her mother naked. She felt as though it was her own body on display. Blood rushed to her face. Boiling her head. Fuming up her eyes.

"Can I tell you a secret?" Su-chen pressed her body against Han's back, head resting on his shoulder. "After the first time we made Clouds and Rain, you said something I'd never forget. You said, 'Su-chen, you are like a virgin. Virgins are interesting only once.' I want to be interesting every time. I thought and thought about what to do. Then I found the answer. Want to know what it is?

Han grunted.

"I'm going to learn the tricks singsong girls use to please men."

"You can never be a singsong girl."

"No, but I can pretend to be one when we make Clouds and Rain."

"That'd be foolish."

"I'll be anything you want me to be."

"That'd be even more foolish."

With mock ruefulness, she said, "Would you rather have a real singsong girl to keep you company?"

Han drank in slow swigs, didn't answer.

"You let singsong girls be seen with you, but you only want to be with me in secret. Are you concerned people would talk because I am your best friend's widow?"

"I'm never concerned about what people say."

"So you wouldn't mind if people knew we're together?"

"What I do in my private chamber is nobody's business."

"Of course not. But sooner or later people will find out. They will be wondering why we've kept it a secret. They will make up all kinds of explanations. Better if we let them know on our own terms. We can announce it to the staff and then start making public appearances."

"Why would we do anything in public?"

"That's what couples do. They do things together in private and in public."

He put down the glass with a thud. "You've been harping on this for weeks. Haven't you got it by now? I do things my way. You can talk until you are blue in the face. It won't make any difference unless it's something I want to do. Whatever is eating you, you need to deal with it. Now could you change the subject?"

His words stung, but she managed a smile. "We don't have to talk at all. Come back to bed."

"Not in the mood."

"You are always in the mood. Your yang is strong and insatiable. We'll make Clouds and Rain through the night and I'll bear your child."

"What?"

"I'm going to bear your child."

"What made you think of something like that?"

"It's the most natural thing."

He eyed her suspiciously. "You're not pregnant, are you?"

"Not yet, but I will be. It's going to happen tonight."

"You can't predict something like that."

"There are days in a month when a woman conceives readily. Today is one for me."

"How do you know?"

"The doctor told me."

He raised his eyebrows. "You talked to a doctor?"

"He is outside the city. I didn't give my name. I was discreet."

"What else have you done?"

She hesitated. "Don't be angry with me. I just want to have your child."

"How long have you been thinking about this?"

"Since the first time we were together. A crown prince for the new Han dynasty. From my womb. I want it more than anything. I know you want it too. A son to carry on your legacy."

"That won't happen without my consent."

"I am asking for it now. You will be a wonderful father. I can tell by the way you care about Jong."

"Jong is more than a son to me."

"He is an excellent chief of staff. But he is half Chinese. He will never be one of us."

"He is devoted to me. That's enough."

"But you want your own flesh and blood to inherit your legacy."

"You keep saying 'legacy' like I already have one foot in the grave."

"So sorry, General, I didn't mean it that way." She added sweetly, "I thought if you need a reason to have a child, that's one."

"I don't need reasons to do anything."

"Wouldn't it be wonderful if I were carrying your child when you came back from Hankow? Your seed beginning to grow right when you launch your empire? The child will be born next spring, the Year of the Rabbit, the luckiest of all signs. It will be a boy and he will grow up to be like you."

He seemed tempted. "How can you be sure it will be a boy?"

"I have my ways."

"What ways?"

"Do you want to know?"

He nodded.

Su-chen had the cue she needed. She returned to the bed, gave a shake of her hair before lying down with her buttocks anchored on the edge of the mattress, feet on the floor, legs wide apart. She began rubbing herself with her index finger, writhing.

"Let me show you how I know. Come…"

Yunna let her body slide down the wall. She clenched her fists to keep herself from breaking into the room and putting an end to the pathetic scene. She felt hot, exploding rage. And crushing shame. My mother. My father's wife. How could she? Only six months since he died. Already she was giving herself to another man. Plotting her next marriage. Her next family.

A crown prince for the Han dynasty.

She wants to be Han Fu-jen, mistress of the Villa, wife of the richest man in China. For that she has turned herself into a whore.

My mother. A whore.

She wants a son. Always a son. Like Sung. Who pushed me from the center of attention. Only because he was male.

A child of General Han would do more.

He is still up, Yunna thought numbly, staring at the light at the back of the apartment. Maybe he sensed I need his company tonight. She knocked and leaned on the door. She was sweating, hot under her clothes, cold on her forehead.

The door opened. She nearly fell. Two arms held her up.

"It's you, Yunna. Are you all right?"

"Can I come in?"

"Of course."

Two candles on the sideboard illuminated a scholar's den. A leather sofa, a set of upholstered armchairs surrounding an oak table with a vase of orchids. A gramophone and a cabinet of recordings occupied a corner. Chinese books in silk casings and English titles in leather-bound volumes lined up side by side on the shelves. Facing the books was a calligraphic rendition of Wang Pu's poem: "Ode to Teng Wang Pavilion."

She sank into the chair by the sideboard. In the wavering light, her face looked ethereal, cheeks pale, eyes burning. He poured two cups from the pot in the tea cozy. She took a small sip, holding the cup with both hands, drawing the warmth.

He pulled a chair next to hers. "You don't look well. Has something happened?"

She didn't answer.

"What is it?"

"Mother…"

"Is she all right?"

"She has no shame."

"What do you mean?"

She didn't reply.

"Tell me."

"I saw her. With the General.

Alarmed, he asked, "Where were you?"

"Grand Hall. They were in his room, doing despicable things."

He was silent.

"I went to look at the crates. I found this pile of jewelry in her room. I've never seen it before. It has to be gifts she received from someone after we left Nanking. It can be only one person. I wanted to find out why the General gave her such expensive gifts and why she sneaks out of her room at night. I thought I would ask the General. Maybe there were reasons. I bypassed the guards and went to the back. There they were. In his room. She was on his bed. They didn't even bother to turn off the light."

I should have anticipated she would find out, he thought. I should have prepared her.

"Did you know?" she asked.

"Yes."

"Why didn't you tell me?"

"It wasn't my place to discuss your mother's private life. And I was hoping it would end before you found out."

"You didn't think I should know?"

"It's a private matter between her and the General."

"I am her family."

"It's her life."

"Her life is part of mine and mine is part of hers. Whether we like it or not."

"She's been through a lot. It could be her way of coping with the loss of your father."

"You're saying because my mother misses her husband—that makes it all right for her to give herself to another man."

"People deal with difficult situations in different ways."

"You don't think it's her fault?"

"No. Not entirely."

"She chooses to go to his chamber. She chooses to behave like a singsong girl. She chooses to forget that she is a widow. How can she not be responsible?"

"The General is a powerful man. He gets people to do what he wants. He doesn't give them a choice. Try to forgive her."

"Forgive her?"

"You may not feel that you can at the moment. But, yes, I hope you can forgive your mother and put this behind you," he said. "Things will change with the General. He'll lose interest."

"She knows. That's why she wants to have his child. To ensure she wouldn't be cast aside. If it happens, the whole world will find out she has betrayed my father."

"She hasn't betrayed anyone. She is a widow."

"My father just died."

"It's been months. She is alone and lonely."

"Other women lose their husbands. They grieve. They turn their attention to the family. They don't behave the way she does."

He got up and ambled to the other side of the room, needing the comfort of darkness, wishing he could block out the images of Han and what he did with Su-chen and all the other women. But they were more vivid in the solitude of his mind. He pulled open the shutters, inviting the night in. The moon was high in the sky, washing distant peaks with light. Its pale glow picked up stretches of distance, silver and white and shades of gray.

"We are human," he began quietly, speaking to himself. "We try to be strong, but we don't always succeed. There are forces more powerful than us. They put us in situations beyond our control. Like what happened in Nanking. Your mother suffered a horrific loss. General Han went out of his way to be kind to her. She couldn't turn down her savior."

"She isn't doing anything against her will. She wants to be with him. She's begging to have his child."

"Emotions evolve. There is little going on in her life. She is in an unfamiliar place. She has no family except you. No friends. Nothing to occupy her time. An attachment like that can become consuming."

"You are making excuses for her. Why?"

"Because hate is destructive and it breaks my heart to see you like this."

He went to her and held her. She was unresponsive and distant. It came to him that what he had said was also true between him and her. With her, he would always be up against forces greater than either of them. His love might never be enough.

"We need to look beyond these walls. The future is out there. Waiting for us," he said, reassuring her. And himself.

"The future?"

"Our future. We will be together. We will live the way we want."

"Will we?"

"Yes."

"How can you be sure?"

"Because there can be no other way. Because we are meant to be. From the first moment, I knew I will be by your side. Every day."

She repeated softly, " 'By my side. Every day…' "

"As long as I live."

"The monk in the temple on Purple Gold Mountain spoke the same words. It was the morning of the Nanking Massacre. Mother wanted to have our fortunes read. That was how he described one of the men in my life."

"One of the men. How many are there?"

"Three."

"Three?"

"That was what he said."

"Did he say who these men would be, when and where they would show up?"

"His descriptions were ambiguous, like a riddle. I was skeptical. I didn't believe fortune-tellers know more about the future than the rest of us. And then things started to happen. Some of his predictions about my mother have been coming true."

"What did he predict?"

"The tragedy in Nanking, our moving here, the General… According to him, it was joss that she would meet someone like him."

"Fortune-tellers have a way with words. They make it easy to interpret them in light of what has already happened."

"That's what I thought, but I can't dismiss what happened. It got me thinking that maybe joss does exist, that we have less say in our destiny than we think, and that there are turning points in one's life that are inevitable."

"I don't want to believe our destiny is entirely in the hands of some unknown force."

"Neither did I. But Nanking changed everything," she concluded. "Let's not dwell on this anymore. If it's meant to be, we will be together."

"Do you want us to be together?"

"My father thought it would be someone like you." She smiled. "You are every girl's dream of a perfect man."

"You make it sound like a flaw," he said in mock complaint, relieved to see her smile. "General Han is going to Yenan and Hankow. The trips are important to him and he wants me to come along. After that, his agenda will be set in motion. The important moves will take place outside Shansui. Risky moves that may make staying here unsafe. It's best that we leave."

"That soon?"

"Yes."

"Where would we go?"

Slivers of moonlight formed a crosswalk on the floor, pointing west. "America."

"You want to find out the other half of you?"

"I've been Chinese all my life. I want to find out what it means to be American. It's a big country, free, with an abundance of opportunities. It'll be a good place to build our new life."

"What would you do there?"

"I want to build real things, houses, roads, bridges. Improve people's lives in tangible ways. I want my efforts to make a difference. Not just to one person, but to a community. I want to work hard and earn my keep like everyone else."

"You don't believe you are doing that now?"

It was a question he had asked himself. He hadn't come up with an answer he could live with.

"What about General Han? Doesn't he count on you to be here?"

"I suppose he does."

"Then you can't leave."

"We may have to leave Shansui anyway."

"Why?"

"General Han plans to move to Hong Kong."

"Why?"

"He likes the feng-shui there, something to do with the mountain range on the island and the shape of the harbor. Fortune-tellers are saying it will be the most prosperous place on earth."

"But it belongs to the British."

"He plans to take it back. He wants it to be the next capital of China."

"Why would that be up to him?"

"It would be—if things happen according to his Grand Strategy."

"The General has a plan to take control of the country?"

"He has been working on it for years. It's an open secret; you might have heard about it from your relatives. After the Sian Incident, his rivals expected him to make the move. The Chinese Communist Party got a big break. Chiang was at his most vulnerable. Han could have taken advantage of the situation, but he didn't. There was speculation that maybe his ambition wasn't political, that he only wanted to expand his opium business."

"That isn't true, is it?"

"The General has never wavered in his goal. He believes timing is everything. He's been waiting for the right moment. It seems the right moment may be here soon. His plan has taken on a quicker pace in the past few months."

"The trips to Yenan and Hankow—are those parts of his Grand Strategy?"

"Yes."

"Are we talking weeks? Months?"

"Only he knows."

"What's going to happen?"

"He said he would defeat the Kuomintang, the Communists, and the insurgent groups in one sweep."

"How?"

"He hasn't told me or anyone I know. That's him—he likes his secrets."

"Do you believe what he said?"

"I don't know what to believe because I don't know what he knows. He is the only one who has full knowledge of his Grand Strategy. The people involved in the operations are given separate pieces of the big picture."

"He wants to be emperor." Yunna said quietly.

"He would begin a new Han dynasty. The second Han dynasty. Pu-yi would be put back on the throne temporarily, as a figurehead. After the country stabilized, the General would retire Pu-yi and proclaim himself emperor. He believes feudalism is the only way to make China great again. He would improve on the merits of past emperors. His rule would be the amalgamation of the best of the past. All the great dynasties in one."

"To make China great again," she repeated.

"With *his* method. *His* kind of greatness."

"*His* dynasty."

"He has many enemies and obstacles."

"The gold. Is it true?" she asked abruptly.

"It's true."

"How much is there?"

"He told me once his fortune was greater than those of all the monarchs in Europe combined. The gold is the profit from his opium trade. The Han family and the British have monopolized the coastal provinces for nearly a century. His claim could well be true."

"Enough to win the war?"

"That's what he's counting on. That's all he's counting on. He is the sole executor of the Grand Strategy. One mind. One perspective. China is a big country. We are in an unprecedented situation where international politics may affect what would happen to China. It has become a much bigger game than Han envisioned. His Grand Strategy may not work out the way he planned."

"He can change his plan."

"Not likely. He believes nothing can or will go wrong. The General is a dreamer at heart. Ideas grow in his head. He convinces himself he can turn them into reality, and he goes ahead, expecting to win every time. It has to do with living in Shansui all his life, being supremely wealthy and always having things his way. Easy to believe one is invincible when one doesn't have to face one's enemies in the flesh."

Let's leave now, he thought. Let's walk along the river in the moonlight. To the other side of the world. Let's forget Han and his gold.

"Has my mother seen the gold?"

"I wouldn't think so, since she is alive. The General has never let anyone who saw the gold live."

"Does my mother know about his Grand Strategy?"

"It's the biggest thing on his mind. He must have talked about it."

Yunna became very pale. "My mother knows one day the General will be the emperor of China."

"It's not going to happen for certain."

"He has a chance."

"A chance. That he has."

"How good a chance?"

"Better than the other warlords. The gold improves his odds, no question there."

He saw something in her eyes. Something hard and unbending. It unsettled him.

She let out a laugh. "You'd think if you've lived with someone your whole life, you would know her. Was I wrong? Was my father wrong? This tradition-worshipping wife. This descendant of the greatest moralist in China. My mother. She doesn't tolerate other women standing up for themselves, but she wants to be empress. No wonder she praised General Han to the skies. She said we should be thanking the gods for a friend like him. Seeing his empire must have driven her wild. His Forbidden City. His piece of the Middle Kingdom." Her eyes were streaming, her voice cracking. "You are wrong, Jong. He wasn't the one who took advantage of her. My mother seduced him. That's why she has been secretive about the relationship."

"The General wants to keep it secret."

"That got my mother really unhappy and she's taking initiative. A son to carry on his legacy, she said to him. That was how a court concubine became Empress Dowager. One male offspring was all it took to attain supreme power. Every wife, every concubine must have tried. It's a tired old trick, but my mother might get what she wants, the way she had Sung when everyone thought it couldn't happen." She went on shakily, "My mother is going to be empress. Who would have thought?"

"Stop, Yunna. There is no need to get worked up about something that may never happen."

"It happened. I saw her. She got the General to go along."

"Let's say the General marries your mother. It wouldn't be such a bad thing. Your mother would have an anchor. God knows it's time the General curbed his appetite, settled down, and took on personal responsibilities. Maybe that would get him out of his golden cocoon. Make him see how distorted his view of the world has been."

Yunna stared at him as though he were out of his mind. "My mother as empress. You can accept that?"

"She is a good woman…"

"Is that enough for China's next emperor?"

"An emperor is a man."

"She doesn't deserve it."

"Who deserves anything? Look at me, an orphan, a half-civilized person. Yet here I am."

"The General made you. He can make my mother too."

"Yes, he made me," he repeated with profound sadness. "I wouldn't be where I am had it not been for him."

"So you know what he can do."

"Yes. I hoped you wouldn't."

She looked at him. "Why do you say that?"

Because it's better to have one's illusions intact. Because the kind of loyalty Han demanded required total surrender. Because more often than he was willing to admit, he wished Han was a different man.

"Something wrong, Jong?"

He was quiet.

"It's the General, isn't it? There are things you don't want me to know."

"It's late. Let me walk you back to your apartment."

"I don't want to be alone. Would you mind if I stayed?"

He managed a smile. "Why would I mind?"

422

"We'll wait for the sun to come out, then we'll take a boat down the river. It's been a while since we did that. The hills will be lovely."

The candles caught a small current of air and flared up. Her face burst into glowing bloom. It was as though they were back in the Frenchman's house and the best part of his life was about to begin. He felt a fierce, irresistible desire to share with her what he knew about love, power, everything.

The flames dwindled. The world was back in shadow.

They talked more about the war, America, not another word about Han. Yunna was drifting away with thoughts he knew he had no part of.

It has been a traumatic night for her. He consoled himself that she was with him. And that together they would watch the sun rise.

21

A light rain had softened the loess soil of the Yenan hills. The jeep negotiated the winding path, the driver gripping the wheel to hold the vehicle steady. Rounding a curve, it skidded and rolled off the road. The passengers were thrown to one side. The driver braked, shifted to lower gear, and put the jeep back on course.

"This is the capital of the Chinese Communist Party?" Han remarked as he straightened up.

"Yes, General, we are in Yang Chia-liang," Jong replied.

"Hardly civilized."

"It's underdeveloped compared to Nanking and Shansui."

"Barbarous."

"They seem to manage all right, making do with basics, being self-sufficient."

"Running a political party out of caves and growing meals from rocks. Mao is downright crazy to live like this.

I thought commune living was something made up by foreign journalists, so they could claim their esoteric cults have imitators in China. Looks like they weren't lying."

"Mao is setting an example for followers of his proletarian revolution."

"Why would a leader want his followers to be like him? A leader should maintain distance from the people he rules. Like the emperors, a figure to be revered and worshipped."

"Perhaps that's why he calls his movement a revolution."

A ceiling of dark clouds gathered. The landscape looked naked and vulnerable in the sudden twilight. They seemed to be the only inhabitants in this gray universe, silent except for the humming of the jeep's engine. At a clearing, a tiny tombstone on the roadside said one mile north. The driver pulled the brakes and checked the map.

"This is as far as the jeep can go, General."

"What's ahead?"

"Mountain trails."

"Can we find our way?" asked Jong.

"Hard to say. There isn't much information on the map."

"If this is where Mao lives, we'll find him," Han said.

As if on cue, four men stepped out from behind the rocks. They formed a half circle facing the jeep, blocking the path. They were holding Mausers.

"What should we do?" the driver asked.

"Mao's guards," Jong said. "I'll speak to them."

He got out of the jeep and greeted the men with a military salute.

"I'm Jong Lin." He pointed to the jeep. "That's General Han Tang-ming from Shansui. We are here to see Mr. Mao Tse-tung."

One man came forward and returned the salute. "We have been instructed to take you to Comrade Mao. Two visitors are allowed. No weapons please."

"We have brought only our good will."

They were satisfied by his words, didn't inspect the jeep or frisk them. The driver stayed behind. Han and Jong followed the guides. They climbed the narrow mountain path single file; their feet slid into shallow grooves molded by the daily footsteps of the young Communists. At the end of the rise, they reached an open plateau, then followed a shaded lane marked by stones. The clouds had dissipated. A thick haze lingered, locking in the humidity. Below, the town was a dust bowl with a smattering of clay houses that seemed to have been there since the dawn of civilization. It's a world of sepia shades, foreboding and remote. For centuries, few people in the province of Shensi knew where the capital was or who ruled.

An unspoiled territory for Mao to launch his revolution, Jong thought.

Ahead, half the ground had been slashed away. The path appeared to be suspended in midair. Caves hugged the steep hillside like giant beehives. The famous Yenan caves. Jong recognized them from photographs. A leveled patch with a vegetable plot set Mao's cave apart from the rest.

"Please go in and make yourselves comfortable. Comrade Mao will be with you shortly."

Inside the cave it was cool like dusk, barely furnished, about fifteen feet deep, twenty feet wide with whitewashed walls. In the sitting area, Jong counted three items of luxury: books, records, and a gramophone. The books were on Chinese history and literature. There were no translations of foreign titles—unexpected for a man who embraced a

European ideology. The stack of recordings was excerpts of Peking operas. Two tallow candles burned on the table. The aroma of a spicy meal issued from an adjoining alcove.

A portrait of Chiang Kai-shek hung on the wall.

Han raised his eyebrows. "What is this?"

"Chiang and Mao are supposed to be partners, fighting the Japanese side by side," Jong replied. "The United Front."

Han straightened the portrait with his thumb and stepped back for another look. "His rival's portrait in his living room. Statement of his public allegiance or reminder of their private feud?"

"Both, I'd think."

A woman in peasant clothes appeared at the door. Her complexion was shades paler than a Shensi native. The cheeks bore a tint of rouge freshly applied; the hair was short and neatly parted. There was a restless bounce in her movements, like a ballerina not completely unwound after a performance. She was at least six months pregnant.

Mao's latest paramour. The Shanghai film actress whose love he had proclaimed indispensable to his revolution. If Mao married her, she would be his fourth wife. Her own marital résumé, Jong had been told, was equally long.

"You must be Comrade Han and Comrade Lin."

She walked up to Han and extended her hand. He stared. She nodded encouragingly, a parent waiting for a child to behave. He obliged, his hand barely touching hers. The handshake, a recent import from the West, was exclusively a male practice in non-Communist China. Jong was next. The woman's palm was cool, her fingers bony and her grip strong.

"I am Chiang Ching, Comrade Mao's loved one."

"What?" Han blurted.

"'Loved one,'" she repeated proudly. "Our Party has done away with traditional terms of feudal hypocrisy and those containing gratuitous deference to the male gender, and have replaced them with a vocabulary that describes social and personal relationships accurately. 'Love' should be the only reason two people are together. Honest and to the point. Not too progressive for you, General?"

She filled a plate with shelled peanuts, grabbed a handful, and popped them into her mouth one by one. She didn't offer them to her guests.

"Where is Mr. Mao?" Han asked.

"He is on his way. Do sit down." She sat on a chair and gave her belly a massage. "The pregnancy tires me out. I hope it's a girl. I like girls. Easy to train, flexible with chores. They work harder than men and never complain. 'Women hold up half of the sky.' That's why men and women should be treated as equals."

Han frowned. "Come again?"

"Nothing less equals. Men have been exploiting women for centuries. Women do the work; men set the rules and take the glory. All because we are told to follow a set of beliefs from a time when people lived like savages."

"You are talking about the age of Confucius."

"Confucius has been dead for centuries. The feudal age is over. Time to make things right."

"How would you do that?"

"Same rules for everyone. If men and women share the same responsibilities, they should be given the same privileges. That's what we believe in and that's why one day I'm going be Party chairwoman."

Han glared. She gave him an insouciant smile and turned her attention to Jong.

"You have a strong profile and appealing features, very appealing. Except your eyes. Fortunately photographic film does not register color. You'd be stunning on film."

"I don't know much about the art of cinema."

"I do."

She stood up and paced around Jong, examining his face from different angles. An uncomfortable silence hung in the room.

"Good looks don't always photograph well. A person must have the right type of bone structure for the camera. I know. I was an actress. Heard of me? Li Yun-he and Lang Ping were my stage names."

"I've been to the cinema a few times in Shanghai, but I'm afraid I haven't seen any of your pictures," Jong replied before Han could say something impolite. Mao's "loved one" had to be the antithesis of femininity in Han's eyes.

"My pictures were shown everywhere. Not only in Shanghai."

"Moving pictures. That's a remarkable technology," Jong said.

"It's an effective tool for teaching the masses."

"Movie houses are your classrooms," Han said with sarcasm.

"We show moving pictures that document the revolution fought by our Soviet brothers and sisters. The events are well attended. Peasants are eager to learn about the evils of capitalism."

"It must be a nice diversion for them," Jong said.

"Not diversion. Education."

"Peasants as students and moving pictures as textbooks," Han said. "Your ideas are indeed too progressive for me."

"Good to have our convictions confirmed," she said with equal sarcasm. "We don't want to have anything in common with the reactionary political party in China."

Before Han could replay, a shadow blocked the door.

All smiles, Han stepped forward and extended his hand. "Comrade Mao, a pleasure to meet you."

He's learning fast, Jong thought. Until this moment, the word *comrade* had not been in Han's vocabulary.

Mao was medium built and lean, his hair long for a man. He was dressed more plainly than Han's chauffeur: a laborer's jacket and baggy khaki trousers, wrinkled but clean. He surveyed the room as if it held a full audience before he sat down on the chair by the gramophone, back straight and knees together. Han had been nervous about meeting Mao, which was unprecedented in Jong's experience with Han. Now he saw that Han's intuition had been right. Mao projected an aura of natural authority. He was in charge the moment he walked into the room.

Chou En-lai was next. The shabby pajama suit couldn't obscure his charm. His dark eyes were full of life, his movements agile and graceful. In one sweep his smile reached everyone.

"Good day, good day. Such a pleasure to see you, General Han and Mr. Lin. It's been a while, hasn't it? Was it Sian or Ningpo that we last met? You look well. Nice journey, I hope."

There was no spare chair for Chou. Jong vacated his.

"Mr. Lin, stay where you are. You are our guest. Let us at least provide this small amount of hospitality in our humble quarters. I do insist."

They vied to be the more gracious. Jong and Chou were of comparable rank, but Chou was senior by a few years. Chou conceded but insisted that Jong move from behind and lean on the arm of his chair.

Chiang Ching began to serve tea. Holding each cup with both hands, she bowed her head as she offered it to the men. Mao, followed by Han, Chou, and Jong.

For all their progressive ideas, Jong thought, traditional protocol was alive and well in throne room of the Chinese Communist Party.

"Comrade Han, what wind blew you all the way from beautiful Shansui to backward Shensi?" Chou began.

"The wind of change."

"Change," Mao repeated. "Do you mean revolution?"

"Change. Revolution. To each his own," Han replied.

"In our Party, an individual is insignificant on his own. We don't function on such small terms."

"Let's be reminded that most big plans are born of small origins."

"And big plans are realized by men with big hearts."

"Like us."

"Well said."

Preamble complete, everyone acknowledged in silence the repartee was a draw. The discussion began. Han opened with a safe topic: condemnation of the Japanese invasions. Chou responded with nods and occasional comments in agreement. Mao remained placid, munching peanuts and sipping tea. He could have been listening to an opera aria in his head. Mao's loved one crouched on the floor like a cat. Her gaze shifted from Mao to Han like a spectator at a tennis match.

Han moved on to the topic of the Chiang-Mao United Front.

"The alliance will not last," Han said firmly.

"What makes you think so?"

"Chiang is a dictator. He can't tolerate a partner, even in name."

Chou nodded. "What do you think will happen?"

"There will be disagreements and conflicts. Things will get worse. A showdown between you and Chiang will be inevitable."

"Who will win?"

"You, Comrade Mao. That is the reason I'm here today."

"You want to join the winning party," Mao said casually.

"I want more than membership in your party. I want to offer you support."

"What kind of support?" Chou asked.

"I have a plan that will benefit both of us. You will get what you need most, and vice versa."

"What do you think we need most?"

"Money. Money to feed your people, purchase weapons, train soldiers, spread your ideas, and whatever else you need to do to carry out your revolution."

"What about you? What would you get?"

"A strong ally. A cooperative partner."

"Assuming we agree, what would be the source of these funds?"

Han tapped his chest. "I'll be the source."

"Are you pledging a financial contribution to our party?"

"In a way."

"Do tell us about this 'way,' General Han," Chou said.

"We will sign a treaty recognizing our coexistence as the two legitimate ruling powers of China. We will be political allies, and if things can be worked out, allies in other ways. Once the agreement is in place, I'll help finance your revolution."

"Two legitimate ruling powers of China," Chou repeated. "I take it you have chosen those words carefully. Are you representing the Kuomintang?"

"I am representing myself."

"Are you prepared to replace the leader of your party, General?"

"Prepared and ready."

"Why do you believe Chiang should be replaced?"

"Chiang should never have been made head. He may be a shrewd politician and he has been lucky enough to elbow his way to the top, but he has neither the skills nor the conviction to govern. Look at the Kuomintang. The administration is farcical. The army is made up of coolies; they take orders from thugs. The civil service is populated by crooks. Every one of Chiang's bureaucrats, from his brother-in-law to the local police chief, is on the take. People are hungry and disgusted. The country is a shambles. Yet Chiang stays in power. Why?"

"You have an explanation, General?" Chou asked.

"He has the backing of the Americans. Since America is regarded as leader of the so-called free world, the alliance legitimizes Chiang. I want to put an end to that."

"You want to stop American aid to the Kuomintang?"

"Yes."

"That's a wonderful idea."

"An idea I will turn into reality."

"Pardon me," Chou said. "I am a little confused. As these are matters of national as well as international importance, I'd like to be sure that there are no ambiguities in our communication. I'm sure Comrade Mao feels the same." Mao nodded. "You said you are not here on behalf of your party. Shall we interpret your views as those of a Chinese citizen, perhaps someone with an impassioned plan to change the course of history?"

Han grinned from ear to ear. "Very well put, Comrade Chou. That's exactly what I want to do. Change the course of history."

"You would be the driving force of this plan?"

"Yes."

Chou's eyes moved from Han to Chiang's portrait on the wall. "Are you planning to succeed Chiang?"

"If succeeding Chiang means I would assume his legacy, the answer is no. That's the last thing I'd want to do. I want to bring China into a new era."

"So do we," Mao said. "Your assessment of Chiang and the Kuomintang is honest and accurate. Let's hear your opinion of the Chinese Communist Party."

"Communism is a novel ideology with a short history. Too early to make a sound assessment. But I don't deny there must be something there. It has helped you to attract ardent supporters from a wide spectrum of society—intellectuals, peasants, laborers."

"Let's for a moment put ideology aside. What do you think of our chances of winning?" Chou asked.

"You will win if you accept my help."

"Do you consider your help the single most important factor?"

"From my perspective."

"What if we don't want your help?"

"You will face a long and brutal fight, with little hope of winning," Han said flatly.

"From your perspective," Mao repeated, stroking a nonexistent beard. "And if we are willing to accept your offer?"

"Victory will be swift. You will take over China, north from Peking to Yenan, south from Sian to Nanking."

"I take it your omission of the southern half of the country is intentional," Chou said.

"There is where our treaty comes in. You will have the provinces north of the Yangtze River; I will take those in the south. You will govern with whatever system of government you choose. As I shall with mine. Between the two territories there will be no aggression and no interference. We will maintain close diplomatic ties and we will cooperate where and when it serves our mutual interests. To the world we will be known as North and South China. Two countries, two systems, one people."

Jong could barely suppress his shock. Where had this come from? Han had never mentioned a plan to split up China. The Grand Strategy was to win the whole country. What had prompted him to come up with this preposterous arrangement? Could he have been so awed by Mao that he decided a concession was needed to win him over? What a concession! It went against everything Han had dreamed and planned. The proposal had to be nothing more than bait. To seduce Mao into an alliance. To isolate Chiang. To win international support—most foreign powers would be glad to see a divided China. Once Han had secured his position, he would renege on the deal.

"It's not an original idea," Han went on. "China was divided before: the Three Kingdoms, the Warring States, the South and North Dynasties, and as recently as the Sung Dynasty. It's a big country."

Jong noticed a tightening of Mao's jaw. Chou's face was blank. Chiang Ching gazed at Han like a child at a new toy.

"What kind of government do you have in mind for this 'South China'?" Chou asked.

"Are we speaking as political partners?"

"*Potential* political partners. What you intend to do with half of the country will be important to us if and when we consider a treaty."

"Constitutional monarchy. Like the British. Modified to suit the Chinese temperament, culture, and values."

"Would you be the monarch?"

"That would be inappropriate and unwise. I don't want anything less than the real mandate. I'll reinstate Pu-yi."

Mao frowned. "Mandate. That's reactionary thinking."

"Not for the rest of China."

"Pu-yi is a halfwit," Chiang Ching put in unexpectedly.

Mao patted her head, a gesture that could have been approval or restraint.

"The progress we've made in the last twenty years would be lost. It would take China—well, half of China— back to the feudal age," Chou said with a shake of his head.

"My new government would be different from the past. Pu-yi's revival would be symbolic. He would be stripped of his former imperial authority, and have no part in running the country."

"But you think he is necessary. As a symbol?" Mao insisted.

"Yes. To give people assurance of continuity and remind them that our glorious tradition is alive and well. Nothing boosts national confidence like a healthy and well-fed emperor. That has been the soul of Chinese civilization for five thousand years."

"The imperial soul is dead," Mao said sternly, very displeased.

Han was unruffled. "I am aware there are other ways to achieve the same result. But I'm a pragmatist. I put efficiency before ideology. The last emperor is a familiar figure in China and abroad. People associate him with the dragon throne. Instant recognition. Instant legitimacy. He is being used by the Japanese for this purpose—why not by me? It will be easy to recruit him; Pu-yi would love to have his old job back. And it will be cheap. Room and board for a man and a small entourage. How much could that cost?"

"It cost a dynasty," Chou said quietly.

"Not mine. The new constitution will ensure that he and his descendants will have no power. The actual governing will be done by the prime minister and his parliament."

"Prime minister. That would be you?"

Han nodded.

"Let me see if I've got it right. You are proposing to buy half the country from us, the more populated, more fertile, and economically more advanced half. With money."

"Not quite, Comrade Chou. China is neither yours nor mine to sell."

"Then I'm afraid you've lost me."

"Shall I speak frankly?"

"Please do."

"There is no question that the Chinese Communist Party has become a force to reckon with. You are seducing starving peasants with an enticing vision of a classless utopia. The idea that everyone is entitled to an equal amount of social wealth is a happy escape from their miserable lives. Few know how this utopia could be turned into reality; or, if and when it was, how the changes would affect their lives. I'll bet you don't know either. You might have read all the books on Communism and you might have visited Russia, but you don't have the experience to make it work."

"The Marxist philosophy provides the framework for our new society. It's not meant to be an operation manual," Mao said.

"You want to install an untested system of government in a culture steeped in tradition. That's a risky proposition."

"Our Russian friends have been doing it for two decades."

"Two decades are but a tiny grain in the sands of time. Even if this new social order works in the Soviet Union, it isn't likely to do so in China. One cannot compare a country of drunken brutes with the descendants of the greatest civilization on earth. Not to credit Chiang Kai-shek in his choice of allies, but we have more in common with the Americans than with our neighbors to the north. We are by nature entrepreneurs, not slaves."

"I take exception to what you said," Mao said sternly. "Our followers are *not* slaves. We are comrades. We work together, fight together, and share the fruit of our efforts together."

"Only time can validate any ideology. We'll have to wait and see."

"We are sure that you wouldn't have to wait very long," Chou said.

"That's good. Let's not to look too far ahead. Let's focus on the situation at hand: survival of your party. People are your sole capital. The *masses*. You have a growing following. But what kind of following? They are poor, underfed, untrained. Not good for much except shouting slogans in the streets. How long can they hold on to their socialist dream if their stomachs stay empty?"

"That's a pessimistic view of what the right ideology can do," Chou said. "Don't you believe in the collective will of the people? If enough people want the same thing, they will overcome the obstacles. Together."

"I am not here to argue the merits of Marxism. I am here to discuss what works. What is the most efficient way to get the job done? In your case, sustain the converted and multiply the fold. You need capital to facilitate your movement. Money to pay for guns and food."

Chou smiled. "You have that much money, General?"

"Give us an estimate," Mao said curtly.

"Of what I have or what I intend to give to your party?"

"Both."

Chiang Ching gazed at Han, fascinated.

"Before we take this further, I need to know if this question translates to preliminary consent to the terms of the treaty."

"Consent may be premature at this point," Chou said. "Let's say you've piqued our interest."

"Premature? You don't need me to tell you that no revolution can succeed without food and no war can be fought without weapons. That's why you are asking the Russians for help. The help won't be free and you know it. They disguise their self-serving agenda with high-minded mumbo-jumbo. The moment you start spending their rubles, your Soviet Big Brother will dictate how you write your constitution."

Mao's face was blank, Chou's thoughtful.

"I am Chinese; you are Chinese," Han reasoned. "We are the same people under the same sky. I have a vested interest in your party because what will be good for North China will be good for South China. Self-interest facilitated by mutual interests. A symbiotic relationship—the most reliable kind of alliance. Unlike the Russians, I will *not* meddle in your government. Honestly, I wouldn't know how and I am not interested. With my money, you can speed up your revolution. It's a far better deal than the one you're getting from them."

Sips of tea were followed by silent reflection. Mao remained immobile. Chou wrapped the cup with his hands, looking at the tea leaves, eyebrows knotted like a fortune-teller reading their meaning. Chiang Ching was looking at Han with moist eyes, as though she had fallen in love. A fly was buzzing around the table.

Mao handed down his verdict. "You've convinced me, General. Your analysis of the situation is sensible and pragmatic, qualities I respect. Our party can use more money and resources. Why not take from one of our own? That's in line with our principles. An individual must share his wealth with his comrades. We'll be glad to share yours." A nod. "To walk a mile one must make the first step. See to it that the Americans get their dirty hands off China. That will be the first step to solidify our alliance."

Chiang Ching smiled knowingly at Mao and he smiled back. Jong observed that in a second she had transformed from house pet to political partner.

"Is this a 'yes' to my proposal?" Han asked.

"Unless you are not comfortable with my word," Mao said.

"A man's word is as good as his gold."

"Most apt in your case, General," Chou said, and drew a round of merry laughs.

"Shall we work out the terms of our treaty in the next three months?"

"Is that the timeline you set for Chiang's political demise?" Mao said.

"Give or take."

"The day Chiang is removed from his throne is the day our partnership begins."

"Not sooner?"

"If you can make Chiang step down tomorrow, our partnership will begin tomorrow. It's up to you, General."

"We are counting on you," Chou added without a trace of skepticism.

"Coming here has nearly broken our backs, but it's worth the trip," Han said.

"There will be no need to put yourselves through the trouble again. Comrade Chou will be in charge of communication between us."

"I hope it means I will get to visit Shansui. My wife will enjoy the scenery," Chou said affably.

Chiang Ching fetched a jug of warm wine and a dish of fire-hot pork from the kitchen. They ate around the wooden table. Mao recounted feuds with Chiang Kai-shek while Han listened, nodding and smiling like a devoted spouse. Chou was watching the pair with a benign amusement Jong found unsettling. Next to him, Chiang Ching kept brushing her knee against his leg. At one point, she dropped her chopsticks, ducked under the table and resurfaced with a grin. Jong had the uncomfortable feeling she had checked out the bulk between his thighs. He averted his gaze and got a wink from Chou. On his other side, Han was roaring with laughter, reacting to something Mao had said. The conviviality was heartening.

Too heartening. Jong felt like an outsider who missed the jokes.

They stayed till sundown. Mao and Han shook hands, four hands wrapped into one fist. The partnership was sealed.

22

On the wall was the *Time* cover featuring Chiang Kai-shek and Soong May-ling as Man and Woman of the Year. Two darts had been stuck into the portrait: one on his forehead and the other on her nose. The room was half office, half mess tent. A trestle table was littered with cigarette butts and half-filled coffee mugs. Cabinet drawers overflowed with paper. In the corner, a dusty American flag drooped from a pole. The window had a view of squatter huts on a rocky knoll; in the distance, the Yangtze River.

Joseph Stilwell, the American military attaché, was medium-built, hard and lean, with a face sun-browned and cracked like a dried river bed. The eyes behind the rimless glasses were sharp enough to penetrate walls.

He pulled two bedrolls from a stack. "The soldiers got all the chairs. Make yourselves comfortable."

Jong arranged the bedrolls side by side. Han settled his rump on one, suppressing a frown.

Stilwell sat on the floor, cross-legged. He lit his pipe, waving off a matchstick. "You've traveled a long way to see me. Let's get to the point. What is the purpose of your visit and how do I fit in the purpose?"

"We are concerned about what's going on between our countries."

"That's very broad. You have something specific in mind?"

Han's command of English was limited; Jong took up the role of principal speaker. "Madame Chiang's relationship with your president."

"As far as any of us can tell, Mr. Roosevelt is devoted to Mrs. Roosevelt."

"We don't mean anything improper. It's a special friendship and few would disagree that it has an influence on Mr. Roosevelt's China policy."

"Mrs. Chiang does seem to get her way with the President—most of the time."

"We want to correct that."

"Good luck. The President is not the only one she has charmed. There are the Congress, the press, the American public, *and* half the world. One has to give Madame Chiang credit. It's not every day that the wife of an Oriental warlord gets to be an object of public admiration in the West. She is an international phenomenon."

"Her popularity is manufactured by the Kuomintang's public relations machine, aided by their ardent supporters at *Time*. The Luces promote the Chiangs as the symbol of hope for China. China's first couple is proponents of Christian virtues and Western democracy. They can turn China into a modern country in America's likeness. Support them and you save a quarter of mankind."

"The Luces are a pain in the butt."

"But their message is powerful. How can people resist, especially when it's printed on the pages of a popular American magazine? You and I know the Chiangs' public image has little to do with who they are and what they do. It's time someone told President Roosevelt the truth. We hope it will be you, Colonel."

"Why me?"

"Because you care about truth and justice. Because you want to put an end to the suffering inflicted on the Chinese people by this senseless war."

There was a new softness in Stilwell's voice. "You over-estimate my influence."

"Not the depth of your conviction. You know there isn't an ounce of patriotism in those Kuomintang merce-naries. You know Chiang's soldiers are not up to fighting the Japanese and he doesn't care. You know if America keeps up this skewed China policy, the Communists will take Russia's offer of brotherly love. They will have to. Who else can counter the American giant? The Communists are motivated; they will fight a good fight. If they win, the Russians will have a lot to gain. They can remake China and the entire Pacific region."

Stilwell nodded. "Such a scenario is not farfetched."

"Moscow is moving into China by way of Yenan. A socialist China will not serve American interests. America needs to act fast."

"Pulling our support won't make the Russians retreat."

"It will level the playing field. If the Kuomintang can't count on the Americans, there will be no compelling need for the Communists to get help from the Russians. Mao isn't stupid; he is aware of Soviet Big Brother's covetous agenda. Given a chance, he will choose not to be beholden to Moscow. On their own, the Kuomintang and the Communists will have to join forces and fight the Japanese. As a true United Front."

"Hard to imagine Chiang and Mao as brothers in arms. The two hate each other's guts."

"Or a better leader may emerge."

"You are a member of the Kuomintang. You and Chiang Kai-shek are on the same side. Even if the Generalissimo doesn't have your wholehearted support, you serve at his pleasure. I find it hard to believe that you are asking us to withdraw support for your party." Stilwell paused, eyes resting on Han. "In China every political move is part of a personal enterprise. What is yours?"

"General Han wants to put China on the path to prosperity. He has a unique vision for the future, an optimal integration of China's heritage and potential."

"A vision?"

"Along with a plan to turn the vision into reality."

"Sounds grand. Why tell me?"

"Hear us out and you'll know why."

A scrutiny of his pipe. "Shoot."

Jong outlined Han's concept of a constitutional monarchy; his plans to rebuild the country and to provide unprecedented social benefits like compulsory education, public housing for the poor, and care for the elderly. He emphasized Han's readiness to use Western expertise in modernizing the infrastructure and his willingness to foster better cooperation between China and its neighbors. He was careful to leave out parts that might alienate the American: the new parliament to be composed solely of Han's appointees; curriculum in the schools to be dominated by Han's brand of traditional teaching; compliance with the Confucian code of conduct requisite for receiving social benefits.

"Pu-yi would be emperor again. Unbelievable," Stilwell said.

"His role will be ceremonial, like the British monarchy."

"You would have a parliament."

"Yes."

"General Han would be prime minister?"

"Yes."

"Would there be a constitution?"

"Yes."

"Elections?"

"Yes."

"With just one party?"

"In the beginning."

"How long is this beginning?"

Han gave his answer. Jong translated: "It will depend on these conditions: How well the Chinese people adapt to the new form of government, people in cities and rural areas, people who are educated and people who are illiterate, all the people. How quickly the country can stabilize after the wars. Hard to put the country together if people's lives are falling apart. How ready are the other parties to become viable political entities? The last point is the most important, as it will have a direct impact on the quality of government. We want new leaders who are capable. We are willing to take as much time as necessary to educate and train them."

"Okay, that's your vision of the future. A future that, if I understand correctly, will take a while to get here. What happens between now and then? You have a dysfunctional central government, a growing Communist faction, and a bunch of warlords making trouble. The country is a mess. What will keep the Japanese or the Russians from swallowing up China before your vision becomes reality?"

The point about warlords making trouble hit a nerve. Han jumped in. "Swallow China? I don't think so. Not so easy. My country has most number people in world. For one Japanese killed, four Chinese killed, not big deal. Chinese population can last very long time. That's advantage of big country. And no country bigger than China. There will always be Chinese on this earth planet. That what you call survival of fittest. We plenty people, we survive."

Stilwell stared at Han, eyebrows straight up like a clown's. Jong looked away in embarrassment.

Han was undaunted. "You don't like honest talk about killing. Too bad. Like or not, it's happening every day everywhere. I want to be more honest. Kuomintang soldiers are bandits, thieves, beggars. They don't fit for normal job. They go fight battle for a bowl of rice, not because they want to save country. Many get killed. Sad, sure. But look at good side. We get rid of most bad element in our society. This war is one big cleansing project. Dirt gone. Leave a good pure China." He slapped his knees, crossed his arms, and resumed his role of taciturn commander-in-chief.

"You people are really something," Stilwell said under his breath.

Mistaking his meaning, Han smiled with satisfaction. "We Chinese wisest people in human race."

Jong had never believed Stilwell could be won over. He and Han were from two different worlds. The American was tough and forthright, a firm believer in democratic principles. Han was a self-centered traditionalist fueled by greed and ambition. But Han had thought he'd found an ally when he heard about Stilwell's criticisms of Chiang. Vinegar Joe will be my Claire Chennault, Han had said.

"What the General meant was: China's long history is filled with unrests and wars, but the country has survived. It's not unrealistic to hope we will emerge from the current conflicts intact," Jong said by way of apology.

Stilwell stood up. "You folks will have to excuse me. It's been nice chatting with you, but break's over. Gotta run now. Hope you don't mind seeing yourselves out."

Han rose and put a hand on Stilwell's shoulder. "Wait, Colonel Stilwell, this is just beginning. We warming up. More important information I tell and you want listen."

Jong also stood up. He said politely, "We only request that you hear us out, Colonel. We did come all this way."

"If you don't like what we propose, you do nothing. No loss to you personal. If you like, you do something and plenty to gain. You have my word."

"Please, Colonel."

They stood in a ring like spectators at a cockfight.

"All right," Stilwell said finally.

They returned to their former positions. Stilwell puffed on his pipe, eyes half closed.

Han had his speech ready and signaled Jong to translate.

"The Chinese are pragmatic people. They don't care about ideology. They want three square meals, a roof that doesn't leak, and a government they understand. There is nothing they understand better than tradition. The country is poor and weak. Why? Because the government is poor and weak. The malaise starts from the top. The remedy should begin there. Strong leadership is needed to revive China. These are my premises. Agree?"

Stilwell tamped the pipe with the head of a nail, taking his time to level out the tobacco.

"You were right when you said this is personal, Colonel. Yes, I am here to make a case for myself. I believe I am the right leader for China. The man to replace Mao and Chiang. I have the vision, the plan, and the resources to rebuild China. I come from an old and respectable family. I have connections all over China and the world. I have built a strong base in and around my province."

"No need to go over your resume. You are a public figure, General. Many of us heard about you."

"But you doubt that I'm the right leader for China?"

"It's not something I think about."

"Come to Shansui. Get to know me. See what I have done, and you will be convinced I am the right person to replace the current leadership."

"There's plenty to do here. I can't take off."

"Come when you can; it's a standing invitation." Han went on, "There is something else you should know. It's a privileged piece of information. I'll let you have it if you give me your word that you'll keep it confidential."

Stilwell didn't seem impressed.

"We were in Yenan. We met with Mao Tse-tung and Chou En-lai. There was much distrust in the beginning, as you and I are experiencing now. I spoke honestly, laid out points of mutual interest, and presented my plan to save the country. They asked questions; I answered them. At the end, Mao and Chou came to see things my way. A pact has been made. We will be partners in restoring peace to China. When the country is back on its feet, we will work out our ideological differences. Equitably, amicably. We will achieve a permanent 'united front.' "

Astute of Han not to mention the two-China scenario, Jong thought.

"Mao chooses you over Chiang? Why?" Stilwell asked.

"Because he recognizes I have the better solution to end the civil conflict. I didn't offer empty words. I promised to feed and clothe his people. Get them out from under the Russians."

"Seriously?"

"Seriously."

"If you cooperate with the Communists, that will be a good thing for China. I mean that sincerely. How will you convince Chiang to step aside?"

"By the only means someone like him will accept."

"Which is?"

"You may be aware that while I keep a relatively low profile, I have been active in laying the foundation for China's future. My plan of action has been carried out systematically and efficiently. By now, unbeknownst to my rivals, their spheres of influence have been undermined and the integrity of their organizations compromised. When I decide the moment, they will be obliterated. Chiang, if he survives, will be left isolated and weakened. He will have no choice but to step aside."

"You've used a lot of fancy words. I just want a straight answer."

"As much as I'd like to, Colonel, you know it is not prudent to disclose one's war plan to an officer of a foreign government. Later, after we've arrived at a firm understanding, after we've become allies, we can have another discussion. A candid, heart-to-heart discussion." A smile. "Never mind my plan. This is what you really want to know: If Han succeeds, what's in it for Joseph Stilwell?

For America? Let me assure you, the questions will be answered before we leave today. Right now, let's focus on the present. What has to be done after our meeting?"

"What has to be done?"

"We have in our possession the Soong family's financial records. They show how the Soongs and Chiang have been redirecting American foreign aid to their personal bank accounts, and how these staggering sums of money have been spent on acquiring assets and properties in different parts of the world."

"When you said 'financial records'—what exactly do you mean?"

"Bank statements, memos, contracts, letters. All originals. I want you to take them to the State Department and your president. With such solid evidence, you will be able to convince them to terminate aid to the Kuomintang. You will achieve great personal honor by sparing your country further embarrassment at the hands of a team of foreign con artists."

"Let's not get ahead of ourselves. How did you get these documents?"

"We have our sources."

"Explain."

"Someone who worked for T.V. Soong. One of his top compradors. He blew the whistle on his boss."

"Why did he do that?"

"He saw the immorality of what he has done and repented."

"No kidding."

"He is a former missionary worker. His religious beliefs must have overpowered his less noble instincts."

"And he went to you?"

"I have a reputation for taking the side of justice."

"Where is this man?"

"He disappeared after he offered the documents to us. It isn't safe for him to stay in China. Soong will hunt him down."

"You paid him?"

"I offered compensation, but he turned it down. He was glad to have done the right thing."

"Out of the blue, someone showed up on your doorstep and gave you these confidential financial records belonging to the heads of government. Just like that."

"Yes."

"Sounds too good to be true."

"It's good and it's true."

"If you say so."

"Does it matter how we came to take possession of the records? As long as they are genuine."

"They will have to be authenticated."

"Come to Shansui with your experts."

"I don't have experts at my disposal."

"Use your judgment. Or trust me."

"Those are not validations I can present to the President of the United States. Give me a sample. I'll find a way to see if they're genuine."

"How much time will you need?"

"As much as necessary."

"Will you promise to take them to your president?"

"I cannot promise anything until I am certain of their authenticity."

"My word isn't good enough?"

"It isn't about whose word. It's about verifying evidence that may have significant consequences."

"Why haven't your State Department and your president taken steps to verify Chiang and Soong's claims that they are spending your foreign aid on defending China?"

Stilwell looked squarely at his guests. "Look, I am not unappreciative of your coming to me. I'm aware of the high regard you have for personal connection. As an officer of the United States Army, I have to follow rules and procedures, onerous as they may be to you."

"We are not asking you to circumvent anything. We are asking you to trust us."

"Can't trust without verification."

"That is not trust."

"That's the way it has to be."

A conspiratorial smile appeared on Han's face. "Of course, Colonel. How insensitive of me. This is our first meeting and we are asking for a huge favor. I understand your reservations. Let me try again. I'll show you how much I value our friendship, and then you'll see the wisdom of putting your trust in me. I heard that you bought real estate in Carmel, California, where you plan to retire. A house is being built on the land."

Stilwell blinked. "What does Carmel or my retirement have to do with this?"

"Plenty, Colonel. First, I can't see someone like you retiring. Retirement is not suitable for an energetic and accomplished man. If you won't be active on the battlefield, why not be active somewhere else? How about Capitol Hill? When you've finished your work in China, why not go into politics? As congressman, senator, or an appointed officer of the President."

"What is this? Daydreaming or fortune-telling?"

"Neither. I will make it happen. For you. You will use your experience to improve America's understanding of China. Too few of your legislators know much about this part of the world. If they were better informed, mistakes like the ones they are making with the Kuomintang could be avoided. With understanding and mutual respect, China and America could become allies. Bring the oldest and the youngest countries together. That will be the Stilwell legacy."

"You are going to get me a seat in the U.S. Congress?" Stilwell asked, amused.

"Have you heard about the Han fortune?"

"That mythical gold mine of yours. Sure."

"It's not mythical. It's more real than your Wall Street and bigger than Fort Knox. It can buy a lot of good will and open many doors. Seat in the Congress, piece of cake. A presidential appointment may require extra maneuvering, but it can be done."

"You are saying your gold can do all those things?"

"Yes, but don't get me wrong. I am not saying the United States of America is as corrupt as the Kuomintang. No, Colonel, your country is remarkable in upholding many principles. But who can say no to money, especially when it comes with the service of a capable man? I will not only get you the office of your choice, I will make sure you have the means to sustain a long and prosperous career in politics."

"How do you propose to do that?"

"Should our meeting today conclude in mutual satisfaction, an account will be set up at a bank in Switzerland, and a sum of American dollars—shall we say in the high seven figures?—will be deposited. It will bear no name. You will be the only person who can access the funds. You can spend the money to finance a political campaign, buy an island in the Pacific, or give to your children and grandchildren. No questions will be asked and no one will find out."

Stilwell remained impassive, his body motionless except for a steady heaving of his nostrils.

"A substantial reward, wouldn't you say? Just for speaking your mind. Others would say it's an excessive offer when exposing corruption is something an upright man like you would do on his own. But I like to show appreciation to friends who share my goal."

"We only met today. We are not friends."

"We do share a common purpose. Let's look at our partnership as an investment. A sound investment for China and America. When you are Senator Stilwell and I am the Prime Minister of China, there will be many occasions for us to work together. We can make great things happen."

Stilwell got up. It was then that Jong saw how angry he was. His face was white and his eyes blazing. He paced the room, his fist hitting his palm like a boxer before a fight. Han had not anticipated the reaction and was visibly stunned.

"Your land is in ruins. You are attacked from all sides. Your people are starving. Your children are dying before they learn to walk. And all you care about is how to become the next emperor. If things keep up, pretty soon you won't have a country."

"I never said I wanted to be emperor."

"You really think people wouldn't figure it out? Unique vision, parliamentary government, my ass." He looked unblinkingly at Han. "If you are honest about wanting to improve people's lives, start with your own backyard. *Stop poisoning the country with opium.* Your opium is doing more harm to China than the Japanese are. It's the number one killer."

"This is preposterous...."

"Don't tell me you don't know how many lives are being destroyed by opium? How many families? How many young girls are forced to prostitute themselves to support their fathers' addiction? How many young men are killed every day because, like you, they want to make a quick buck peddling the poisonous drug?"

"These are hard times. People do what they have to do to make a living."

"With opium, they don't make a living; they become the living dead. I wouldn't touch your gold even if I had to make my living cleaning toilets. Your gold is blood money. The bars that sit in your vault are not gold. They are the corpses of people who died on account of your greed."

"My gold can do a lot of good for China."

"Prove it. Use the gold to buy food for the hungry. Build hospitals, schools. Repair the damned roads. That's what China needs. Not another Forbidden City to house your new dynasty." Something savage came into Stilwell's eyes. He stopped in front of Han. Han shrank involuntarily. "Until you are willing to give up your opium business, you are no different than Chiang and all the other warlords who are robbing the country blind. Constitutional monarchy indeed. God, I am sick of you people."

Silence.

No one had ever been this blunt with Han.

Jong found himself reacting to Stilwell's outburst with a mixture of shock, admiration, and shame. Over the years he had watched Han traffic his opium, hoard his gold, and ruin lives. Not once had he had the courage to urge him to stop. Today, this cranky foreigner, this soldier from the youngest country in the world, this man who would rather clean toilets than accept Han's gold, had articulated what he should have said years ago.

Han's eyes were two smoldering points ready to burst into flames. "You listen to this very carefully. How I earn or spend my money is nobody's business but my own. How China should be governed is no other country's business but China's. I did not come here to be judged by you. I am here to offer a once-in-a-lifetime opportunity for you to make a name for yourself. If you were as smart as you have led the world to believe, you would be expressing profound gratitude that I have chosen you and not harangue me about my business affairs."

"Okay, I'm grateful. Thanks, but no thanks. Amen."

Jong stared at a caravan of ants transporting a bread-crumb, thinking about the coolies who had transported Han's gold to the vault. Han had killed them all. The five hundred men were few compared to the thousands who had died on account of his opium.

Han shook his head, expressing regret at the impasse. "Colonel Stilwell, you think you know best because at this point in history, your country happens to be the most influential power in the world. You believe you represent the future and other governments should imitate yours. Your way of governing is the model for mankind. You can do no wrong."

"I'm sure we are not perfect."

"No, you are not. But you don't doubt that you are on the right side of history. This excessive confidence makes it possible for people like Chiang and his wife to exploit you.

They wrap your president around their little finger by saying they are remaking China in America's image, and Mr. Roosevelt is thrilled and proud. Here I come and tell you something different. Not along the lines of Western-style democracy. Not one hundred percent America-inspired. Right away you conclude my ideas can't be any good. Are you familiar with the saying 'Principles are luxuries until people's basic needs are met'?"

Stilwell nodded.

"That is China's situation in a nutshell. How can people make sensible political choices when they don't know where the next meal is coming from or whether there will even be a meal? I want full control because it is the most efficient way to put China back on its feet. You know how urgent the situation is. There aren't years to nurture a new political system. There are months. Before you dismiss me, let me ask you this. Have you, your president, and your Congress taken the time to consider this reality: What works for the United States may not work for a country as old as China?"

Stilwell's face was reflective, somber. "Some of what you said is valid."

"I'm glad we've found common ground. Will you take the documents to your president?"

"After they have been authenticated. *And* you give up your opium."

Han was incredulous. "We are back to square one."

"We were never anywhere else."

"None of what we said made any difference?"

"The terms are non-negotiable, if that would answer your question."

"No maybe? No more time to consider?"

"No."

"Why?"

"I don't trust you."

Han's eyes narrowed. "Pardon me?"

"I don't trust you."

Another tense silence.

"That's it?"

"That's it."

"Fine," Han snapped. "We wasted a day. You are not the only one who can deliver a message to Washington. There are people in your country who will gladly take up the offer. Many."

"I'm sure you're right."

Han turned to Jong. "You will go to America. Take advantage of this freedom of the press America so prides herself on. Show the documents to the newspapers and the magazines. Let them tell the world that their government is being played for a fool." He glared at the *Time* cover on the wall. "Start with Soong May-ling's number one fan, Henry Luce." To Stilwell: "You lost your big chance, Colonel. It will never be offered to you again. As soon as I'm out of here, I'm done with you. You'd better pray to your god that our paths do not cross."

Jong was aware that he was left to make one more try. Alone with Stilwell, he felt he was the one who needed assurance, from the man who had spoken the words he hadn't had the courage to say. He had an overwhelming urge to unburden himself. To talk about the years he'd spent with Han, as confidant, co-conspirator, son. How heavy the roles had become. The compromises, the lies, and the abhorrent things he had done in the name of loyalty. The public man who was growing more estranged from the private one. How weary he was. And disgusted. He wished he could have the American's friendship. Even for one day. It would be the beginning of the road back.

"I am sorry," Jong said.

"So am I, in a way."

"I hope you will reconsider. You are here, Colonel, you see things firsthand. The problems are overwhelming. We can't solve them alone; no one can. The General is sincere about needing your help. When you are ready, I can send a plane for you, or I can deliver the papers in person. There must be a way for us to work this out."

"I do my best for China. As an officer of the U.S. Army. That's the way it has to be."

"All we ask is that you take a look at the papers, and then decide."

"I don't see how I can change my mind." Stilwell gave a tug at his eyeglasses. "Those financial records—they're probably genuine. I am aware of the rampant corruption in the Kuomintang. But I cannot, nor do I want to, be Han's spokesman, unless he is willing to give up his opium. And we both know it will never happen."

Jong was quiet.

"Han wants you to go to Luce. I fully support it. It won't be easy to convince him. The man is a tyrant, with an ego as big as America. He and T.V. Soong are thick as thieves. He wouldn't want to admit he has been betting on the wrong side. But he may wise up if the evidence is overwhelming and he wants his magazine to break the story. Who knows? If you can pull it off with *Time*, it would be better than anything I could do." Stilwell added without rancor, "There was no need to offer me anything. It was absurd. You asked my help to put an end to corruption, and then expected me to accept a bribe."

"The General made some assumptions before we came. They were based on practices he is accustomed to. Not on what we know about you." Jong added, "He is not sensitive to the contradiction."

"But you are."

Jong nodded.

"This can't be the first time you've witnessed the contradiction."

"No."

"Does he always leave you behind to make the final pitch?"

"Yes."

"Do you always succeed?"

"No. Not always."

"But you do your best for him."

"Yes."

A pause. "It must be hard."

Jong looked away. "I can't say that. I have been lucky, very lucky."

"Luck can be a double-edged sword," Stilwell said. "I heard your father was American."

"A missionary from Boston. That's what some people said. It seems to be a plausible story." He returned his gaze to Stilwell. "It must be a different world out there. In America."

"It's a young country. Big-hearted, a little naïve. On the whole we're okay. You've never been there?"

"No."

"You'll be going there soon."

"Yes."

"Maybe you'll like it there."

Their eyes met. Jong saw something of himself in the American. Something he had not revealed to anyone. He wished he could hold on to the moment.

Stilwell glanced at the door. "He is like a father to you, isn't he?"

"Yes."

"A good father?"

"The best any orphan could wish for."

"You must love him."

"Yes."

"You are going to help him succeed?"

"It's my job."

"Do you believe in him? And the things he said about bringing back the past?"

Jong didn't answer.

"It's hard to do your job if you don't believe in what you're trying to achieve. But you must know that already."

"He counts on me. He has no one. I don't have a choice."

"You do. It will be the toughest choice you ever make, but you will make it." Stilwell put his hand on Jong's arm like an old friend. "Cheer up. Right or wrong, life goes on. I hope he won't blame you for my stubbornness."

They walked to the door.

"Good-bye, Mr. Lin. Maybe we'll see each other again. Maybe we won't. I hope things work out for you."

23

Lillie sat in the back seat of the car parked a few yards from the entrance of the bank, watching from behind dark glasses. Promptly at 5:30 p.m., Chiu walked out of the building. The chauffeur opened the door and he climbed into the black Vauxhall.

She tapped the driver's shoulder. "Go."

The Vauxhall headed east. It was rush hour. The streets were congested, cars jostling with buses and rickshaws. At a light, Lillie's car pulled alongside Chiu's. She caught a glimpse of the banker's ruby cufflinks and the racing page he was reading. They were driving away from the Central District. High-rises became scarce. Crowds thinned out. The Vauxhall turned south, heading to Happy Valley, a residential district built around racetracks. The car drove past the new Royal Cricket Club and up Broadwood Heights to Chiu's house.

He lived on the top-floor of an Edwardian townhouse with two amahs, according to the private investigator, a former sergeant in the Hong Kong Royal Police called Luo. Lillie had hired him to look into Chiu's life. The property was paid for in full and with the title in the wife's name. No doubt who's boss in the relationship; the missus was a Soong. Chiu wouldn't be where he was without help from her relatives. The family never let him forget his humble origins; they treated him like help. After six years, the marriage soured. The couple began to lead separate lives. Chiu moved to his own apartment in Shanghai. Mrs. Chiu and the children stayed in her family's mansion. When the bank in Hong Kong was looking for a new chief executive, he volunteered.

The banker seemed to find the bachelor life more suited to his temperament.

His flat had four bedrooms with an unobstructed view of the racecourse. On Saturday afternoons he watched the races from his balcony, binoculars and notepad in hand. Disciplined fellow, the investigator had observed; never placed a bet, not even on his own horses. They were part of his personal investment portfolio, growing fast as he gained influence as a major player in the Colony's shady world. He owned eight horses, a stable to house them, and three off-site betting stations that took in thousands every week. Not a cent went to the joint account with his wife or Inland Revenue.

"Sounds like our typical wheeler-dealer living the high life," Lillie had remarked.

"Wheeler-dealer extraordinaire. But there is more to this one," Luo had concluded solemnly. "Complicated man, our Mr. Chiu is. Lives two lives. I don't mean the usual romping in cathouses after a day at the office. The man has a very strange hobby."

The Vauxhall stopped at a terrace of red brick townhouses set back from the street. White curtains framed the windows. Brass knockers shone on black doors. The lawns were close-cropped, the borders marked by rows of pink and white impatiens. English schoolchildren were playing hopscotch on the pavement; a Chinese amah looked on. Chiu got out of the car, walked around the children, and headed to the gated garden. The Vauxhall drove away.

"Go to the back," Lillie said to the driver.

It was a private road for the townhouse residents. Lillie's car stopped behind the red column of a Royal Mail drop. She watched Chiu reappear from the side door next to his garage, minus attaché case and newspaper. A quick look before he sprinted away, so swiftly that had Lillie not been warned, she would have missed the figure ducking into a waiting taxi parked at the mouth of the road. He never used his car for his evening excursions, Luo had reported. The chauffeur was on the company payroll and that automatically cast him in the role of informant for his wife. The banker was paranoid like a Russian. He thought the flies were spying on him.

Chiu's taxi followed the loop of the racecourse, going east again. At the open-air market by the tram depot, it stopped in front of a bean curd shop. Chiu owns the building, Luo had said. The shop was a front. It didn't sell enough merchandise to pay the electric bills. The real business was in the back and it was a gambler's dream. A full-service mini-casino offering mah-jongg, blackjack, fan-tan, and a weekly lottery. The clientele was as diverse as the neighborhood: housewives, call girls, doctors from Blue Pool Road. The police looked the other way because they were on the take. Fortunate for Mr. Chiu, most of them like to gamble and re-deposit the money back into the house.

Lillie told the driver to park a few spaces behind Chiu's taxi. She got out. Checking numbers like someone looking for an address, she slowed down when she approached the shop. It was lit by a single fluorescent tube. One end blinked sporadically, producing a macabre effect on the pathetic showroom. A few dozen salted eggs in rattan baskets, fermented bean curd in earthen pots, jars of rice wine. They could have been there for ages. The containers were covered with a thick film of dust. The labels had faded. A radio was blasting a Cantonese opera at full volume. An old man sat at the cash register, eyeglasses on his nose, reading a thick novel.

Chiu reappeared from behind a column of wooden crates. Inspection of the premises must have been satisfactory, he was all smiles. He stopped at the cash register. Without a word, the man took out a fat cylinder of bills tied with a rubber band and handed to Chiu. Chiu peeled off a few and handed to the man. He accepted them with a nod and slipped them between the pages of the novel.

The taxi continued eastward. The streets narrowed as they left posh Happy Valley for middle-class Causeway Bay. The sidewalks were more crowded, fewer trees. Drab apartment blocks replaced terrace houses. Flags of laundry fluttered from bamboo poles hanging over balconies. The taxi rounded a corner and pulled up to a shop. A bilingual sign over the door offered Oriental antiques with a special-ization in Ching Dynasty relics. Closed for the day.

The taxi meter flag stayed up while Chiu headed to the shop. He knocked. A hand unlocked the door for Chiu.

"Mr. Chiu is a special customer, very generous. He gives the shopkeeper a nice bonus when he finds something rare," Luo had said. "Miss Lillie, you would never guess what he buys there."

"Antiques to launder his illegal income?"

"Antiques? Marginal. Chiu may be the only collector of his kind. He is set to own every pattern, every size that existed. The more decrepit the more desirable. His collection fills up a room in his flat, floor to ceiling, each pre-served in its own hand-carved pinewood coffin."

"Pretty revolting."

"Wait till you hear what he does with them."

"Do I have to?"

"If you want to understand the man."

"Obviously he has a foot fetish. I've seen a few of them in Shanghai."

"People like that get their fix from women, women who are alive. Our Mr. Chiu is different."

"Oh dear."

"Every other evening, he locks himself in the room, lights a circle of red candles and puts a stack of Shanghai love songs on the gramophone. He picks out a pair from the collection and puts it on the center of the mattress. Then he strips himself naked. He climbs on top of the mat-tress and positions himself…"

"I get the picture. But if he locks the room, how can the amahs know what he does?"

"You know amahs; you can't keep anything from them."

Fifteen minutes later Chiu was out of the shop, package in hand, face brimming like he was making off with the Mona Lisa. As the car drove past the antiques shop, Lillie caught sight of a display window filled with opium paraphernalia. A pale man with slick black hair watched behind the counter.

What is it with fetishists? Fulfillment of some dark, unrequited yearning? Fascination for the outlandish? Or just plain crazy? She had seen men neglect pretty young wives to copulate with senile women; men who couldn't achieve potency unless being subjected to unspeakable abuse. But sexual congress with the worn shoes of bound-footed concubines dead more than a century, she admitted, had to be the most bizarre.

At the midsection of King's Road in North Point, Chiu's taxi turned to the waterfront. Its destination was a three-story building in the middle of a narrow street; the lots around it were vacant. A fluorescent sign blazed in English and Chinese: Mayflower Restaurant and Ballroom. On one side of the glass double door, a book-size plaque announced: *Hourly rental rooms available. Inquire inside.*

She placed the business two notches below the Paramount for its out-of-the-way location.

Chiu paid the taxi. It drove away.

An Indian bellboy greeted Chiu with a bow reserved for the best customers. Chiu pulled down his hat and sidled in. Through the glass door Lillie watched him hand the parcel to the maître d'. He accepted it with both hands and carried to the storeroom behind the reception desk. By the movements she could tell it was something they did habitually. Chiu pushed the second double door of opaque glass and disappeared into the dark interior.

"Private party tonight. Guests must have invitation to enter," the bellboy said, barring her way.

"I'm not here for the party." She stuffed a wad of bills in his gloved hand. "I want information. Can you help?"

"I'll try, ma'am."

"How long have you worked here?"

"Since the place opened."

"You should be able to answer my questions. Is the owner from Fukien?"

"Whole family from Fukien."

She fired off more queries about the owner and confirmed Luo's report. Seafood merchant and family had fled to Hong Kong. Wife wanted to get far away from the Japanese—California was the destination and Hong Kong the first stop. They hoped to make a quick fortune to launch their new life in America; hence a bordello. They were conventional retailers and they had little clue how to run a pleasure parlor. Business had not met expectations. They could pay the bills, but there was little profit for their big dreams.

"The man who just went in. Do you know him?"

"That's Mr. Chiu. Successful banker and political celebrity." He wiggled a finger. "Not wise to talk about important men like him."

"Good that you are discreet. You won't tell anyone about this conversation, understand?"

He nodded.

"Does he come often?"

"Wednesdays and Fridays. Rain or shine. Punctual man. You can set your watch by his arrival time."

"Stays the night?"

"No."

"Never?"

"Never."

"What time does he leave?"

"Two a.m. the latest."

"What kind of girls does he like?"

"Pretty, young, curvy."

"Does he have a favorite?"

"Mr. Chiu likes variety."

"So most of the girls know him."

He nodded.

"What do they think of him?"

"They don't like him. He is moody and unpredictable. One minute he's jolly, the next he turns violent because the girl doesn't look at him when he talks. The worst part is the games."

"Tell me about the games."

"I don't know much. The girls said his yang is not efficient. Needs tricks to get started. Nasty tricks. They don't like to take part, but they cannot say no. His cousin is a big shot in China. Everyone is afraid of him."

"Does he use drugs? Opium? Heroin?"

"Brandy after dinner, that's all. The girls say what he does in bed is worse than drugs."

"Good tipper?"

He flipped his palm. "So so."

"Does he show up alone?"

"Always."

"No bodyguards?"

"No. I would have noticed."

"Friends?"

"No."

"Someone like him must have many friends."

"He doesn't bring them here."

"He doesn't want his friends to know."

"He calls himself Mr. Lee. We know who he is, of course, but we go along."

"How does he pay?"

"The owner lets him use the services for free."

"Why?"

"He is influential with police and gangsters. Wise to be on his good side."

"Of course."

"Something else you'll also want to know, but you didn't hear from me."

Lillie nodded.

"A month ago, a girl disappeared after spending an evening with Mr. Chiu. She left all her stuff behind, even some valuable things. So either she must have gone in a big hurry or she was.... We still don't know what happened."

"Go on."

"Some of us thought Mr. Chiu must have been playing one of his games and something went very wrong. The girl was scared and she ran away. But if that's what happened, she would have come back for her things. It'd be easy for her to show up on the nights he isn't here."

"You never saw her again?"

"No one did. It's like he performed a magic trick and made her disappear."

"Did anyone ask Mr. Chiu what happened to the girl?"

"We didn't dare."

"No one contacted the police?"

"The owners didn't want police on the premises. Maybe they knew more than they were willing to say. The girls are praying Mr. Chiu will find another house to patronize, but he seems to like it here."

Lillie stepped back for another look at the ballroom. Hope surged. She'd found the link to T.V. Soong, the man who held the answer to Victor's fate. She did a quick calculation in her head. Real estate prices were on the rise, but she could more than afford to buy the building and the business. Ten gold peaches should convince the owners to sell. Tomorrow she would retrieve them from the safe deposit box, take them to the jewelry repair shop on Temple Street and have Han's seals removed. The owner was Portuguese and couldn't read Chinese. She would sell them one at a time to different goldsmiths. Then she would retain a solicitor to represent her in making the offer for the Mayflower. She knew the business, the kind of men who patronized these places, how to motivate the girls, and what it took to be a good boss. She could make a go of it. Turn the Mayflower into her Paramount. Why not? It was likely she and Pierre would have to stay in Hong Kong for a while. It would make sense to invest some of the gold.

And twice a week she would spy on the most intimate aspect of Mr. Chiu's many-sided life. She expected to uncover more titillating details. As number one hostess at Shanghai's number one club, she had learned that there was nothing like firsthand knowledge of a man's bedroom habits to bring him down.

24

A cool spray woke Han. He opened his eyes to a sky streaked with the orange rays of the evening sun. How long have I been sleeping? An hour? Two? He leaned over the edge of the boat, scooped water from the river and splashed it on his face, feeling refreshed. The river was a curvy band of rusty gold. In the distance, the forest seemed on fire. The hour before nightfall, his favorite time of the day.

What time was it in America? It had been three days since Jong left for New York. By now he would have contacted *Time* and showed them Soong's financial records. He would be negotiating the terms for publication. Han had no doubt that Jong would get his way. He was a natural when it came to handling foreigners. Didn't matter that he had never lived outside China, he understood them instinctively and in turn they treated him like one of their own. Han could see him talking to the Americans with the right mix of charm, firmness, and candor, making them feel they were with a friend. He would guide them along and make sure they do what he wanted. It wouldn't be long before people read about the Kuomintang's crimes. The headlines would stun the world: China's first family are thieves and crooks. Things would move fast. America would stop the flow of cash into China—they would have to, the public would be clamoring and Congress would have to act. Soong would be fired from the Ministry—more likely, the arrogant bastard would resign, feigning outrage at being wrongly accused while scrambling to hide his ill-gotten gains. Chiang would probably form a provisional government to buy himself time. Without American support, he would have no resources, no clout, no allies. It wouldn't be long before he had to step down in disgrace. Even if Soong and Chiang managed to hang on to power, the damage would have been done. Things would never be the same for them. They would lose authority at home and credibility abroad. The Party top brass would seize the opportunity to jockey for control. They would fight among themselves the way they always did, frantic, haphazard, without planning. Mao would rally his guerilla soldiers and try to get into the game. None would go far. None would be as prepared as he.

The other part of his Grand Strategy was also on schedule. Yesterday the long-awaited message had arrived from Klaus Ganz, the German arms dealer in Tsingtao, who had returned from five days of tough negotiations in Berlin. The escalating conflicts in Europe were speeding things up, the message had said. Germany was pushing the research full-throttle. Scientists were working round the clock. A breakthrough was expected any day. Ganz had obtained the assurance that Han would be first in line to procure this new invention. It could be a matter of weeks.

If things went as planned, the country would be his next year.

If things went as planned.

What if they didn't?

What if something went awry? A mistake by a foot soldier. An obstruction from an overlooked rival. Natural disaster. His own miscalculation. One of the many innocuous incidents littered throughout history that changed the trajectory of events. What if any one of those occurrences happened in the course of his Grand Strategy? Should he have a fallback plan?

A fallback plan would mean he considered failure—a state of mind Han had avoided. He had kept his focus, wouldn't let himself question the certainty of his success. He believed supreme self-confidence was a requisite of the mandate—the gods wouldn't choose a ruler who didn't have complete faith in himself. Even if the gods didn't come through, how could the owner of the world's largest gold reserve not get what he wanted?

The sun dropped below the horizon. In a wink, the golden universe became a limbo of half darkness. Shapes lost their edge. The river became an inky ribbon of liquid; the mountains turned into crouching monsters. The boat seemed to be sailing toward an immense hollow. Icy currents swept from the dark water, chilling his bones.

He shivered.

Strange that it gets this cold in Shansui, Han thought. Last night it had been warm enough to bathe naked in the river. Half drunk, he had emulated the poet Li Po, trying to scoop the moon out of the water... He felt light in the head. It had to be the bottle of rice wine before the nap. He had drunk the last drop without food. A cup of hot tea would be good. He raised his hand halfway when he realized he couldn't tell where to look. His eyes wouldn't focus. He was back to a half-finished dream. The world around him contorted and blurred out. Images poured in. Scenes of past battles. Faces of men he had killed. He smelled the stench of the corpses, the metallic odor of spilled blood. He gripped the edge of the boat, forcing his mind on tangible things. Jong in America. The upcoming trip to Tsingtao. His gold, his lovely treasure...

It came to him, clear as a message written on the sky, that he would not grow old. That his life, like the scenery around him, would burst into momentary brilliance, and then fade away...

"Row, row, row the boat to Grandma's house, and Grandma will keep us warm, Grandma will make rice sweet as lotus seeds, and let us sleep in her bed soft as snow, Row, row, row. To Grandma's house we go, to Grandma's house we go..."

What was it? A voice from his childhood?

Someone was singing. Close by. He heard every word of the familiar song. He opened his eyes and looked for the source.

Near the shore. A moving shadow. Barely visible in the last rays of the day.

A lithe figure.

A girl.

She was learning to swim, singing to herself as she tried to master the skill of staying afloat. Her movements were stiff and uncoordinated. She managed a couple of strokes at a time. When she sank, she picked herself up, shook off the water and tried again, letting out peals of laughter. They gilded the air like an early nightingale.

The world came back to life.

The chill had dissipated, along with the monsters of the night. The river was calm as a pool. Threads of pale cirrus touched the heavens. The earth was reveling in the first beams of the moon.

He waved a guard over. "The girl on the beach. Who is she?"

"Mrs. Li's daughter, General."

Su-chen's daughter.

When was the last time he'd seen her? It must have been when he had visited Henry in Nanking. A couple of years ago. He couldn't recall the face exactly. But he remembered its prettiness. Yes, very pretty. Why hadn't she been presented to him when she arrived in Shansui, and the months following? It had to be Su-chen's doing. She must have gone to great lengths to keep her out of his sight. She didn't want him to set eyes on her beautiful daughter.

"Do any of you know why she is here?"

"Miss Li likes the outdoors."

"Is she always alone?"

"No, General. A maid usually keeps her company, or Mr. Lin."

"Bring her on board."

A dinghy was lowered over the side of the boat. A guard jumped in and rowed toward the shore. The girl heard the noise and turned to the boat. She stopped swimming, standing in the shallows; the waves were beating against her calves. A lone mermaid on the beach looking out to sea.

Han waved.

She tilted her head at an angle and waved back.

In the burnished light she was breathtakingly beautiful, taller than Han had remembered. The dark liquid eyes and the perfect mouth were familiar, yet more enticing set in the freshness of youth. A young Su-chen. An untouched Su-chen. In the soaked clothes she was more naked than dressed. She could use something to cover her. But he liked her this way. He could make out the hollow between the swell of her breasts, the nipples like two tiny buds. He wanted to put his arms around her fragile waist, locking her to him.

"So sorry to have caused you trouble, General. I shouldn't have stayed out so late," she said politely.

"No trouble at all. I thought you might be cold; it's warmer on the boat. What is your name?"

"Yunna."

"*Maid of perfection*, yes, I remember," Han muttered. "How old are you, Yunna?"

"Seventeen this autumn. I was born on the fifteenth day of the eighth moon."

"Mid-Autumn Festival. The night of the brightest moon."

"The perfect moon."

"You like to swim?"

"I don't know how. I want to learn."

"On your own?"

"It's the best way to learn anything. For me."

"You were by yourself. In the dark. You were not afraid?"

"What was there to be afraid?"

"No. There is no need to be afraid, not around here. But it must have been lonely."

"Being alone is not the same as being lonely."

"But it would have been nice to have some company."

"The right kind of company; otherwise I prefer to be alone."

Han smiled. "You are your father's daughter."

"I am."

A flicker crossed her face. His heart knocked.

"You look like your mother."

"I am not like my mother, General."

"You are younger and prettier," he said quickly; he didn't want to talk about Su-chen. "And you have a sweet voice. How do you know the song?"

"I learned it from a maid."

"It was my favorite song. I used to sing it when I was a little boy. Maybe you'll sing for me some time."

"If you want me to."

She was standing by the oil lamp. Its glow threw her body into relief. The outline of her camisole under the tunic, the delicate pink of her skin and, disconcertingly, the hint of the shadowed triangle between her legs.

"You are very beautiful," he said hoarsely, returning his gaze to her face.

A breeze frothed her fringes, caressing her eyebrows. His throat was dry. His yang was rising. What magic it would be if he were inside her...

As though responding to his thoughts, she blushed.

He wanted to put her at ease. "I came to your house in Nanking. That must have been two years ago. Do you remember?"

"It was summer. You planned to stay for five days, but you left after two days for a meeting in Shanghai."

"You have an excellent memory."

"Your visit was an important occasion to us."

"I enjoyed myself thoroughly. You were a child then; now you are a young woman."

"Much has happened since."

He took her hand—it was soft and cold like a bird—and led her to sit down with him. "You like Shansui?"

She gave a small nod.

"Do you feel this is your home now?"

"I am comfortable, General."

"Comfortable. I see. But it's not home?"

"No."

"Shansui is not a big city like Nanking. You need time to get used to the change."

"I don't think it's a question of time, General."

"No? What is it a question of?"

"I have the use of nice things. But nothing here is mine."

"You don't like that?"

"Would you?"

"No, I wouldn't. You speak plainly; I like that." A pause. "That's the difference between you and your father. He was tactful, always mindful of my feelings. Maybe it was his way of showing respect, but I wished he had let me know what was going on his mind, good or bad. It makes things simple—if what we think and say are the same... I suppose it couldn't be helped. Your father was a private man."

"My father is dead," she said with unexpected force and extracted her hand from his grasp.

"Sometimes it slips my mind that he is not here anymore. You miss him?"

"Yes, I miss my father."

"So do I. There isn't a day goes by that I don't think of Henry."

"He was murdered."

"By unscrupulous men. Bad times we live in. Terrible."

She faced Han. "Who killed him? Who gave the order? Why?"

"I wish we knew."

"Do you, General?"

"My men have been looking for the killer, trying to find out what happened."

"But all these months. Nothing."

"Rumors have been going around that top Kuomintang officials were involved. They may be just rumors, or there may be some truth to them. In the current political climate, it wouldn't be easy to sort them out. It seems the Party is getting nervous that things might get out of hand. They've ordered a blackout. No more searching for evidence. No more interviewing witnesses. Nanking is not under my purview. My men's hands are tied."

"Top Kuomintang officials. Do you mean my mother's relatives? Did they have my father killed?"

"It could be them. It could the triads acting on someone's orders. It could be rumors started by a rival to implicate your relatives."

"My father was a scholar. What had he done? Why did anyone want him dead?"

"He was a member of Chiang's cabinet. Maybe he got in someone's way."

"But he was family."

"It puzzles me too, but I don't have the answer."

"But you are an important man in the Party."

"I have membership and a title, but I am really an outsider."

"You don't mind?"

"I don't need to belong to a party, any party."

"You make your own rules?"

"Yes."

"No one can stop you from doing what you want to do."

"That's right."

"May I speak frankly?"

"Of course."

"The investigation may be blocked, but there must be a way around it." She added, "If you can't find out who killed my father, no one can."

"It'll need time. The situation is complicated."

"Political situations are always complicated. Father was devoted to you."

"The feeling was mutual."

"Was it, General?"

"Should there be any doubt?" he said, taking her hand again; he craved the touch of her soft cool skin. "Your father was my best friend. We lived apart, but I always felt our closeness." A fond smile turned sad. "You can doubt anything else about me, Yunna, but never doubt my affection for your father. I promise I will find his killer."

"Will you?"

"You didn't think I would let the killer get away, did you? Someone who murdered my best friend and hurt his family. That's no different than hurting me." Both hands grasped hers. "I will do everything I can to solve his murder. Trust me."

"Everything?"

"We won't stop until we find out."

He felt a release in her, a letting go of doubts and a renewal of hope. It was clear how much her father meant to her and how long she had been waiting for this assurance from him.

"One thing has been haunting me: If I had asked Henry to move here sooner, he would be alive."

"You asked Father to move here?"

"I wanted him here. To share my work and my life. Your father gave me a lot of valuable counsel over the years. I thought it was time for him to have an official position. It would have been a personal wish coming true, having my best friend close by."

"And we were coming with him?"

"Yes. He and his family would live inside my compound. My work would be his work. His family would be my family. We would share everything." The moment was right. He played his customary seduction card. "In spite of my power and my wealth, Yunna, I am a lonely man. There are few people I can trust. Your father was one. What happened in Nanking ruined my hopes. I lost more than a friend. I lost a part of my future."

"I didn't know."

"My offer got there the day before the disaster. There wouldn't have been time to leave. It's not important now. We can't torment ourselves speculating what might have been."

"Did Mother know about your offer?"

"Your father must have told her."

"Did she want to move here?"

"She must have. She had someone contact me when you were in Shanghai and ask for my help."

"Does she talk about Nanking?"

"Sometimes."

"Does she talk about my father? When she does, is she sad or is she relieved? Does she want to share her future with you, now that her husband is dead and she is free to conduct her life as she pleases? Do you think of my father where my mother is concerned? Do you, General?"

He didn't like the accusing tone. No woman had ever spoken to him this way. But he sensed her pain, so deep that he knew it had been consuming her. To his own surprise, he was ashamed to have been the cause.

"You are sharing my present. And my future. Both of you."

"Please do not speak about my mother and me in the same breath."

"That's an unusual thing to say."

She looked away.

"What is it? Tell me."

"I know what she has done. With you."

"What did she tell you?"

"She didn't tell me anything. My mother and I seldom share confidences. We don't get along very well. It was easier when Father was around. He understood me and he knew how to handle her." She added unhappily, "Everyone in the Villa knows. I was the last to find out."

"How did you find out?"

She didn't reply.

"Someone told you?"

She shook her head.

"I didn't set out to hide anything from you. I saw no point in telling you, a child…"

"I am not a child."

"You are right, you are not a child," Han said calmly. "You are a young woman, Yunna, so I'll treat you as one and tell you the truth though it may be difficult to accept. When I saw how devastated your mother was, my heart went out to her. She reminded me of my attachment to Henry. My loss. I wanted to comfort her. On Henry's behalf. Not a sensible role to take on; I see that now. How could I replace your father?"

"How could anyone?"

"Indeed. At the time it seemed an expedient way to heal our wounds, together, two people who shared a common love." He sighed. "In despair one can be driven to do things one might regret afterward. It was one of the darkest hours in my life when your father died. My heart was ripped apart. I wasn't acting with reason. I can only describe what happened between me and your mother as an aberration. At least it was for me."

"*Was?*"

"Yes, *was*."

"I don't believe she feels the same way."

"That would be unfortunate."

"Does it matter to you how she feels?"

"To my conscience. Not to my heart."

Calmer, she asked, "You said you were regretful?"

"Deeply. Especially now, when I see how much it hurts you."

"Me?"

"Yes, you. Yunna."

"Because I am your best friend's daughter?"

"Because you are you. Because I want to."

He took her in his arms. She was hesitant, shy, yet thrilled. He could see the tiny tremors of her eyelashes. He placed his palm on her hair, caressing lightly until she grew comfortable with his touch. He drew her gently to him and she rested her head on his chest, naturally, trustingly, as a child with her uncle, a girl with her mentor. He felt her longing, her need for an anchor. I've crossed the threshold and I've won her trust, he thought and decided that his version must be all she would know about his liaison with Su-chen.

"I will make it up to you," he said. "For your pain and your loss."

"It won't be possible to replace what was lost."

"I can do things few men dare to dream."

He felt her warm breath on his throat and it drove him wild. He could barely control his own breathing. He could take her now. They were in his boat; she was in his space. And she was in awe of him. The light in her eyes when she stepped onto the boat had betrayed enough. It crossed his mind that their meeting might not have been accidental. The childhood song. The spot on the beach where she would be seen from the boat. Her readiness to speak her thoughts. It wouldn't surprise him if she had planned the encounter. She was not a simple girl; she had her father's manipulative intelligence. What had prompted her to orchestrate the evening? Was solving her father's murder the only thing she wanted from him? He decided he didn't care if there was a hidden agenda. The thought that she had deliberately set out to meet him was pleasing enough. Whatever she wanted, he would give her. Why wouldn't he? She would be his. All of her. Remarkable how easy it had been to win her over with the confession of his liaison with her mother. A young girl is gullible, even a smart one. A cup of warm wine, compliments about her looks, a few caresses at the right places and she would be his.

He wouldn't do that. Not yet.

He wrapped a blanket around her shoulders, then lifted her chin with his finger. In her eyes he saw his own, filled with an unfamiliar tenderness. He was entering a sublime place, and he was supremely happy. It became certain the role she would play in his life.

"Come to my chamber tonight, Yunna. There is something I want to show you."

25

"I've heard of General Han, though I can't remember if I met him. It was a quick trip and we had a full agenda. Hard to keep track of everyone we met. But it was quite enjoyable. I loved the monuments. And the people of course," the American said, crossing his legs. "What can I do for you, Mr. Lin?"

The American was David Moore, special assistant to Henry Luce, publisher of *Time*. Moore was a lanky man with salt and pepper hair, sallow cheeks. His hands were too large to fit anywhere; he shifted them restlessly. His clothes were well made, but a trace ill-fitting. He reminded Jong of a mid-rank British colonial officer, with the same haughty nonchalance typical of the lower echelon of the ruling class. Youngest in Luce's executive team and the only name that did not appear on Soong May-ling's guest lists. Jong picked him for the initial contact.

After checking into the Waldorf-Astoria, Jong had invited him for a meeting in the suite.

"We want to take the Sino-American relationship to the next level," Jong replied, offering a box of Cuban cigars.

Moore selected one and sniffed. "I'm all ears."

"You may not like what I'm going to say, but do be reminded that we have the best of intentions for both countries."

"Okay."

"*Time* has been promoting a positive image of the Generalissimo and his wife. An expertly crafted image that reflects more of Mr. Luce's friendship than the couple's accomplishments. Articles in your magazine read like fan mail. There's something in every issue. That's powerful advertising, and you've gotten results. Public opinion of China's first couple has grown favorable and it exerts influence on policy decisions in Washington. Your president has been giving generous sums of money to Chiang's government, in foreign aid and in loans."

Moore clicked the lighter, lit the cigar, and took a puff. "I am sure Mr. Luce would be happy to take credit for playing a role in shaping America's China policy. Part of his interest stems from friendship, sure, but his concerns go beyond a small group of people. He supports the Kuomintang because he believes they are the hope for a free China. A free China will be good for America and for the world. The American people agree with him."

"Mr. Luce is the Kuomintang's most effective lobbyist."

"If that's your way of acknowledging his contribution to bringing democracy to China, I'm sure he wouldn't mind. The Chinese people certainly deserve it. Your people have had such a rough time for so long. Poverty and your feudal way of life were causes of the misery, but some of the things my fellow Westerners did to you, I have to admit, were downright shameful."

"Lofty goals aside, you are journalists. Your primary responsibility is to report events as they happen and how they happen, objectively. Not to advance the agenda of a few individuals."

"Not a few individuals. The whole country. Democracy for China, that's what we advocate."

"There is a line between journalism and propaganda. With the Kuomintang, *Time* has crossed the line. Your reporting on China has been selective. Facts have been overlooked or skewed to protect Chiang."

Another puff. Moore said unhurriedly, "What kind of facts have we overlooked or skewed?"

"Let's focus on the centerpiece of the Sino-American relationship. The millions you've sent to the Chinese treasury. Has anyone checked to see whether the money has been spent on the intended purposes?

"Someone might have checked. I wouldn't know."

"If someone had checked, he would have gotten the answer easily. Most of the funds haven't been spent. In fact, they are sitting right here, in personal accounts owned by the Kuomintang leadership. They haven't tried very hard to hide the windfall. As soon as American aid started to flow into China, Mr. Soong's personal fortune realized a meteoric rise. He is now one of the richest men in the world. Has anyone questioned how the son of a missionary could amass such staggering wealth in such a short time?

"This is a grave accusation. You are alleging criminal activities committed by a head of state and his minister. I take it you are *not* speaking as an officer of the Kuomintang, and you are aware of the implications of what you've said?"

"Yes to both statements."

Moore fixed his gaze on the cigar. "You didn't travel halfway around the world to talk about public opinion and someone's personal fortune. What do you want from us?"

"We want you to expose the corruption."

"Assuming what you said about diverting the aid to personal accounts is true, we can't just walk into banks and demand to see the records. We are not law enforcement."

"I'm sure you could find a way if you wanted to. But to make things easy, I've brought the evidence."

"What kind of evidence?"

"Papers, financial records. T.V. Soong's. Not only bank statements but documents pertaining to his many investments, deeds, incorporation papers, stocks, bonds. Mr. Soong doesn't seem to have much faith in his own country; he has used the funds to acquire assets outside China. Buildings in New York. Land in California. Properties in Europe. Mines in Africa… You get the picture."

"How did you obtain these papers?"

"We don't disclose our sources."

"Originals?"

"Yes."

"Let me see."

Jong reached into the briefcase, pulled out some of the files Victor had brought to Shansui, and arranged them on the coffee table.

"This is a sample of the documents in our possession. The complete file has records going back five years."

Moore picked up the file on top. He held it by the corner as if waiting for the paper to dry before he flipped the cover.

Jong got up and ambled to the window. A sunny day on Park Avenue. The high-rises looked like fancy beehives; the windows shimmered with reflections of a late afternoon sky, behind them glimpses of well appointed rooms. They said the rich in New York live on Park Avenue. How rich would be considered rich in American terms? What was the price of an apartment? Fifty gold bars? A hundred? He had no idea. His life had been as insular as Han's. When he left Han's golden cocoon, he would have to learn how the rest of the world lived, starting with the basics, like someone released from a long prison sentence.

He gave the American fifteen minutes.

Moore's face was filled with alarm. "Some of these are in Chinese. I'll need a translator. How long can I keep them?"

"I'll get a translator. You can take as much time as you need, but nothing leaves this suite."

"I have to read them here?"

"General Han's instructions."

"I will need more than a day."

"Take as long as you need. You can use one of the rooms here."

"Room at the Waldorf—that's an unexpected perk," Moore said unhappily. "I may want them photographed."

"A photographer will be at your disposal."

"One thing must be clear. Am I the only journalist who is being given this information?"

"There is a saying in China: 'Let the person who tethered the bell be the one to let it ring again.' We want *Time* to expose the crimes of the Kuomintang. The first-refusal rights are yours."

"I am not in a position to make promises. Whatever happens next will need Mr. Luce's approval."

"We expect that. We also expect you will convince Mr. Luce to publish your findings."

"I'll try."

"If you can't convince him, I'll take them to another publisher."

"I said I'll try."

Jong handed him a package wrapped in brown paper. "Greetings from General Han."

"What is this?"

"A present."

"Heavy."

"Open it."

Moore was hesitant at first, as if the package might be a prank. After a glimpse of the contents, he tore away the wrapping. It was a replica of the Empire State Building the size of a baseball bat. Solid gold.

"Is this real?"

"The purest grade."

"'Gold Fox' is true to form." Moore pulled a grin. "Not too tactful to have said that. You want me to deliver this to Mr. Luce?"

"It's for you."

"*Me?*"

"Yes."

"What do I have to do?"

"Your job."

"That's it?"

"That's it."

"It's an extraordinary reward."

"Not if you do your job well," Jong said. "There's plenty more where that came from and we don't keep records of our gifts."

Moore stared at the miniature building, tightening his grip.

"This must be worth at least…" He looked up, awed. "My God, I may never have to work again."

"We take care of our friends."

"I guess I should say thanks."

"We prefer that you not say anything to anyone."

"No, of course."

Moore repacked the statue. Holding it under his arm, he stood up, as tense as though he had been passed the loot from a crime. Which, Jong thought, was what the gold was.

He saw Moore to the door. "Are you married, Mr. Moore?"

"What? Oh yes."

"Your wife is accustomed to you spending the night away from home?"

"I travel frequently."

"A woman can be arranged."

"You mean a… I'm not sure that'd be a good idea."

"She'll be anything but an idea."

Moore let out a nervous chuckle.

"After a day of work, you could use some diversion."

"And you want to keep me in the suite."

"That too."

"Well, then."

Jong watched the American walk down the hallway with the package under his arm, head down, gait furtive, looking humbler than when he had arrived. Undeserved reward had a way of diminishing the recipient's dignity.

Jong closed the door.

He was exhausted from the long journey. Between Shansui and New York there had been five changes of planes. His day had been turned upside down by crossing the time zones. He would stay in and write to Yunna, tell her about his impressions of America. On second thought, mail to China would take weeks; he would be home before the letter arrived. He could put a call through to Shansui. There was no telephone in the east wing apartment. The closest was the one in Han's office. He would have to ask Han to find Yunna. Han might be surprised by the request, but he wouldn't refuse.

The hotel operator secured the connection to Shansui after the second try. The telephone rang and rang. Early morning in China, Han should be back from his ride. He would be reading reports in his office. Maybe he'd stepped away. Jong hung up and tried again after fifteen minutes. No answer.

What had made Han change his sacred morning routine? Had he left the Villa? Was he ill? If there was an emergency, Jong would have been notified by wire. It had to be something innocuous.

Dusk was descending on the city. Shadows lengthened. Across the street, halos of lamplight beamed warmly through curtained windows, framing pictures of families around dinner tables. He felt despondent and out of sorts.

I feel this way because I am half a world away from her.

He left the suite and rode the elevator to the lobby. Café society was at its peak. Below the famed murals, waiters pirouetted through the throng with crystal goblets of champagne. A man in a cocktail suit was playing Broadway tunes on the grand piano. Couples in tuxedos and gowns gathered; their lighthearted chatter punctuated by laughter. The scene had the hyper-reality of a Hollywood movie. He was in a happy, carefree world. Here, war existed only in newspaper headlines; poverty and starvation were abstractions. He moved through a fog of cigarette smoke and expensive perfume, like a ghost amid the gaiety.

Leaving the crowd, he walked past the lounge and stepped down to the shopping arcade. A carpeted tunnel, quiet like a cave. The shops were closed. Luxury goods were arranged in glass cases like museum displays. As he rounded a corner, an attractive woman in a black dress and a white fur stole was walking toward him. Recognition came into her eyes, as though she remembered having seen his face. She held his gaze as they crossed, waiting for a signal from him. Odd that someone would find him familiar. He thought about chameleons and what he had said to Pierre: I am Chinese when I am in China.

What am I in America?

Next morning Moore returned with an overnight bag. A translator and a photographer were waiting in the suite. The translator was a former diplomat called Cornwell. He showed up after Jong wired the request to a contact in Hong Kong. Tall and blond with a handsome face, he chatted in flawless Chinese with the guards. The photographer, a Hungarian from Brooklyn who went by the name of John, knew five words of English, a vocabulary he deployed sparingly. After introductions, the three men set to work in a bedroom with guards posted at the open door. The files were spread on the bed. Moore pored over them, taking notes and selecting documents to be photographed. Cornwell pulled a chair to the bed; he translated the documents as they were passed to him. The Hungarian perched on the windowsill, blowing smoke rings to the sky. He only left the spot when his services were required. The trio developed a silent routine; work was progressing. Moore didn't protest when a guard followed him to the bathroom. Lunch was ordered from room service and delivered by Jong's guards. The men ate and went on working.

Jong looked in at six. Cornwell and the Hungarian had left. Moore was alone in the room, doing stretching exercises in front of the window. Jong collected the papers and locked them in his room.

"That was some explosive stuff. Who'd have thought? All that money went from the U.S. Treasury to one family," Moore said when Jong joined him in the living room. There was a fatigued brightness in his eyes. "It's going to be the story of the century."

"Made good progress?"

"I went through a third of the files. I should be done the day after tomorrow."

"When will the story go to press?"

"Can't say at this point."

"When?"

"The editor-in-chief decides. It'll be on a fast track, that much I can assure you. Give me a day, I'll find out."

"I want the answer tomorrow."

"You will have the answer as soon as I do."

"Tomorrow."

"I'll call the editor first thing in the morning. Look, I want to see this come out as much as you do. It will win all the prizes and get me a seat at the big table." Moore sauntered to the bar, then mixed himself a drink and took it to the sofa. "When will the girl be here?"

"Any moment now."

"Is she staying the night?"

"She's paid to stay. It's up to you," Jong replied. "I can only send for someone who has passed our security check. I hope you don't have strict preferences."

Moore slouched down, hands locked behind his head and feet up on the coffee table. "No problem. I've always had a taste for Orientals."

"She's White Russian."

"Did you ship her from Shanghai? From Moscow?"

"I can't tell you anything other than she doesn't speak a word of English."

"A mute. Great."

"It eliminates the temptation to talk about what you've been reading."

"As long as she's not one of those frumpy broads wandering on Canal Street."

"She is nice-looking."

"Good figure?"

"She commands top dollar."

"Okay. What the hell."

"What did you tell your wife?"

"That I had to be in Albany for some state legislature business."

"Told anyone else?"

"Mr. Luce."

"What did you tell him?"

"Who you are and the reason you're here".

"Anything else?"

"I told him what I knew at the time."

"What was his response?"

"He asked to be briefed when I'm done."

"Did he have questions for me?" Jong asked.

"No."

"Did he give the go-ahead to publish?"

"He didn't say and it's not my place to pressure Mr. Luce. I'm sure we'll find out soon enough." Moore picked up the room service menu. "I feel like celebrating. You want to join me for dinner?"

"I'm going out."

"A date?"

"To look around."

"Want a list of the landmarks?"

"I'll get a cab and ride around."

"Exciting city. You'll have a grand time. You wouldn't mind if I helped myself to a dinner with all the trimmings? They have an excellent wine list."

Step one of the mission completed, Jong thought. In two days Moore would be done. If Luce decided against publication, he would contact others. He had the list ready.

"Where to, sir?" the taxi driver asked.

"I'd like to see Times Square. After that, drive around Midtown and then drop me off in Chinatown."

"First time in New York?"

"Yes."

The driver looked at him in the rear view mirror. "We are getting visitors from Europe. They want to start a new life in America. Things must be bad over there."

"Must be."

"You are not from Europe?"

"No."

Manhattan reminded Jong of Shanghai, though the Chinese city was a village compared to this super modern metropolis. Everything was bigger and taller and brighter. Glittering skyscrapers jabbed into the sky. Automobiles streamed in tributaries of light. At an intersection in Times Square, the taxi stopped at a traffic light. Pedestrians poured from the curbs. A man with a toddler in his arms crossed the taxi's headlights. Father and son. Dark hair, similar profile. Something about the boy caught Jong's eye. He rolled down the window. The child also noticed Jong. His blue eyes stayed on him until they reached the pavement. Jong thought about the missionary from New England, the man who might be his father. John Linden. There was no memory attached to the name, yet his connection to Linden seemed more plausible here. An old longing stirred. There must be a way to find out whether Linden was alive. The distance from New York to Boston was manageable. He could make inquiries at churches. A former missionary who had lived in China around the end of the Ching Dynasty. There couldn't be many who fit the description. He imagined a kindly, soft-spoken man preaching in a white clapboard church, with pictures of old China hanging in his rectory and jars of fragrant tea in his cupboard.

The cab let him off at an entrance to a subway station. Ahead, a forest of Chinese signs. The sidewalks were cluttered with discarded paper boxes and overflowing garbage bins. Except for the English words above the shops, the place seemed disconnected from the city. Darker, dirtier, filled with secrets. Heads peered from half-open doors, registered a momentary interest in Jong's Eurasian face, before they returned to the task at hand. At a shop selling tourist gifts, he bought postcards and, as a tribute to Han, a replica of the Statue of Liberty painted in gold. He would send them to Nan-fei. She would be thrilled to know he had been to America.

The restaurant was decorated like a Chinese curio shop. In the foyer, cloisonné vases and ivory carvings lined up on rosewood shelves. A woman dressed like a Ming courtesan greeted him. One look at Jong's eyes and she switched to English as she led him through a silk screen partition to a booth. The diners were Caucasian, handling their food with forks and pouring ketchup over steamed rice. This might be their only contact with this exotic culture called China, Jong thought. Five thousand years of civilization shrank down to a plate of chop suey. Little wonder that they bought the lies: China's problems could be solved with American cash, Soong May-ling was an exotic goddess who would save the country with her Christian virtues. Fairy tales custom made for the American public.

After dinner, he set out for the clearing in the rows of buildings. Across the shore, lights blinked like a belt of sequins. The city was veiled in a silver haze. A pale green monument rose out of the dark water, swathed in skeins of lighted fog. The Statue of Liberty. Smaller than he had imagined. He leaned on the railing and drew in the cool night air. He tried to imagine living in a country where he could take freedom for granted. Where he could be his own man.

The moment Jong stepped out of the elevator, he sensed something was wrong. The air unsettled him. He took out his pistol and moved on cautiously. He was alone in the hallway. The place was still as a tomb, but the quiet didn't allay his fears. He fitted the key into the door of his suite. Not locked. A chill rose inside him. He flattened his body against the wall, cocked the gun and grabbed the doorknob. He pushed the door gently, and then kicked it open.

Every light was turned on.

All the doors were open.

The Russian woman was lying spread-eagled on the blood-soaked bed in Moore's room, face up, naked. Two bullets. One in the forehead and one in the chest. No sight of Moore or his personal belongings. In his own room, Jong found the guards on the floor in pools of blood. Surprise locked their faces. Their guns were still strapped to their belts—there hadn't been time to fight back. It had been a swift ambush. The intruders had known exactly what to do. He checked their pulses, knowing already that they were dead. Five of his best guards. He had picked them because they were bright young men, eager to see the world outside China. Now they became the first casualties of Han's Grand Strategy.

Jong looked around. Except for two overturned chairs, there was no evidence of disturbance. Moore must have let the intruders in, right after the woman arrived and before the guards took their dinner break. They had not been aware until shots were fired at them.

Jong sidestepped the corpses and headed for the closet, knowing before he looked that the files would be gone.

A type-written note was pinned on the wall.

America is our territory. What nerve to presume that you could ask our friend to take part in your treachery. This time we only took back what is ours. Do not expect the magnanimity to be repeated. We've spared your life only so you can take this message to General Han. Tell him his time is up.

Jong folded the note and slipped it into his pocket. He was sure that between Soong and Luce, they knew people who could cover up the murder of six foreigners. They would intercept the translator and the photographer when they showed up in the morning. The pimp wouldn't go out of his way to look for a missing prostitute. The more pressing question was: How much should he believe that Soong would let him leave the country?

He was on a visitor's visa. Han had no influence here. If he were implicated in the killings, it would cause diplomatic and personal havoc that might take months to resolve. He had to get out of New York. Fast. And the country as soon as he secured passage on a plane. He took only his passport and money. Leaving everything as he had found it, he locked the suite and threw the "Do Not Disturb" sign over the knob. It would give him an extra hour when the maids showed up in the morning. He dropped the room key into the garbage chute. Not wanting to risk being remembered by the elevator operator, he found the stairwell and ran down twenty-five floors.

He assumed a normal pace as he made his way through the lobby. The crowd was smaller than last night. In a sweep,

508

he identified two possible watchers: a woman on the public telephone and a man standing by the restroom. They had positioned themselves to have full view of the lobby; there was an extra alertness in their glance. They might not be the only ones; there could be a string of them in and around the hotel. Jong had no doubt that Soong's agents had been watching since his first meeting with Moore.

He kept moving.

He made it to the exit. He allowed himself a sigh of relief as he stepped to the edge of the curb. A line of taxis had queued up. Boarding one here would leave a solid trace for his watchers. He walked on. At the corner of Madison and Forty-eighth Street, he waved down a passing cab. He told the driver to take him to the airport.

The last flight of the day had departed an hour ago. The airport was deserted. He was alone in the empty hall. Was this normal? Airports were like train stations; people were always coming and going, round the clock. Where were the other passengers? Airline personnel? Airport staff? He felt both trapped and exposed. I can't wait here. There must be a way out. Taxis were available on dispatch. He could call one and go to a town outside the city, get some rest and arrange his escape route tomorrow.

He looked around for a telephone booth.

Out of nowhere, a team of janitors appeared, holding brooms and dustbins, marching like a platoon of soldiers. He stared as his nightmares multiplied. The door. Why had he locked the damn door and left fingerprints on the knob? The lights. He forgot to turn them off. People in the street would notice when the city shut down. Why did he put up the "Do Not Disturb" sign? That was foolish. It gave away his intention to hold off the housekeeping staff. It was circumstantial evidence, but together with his disappearance, they would be enough to cast him as prime suspect.

The janitors walked past him.

He hurried out of the building.

Outside, he was startled to see a full moon, so luminous that it eclipsed the streetlamps. He gazed at the perfect circle of yellow light. A wave of new hope came over him.

He'd been spared.

To go forward with his own plan.

Jong crossed the street to an all-night diner. It was bright as day and packed with airport workers coming off the late shift. He chose a table by the rear exit. He would wait until morning and take the first plane out. Meanwhile, he would figure out how to stay alive for the rest of the journey. How to deliver the bad news to Han. And what he must do to end the madness.

26

"I've become a joke, haven't I? You think you can make fun of me with your stupid lies. You think I can't tell what's true and what's not," Su-chen said. She picked up a vase and threw it across the room. It flew over the maid's head, hit the wall and exploded. "I won't let you get away with this."

Hands over her head, the maid said, "Mrs. Li, please, who would dare to make up something like that?"

"You would. You daughter of a cheap whore."

"The General's personal attendant delivered the summons. He told me to wake you up. The General wants to see you right away."

"He sent his personal attendant?"

"Yes."

Su-chen calmed down somewhat. "He wants to see me now?"

"Yes."

Since returning from Hankow, Han seemed to have forgotten her entirely. She had Ah Ching deliver messages to him; he had not replied to any of them. The few times she succeeded in crossing his path, he had been aloof. She couldn't muster the courage to prolong the conversation. With little to occupy her time, she had examined every detail, every nuance of their encounters. She couldn't find cause for his indifference.

"Please, Mrs. Li, the General is waiting."

He had never sent for her in the morning. "Did he say why he wants to see me?"

"His attendant didn't say and we didn't dare ask."

"If you made this up, I'll kill you."

Groggy from having lain in bed too long, Su-chen staggered the few paces to the dressing table. A look in the mirror set her off again. She called the maid to attend to her appearance. Immediately. And she needed a cup of strong tea. While the maid fixed her hair and applied makeup, her mind was going in different directions. One moment she thought, he has been traveling and conducting negotiations with Mao and the American attaché. He has important things on his mind, that's all. He misses me, that's why he sent for me. But why did he let me wait this long? I have been here, waiting, day and night. He couldn't have been that busy. The other day he ordered a showing of films starring a Shanghai actress. The servants said he watched alone through the night.

In a state of trembling anticipation, she went through the entire wardrobe, finally settling on the outfit she had worn on the first evening with Han. Purple cheongsam and black shawl, this time with lots of jewelry and perfume and her lips painted a bright red. A sedan chair from Grand

Hall was waiting outside the apartment. The maid hadn't lied. Too bad, I'd have enjoyed wringing the little wrench's neck, Su-chen thought savagely. While at it, she would find Ah Ching and wring hers too. The double-crossing bitch probably hadn't delivered any of her messages. She sensed Su-chen was losing favor with Han and didn't want to bother.

Su-chen climbed into the tiny cabin. The sedan chair took off. She noticed the coolies chose the shortest route via the main artery. The sedan chair was visible to sentries and servants. It came to her that the summons was official. Whatever his reason for seeing her, it had nothing to do with the bedroom. Passing the watchtower, she imagined climbing to the top and throwing herself to the ground. Marking the spot. Forever. Every time Han looked at the watchtower, he would be reminded of her...

The sedan chair toddled on.

Approaching Grand Hall, she was surprised to see Han on the steps, watching the approaching sedan chair with a smile. Last time he welcomed her out in the open had been her first day at the Villa. An age had passed since then. I would do anything to bring back the moment and make it last, she thought.

The sedan chair stopped. She got out and hurried to Han.

He came down the steps. "Gorgeous day, isn't it?"

"So happy to see you. How have you been?" Su-chen took his hand. It was against protocol but she didn't care.

"Fine, fine."

To her disappointment, he let go of her hand. He strode off, briskly and purposefully. She could barely keep up. He walked down the length of the building to the garden in the back. He was two steps ahead of her; she couldn't read his face.

He pointed at the pavilion. "We'll talk there."

They crossed the lawn. She sat down on one side of the marble bench, expecting him to join her. He remained standing on the elevated threshold of the moon gate.

"Want anything? Tea, wine, food?" he asked.

Su-chen shook her head.

He nodded. "We have no need for distractions on such a beautiful day."

His heels were rocking to an inaudible beat. His face brimmed with boyish exuberance, eye captivated by something visible only to him.

He is happy, she thought. Without me.

"Why am I here?"

"I'll get to that. First, Su-chen, tell me, have I been an adequate host?"

"More than adequate, General. I have never been better provided for."

"Excellent. What would you say if I asked you to live here permanently?"

She couldn't believe what she heard.

"Would you accept?"

"Of course, I'd accept. You mean it?"

"And your daughter?"

"It'll be fine with her, I'm sure."

"Do you have any plans for her? Plans you and Henry made?"

"This is so unexpected, so wonderful. You don't know how long I've been waiting...."

"Plans for Yunna — are there any?"

"Nothing has been decided, but..."

"Go on."

"Henry always insisted Yunna should decide her own future. She could choose to do the things he did when he was a young man—travel, study abroad, even pursue a career. I didn't agree. I wanted, I want, her to follow the traditional path, be a wife and mother, and stay home."

"I am with you. A woman's life is with her husband. She is to support and serve him, bear him children. It has been so for generations and it should go on for future generations. There is no reason to change. I am glad you have not been swayed by Henry's progressive views. It shows strength of will and respect for our culture. You set an excellent example for young women in China."

His solicitude was unfamiliar and it made her nervous. "Has Yunna done anything? If she has displeased you, let me apologize on her behalf. Henry spoiled her; she can be willful."

Han sat down on the opposite bench, elbows anchored on the marble table and eyes fixed on her face. "I want you to know that I am absolutely serious. This is why I am following protocol and making the request to you."

"What are you saying?"

"I will not offer her anything less than being my supreme wife."

"*Her?*"

"Your daughter."

"What about her?"

"I want to marry her."

She stared without comprehension.

"I want to marry your daughter," he repeated.

The shock was too much. She couldn't speak.

"Incredible, isn't it?" he went on. "I can't quite believe myself. All these months she has been here and I haven't even seen her."

"Why should you have? She's just a child. There's no need for her to see you."

"It turned out it was good that we didn't meet until the other night; otherwise it would have been awkward and inconvenient."

"Because you were bedding her mother?"

"Yes," he replied, unmindful of her distress.

"How *did* you meet her?"

"I was on the boat. I heard someone singing a song from my childhood. I looked for the voice and there she was, swimming on the beach alone. It was getting dark. I invited her on board. She was shy. To be honest, I was too. We were tentative at first, feeling our way until we warmed up to each other. She is an astonishing girl. Completely enchanting. I thought, Here she is. The one meant to be."

"Meant to be what?"

His eyes were closed. "Never have I been so moved by a woman. Those eyes, dark and expressive. They are the pools of my destiny. Right there as she stood with the moon rising behind her, I knew what to do. It was the easiest decision I ever made. I asked her to come to my apartment."

"Your apartment?"

"Yes."

"When?"

"That night."

"*Night?*"

"I want her to see the vault."

"The vault?"

"Stop repeating everything I say. I took her down to the vault. I showed her the gold. I told her what I plan to do with it. The role I am destined to play in history."

Horror swept over her face. "You let Yunna see the gold?"

"I did."

"You said anyone who sees the gold won't be allowed to live."

"I made an exception for her. She didn't disappoint me; she became as convinced as I am. It was as though all along we had the same thoughts, dreamed the same dreams. 'It will come true,' she said. 'The country needs a strong leader like you. Someone resourceful, visionary, wise. You are going to make China great again.' We talked until the sun came out, and the next day. Never done that with a woman. We didn't feel tired. Just exhilarated, happy."

Su-chen's eyes were fixed on his, unblinking.

"What are you looking at?"

"You *are* serious about marrying her."

"Haven't I just said so? The wedding date will be set soon, before the Japanese move further inland and things get messy with the Party. I want to be married before I make my big move. Yunna is going to bring me good luck. I know she will."

Su-chen swallowed. "Yunna is so young. You are…"

"What about me?"

"You are older than her father. There are decades between you and her."

"You tried to marry her off to a man my age. You didn't seem to mind then."

"She told you that?"

"We talked about everything."

"You were her father's friend. You were my…"

"I am a friend of the family."

"Marry someone else," she snapped. "Yunna is not the only girl in China with a pretty face."

"I don't want someone else. I want her."

"How could you say that to me? What about me? What are you going to do with me?"

"As I said, you can stay here. I'll set you up in your own apartment in Outer Court."

"I stay here. As your mother-in-law?"

"Let me put it this way. You are Yunna's mother; therefore you are family. I'll see to it that you are provided for. You can stay here or you can go somewhere else. It's up to you."

"Yunna's mother," she repeated, furious. "On my own I am nobody to you. You have done with me for good, is that it? Is that what I've become? A woman to be cast aside, like one of your waitresses…"

"Get hold of yourself."

"Why did you make me do those things with you? Why? I am so ashamed."

"Ashamed? Whatever for?"

"They were against everything I believe in. They were immoral, wrong."

"So why did you do them?"

"I thought you cared about me and you wanted me to be part of your life. I thought we were going to be husband and wife." She added bitterly, "I wouldn't have let you seduce me if I had known I was no better than one of those cheap women who shared your bed."

"Let me seduce you? What impertinence."

"You lured me to your chamber. You drugged me, and then you defiled me."

"You were so hungry for me, you would have crawled to my bed."

"I'd lost my husband. I was lonely. And I was in awe of you." The sight of him pained her; she had to look away. "I still am. I worship you. There is nothing I wouldn't do for you."

"Be thankful that I am marrying your daughter—that's what you can do." His voice softened. "You've known all along I haven't been interested in lengthy attachments. I had the maid inform you of my habits before you came to my bed, to make sure there were no unrealistic expectations. Making Clouds and Rain was recreational for me. Nothing more."

"Even with me?"

"We shared some pleasant times. Let's leave it at that."

Her face crumpled. "I gave you everything. I live for you. I would have died for you."

"Don't be morbid. All right. I believe you were devoted to me."

"That's all you can say?"

"About our past, yes."

"I am now your past?"

"I don't see another way to describe it."

"My daughter is your present?"

"My present. And my future."

"Everyone knows I am your mistress. If you marry my daughter, how am I going to face the world?"

"Not everyone. Only a few. They will regard you as someone who had been given an enviable privilege."

She closed her eyes, her face pale and taut. "Never mind the world. How can I live with myself? My husband was barely dead when I, a descendant of Confucius, gave myself to another man. I did so with the most sacred intention. Only to find out I was just another whore…"

"I never promised you marriage."

"You said I'll stand by your side and share your future."

"When I rule the country, every man and woman will share my future. Look, you were a wreck coming out of the mess in Nanking. I felt sorry for you. You're an attractive woman. I've never bedded a friend's wife. I thought, Why not?"

She flew at him, her curved fingers digging into his chest like claws. Han's hand shot out and locked her wrists together, squeezing hard.

"Control yourself, Su-chen."

"I will not let Yunna marry you. I will not let her marry the man who violated her mother."

"Violated you? What nerve."

He smashed her flat-handed across the face. She staggered, steadied herself, and tried again, throwing her whole weight at him. Losing her balance, she pitched forward. Before she could fall, he gripped her shoulders and held her upright. She shook him off, violently, letting out a loud wail, like an animal being slaughtered. He locked her wrists again and proceeded to wring them like they were a piece of dripping rag. He kept twisting until her skin turned red. She shrieked.

With one yank, he let her go. She sagged to the floor.

"You are a despicable man. I hate you, Han Tang-ming."

She climbed back to her feet. One cheek was swollen; her wrists were bruised.

"Let me remind you that you are alive today because I saved you," Han said. "You could have died with the other three hundred thousand people in Nanking. You owe your life to me. Your daughter owes her life to me. That means I own you both."

A tense silence.

Su-chen let out a shrill laugh. "Yunna doesn't love you. She loves another man."

"What?"

"She loves someone else. A younger man."

"Who?"

"You don't know? He's right here and you don't know."

"Who?"

"Jong."

Silence.

"Yes, Jong. Your spiritual son. Your most loyal companion. The only man you trust."

"He never told me."

"Why would he tell you? You are not part of his future. He is getting ready to leave. He wants to make a new life outside China, with Yunna."

"He said he will never leave. He promised to stand by me."

"That must have been before he met Yunna."

"Jong is not someone who breaks his promise."

"That's what you believe. But do you really know Jong? Do you know he is tired of taking your orders and he doesn't want to fight your war?"

"How do you know?"

"I just do."

"Did Jong tell you?"

"He didn't have to."

The muscles in his face relaxed. "You made this up."

"It's going to happen. Jong is going to marry Yunna and they are going to leave Shansui together."

Han had arrived at a satisfactory explanation for himself. "I can see how the attachment was formed. It's quiet here. They spent time together and they became good friends. He likes her—who wouldn't? If he fantasizes a future with her, it's just one of those things that come with being a young man in the company of a beautiful girl. There's no need to read too much into it."

"He *loves* her. Jong and Yunna have been in love since they met in Shanghai."

"Even if she did, she doesn't anymore."

"After seeing the gold, who wouldn't choose you?"

"Yunna isn't that kind of girl. She is principled, idealistic…"

"And smart, calculating, ambitious. Do you really believe she is not affected by the gold? If you do, you are a fool." She paced around Han, glee mounting. "Let me tell you something about my daughter. Since childhood, she has set her sights on the unattainable. She said, 'I don't want the stars, I don't want the moon. I want the sun and I want to outshine everyone.' To be the fourth reigning empress in China—that's her dream."

"I'll make her dream come true."

"You better do that, because that's the only reason she fell willingly into your lap. Oh, maybe *you* were the one who fell into hers? That crafty little witch must have planned the encounter on the beach. She is more than capable of something like that. She used to stage political demonstrations in the streets and rallied crowds. It would have been easy to figure out how to lead one lecherous man by the nose. You and your gold fit nicely into her plan. You are her magic carpet to supreme power. That's what she sees when she looks at you. 'Pools of your destiny.' Ha. Whose destiny? Did you do it right there in the vault, add her to the list of virgins you have deflowered?"

"It didn't happen like that. Yunna touched my heart."

"Really? Did you touch hers? Or did you touch something else in her? Are you so taken by her looks that you don't see the obvious?" Her voice grew fierce. "She doesn't love you. *She loves what you can do for her.* In a few years, when you are an old man, when your body is weak and your mind is feeble, she will be in her prime. She will step over you and rule behind a curtain, like the Empress Dowager. My daughter has everything planned."

"In a few years I will be the emperor of China and she will be my empress. That's what's going to happen."

"Jong won't let you marry her."

"I am not worried about Jong. He puts me before everything else."

"Does he? We will have to see, won't we? How could you understand how he feels? You have no idea what it means to love a woman."

"I do now."

"After all these years, the great General Han learns about love." She choked, laughing. "How fantastic. How touching. How comic."

"I asked you here as a courtesy, you being Yunna's only parent. Whether you approve or not, she will be my wife."

"If Henry were alive, he would never let you so much as touch Yunna's hand."

"Your husband," Han spoke deliberately, "if he were alive, would be delighted to see his daughter marry me."

"That would only be so because he never knew the real you. He thought you were a just and moral man."

It was Han's turn to laugh. "Henry knew me and I knew him. We had no illusions about each other. He would have wanted his daughter to marry me because he would have known what the alliance could do for him. He wouldn't pass up the benefits."

"Henry was a man of honor and principle. He wouldn't have married off his daughter for selfish reasons."

With unerring regret, he said, "Was that how you saw your husband? I'm not surprised. You are naïve about people. Let me tell you about the real Henry Li. The man only I knew."

She read something in Han's face and was suddenly afraid. "Leave Henry alone."

"Henry never told you what he did for me, did he?"

She hesitated. "What should he have told me?"

"Nothing. Your dear husband didn't want you to know. Can't blame him. He didn't have a choice. You are a staunch moralist. You see the world in simplistic terms. Good is good. Bad is bad. Nothing in between. You wouldn't have been able to understand the intricate nature of his work, the complexities of the maneuvers and the ruthlessness required to execute them. We couldn't risk the chance of being compromised. He also thought you might have resented it. He wasn't sure what you would do when the chips were down and you had to choose between him and your family."

"Why would I have needed to choose?"

"He was working against your family. To be precise, your cousins."

"He was working against the Party?"

"On my behalf."

"What did he do for you?"

"In the beginning he stole secrets from your relatives and passed them to me: Who had contracted an unnamable disease. Who had stolen from the Party till. Who had taken a contract out on whom. Tidbits of personal nature, useful for blackmailing and swapping favors."

"Things I told him?"

"That's right. From your cousin Soong May-ling to the Generalissimo's trusted lieutenants. You were his best source of intelligence. It never fails to amuse me how willingly women share secrets, especially with their husbands. Henry compiled dossiers on your relatives. That went on for a couple of years."

Su-chen was immobile.

"He had a good run, but he got tired of gossip and bedroom drama. He wanted to expand his territory, fight real battles, command real soldiers. I gave him a bigger job; he had proven himself. By then I'd gotten to know him well. Knew at heart he didn't care for politics. That was a big point in his favor. He did what he did for money. No complicated motives, no hidden agendas. Made things simple. I let him run my underground networks, first the one in Nanking, and then those in the eastern provinces. He was a marvelous agent runner. World-class manipulator. Deft, meticulous, smooth. When it suited our purposes, he killed."

"Henry was not a killer."

"Not with his own hand, of course; Henry was too smart for that. The fact is, your husband was responsible for the destruction of many lives and careers. I can give you the list. You know a good number of them."

"This can't be true. Henry wouldn't have done that to people who trusted him."

"Do you seriously believe Chiang trusted your husband?"

"He gave Henry a position in his cabinet. He wouldn't have if he didn't trust him."

"In politics, trust is synonymous with usefulness. Chiang must have found him useful, or Henry was able to convince Chiang that he was useful. Whatever there was between the two men, it was gone when it ended. About the time the Japanese began their move on Nanking, Chiang found out what Henry had been doing for me. That was the reason you were to be left behind when your relatives boarded the plane for Chungking. Chiang didn't want to rely on the Japanese to get rid of Henry. He sent his trusted Blue Shirt Gang on the day of your son's birthday banquet. Henry was killed by a Blue Shirt."

"But, you said you never found out who killed Henry."

"I lied."

She breathed. "Kai-shek killed my husband?"

"There is solid proof. In fact, for those of us in the know, it's an open secret that Henry was duly punished for his betrayal."

"Henry wouldn't have done such terrible things. You must have forced him."

"Henry did what he did because he wanted to. He loved the work. The life he had before me hadn't been much: teaching, raising a family, living within his means. One day the same as the next. Playing supplicant to your family— that was the part he loathed most. You didn't know, did you? And that was the other thing that exasperated him.

His wife didn't have a clue that he was unhappy. But what could he do?"

"He could have told me."

"Then what? He'd married into China's first family. The moment he became your husband, he was cast in the role of an adjunct. Irrevocably. Never mind his family had been prominent in Nanking—yours would always eclipse his. He might have been progressive in certain ways, but he was not free from tradition. No man likes to be upstaged by his wife's relatives. Working for me saved his pride and his spirit."

"I knew he didn't enjoy socializing with my family. I thought he preferred the company of academics."

"That's what he wanted you to think," Han said with a nod. "Henry was good at what he did. He could get anyone to believe what he wanted them to believe. Espionage was his true calling. He enjoyed pulling strings behind the scenes. It gave him a sense of power nothing else in his life could match. It was also a spectacular way to get even with your family. And there was the tangible benefit of money. A professor's salary couldn't have afforded the luxuries you took for granted. The house, the motorcar, the servants, and the things you purchased to make life stylish and comfortable. They were all made possible by me."

"I thought it was his family's money."

"That was long gone. I paid him well. In turn, he did a splendid job for me. Ours was a symbiotic relationship. The best of its kind."

She pressed her hands to her ears and shook her head. "Lies. All lies. I don't believe a word."

"Believe whatever you want; I don't care. But listen to this: As of this moment, you are forbidden to speak about our prior intimacy, in public or in private. I'll marry Yunna on a date set by me. You'll be invited to the ceremony, but your attendance will not be expected. I change my mind about having you live here. You'll move out of the Villa after the wedding. You can go back to Nanking; but if you stay in Shansui, I'll decide where you live. For as long as Yunna is my wife, you'll receive a stipend, a sum more than enough for you to live comfortably. You'll show your appreciation by keeping a respectful distance. You will not see your daughter or your grandchildren without my approval."

Hope had gone out of her. Life had gone out of her. She was as motionless as a block of stone.

"You have your orders now. You may go."

Her arms hung at her sides, lifeless. "I can't give you up. I can't."

"It's no use, Su-chen."

She jerked back into motion and grabbed his hand. "Don't do this. Give me another chance."

He extricated himself. "I'll have the sedan chair pick you up."

"Please, listen, and then decide about Yunna." She made an effort to keep her voice even. "I know you, Tang-ming. You are a virile man. You always like a new woman, the waitress from Canton, the farm girl from the next village. I knew about them and the others too. I didn't mind because I knew sooner or later you'd tire of them. Yunna won't be different. She is a passing fancy. But marriage is forever. When the excitement is gone, you will be stuck with her. My daughter is not ready to be General Han's Fu-jen. She still has a lot of growing up to do. You are wise. You must see the problems of having an immature girl for a wife." She took a deep breath and forged on. "If you want her, have her. Like you had the others. I can live with that, as long as it's temporary. I'll let you make Clouds and Rain with Yunna every night. One month. Two months. However long it'll take to satisfy you. I'll stay out of your way. I won't complain and I won't hold it against you. When you've had enough, you will send her away. I'll come back and we'll be together like before."

"Are you done?"

"I want you to know how much I'm willing to put up with. Just so I can be with you."

"I heard what you said. It doesn't change my mind."

"But I am entitled to be your Fu-jen. I have earned it."

"I don't want to hear another word. Guards. Take Mrs. Li back to her room."

Her eyes were blazing. "You can't throw me out. I am not just any woman. I am a descendant of Confucius. I am cousin to China's first family. There is no other woman more qualified to be your Fu-jen."

Two guards arrived. She backed away. They stepped up, grabbed her arms, and frog-marched her out of the pavilion.

"I won't let you get away with this. I won't. I swear..."

27

"I hope the short notice hasn't caused any inconvenience," Jong said to the Englishman as they shook hands.

"None whatsoever, though I admit your wire from San Francisco caught us by surprise. We didn't expect you would come in person for a routine transaction. But always a pleasure to see you, Mr. Lin," replied Clive Boyd-Jones, head of Hong Kong's Trading Liaison Services. "To what do we owe the honor of your visit?"

"Hong Kong is on the way. Haven't been here for a while. I thought I'd stop by. I noticed there is quite a lot of new construction."

"Money is pouring in from Shanghai and Canton, as are people. It's inevitable, I suppose. We are the only European-managed municipality in this part of the world that can guarantee security for its residents. And we are steps from the China border; they can jump over the fence, literally," Boyd-Jones said, flicking nonexistent dust off his blazer. His hands were bony and blue-veined. "How was America?"

"Business concluded sooner than expected."

"The Yanks are efficient in their own way."

"They are."

The two men were in the basement garage of the Admiralty, a British military base on Victoria Harbor. The room used to be a parking attendants' office, a large kiosk with windows looking out on rows of jeeps. The interior was ten feet square and skimpily furnished: two chairs, a chipped metal desk, file cabinets, a dust-laden electric fan. A photograph of King George VI and a map of the Colony hung on the wall. As far as Jong remembered, this was where meetings with the British had been held. Tens of millions dollars' worth of opium trade handled in an underground cell.

Boyd-Jones picked up a thin stack of papers from the desk and handed it to Jong. "The deed to the lot on Victoria Peak. The accompanying documents list the particulars of future site improvements. The title was prepared according to the instructions in your wire. The purchaser will own the land as long as Hong Kong is under British rule, which is as good as perpetuity."

The top sheet was a property transfer deed. The price: one pound sterling. Name of the new titleholder was left blank.

"I can arrange for you to inspect the property, perhaps you'd like to do that before you leave." Boyd-Jones sat down behind the desk. "Do bear in mind that most of the parcels on the Peak have been assigned to Foreign Office staff and to British citizens who are overseeing long-term developments in the Colony. The unclaimed lots are not of premium quality. If you don't find this one satisfactory, it may not be easy to identify a comparable replacement."

"It will be satisfactory if it has what General Han asked for," Jong said. He remained standing as he read the attachment pages.

Boyd-Jones recited, "Acreage with unobstructed views of Victoria Harbor and Kowloon Peninsula. At least five hundred feet above sea level. Compliance with the following feng shui requirements: backed by slope of even gradient, no graves, past or present, on site or in sight, flat road frontage, faces northeast at thirty-three degree angle, minimum of three mature trees on the premises, blah-blah-blah… There is enough land for a compact Taj Mahal. Plan to build soon?"

"The date hasn't been set."

"I hope General Han is aware that he will be the only Chinese resident in the neighborhood, should he decide to live there."

"What is wrong with the area?" Jong asked pointedly.

"Nothing. We want to keep it exclusive."

"Like one of your clubs."

"Segregation makes life and politics simple. We learned that in India." A measured glance at Jong. "But you are not Chinese, Mr. Lin."

"My nationality is in the eye of the beholder."

"Well put."

Jong sat on the other chair. He took out Han's seal and stamped the appropriate spaces on the deed. For ownership of title he wrote in Han's name alongside his, "as joint tenants."

Boyd-Jones looked on, his thumb inserted in the pocket of his waistcoat, fingers tapping contemplatively.

How much had the Englishman guessed? Jong wondered. What would ensure his discretion? How would Han react if he found out the land reserved for his second Crescent Moon Villa had been appropriated by him?

Jong handed the papers back to Boyd-Jones.

"I'll forward them to the Registrar's Office." Boyd-Jones slipped them into an envelope and closed the clasp. "They will record the deed today. You can have them before you leave Hong Kong. Shall we send them to your hotel?"

"I'll pick them up at the Registrar's Office, if it can be arranged."

"You? Or your staff?"

"Me."

"You're traveling alone?"

Jong didn't answer.

"I'll leave word that the documents are to be released to you." Boyd-Jones leaned back in his chair. "Do you have a moment, Mr. Lin?"

Jong nodded.

"We thought this would be a good time to discuss a few things. First, there is a message we'd like you to take back to General Han. It concerns his intelligence operations, in Shanghai and elsewhere."

"Why would General Han's operations concern you?"

"When we come across information useful to our friends, we pass it on. Let's begin with the assassination of Henry Li. Are you aware that the Blue Shirt Gang was behind it?"

"The case is under investigation."

"That's what you tell the public."

"Why do you think the Blue Shirts are involved?"

"This is what our men found out. The Blue Shirts sent one of their men to Li's house, on the day before the Japanese attack. The next morning he killed Li just when all hell was breaking loose. He messed up the place so it would appear the Japanese were there, and then he vanished into the mayhem. There was so much confusion that it was impossible to trace the killer. Ingenious timing. Maybe it was luck. Not for the people of Nanking, of course." Boyd-Jones added, "The assassination of Li was the first phase of a bigger plan—that's the information we want you to have."

"Go on."

"The Blue Shirt Gang is in the process of annihilating General Han's intelligence network. As the saying goes: 'To kill the dragon, one must first hack its head.' Li was the head, therefore the first to go. The next is your biggest operation, the one in Shanghai. You know, of course, the Blue Shirt Gang means the order came from the Generalissimo." Boyd-Jones retrieved a file from a drawer. "Take a look, Mr. Lin."

The cover page was a street map of Shanghai, with points marked in red and dates scribbled along the side. The red marks were locations connected to Han's covert operation—safe houses, offices, and drops. Jong noticed the dates were in the future; the timeline covered the next three months. The pages that followed were a list of Han's agents in Shanghai, addresses, physical descriptions of individuals and their families, detailed records of daily routines, codes, and bank account numbers. It was the entire roster. Most startling were the details related to codes and accounts. Han had never allowed this type of information to be included in written communications. Henry and the local section chiefs were the only ones who knew, and they had memorized the numbers.

"How did you get these?"

"Our intelligence people have their methods. They are not sharing them with me." Boyd-Jones concluded casually, "If General Han wishes, we can pass future findings to him."

"So you intend to keep up your efforts?"

"It's to our benefit that General Han's interests are protected. Ours has been a long and profitable relationship. We have no desire to change business partners."

"Do the Blue Shirts have similar plans for the other generals?"

"They might have, but those don't interest us."

"You have been keeping tabs on us and us alone?"

"Not *on* you. *For* you. We have been looking out for you."

No surprise that the British had been spying on Han's operations. Han had agents working exclusively on the British in Hong Kong, India, and the British Isles, keeping close watch on his business partner. No one trusted anyone when so much was at stake.

"Don't you wish we could tell the world how well we get along?" Boyd-Jones continued. "Forget treaties and alliances; nothing bonds relationships like a profitable enterprise. They could learn from us."

Even when the enterprise was poisoning one country's people.

"Speaking of enterprise, I'd like to bring up the next topic," Boyd-Jones continued. "One of the pleasures of working with someone like General Han is knowing that we can count on his pragmatism. The end justifies the means. He makes choices that get the job done, doesn't waste time on grandstanding or on namby-pamby polemics." There was a new eagerness in Boyd-Jones's tone that put Jong on guard. "Our people in London have put together a proposal for General Han's share of our joint enterprise. In view of the Blue Shirts' plan and the war with Japan, we believe he may be amenable to other ways of protecting his assets."

"What are you proposing?"

"Change the way we manage the dividends of our business—the logistics, not the apportionments. The percentage of General Han's share of the profits will continue as stated in our agreement. We believe it will be to his advantage that his assets be protected under British domain. For security, improved management, and other reasons of a political and legal nature. I would elaborate if you want me to, but I am sure you are more aware of them than outsiders like us."

"What are you saying?"

"We are offering a new home for General Han's gold."

"I didn't know it needed one."

"It's fine where it is, provided General Han can keep the location secret and secure."

"It's secret and secure."

"For now. What happens when he runs out of space, or if the Japanese get near Shansui? It's never too early to plan ahead. We hope he would consider a different storage method, a better storage method."

"What would you like him to consider?"

"The golden rule of investing: diversification. Not keeping all his eggs in one basket as they are now. Gold bullions in the basement. It's neither the safest nor the most profitable way to handle one's money. Rather primitive, if I may say so," he said with mild disapproval. Boyd-Jones used to be a banker. The notion of vast wealth lying fallow must have been exasperating to him. "This is no longer the Han Dynasty—if you'll pardon the pun."

"How should he diversify his assets?"

"By depositing his earnings in a British bank, with dividends at the most favorable rate."

"General Han doesn't want someone else manage his assets. Least of all foreigners."

Boyd-Jones leaned back and hooked his fingers in the pockets of his waistcoat. "Our banks have a long tradition of excellence. They are rock-solid institutions; his money will be in good hands. That's what we want these days— getting and keeping as much as it is within our power to do so. In General Han's case, the stakes are enormous, the circumstances precarious, more so as the war escalates. Shansui is one of Japan's priority targets. Like everyone else, they want the gold. There is also the civil war. What happens if the Communists win? They would love to turn General Han into their poster boy of criminal imperialism."

"Regardless of what might happen, General Han is keeping his assets inside China."

"And run the risk of being robbed, kidnapped or killed?

"General Han, like his father and his grandfather, is aware of the risks associated with the opium business."

"One hopes that someone who cares about him would want him to take precautionary measures and minimize the risks. That's why we thought you would be the best person to make the pitch on our behalf. Assure General Han that every transaction will be handled with absolute confidentiality. Airtight security measures will be set up for the account. The bank has plenty of experience with this type of arrangement. Similar accounts have been set up for heads of state, royal families in exile, and other dignitaries in sensitive positions." With deliberate casualness, Boyd-Jones added, "Part of the dividend will go into an account in your name, as acknowledgment of your persuasive efforts, should they prove effective."

"I see."

"We hope you will convince General Han of the wisdom of putting his money in the hand of his most trusted partner, and the one of longest standing. An alliance three generations old and growing stronger by the day. Our partnership has lasted longer than some dynasties."

"What will be the instrument for evaluating these 'persuasive efforts' of mine?"

"The reward will be in direct proportion to the size of the General's investment."

"A broker's fee."

"You could say that."

"That will also be handled with confidentiality?"

"Absolutely." Boyd-Jones extracted a sheet of paper from the pile. "Here are the particulars. Percentage of the commission and scale for future bonuses. Method of deposit and withdrawal. Codes, telephone numbers, contacts."

"Never thought of myself as a salesman working on commission."

"It's not an undesirable situation. Free money any way you look at it. Leaves one plenty of time for cricket."

"I don't play cricket."

"Mah-jongg, chess, whatever." His pale eyes bored into Jong's. "We all play games of some kind."

Jong ambled to the other side of the room, his back to the Englishman. He gazed at the reflection of light bulbs on the hoods of jeeps, thinking about the lights in the Waldorf suite shining on the dead bodies. And what Stilwell had said to him when they were alone.

"I will brief General Han on his British friends' discovery of intelligence related to our operation in Shanghai. And I will speak to him about your proposal of the new financial arrangement—but only after you have provided the following: the name of the bank and a complete inventory of its assets and liabilities going back ten years, résumés of officers and directors and their financial interests, the bank's policies and procedures, British and international banking regulations pertaining to this type of account, the terms of the guarantee provided by the Foreign Office, and a list of clients with similar arrangements."

"Our courier will deliver the documents to your hotel."

Jong turned to face Boyd-Jones. "For my part, I do not want a reward in monetary terms."

"Whatever you wish, we'll do our best to accommodate."

"British citizenship for myself and the girl I am going to marry, status identical to that granted to British-born citizens, not the second-rate standing for colonials. If we decide to settle in the West, unconditional immunity from prosecution of any crime—civil, criminal, war —-resulting from my association with General Han. I want a written guarantee signed by your prime minister. The first deposit will not be made until these conditions are met. This agreement must be held in the strictest confidence. You will provide the names of people who will be privy to any part of this conversation before I leave here. I prefer the number to be as small as possible, and any change must be approved by me in advance. Your continued honoring of this agreement will be reciprocated by maintenance and appropriate increment of General Han's deposits in his British bank account."

If Boyd-Jones was surprised by what he heard, his face didn't betray it. "Your requests exceed the authority of the Liaison Office. I'll have to consult London and the prime minister, though I don't foresee any problem in meeting your terms. I can have the answer for you this evening."

"Call me at my hotel."

"Do you plan to leave China soon?"

Jong didn't answer.

"A schedule will help us to move things along."

Again, no answer.

"If and when you come to the West, Mr. Lin, keep in mind that your talents and experience will be welcomed. Our Special Services will find you a suitable position, in Hong Kong or London. If you wish to make your home further away from China, I am sure the Americans would be glad to have you. Their State Department has a constant shortage of China experts."

"Should the occasion arise, I'll remind myself of your recommendations."

"It'll be my pleasure to report to London what we've accomplished."

They shook hands.

"Welcome to the British Empire, Mr. Lin."

28

The orchestra was playing a Shanghai love song currently popular on the radio. Couples swayed to the music.
Tiny ceiling lights picked out faces and bare arms. Only
two out of nineteen tables were not occupied. Not bad
for a Wednesday night, Lillie thought, observing from a
small window in the enclosed loft. Since she bought the
Mayflower, she had improved business by hiring younger
girls and bringing in a live band for the tea dance hour.
Refugees were pouring in from China. Hong Kong's population had doubled in two years and was expected to redou-
ble in the coming six months. The Mayflower could turn
into a money-making machine like the Paramount in its
heyday. Even after paying exorbitant amounts of 'protection money' to the triads and the police, the Paramount had
realized substantial profits. It's not different here. She paid
out a fifth of the receipts to stay on their good side, and
no guarantee that the amount would remain the same. She

was an easy target. A single woman running a cash business. They would pick on her first. She needed to cultivate relationships with people who had clout... She tried to keep her mind on unrelated things because she was tense and nervous.

She checked the clock. 12:48 a.m.

Any second now.

She pulled the drapes. Without the view, the room seemed quieter. She poured black coffee from the thermos. A stiff whiskey would calm her nerves, but she needed to stay alert. She lit a cigarette and started to go over last week's receipts, making an effort to concentrate.

1:13.

A knock on the door.

"Who is it?"

The door opened a slit. A maid popped her head in. "Miss Lillie, something happened in one of the rooms."

Lillie heard the fear in the voice. It's done.

"What room?"

"The Cathay Suite."

She put on a weary look. "What is it this time? Problem guest or uncooperative girl? I am getting ready to leave. Get Nick. He should be done with the band."

"Annabelle's dead."

"What?"

"Annabelle. She's dead."

"The new girl?"

"Yes. She was strangled."

"Come in and close the door." The maid obeyed. "Who strangled her?"

"It had to be the guest. He was the only one in the suite."

"Are you sure she's dead?"

"She looked terrible, all white and... She wasn't breathing."

"We'll call the police," Lillie said without hesitation.

"The guest was Mr. Chiu."

An audible gasp. "*The* Mr. Chiu?"

"You know the kind of games he likes to play. He must have gone too far this time."

Lillie sank back in the chair. "If we call the police, we'll run the risk of offending an important man. If we don't, we'll be covering up a crime." She looked up. "Where is Chiu?"

"He has locked himself in the bathroom. He is very shaken."

"What about Annabelle? Where is she?"

"In the bedroom."

"Has she been moved?"

"No. We didn't dare."

"'We'? Who else knows about this?"

"Ah Feng. He was the tea boy on duty. Mr. Chiu ordered the deluxe dinner. I couldn't carry all the trays. He helped me."

"Chiu ordered food after he strangled Annabelle?"

"The order was placed ahead with instructions to deliver at one a.m. Mr. Chiu usually eats at midnight, and prefers something light, but that was what the order said. When we showed up, he said he hadn't ordered anything."

"That's when you saw the body?"

"Not right away. We asked Mr. Chiu what to do with the food. He kept shaking his head and saying he didn't know how it happened. It was clear something was wrong. We thought we would take the food back and leave him alone. He blocked the door and wanted us to get a taxi. We told him it was too late. There were no taxis in the streets. It had to be a special dispatch. When he heard that he ran to the bathroom and locked himself inside. We thought we would find out from the girl what was going on. The bedroom door was open. Annabelle was lying on the bed. Ah Feng tried to wake her. She didn't move."

Lillie stubbed out the cigarette. "You and Ah Feng are not to say a word about this. We don't want the other guests to find out. They would panic and things would get out of hand. Go back to the suite. Guard the door. Give Chiu brandy; he needs it."

"What if he wants to leave?"

"Tell him you called a taxi and it's on its way. Don't let him out of your sight until the police arrive."

"Are you really going to call the police, Miss Lillie?"

"It's the right thing to do. Annabelle didn't deserve to die like that. I can't in good conscience ignore what happened."

"But, Mr. Chiu isn't just anyone..."

"Maybe there's a way to handle this. I need to think."

"Do be careful, Miss Lillie," the maid said bravely and left.

Lillie picked up the telephone and dialed. Her call was answered on the first ring.

"Now," she said and hung up.

The Cathay Suite was at the end of the hallway with its own foyer for extra privacy. The maid and the tea boy were standing at the door.

"Are the police here?" Lillie asked.

"Yes, the detective is inside, talking to Mr. Chiu."

"Have you seen anyone? Guests? One of our girls?"

"There has been no one."

"Take the rest of the night and tomorrow off." She gave each an envelope filled with cash. "Go home now. Remember, not a word to anyone."

"Yes, Miss Lillie."

She waited until they disappeared into the stairwell before she opened the door of the suite. The trays of food were on the dining table, untouched. Muffled voices were heard in the bathroom. Two men in the thick of an interrogation. The bedroom was a disaster. Bed linens and clothes, Annabelle's mostly, were strewn across the floor. The air stank of vomit and sex. Lillie's eyes went to the bundle on the bed. Pillows, towels, and sheets were heaped haphazardly over the body. Chiu had been terrified and had made a clumsy attempt at cover-up.

She pulled back the layers of clothes and nearly screamed.

The bulging eyes were milky, staring at the ceiling. The face was swollen, her eyes staring blindly up. The tongue protruded like a piece of liver. Foam had dried around the girl's nostrils. Dark bruises on her neck, scratch marks on her shoulders and breasts. The skin underneath the nails had turned blue. The postmortem—if there was one— would find that the girl had died of an opium overdose.

Lillie felt sick. She rushed to the balcony and threw up into a flowerpot, then gripped the railing to steady herself. Calmer somewhat, she wiped her mouth with a handkerchief and drew in gulps of air. The world was jarringly normal. The city lay dark under a cloudless sky. The harbor seemed close by; she could hear the waves beating on the concrete embankment. In the distance, a car honked.

I killed the girl.

I killed her as Japanese soldiers killed Chinese civilians. Murder at random, but murder no less. Annabelle happened to be there when I needed a pawn. She was a perfect candidate for what I had in mind: new in town, no family, no experience with men. I sweet-talked her into offering her first night to Chiu, expecting him to give her the treatment after I found out his kinky routine with virgins. I overdosed her with opium ahead of time, because the girl had to die for the plan to work.

Tomorrow I'll invite monks to bless the place and to give Annabelle a proper sendoff to the Great Beyond. For an extra fee, they will perform the special ritual, urging the gods to reverse her karma. Bring her back as the firstborn son of a wealthy family. Let her live a long and prosperous life...

Lillie could only hope that gods did exist, and that they would understand why she had to do what she did, and forgive her.

The necktie was under the bed. Soft silk, an Italian import. A local tailor had sewn Chiu's initials on the broad end. It smelled of sweat and Annabelle's perfume, and was wrinkled in the center where the knot had been. Chiu had done the expected. Lillie knew the game. An arcane sexual kink. The man puts a noose around the woman's neck, tightening it just enough to constrict her carotid. He increases the pressure while he keeps up at the other end. The act produces wild sensations for the woman and a vicarious sense of achievement for the man. In the frenzy, things can get out of hand. An untimely prolonging can cause death by asphyxiation. Chiu must have thought what had happened. Lillie slipped the necktie into her pocket.

At the bathroom door she waited for a pause in the conversation. She knocked. "This is Lillie. I'm the owner and manager. May I come in?"

"Door's not locked."

Chiu sat on the toilet lid in a half crouch, shoeless, shirt open, knuckles on his temples. He averted his eyes from her. Facing Chiu, a bespectacled man in a trench coat perched on the windowsill, pen and notepad in hand.

"Good evening, Mr. Luo. I was hoping it would be you."

"I was on duty when the call came. What an awful mess."

She nodded. "Terrible."

"The girl was new?"

"Hired last week. This was her first day on the job."

"How old was she?"

"She said she was eighteen."

"Looks younger to me. Have you checked her papers?"

"No, I haven't. So sorry. I was going to do that after she passed probation."

"Her name?"

"She was known as Annabelle. The girls here are given English names; the clients like that. Annabelle's Chinese name was Sau Yan something, I don't remember. I have it written down in the office. I can look it up."

"Do that before I leave. She didn't look Cantonese. Where did she come from?"

"She told me she was a native of Ningpo. She sounded vague about how she got here. She could have smuggled herself into the Colony. I can ask the other girls. They might know."

"My men will interview the staff. Did she have family?"

"She grew up in an orphanage. No relatives. Didn't know anyone in Hong Kong. She was illiterate and had no skills, and she needed to support herself. That was her story."

"This Mr. Lee here. Was he her first customer?"

"Yes."

He turned to Chiu, "Breaking in new girls—is that your thing?"

Chiu's face reddened. "That's none of your business."

"Now that you've killed one, it's our business."

"You can't accuse me of something like that. You have no proof."

"There is plenty of proof. A whole roomful."

"She might have picked up an infection somewhere and she wasn't aware of it," Lillie reasoned. "She could have been ill the whole time. She didn't look very healthy."

"No illness would give her those marks around her neck. But no need for anyone to guess, the cause of death will be confirmed by an autopsy." Luo slapped the notepad shut and stood up. "Lock the suite. Tell your staff not to touch anything. The forensic team will be here soon. I am taking the suspect with me."

"You mean Mr. Lee?" Lillie said.

"I want my solicitor. You cannot do anything until my solicitor is here," Chiu protested.

"I let you make the call. You said the one in your employ is not suitable."

"My solicitor doesn't practice criminal law because I am not a criminal. I need time to find some-one else."

"There will be plenty of time after we book you."

"You can't do that. I am not just anyone. I know people. I'll file a complaint with the chief of police."

"File away. The chief is a Brit, young and gung ho on proving himself. He'll be happy to throw you in jail, get his name in the headlines."

"Keep the reporters out of this."

"We can't. They are always hanging around the station, waiting for the big story. This one is sensational. Sex, mur-der, money. Your picture will be in all the papers."

"That'd be awful. Mr. Lee is a highly respectable citi-zen," Lillie objected, alarmed.

"It doesn't make any difference if you are the gover-nor's number one son or a coolie. You committed a crime, you go to prison. Everyone is equal under law. That's the Brits for you."

"But, at this point, nothing is certain?" Lillie asked.

"No."

"Isn't it true that according to the law, a man is inno-cent until proven guilty?"

"That's correct."

Sensing an ally in Lillie, Chiu said boldly, "Why would someone like me, a man with money and influence, kill a nobody like her? What is the motive?"

"That's for your solicitor to explain to the jury."

"If I were guilty, I would have run away. I could have done that, easy. But I didn't. I was here when you showed up and I told you what happened."

"That you did."

Lillie said to Luo, "Would you mind if I had a moment with Mr. Lee?"

Luo thought.

"It won't be long."

Luo looked at his watch. "Ten minutes."

Lillie closed the door and crossed the small space to sit on the edge of the bathtub. She looked levelly at Chiu.

"I'm sorry the police were called before I was told about the accident; I would have handled the problem differently. Nothing like this has ever happened here. Understandably my staff was shocked and confused." She paused. "It's unfortunate that Mr. Luo has seen the crime scene. We'll have to find other means to salvage the situation."

"You can make this go away?" Chiu said.

"It's possible."

"How?"

"I want you to know that you are with a friend."

"Friend?"

"As in people who help each other through bad times."

"I don't know you," he said uncomfortably. "Why would you want to help me?"

"Because when I help you, I help myself and my business. Whether Annabelle died of natural causes or not, I don't want word to get out that the police were called at the first sign of trouble. No man of position would patronize an indiscreet house. I want my customers to know they can count on us to guard their privacy." A pause. "Mr. Luo, though a policeman, understands my concerns."

"He seemed determined to book me."

"He has rules to follow. That's his official side."

"Is there an unofficial side?"

"Doesn't everyone?"

Chiu was quiet.

"In order for me to help you, Mr. Chiu, please tell me what happened."

Only his eyes betrayed surprise at the mention of his real name.

"Hong Kong is a small place. Hard not to notice someone as famous as you." She added, "I've heard of you for many years."

"You are from Shanghai?"

"Yes."

"How much do you know about me?"

"You rose from poverty to become a legend in the international banking world. From a room in Nantao, you moved to a villa in the French Concession, sharing the same street with our Minister of Finance. Like most people in Shanghai, Mr. Chiu, I've followed your illustrious career with admiration. I know many men who aspire to be you. Many women who dream of marrying someone like you. Many women."

Chiu ambled to the window. He pressed his body against the sill and gazed at the rows of streetlamps on King's Road.

"Never had any problem with women. Not here. Not in Shanghai. Not anywhere. Every girl I met loved me, and I loved her back. I have an infinite capacity to love, though my wife is unwilling to recognize it. She didn't know how lucky she was. It's sad, but I have given up trying to convince her. Young girls sense the love in me; they respond naturally."

"You must have had the same effect on Annabelle."

He turned and rested his eyes on Lillie's face; his voice took on a collegial quality. "This girl fell in love with me the moment we met. She said, 'I'm happy you are my first. You are sweet and you have class.' We were tender with each other, like a couple on their wedding night. A lot of kissing, caressing; we felt connected. She was a special girl, vivacious, responsive and uninhibited. Not like girls her age. She was thrilled to be with me. I showed her the ways to prepare for love, gave her so much pleasure that she wept and laughed." He breathed. "Without warning, she started having a fit, arms and legs jerking, shaking all over."

"You must have been concerned."

"More than concerned. We hardly knew each other, but I cared about her. I did my best to calm her. After a while the shaking stopped but she was feeling dizzy. I thought making Clouds and Rain would help. It was her first time, so it was a little painful, but she got over it. Before I could catch my breath, she was aroused again. That's my effect on women. Once is never enough. I thought, why not teach her a nice game, and make her first time an unforgettable experience?" A light flush appeared on his face. "She loved it. She didn't want to stop. She kept saying, 'More, more, it's heavenly.' What else could a man do but give the girl what she wanted? All of a sudden, she'd stopped breathing..."

"The girl was inexperienced. You were guiding her?"

"I am a seasoned lover. I know what a girl wants."

"You wanted her to enjoy herself."

"I take pleasure in giving my women pleasure."

"You had a good time too?"

"Of course."

"She lost control?"

"Nothing could have slowed her down."

"This game—you've played with other girls?"

"Many times."

"They liked it?"

"The adventurous ones did."

"But they all went along?"

"I'm irresistible."

"Have there been other situations where things got out of hand?"

"There was one in Canton and then one in... I don't see how they can be relevant."

"What is relevant, Mr. Chiu, is that Annabelle did die after you instigated the game." Lillie whipped the tie out of her pocket. "I found this under the bed. These are your initials. This piece of evidence, plus the forensic traces in the room and testimony from witnesses, will go into the police report. The best solicitor in the Colony will not be able to refute them. It may not have been your intention to kill her, but you are responsible for the girl's death. Furthermore, the victim was fifteen, legally a child, a fact that will make her more sympathetic in the jury's eyes and her violator correspondingly more punishable—if this goes to trial."

He was stunned by the unexpected harshness in her tone. "But didn't you say there is an unofficial way to deal with the situation?"

"I did say that."

"Make this go away. I'm not without means."

"And you don't want what happened to leave the room."

"If the situation can be resolved quietly, I'll appreciate all the more. I have never forgotten anyone who has done me a favor."

"A favor for a favor?"

"Fine."

"Any favor?"

"Whatever I can do."

"You are giving me your word?"

"I am giving you my word."

"Let's look at the situation from another angle. Annabelle was alone in Hong Kong. No one will miss her. A story can be made up about her disappearance that will satisfy the few who knew her here. She found another job. She ran into a relative who wanted to take care of her. Girls come and go. Quick turnovers are not unusual in this business. We'll clean up the suite. The only witnesses are the two employees who found you with the body. The proper incentive will convince them to keep their mouths shut. Luo is our only obstacle."

"Ask him to name his price."

"Too direct. He won't like it."

"Whatever it takes, all right? You know him; handle it your way. I don't care as long as you get him off my back. I am a man of the world. If you want a cut, we can work that out too."

"Good to know, but that's not what he has in mind, Mr. Chiu."

"Find out what he has in mind," he said impatiently.

Lillie examined her manicured fingers as though they were clues to solving their dilemma. "It won't be anything in monetary terms."

"You know what it will take for him to look the other way, without talking to him?"

"I know because Mr. Luo and I want the same thing."

"What same thing?"

"Something only you can do for us."

"*Only* me?"

"Yes."

"Is this some kind of game?"

"We are dead serious."

He reassessed her and his own predicament, eyes locked on her face, as if he was trying to force the truth out by sheer force of will.

A sober awakening came upon him.

"Police don't work alone. They work in pairs. A forensic team always arrives with the detectives. They seal off the crime scene, take photographs and dust for fingerprints. None of those things happened here. A real policeman wouldn't have let me talk to you in private. Who is that man out there?"

"Mr. Luo is connected with the Hong Kong Royal Police. He is also a good friend. Up until this moment he is not acting in an official capacity. That can change, easy. He can put in a call to the police station and get the team of forensic experts to come—if that's what you want."

"Who are you?" Chiu asked.

"Owner of the Mayflower. That's all you need to know."

"You own this place?"

"One hundred percent."

"The Mayflower was never on the market. You made an offer to the couple."

"I paid them a good price. They were happy to sell."

"Did you know I was a regular before you made the purchase?"

"Quality of the clientele is important in any business investment."

"You bought the place so you could get to me?"

"That would have been an outrageously expensive introduction. Your patronage adds value to the business, sure, but I bought the Mayflower because I want to make money."

"This place wasn't making money. The couple barely took in enough to pay the bills."

"I've turned things around. Haven't I?"

"You have been keeping tabs on me."

"You are a special customer. Special room. Special rate. Special requirements. Hard not to take notice."

"You found out what I like to do with young girls. You sent Annabelle to me on purpose?"

"It's my responsibility to find out what my customers like and do my best to satisfy them. All customers."

"You must have done something to make sure she would die, so you could pin the murder on me. You set me up."

"You can speculate all you want, but there's no evidence to support your accusation."

He shifted his posture, tensing up like an animal ready for a fight. "What if this something you want is not in my power to give?"

"It is in your power to give," Lillie assured him. "However, if by inability you mean unwillingness, you should know that you have been speaking into a microphone installed behind these walls. Your confession and the lurid details of your conquests have been recorded. You should also know there are three microphones in the suite. One here, one in the living room, and one close to the bed. The machine was turned on when you occupied these rooms."

His eyes darted around the walls. Helpfully Lillie opened the medicine cabinet and pointed at the mesh top of a microphone.

"I also have a dossier on you."

"What?"

"Records of your dealings in Hong Kong. Only the shady ones—they are so much more interesting. Betting stations, mah-jongg centers, a slaughterhouse for dogs sold to unlicensed restaurants, to name a few. We were impressed by your business acumen, especially how clever you are in hiding your profits from Inland Revenue."

"I'm not the only one in Hong Kong who looks for ways to pay less taxes."

"Of course not, but you are easily the most creative. You are set to beat the system, by whatever means at your disposal. Why would a wealthy man like you risk breaking the law just to save a few bucks? We were intrigued. We thought we should get to know you—not just how you make your fortune, but everything else. We looked into your personal life. Nothing reveals more about a man than what he does when no one is looking." She smiled warmly. "It turned out you are not only obsessed by money. You are obsessed by other things, things that normal folks wouldn't want in their living room."

"What are you talking about?"

"Your unusual hobby of collecting antique shoes and what you do with them in that special room in your townhouse were fascinating discoveries."

"You found out about…"

"Imagine how the jurors would react if the information were to surface during a trial."

Chiu turned pale; a spasm pulled at the corners of his mouth.

"Given a choice, we would rather put the tape recordings and the dossier in the furnace. We are discreet people. We don't like to interfere with other people's business, legal or otherwise."

"Tell me what you want from me. Now."

"You've heard of a company called International Airsea?"

"It's a common name."

"There is only one by that name owned by Mr. Soong."

"The one in Shanghai. It was closed down."

"What happened to the people who worked there?"

"They were paid off. They went on their way."

"Do you know where they went?"

"No. I don't know where they went. I don't know who those people were, never met them, never had any dealings with them. Look, I am a banker, that's what I do for Mr. Soong. I'm not involved with his other businesses."

"Didn't he send Airsea's manager to you?"

"The Frenchman?"

"Yes."

"I was told he would see me about an account."

"Were you told anything else?"

"Like what?"

"How long he would stay in Hong Kong. What else he would do here. Where he could be reached."

"I wasn't his chaperon. I was told to handle a fifteen-minute confidential transaction with the former manager of Airsea. That's all the instruction I had."

"Did he show up?"

"No."

"Did he cancel the appointment?"

"Never bothered."

"Did he call?"

"No."

"Did anyone else call on his behalf?"

"No."

"Where is he?"

"Where is he? How would I know?"

"You were his contact in Hong Kong, you must know."

"He was the one to initiate contact. I was given a name, a date, and an account number. I have nothing else."

"Shouldn't you have followed up when Victor missed the appointment?"

"Why would I do that? If the man didn't want his money, that's his business."

"What about the staff at the bank? Have they heard from him?"

"No."

"Did you ask?"

"I didn't need to ask. They would have told me. It was a special account. Anything related to it went directly to me."

"Do you know his other contacts? In Hong Kong? Shanghai?"

"Didn't you hear what I said? I am a banker. I manage money. I don't manage people."

"Did you tell Mr. Soong when Victor didn't show up?"

"Of course I did."

"And what did he say?"

"He didn't say anything."

"He wasn't surprised?"

"I wouldn't know. I sent him a wire when the Frenchman missed his appointment. I didn't get a reply from him."

"Does he always ignore your wires?"

"He replies to those that need a reply."

"What about the money?"

"What about it?"

"Is it still there?"

"That's none of your business."

"Is it still there?"

"It's still there."

"Mr. Soong didn't tell you to close the account?"

"No."

"Would it mean that he still expects Victor to show up?"

"I have no idea."

"Are you telling me everything you know?"

"You expect me to tell you the whereabouts of someone I've never met. You can keep asking the same questions. I have nothing more to tell."

"Who knows where Victor is?"

"Mr. Soong might know. You'll have to ask him."

"That's exactly what I'll do."

"He won't see you."

"In that case you will make sure that he does, Mr. Chiu. You will arrange the meeting so I can ask him."

"You want to interrogate Mr. Soong? You must be nuts."

"A casual introduction next time Mr. Soong is in town. When I say 'casual,' I mean you are not to tell him ahead of time who I am and what to expect. You will bring me to him and I will do the talking. That is the favor I want from you."

29

"So things went well in New York?" Han asked. They were in Han's office in Grand Hall. It was the morning after Jong's return.

"On the whole I'd say so, General. Luce's men didn't want to believe a close ally would have stolen so blatantly."

"But you convinced them?"

"The files did. It's all there. In black and white. I let them read everything front to back and photograph what they needed. Then they wanted to call in their experts to look them over. I told them I hadn't traveled half the world with forgeries. But they insisted it was standard procedure to authenticate documents from an unverified source. There was no way around it."

"It will be a thousand years before they understand the meaning of personal trust."

"After the experts are satisfied, the editor-in-chief will assign the piece to reporters. They may want to do more

investigating, come to China, see things firsthand, interview witnesses. You know how they are. Every detail must
be checked and rechecked."

"How long do I have to wait?"

"A month if things go without a hitch; two would be
realistic. They'll let us know as soon as they decide on the
date."

"Two months. That should be fine."

"It doesn't mean it will be published for certain."

"Why not?"

"We are depending on strangers thousands of miles
away. We have no control over what they do. The reporters
might find something they can't verify. Luce might cave in
to Soong. For years he has been painting a rosy picture of
his Chinese friends. He would have to admit he has staked
his reputation on criminals. But the shock value will be
hard to resist. The story will put his magazine over the top."

"How likely will *Time* let us down?"

"Not likely if it were up to the journalists. They agreed
it will be the story of the century. Luce would be the only
obstacle. If *Time* doesn't come through, I will contact others. It may mean a longer wait."

"We'll revise the timeline after the trip to Tsingtao."

"I stopped in Hong Kong and locked the files in the
safe house."

"You did? Why?"

"Any publisher wouldn't pass up a story this big. If Luce
turns it down, there could be only one reason. Soong inter-
vened after Luce told him we got his files. Soong will do
everything he can to get them back. If we kept them here
and later we had to deliver them overseas, he would intercept them. Whatever transportation we used, it wouldn't

be hard for him to make trouble the moment we left the province."

Han nodded. "He has the Party's apparatus at his disposal."

"That will be the risk to avoid. That's why I left the five guards in the safe house. The papers are being watched round the clock. If and when we need to identify someone other than *Time* to publish the story, I can contact them by wire. We can have the guards deliver the files to their representatives in Hong Kong. The safe house is steps from the Foreign Correspondents' Club."

"Hong Kong is out of Soong's jurisdiction and the Brits wouldn't do anything to get on my wrong side," Han said. "The files should be safe."

"I also closed the deal on the lot on Victoria Peak. I remembered you said you want to have the second Villa up in a year."

"Good. I was going to contact Boyd-Jones about that."

"Something else came up at the Liaison Office." Jong gave a summary of Boyd-Jones's pitch to deposit future proceeds from their partnership in a London bank.

"What was your reply?"

"I told him I'd need the terms in writing before I could make a recommendation to you. He sent them to my hotel. The terms are sound as far as I can tell. But if you decide to go forward, we should have our solicitors look them over."

"What about the dividend rate?"

"The rate is higher than market."

"Why did they make the pitch to you?"

"They preferred to discuss in person. I was there and they made use of the occasion."

"With the Brits, there is always a hidden agenda. Did you get a sense of what it was?"

"They said they were concerned about mounting instability in China. They have collected intelligence indicating our networks might be attacked in the coming months. Total annihilation, according to their spies. If the peril is real, it will affect your end of the partnership. They don't want to see it jeopardized."

"Of course they don't. The money is too good. Any validity to their intelligence?"

"The level of urgency might have been exaggerated, but I don't doubt the dangers are real," Jong replied. "With Henry gone and the new man learning the ropes, it's a vulnerable time for the field operators."

"I'll order them to take extra security measures."

"They will not be enough. We should have all the codes changed. Revise the routines and move our people out of current locations."

"That bad?"

"The Brits know our operations in Shanghai, inside out. They also found out what the Blue Shirts plan to do."

"How?"

"Boyd-Jones wouldn't say," Jong replied. "Should we look into this?"

"The Brits are not the enemy. Whatever they know now won't be relevant. Their intelligence will be out of date. Our operations will have a new set of targets and the Blue Shirts won't have a chance to do what they plan to do. What do you think of the proposal to deposit in their bank?"

"It's worth considering. Not so much as an investment or a place to park your assets, but as a way to show your trust in the partnership. It can buy a lot of good will."

"There will be plenty of opportunities to call in the favor later. Go ahead."

"I'll wire Boyd-Jones and he can set it up. When will you want it to begin?"

"As soon as possible. Why not?"

"How much would you like to put in the account?"

"It's your deal. You decide."

"How about we begin conservatively? See how things go. If you are satisfied with the way they handle the account, we'll increase it at intervals. Any time you find their performance unsatisfactory, we'll stop."

"Fine. Do whatever you think will work for us," Han said, too pleasantly.

Han had bought his fabrications and recommendations without expressing any doubt. And the tone had been casual. Too casual. As if they were chatting about happenings in the world, not events that would directly affect the execution of Han's Grand Strategy. From across the desk Han was gazing at him, eyes intent, probing. Jong sensed a different train of thought was going on in Han's mind. Why did he feel Han was assessing him? Could his guilty conscience be playing tricks on his perception?

"Everything all right while I was gone?" Jong asked.

"Should it not have been?"

"Of course not. I didn't mean it that way."

"Actually, something did happen while you were away. I have decided to get married."

It was the last thing Jong expected. "I didn't know you were thinking of marriage."

"Neither did I. I never thought I would marry again after the fiasco with my first wife. But after I met her, everything changed. I changed." His face lit up. "It was as though my eyes were opened by the gods. I was able to see what I have been missing."

"Who is this special woman?"

"Yunna."

"Yunna?"

"Yes. Yunna. I have chosen her to be my new Fu-jen."

Jong couldn't speak.

"You look surprised."

Jong managed a small nod.

"So was I. Very happily surprised."

"Yunna," Jong said again with difficulty.

"The most beautiful girl in China."

"But you always said you had no need for a wife."

"I did say that, didn't I? And meant it too. I liked being a bachelor. Having as many women as I wanted. Keeping them as long as I wanted. Not having to put up with their moods and silly demands. I thought that's what I'd do. Didn't expect I'd lose my heart." He breathed. "What you said about falling in love—I didn't think it would happen to me. But it did. Who would have thought? Having met her, I can't see myself with anyone else. Incredible, isn't it?"

"Yes," Jong said weakly.

"It's a wonderful feeling. I wish there was a way I could share it with you."

As the reality of the news started to sink in, Jong's mind churned with shock, confusion, anger, hurt. How could this have happened? How could things have gone this far in such a short time? What did Han do? Drug her? Put a spell on her? How could the man he loved want to take away the girl he loved?

"Does she know how you feel?" Jong asked.

"Yes."

"Are you sure?"

"Sure I'm sure. I told her. And I showed her the gold."

That said everything. Jong's heart sank.

"I wanted Yunna to know she is different from the women in my past. She will be my Fu-jen. My one and only supreme wife. I followed protocol and asked her mother for her hand. Well, the fling I had with her didn't help. It took some convincing before Su-chen gave in."

"She did?"

"After a nasty scene. I wasn't surprised. Henry said she could be dogmatic and possessive. It's her upbringing. She thinks she is entitled to have whatever she wants because she is a Kung. Anyway, I set her straight."

"She is devoted to you."

"She was devoted to Henry too. You know how women are."

No, I don't. Not anymore.

"I had the fortune-tellers check the astrological almanac. The fifteenth of next month is an excellent day for weddings. I'll have a big banquet with the ceremony."

"Will there be enough time to get ready?"

"The staff is working round the clock. I don't want to wait; no point in putting off happiness. I'd marry her tomorrow if we could postpone the trip to Tsingtao. But Ganz said everyone is breathing down his neck. He needs to have a decision from me. Why are you looking at me like that, Jong?"

Jong was wrestling with tidal waves inside his head. He managed to articulate the least significant point. "Yunna is awfully young for you."

"Why is everyone concerned about our age difference? I am in excellent health. She is marrying the most eligible bachelor in China. There are a few years between us; so what?"

"What if she doesn't want to be Han Fu-jen?"

"Every woman, every girl in China wants to be Han Fu-jen."

"Yunna isn't just any girl."

"No, she isn't. And not a fool."

"She can't have any feelings for you."

Han raised his eyebrows. "That's an odd thing to say."

"She hardly knows you."

"I've been a friend of her family since she was a little girl. I was an important figure in their lives. Her father must have talked about me. Even if she didn't know me well before, she does now."

"In such a short time?"

"That's the marvel of it. Since that first evening, we have been together every hour of the day. If you had not been away, you would have seen how close we've become."

If I had not been away, Jong repeated silently, would this have happened? What did our love mean if I could lose her so easily?

"Something you want to say, Jong? You know you can be frank with me."

Can I?

"She and I…"

"What about you and her?"

"We…"

"Tell me."

Jong did his best to speak calmly. "When Yunna arrived in Shansui, she was devastated by what happened in Nanking. She is a strong girl and she keeps things to herself, but I could see how heartbroken she was. I wanted to make her feel this was her new home, and that given time, things would be fine. I reached out to her. We became friends. Close friends."

"I am glad Yunna has a friend."

"We spent time together. We trusted each other. We talked about things close to our hearts."

"That's what friends do."

"We talked about the future. Things we'll do after the war. Places we'll see. People we want to be with…"

"Who did she want to be with?"

Jong didn't answer.

"Are you trying to say those plans didn't include marrying someone like me?" Han looked at him archly. "Do you know what kind of man she wants to be with? Does she have a special someone? Is there an attachment I am not aware of? I want you to be truthful with me."

I am the special someone. Yunna is attached to me. We are each other's future. But Jong couldn't say the words. Han's face forbade it. His loyalty forbade it.

"I'm afraid I can't say, General."

"Why not?"

"It would be presumptuous for me to speak on Yunna's behalf."

Han laughed uproariously.

"Should my answer have been different, General?"

"I've always suspected, and it turns out I'm right. You *are* a Westerner at heart. No Chinese man would consider it presumptuous to speak on a woman's behalf."

Relieved that Han's observation had nothing to do with what was on his mind, Jong said, "Most Westerners don't see me as one of them."

"Maybe not now, but the day will come when you will be one of them."

Jong detected an edge in Han's voice. "That would only be possible if I left China and lived somewhere else."

"Would you like to do that?"

"Such a future has never occurred to me," Jong answered, more readily than he should have. What if Han had learned of the conditions he'd proposed to Boyd-Jones?

"It's not a bad idea. Travel, experience cultures of younger countries. Surely you want to find out the non-Chinese half of you."

"Only when I am not needed here. My life is with you, General."

"You still feel this way? After living in my shadow for so many years? Wouldn't you want to strike out on your own?"

Han had asked the same questions before. On the day before the Nanking Massacre. This time the tone was different. Jong sensed neither curiosity nor concern, but a need for information.

"If such thoughts have been contemplated, you can tell me, Jong. I'd prefer that you didn't go, of course. I can't see my life without you. But nothing lasts forever. Not even us. If leaving is something you want to do, I won't stand in your way."

"It's not my wish to leave you or Shansui."

"Not ever?"

"No."

"You will stand by me no matter what?"

"Yes."

"Nothing and no one will come between us?"

"No."

Han shifted his gaze to a spot beyond Jong. "I am glad to hear that. Very glad."

"I mean it, General."

"Of course you mean it. I'd never doubt you, Jong, you know that."

A wall of distrust has been erected, Jong thought, though the first brick had been laid long before today. The first time Han had told him about his plan to be emperor, Jong had known in his heart that Han was embarking on a disastrous undertaking. If it succeeded, it would bring vast suffering to China; if it failed, their own destruction. But it was at this moment that they arrived at the watershed in their relationship. Jong felt the fracture as acutely as the grinding hollowness in his stomach. From now on, every word would be weighed before and after it was spoken. They would move away from each other toward futures they would not share. But in his wildest dreams he would never have imagined Yunna the catalyst.

"Is there anything you want me to do before we leave for Tsingtao?" Jong asked.

"Have a good rest. Everything is set."

"When will we take off?"

"We are booked on the midday train."

"You changed the plan?"

"Yes."

"Why the train?"

"Because it's something no one would expect me to do. We need this added measure of security. Ganz is well known in Kuomintang circles. He is their broker of choice for certain types of goods and weapons. It's not a secret that he and I do business now and then—he does have a broad clientele. But at this moment, it's best not to call attention to our relationship. I also want to see the countryside. Get a closer look at how peasants are coping with

the war. It would help me to understand why they are joining Mao's revolution. We'll travel incognito. No entourage,
just a couple of bodyguards. You haven't met Ganz?"

"No."

"I've known him since he was a kid running his own
poker franchise. His family is from Bremen. He's an engi-
neer by training; international trading is what he does. He
can get anything from anywhere—and I do mean anything.
He's working on a special project for me."

"I didn't know Tsingtao was in your plan."

"Tsingtao is not in my plan; Berlin is."

To signal he didn't want more said on the subject, Han
adjusted his posture, leaning back and resting both elbows
on the arms of the chair. He turned to the window.

He began in a voice of quiet reminiscence, "Remember
the first time we met? The Majestic Hotel in Shanghai. You
were how old?"

"Fifteen."

"I'll always remember the day. I was sitting by myself,
behind a pillar; I didn't want to join the party. Those situations
bore me. I planned to make an appearance and then leave. You
came to me with the tea tray. I saw the color of your eyes and
I was intrigued. You looked at me as if you had known me for
years and talked to me like an equal. Never had that happened
to me. Certainly not with a child. I liked your confidence. It
reminded me of myself when I was that age. And your intelligence—it shone like a beam of light. It was clear that you
didn't belong there. I decided then that I would remake you.
You would be the son I should have had. When I brought you
home, people were surprised. They thought it was unwise to
have chosen a half-breed child. Adopt a real Chinese boy, they
said. Half-breeds are born with half a mind. They were wrong."

A smile straight from the heart. "Bringing you here was one of the best things I've done for myself, Jong."

Han's words—as intended, a part of Jong observed—evoked a rush of nostalgia and gratitude. The rest of him was conscious of the unspoken reminder: You are who you are because of me; you should live your life as I want it.

"You changed my life. I will always be grateful, General."

"Gratitude. Is that all you can give me?"

"I will give you whatever is in my power to give. I will do whatever you want me to do." What else should I say?

"Then let me tell you what I want from you: your life-long commitment. As I shall give you mine. Our lives insepa-rable, as they are meant to be. I will make our relationship official. I will adopt you as my son and you will be my heir. In the event of my death, you will be the executor of my estate. If Yunna bears me a son, you will act as his guardian regent until he reaches the age of nineteen. If I should have no son, you will marry a Chinese woman. Your son will be given my name and he will continue the Han family line."

Jong was speechless.

"Will you do that for me?"

"It's a magnificent gift, General."

"Will you accept?"

"I…"

"Will you accept?"

"There may be other considerations."

"Like what?"

"Yunna might not like being my adoptive mother. It would be awkward."

"Didn't you tell me she trusts you? Your being my son will bring you closer. You will be family."

Family. What irony.

"You think I may be making the decision on impulse, because I am in an exceptional mood," Han continued. "Yes, I am very happy, but there is nothing impulsive about this. It has been on my mind for a long time. You didn't think I would keep you in an unofficial limbo? Son in substance, not in name?"

"I have never minded, General."

"I know, but that doesn't mean it should go on." Han leaned forward. "Let me tell you why this is the right time to do this. Precisely because I am getting married. Yunna is young. I expect she will bear me children. As much as I abhor the thought, I have to prepare for the day when I won't be around to take care of them. I will need someone who will do that for me. Someone whose loyalty neither I nor Yunna will question. Someone who will be the faithful custodian of my legacy. Someone who cares about her, who will protect her and our children."

Someone who cares about her. So deeply that he is willing to put her life before his own. Was Han's instinct so sharp that he could select the perfect understudy without knowing the truth? Or was it more than instinct?

"I may not be up to the job," Jong said.

"If you are not, no one is. You said you would stay with me as long as I need you. That was a promise you made. Promises can be broken. I am not unrealistic about the inherent fickleness of human nature." He paused. "Once you become my legal heir, there will be personal and public obligations. Irrevocable life-long obligations. They may exceed what you have in mind. If you have reservations, tell me now."

"Whether in an official capacity or not, I'll carry out your wishes."

Han nodded to indicate he wouldn't have expected anything less. "I'll make the announcement after the wedding."

After the wedding. As insurance? Reward?

"I'll do my best, General."

"I can't tell you how pleased I am." Unexpectedly Han changed the subject. "Did you find out more about your parents?"

"Nothing new. It's the same stories. None seems to be based on fact. The one about my father being an American missionary may be the least implausible."

"Do you intend to pursue it further?"

"Not unless there is a convincing new lead. I honestly don't know what more I can do."

"You did all you could. Time to put it behind you," Han said firmly. "Not every child takes after his parents. What matters is the man you have become."

Not for the first time, Jong wondered whether Han knew about his parents, and if he did, why he hadn't told him. But this was not the moment to pursue the query. He needed desperately to be alone. To sort out the tangle of feelings. To decide what to do with Han's plan to marry Yunna and his own future role as regent of Han's dynasty.

Jong stood up. "I should get ready for the trip."

"If you wish to offer your good wishes to Yunna, you'll have to wait. She is in retreat."

"Where is she?"

"In a secluded place. She will not receive visitors until the wedding."

"Why?"

"Once she becomes Han Fu-jen, she will be faced with many demands. This may be the only time for her to have a good rest. I don't want her disturbed."

Their eyes met. Her presence fell between them like a sword.

"Is she alone?" Jong asked.

"There are servants and guards."

"Is she inside the Villa?"

"No."

"In Shansui?"

"You will see her on our wedding day."

Han stood up and saw Jong to the door.

"It has been an eventful month, wouldn't you say?" Han said.

"Yes."

"Soon we'll reap the fruits of our efforts."

"Yes."

"We have gone far, Jong, you and I. We will go farther. The sky is the limit."

Tsingtao, and then the wedding, Jong thought. Twenty days are all I have. To do what must be done.

There wasn't any doubt now. Han had given him no other choice.

Twenty days. And the rest of my life.

༄

"Meet my friend Klaus Ganz," Han said, making introductions on the platform at the Tsingtao railway station. "Klaus, my chief of staff, Jong Lin."

Ganz had green eyes, long blond hair tied back. He was barrel-chested and broad shouldered. He wore an ankle-length shearling coat and black leather boots. A decoration on a ribbon peeped from under the collar of his shirt. His manner was brusque and decisive.

They shook hands. Ganz's grip was firm, as was his gaze. Not someone to pick a quarrel with, Jong thought.

"General Han talks about you whenever we meet. I feel I know you already. First time in Tsingtao?" Ganz said in perfect Chinese.

"Yes."

"It's a little out of the way. You'll find that it's a special place."

"I'm sure it is."

Ganz's entourage cut through the crowd like royalty. The German was a local legend, Han had told Jong on the train. His father had been a member of an engineering team commissioned by the German government to build the city. When work was completed, his parents had returned to Germany. Their eighteen-year-old son had stayed, supposedly for two more years to finish his university degree. Free of parental supervision, Ganz had turned his full attention to his passion: gambling. In weeks he had lost everything, including his father's house. When those he owed came to take possession of the property, Ganz had vanished. Eight years went by before he resurfaced, teenage gambler transformed into successful international businessman. He had bought back his father's house and set up the trading company.

"Handsome-looking things," Han said, admiring the three new Mercedes sedans parked nearby.

"Latest model, engineered like an airplane. Only two hundred were built. I can arrange a delivery from Stüttgart if you'd like."

"Three. For myself, Jong, and my new wife."

Ganz led them to the last car. Two men with Ganz's build dressed in identical outfits climbed into the first two cars.

"Do you always travel like this, Mr. Ganz?" Jong asked as the car took off.

"Klaus, please," he replied affably. "I have to. Police presence in Tsingtao is negligible. The streets are not safe and they are getting worse by the day. Most people here know who I am and the extent of my assets. Extra caution is necessary." He nodded at Han. "I don't expect the bad times to last. I am counting on General Han to make the country safe."

Ganz took out bottles of beer from a thermos box under the seat, opened them and filled three mugs.

"To China's new dynasty. I'll build a brewery in your honor, General. And you'll make everyone learn the pleasure of beer."

Han cheerfully took a gulp. "First you'll have to convince me this is not made from foamy piss."

"Certainly no match for your mou-tai, which is concocted from bathwater in Canton whorehouses."

"Whores with the pox."

"Pox from *kweiloh* yangs."

"Cheers."

They rode along tree-lined boulevards, passing cobble-stoned alleys and half-timbered houses with geraniums in window boxes. Tsingtao had been a German concession until 1914. What the Germans had built remained intact. Magnificent churches and towers dominated the streets. After a loop around a quaint town square, the cars headed uphill. The air turned damp and chilly. They were moving alongside a cliff through thin patches of fog.

On a bluff overlooking the sea, a Bavarian castle stood, surrounded by stone paths and an apple orchard. A circular brick driveway scythed through a perfect lawn. Passing the gate, the other two vehicles veered off to the row of garages behind the house. Ganz's car pulled up at the entry under a carriage porch. A team of Chinese amahs appeared and carried the luggage from the trunk of the car into the house.

The interior was high-ceilinged with dark beams. The living room was furnished like a nobleman's den. Antlers hung on the walls. Velvet drapes cascaded over high windows. Two maids offered coffee in gilded porcelain cups. Ganz and his visitors sat on armchairs around a massive slab of black marble. After a brief chat, Han and Jong were escorted to the guest quarters.

"Tell us more about this hush-hush invention," Han said when they convened in the library after dinner.

Blackout drapes were drawn over windows. A mahogany mantel shaded a thriving fireplace. Hanging on the walls were Dutch oils Jong estimated to be worth more than all the Mercedes sedans in Shantung. They sat on gray damask sofas. A portable bar was parked beside them, holding cut-crystal decanters and silver-jacketed tumblers.

Ganz lit a meerschaum pipe, waved the flame from the matchstick. "As I said in the wire, General, it's a bomb."

"Not the usual bomb?"

"No, there's nothing usual about this one. It's the invention of the century. A bomb to end all bombs. Imagine, if you can, a village flattened by a single blast, the city of Canton wiped out in half a day."

"How does it work?"

"It's an immensely complicated weapon. It would take a team of scientists hours to explain the intricate design and functions. There is an abundance of technical data, most of which comprehensible only to people who work in the laboratories. I'm not sure if I can interpret the information in the reports I've read. The science is too advanced for me. What I can do is give a summary in layman's terms. All right with you?"

"I don't need a detailed explanation. Just tell me when it will be available and how it can work for me."

Puffing on his pipe, Ganz began, "The source of the bomb's explosive power comes from the fission of atomic nuclei. When the nucleus of a heavy atom, in this case uranium, is split, a staggering amount of energy is released. An unprecedented amount. On a kilo-for-kilo basis, it produces one hundred million times more energy than a chemical explosive such as TNT."

"Come again."

"*One hundred million times.* I did a double take too, and had the number verified. Let me put it in concrete contexts. Its velocity is a hundred times more powerful than the biggest tsunami or earthquake experienced in the last hundred years. It can uproot a forest, tear buildings off the ground, and toss crowds into the air. The heat emitted is so intense that it can melt roof tiles miles from the explosion. Chance for survival for anyone within a fifteen-mile radius is nil."

The room was quiet.

"It can be dropped from a plane?" Han asked.

"That is the integral part of the design. The bomb is no bigger than a sampan. It fits into a plane and can be deployed from the air."

"The target won't have time to defend itself. Vast destruction in a matter of minutes. I like it."

"Are you talking about the atomic bomb?" Jong asked.

"In Germany we call it U-235, after its primary ingredient, uranium-235, or actino-uranium."

Jong's chest tightened. He had read in foreign newspapers about the invention the Western powers had been racing to build. Germany and the United States were current front-runners. The bomb was believed to be the deadliest weapon ever made.

"You are saying the atomic bomb is available to us?" Jong asked.

"On a very exclusive basis."

"How exclusive?"

"At the moment General Han will be the only customer. If it's up to me, it will stay that way. But I can't control what Berlin does."

"Germany is willing to sell this brand-new weapon to a foreigner? I find that hard to believe," Jong said.

"Countries sell weapons to other countries, nothing out of the ordinary there. And General Han isn't just any foreigner. But this is a brand new invention and we are in uncharted waters. I didn't want to take anything for granted. I waited until I had the right people giving me the go-ahead before I draw up the contract."

"Isn't it still in development and no one is certain of the outcome?"

"It is in development in the United States and Britain. The Americans got a late start. They are making frantic efforts to catch up, building laboratories, recruiting scientists, hot debates on Capitol Hill. The usual Yankee bravado. More bark than bite, if you ask me. It will be a while before they get on track—*if* they get on track. At the moment our British friends are ready to give up. They're running out of material and brainpower. Germany is ahead of everyone. We expect to have our first atomic bomb within six months."

"Six months," Han repeated with a frown.

"My source assured me a prototype can be ready in three."

"Who is this source?" Jong asked.

"Berlin."

"Can you be more specific?"

"The very top."

"Names?"

"No names."

"Departments? Agencies? The project must be under someone's purview," Jong persisted.

"I can give you the list of agencies involved and names of the people in charge."

"Those I can look up on my own. What about the identity of your contact?"

"It's confidential."

"We are not a security risk."

"Of course not. But I have given my word. I can't breach my promise."

"There must be a way to verify what you've said."

"You want to verify the source or the status of the bomb?"

"Both."

Ganz pointed the pipe like a pistol, aiming at Jong. "Are you questioning my integrity or my competence, Mr. Lin?"

"I'm asking if there is a way to confirm your statements."

"You don't trust me?"

"This is not a matter of trust." Jong replied. "As you said, it's a brand-new invention developed in total secrecy with the potential to do vast damage. So far, you have not supplied us with enough information to make an educated decision. We'd like some proof of your claim. Concrete proof."

"You are not shopping for stocks on Wall Street. This is *top top top* military intelligence."

"If you want to sell the bombs to us, you owe us every piece of information in your possession."

"It'd be more accurate to say General Han wants to buy than to say I want to sell."

Han cut in. "How much can you deliver?"

Ganz thought. "Fifty kilotons."

"How far will that go?"

"Enough to obliterate most of Shantung Peninsula."

"Price?"

Ganz proposed a sum that could be half the national budget. "One third in a week; another third when the goods leave Germany; the rest on delivery. I can give you the exact delivery date in a month."

"I want exclusivity in Asia. For a period of twelve months."

"I have already included that in the terms. It's not only because we are good friends, it's a consideration for my personal safety. I don't want anything like that to blow up at my doorstep. With you, I know precisely where the bomb will go."

Jong asked Han, "What are we going to do with the bomb?"

"Take the country back from the Kuomintang and the Communists. Get the Japanese out. Reassert China's authority abroad."

"Do you think the threat of an atomic bomb would be enough?"

"It won't be just a threat."

"You mean..."

"We'll drop the bombs on the island of Formosa. That's about the size of Shantung Peninsula."

Jong was stunned. "We are going to use the bomb on our own people?"

"The people of Formosa may share some history and physical characteristics with us, but they consider themselves an autonomous tribe. They have their own culture, and they think they should have their own government. Right now it's a Japanese colony. A showcase of China's shame. When the Japanese are gone, the natives will make trouble for us. The bomb will wipe the island clean."

"General, you can't. You will be massacring innocent people."

"I knew you'd object, Jong. That's why I haven't let you in until now. Your concerns are commendable, but unrealistic. Think. Who could resist a weapon like that? If not me, someone else will get his hands on the bomb. He could use it on Peking, Chungking, even Shansui. Innocent people die. That's what happens in wars."

"But..."

"I am not setting any precedent. Chiang Kai-shek bombed the dikes on the Yellow River to block the Japanese from advancing. Just so he could reserve his weapons and troops to fight Mao's guerrillas. We witnessed the consequences of this ingenious little feat. Four thousand villages flooded, two hundred thousand people killed, ten times more made homeless. No one has called Chiang a murderer, not publicly. No damage has been done to the man's political career. One does what is needed to win. That's the only rule of the game."

"There are *millions* of people on Formosa…"

"I want a target commensurate with the bomb's power."

"Why not choose a foreign target?"

"Foreign territories have foreigners on them. I'm not interested in starting a war outside China."

"What about somewhere less populated? You could drop the bomb on Outer Mongolia. There are a few spots where it's inhabitable. You would show the power of the bomb without hurting anyone."

"The impact would have no consequence. People would say Han is a paper tiger."

"People can say what they want, but you would have shown them what you can do."

"Then what? Wait for them to surrender? The target has been chosen in accordance with my Grand Strategy. Cities with historical monuments must be preserved. Peking is out, as are Nanking, Sian, and Wuhan. My key operations are in Shanghai. Canton is too close to Hong Kong, where I'll build my capital. Formosa is an ideal target. It's off the coast. Fallout from the explosion, if any, will have minimum effect on China proper."

"We've worked out other game plans, General. They can get us what we want with less risk, less bloodshed."

"Not if I want a swift and sweeping victory. There is one more compelling reason. The Soongs are investing heavily on the island. Chiang has cut a secret deal with the Western powers. America will intervene and they expect to win. They will take the island back from the Japanese and give to the Kuomintang as a consolation prize."

"We are looking at months down the road. This scenario may not happen as planned."

"But there's a better chance that it would. I won't let Chiang have his empire, small and pathetic though it will be."

Jong said to Ganz, "How soon do we have to decide?"

"I am giving General Han first-refusal rights. We are friends and he was the one who spurred me to seek it out. But this is a business agreement, not a topic for political debate nor a cause for moral dilemma. Time is of the essence. A break-through may be happening in the labs as we speak. I need a decision from you before you leave. I am going to Berlin with a purchase agreement—yours, I hope. If you can't make up your mind, it would be best that we stop the conversation." Ganz turned to Han and raised his eyebrows as if to say: I thought the decision was made—why the argument?

"Are you implying you have other customers?" Jong asked.

"We live in volatile times. There is no shortage of ambitious people who would seize any chance to take over the world. None as deserving as General Han, of course."

"I'm not interested in generalities. Do you have a list of prospective buyers?"

"Count the number of generals and triad leaders."

"How many have you approached?"

"None. As I promised General Han."

Jong changed to a southern dialect and addressed Han, "The atomic bomb is an experiment. Its capabilities are not tested. We won't know how it will work—if it will work. Even if it does work, will it work the way we want it to? What if there is a problem? Who's going to fix it?"

"Ganz already thought of that. The deal will include a team of experts from Berlin. They will oversee the operation from start to finish. If there is one thing we can count on the

Germans, it's their high level of technical excellence. They are betting on the bomb to win the war. It has to work."

"We will have to rely on strangers. Foreigners. We will have to trust them with our lives. It will be a huge risk."

"There is always risk in any wartime operation. Let's not get worked up about this. It's a bomb, only more powerful. We'll handle it like any other bomb. Select the target, aim, and make the drop. If it's not done right the first time, we'll do it again."

"We can minimize risk if we have full knowledge of how the weapon works, our own team of experts, and our own safeguards."

"It will take time to do all that. The longer we wait, the greater the chance of it being leaked. If Chiang finds out I have the atomic bomb, he will go berserk. He will run to the Americans and scream for help. A weapon like that can change the balance of power overnight. The Americans would get behind him in a big way. That would not be good for me."

"I am not convinced a private citizen can procure a top-security weapon from his government for a foreigner. Why would Germany want to give their invention to us?"

"Berlin is not happy that Washington is cozying up to the Kuomintang. They don't want America gaining undue influence over the largest country in the world. I'll help them to obliterate their rival's ally. An insider who will do the dirty work for them. That was the selling point Ganz made to Berlin. And they are not giving anything away. I am paying good money."

"Everything we know about this yet-to-be-invented weapon comes from Ganz. He lives here. How can we be sure of his Berlin connection?"

"Germany is his home and where his sources are. He has made countless deals with the German leadership—some of them on my behalf. He has an impeccable record."

"What if he's lying about the atomic bomb?"

"Why would he do that?"

"The money. For one."

"He knows better than to lie to me. He would be signing his own death warrant."

"He would be out of China. With a staggering sum of money."

"I've known Ganz for years. He is a professional. The best. He has never reneged on a deal."

"This is far too important a decision to base on one man's word."

"Ganz has researched the market, tested prototypes, and approached dozens of suppliers all over the globe. He has been reporting his progress every step of the way. When he first heard about the atomic bomb, he was skeptical. He recruited experts to conduct a thorough assessment before he made the proposal to me."

"The stakes are enormous, General."

"As will be the outcome. The bomb will give me China."

Ganz leaned on the sideboard, puffing his pipe from the side of his mouth. "Would you like more time for your private discussion? I can smoke my pipe somewhere else."

"Stay where you are. We will close the deal now. You will go to Berlin with my purchase agreement. Jong will arrange the first installment. What do you prefer, cash or gold?"

"Cash. To be wired to an account in Geneva."

"Consider it done. I expect to hear from you within a month."

"You will, General."

Alone in his room, Jong stared at the piece of paper with the number of Ganz's Swiss bank account. This is the sum total of decades of planning: the massacre of innocent people using an unimaginably destructive weapon purchased with opium money.

Would things have been different if he had made an effort to steer Han from this path?

Would there be time to stop him?

Jong put the piece of paper in an ashtray and lighted a match. The paper crumbled, blackened, and turned into ashes. He stared at the gray remains, imagining a miniature scenario of an atomic explosion. For all his objections, he knew Han was right. They were in a war. Someone would use the bomb on innocent people. To win, Han needed to stay ahead.

He took the ashtray to the window and poured out the contents. The flakes whirled like dead butterflies in the night. The sky was starless. A thin moon cut through the darkness like a swath of silver.

He listened. The night had no answer for him.

From the bottom of his suitcase he retrieved a folded piece of paper and spread it on the desk. A topographic map of southern China. He sat down and switched on the light. With a pencil he traced the route. Avoiding main roads and military checkpoints, he glided the line from Shansui, heading southeast, passing the border of Kwangsi and turning southward through Kwangtung Province to the Pearl River. He measured the length of the route with a piece of string, checked the scale and converted to miles. Going nonstop, it would be possible to complete the journey in one night.

One night.

The night.

There might be unanticipated peril, a change in weather, rough terrain, mechanical problem, ambush. All he could do was to be prepared.

He picked up the telephone and called the treasurer in Shansui.

"The entire amount to Switzerland?" asked the surprised voice at the other end.

"Have our man at the bank handle this. Only him. This is a highly confidential transaction. Tell him to put the money in a transit account. It will have no account number. No name. No address. The funds can only be accessed with a password I will provide."

"Do you mean the money will be moved?"

"Yes."

"Where?"

"It won't be your concern."

"The bank will ask. They need the information for this type of account."

"Tell them they will hear from me. And they are to accept instructions from me. Only me. This point must be absolutely clear."

"What about expiration date?"

"No expiration date."

"This is highly unusual…"

"Yes, it is. That's why it must be handled with absolute discretion. Don't say a word to the staff or anyone."

"Yes, Mr. Lin." He hesitated. "You said the order is from the General?"

"You want to verify?"

"It's not that I don't trust you, Mr. Lin. It's just that this is a huge sum of money."

"I understand. Tomorrow I'll ask the General to call you from where we are. He will confirm the amount. That's all he will do. He is not accustomed to explaining his decision to his staff. Satisfied?"

"Yes."

"If you have more questions, ask me. Use the telephone."

"Yes, Mr. Lin."

He hung up.

He re-dialed the operator and requested an overseas line. He gave a number in Hong Kong.

An English voice answered.

Jong recited a code. "Calling for progress report."

"Project completed as planned. The documents are ready."

"Two sets?"

"Two sets. Names according to your instructions."

"Forward to the contact in Canton. Use established procedure. They will be picked up in due course."

"London asked for an arrival date."

"Why?"

"We want to make sure your settlement will be handled properly."

"I won't need any handling."

"There are ways we can help."

"No help needed."

"They are insistent."

"So am I."

"Any message you want to forward to London or other destinations after Hong Kong?"

"I have no message for anyone. Good-bye."

Jong took out a sheet of paper and began to write. He would only tell her the part of the plan that involved her, nothing that would cause her undue anxiety. Han wouldn't have her locked up. There must be a way to deliver the letter to her.

Sharp gusts of wind beat insistently against the windows. Joss is knocking. In his mind he saw again the whirling ashes in the night. And Yunna's face.

It's my war now.

Our war, if you join me.

30

It was a castle with Gothic towers and stained glass windows on the hillside overlooking Repulse Bay, a beach resort on the southwest side of Hong Kong Island. A pergola of pillars rose from a half-moon terrace. An outdoor bar stood on the lawn, round like a bandstand, shaded by a blue and white awning. The grounds were deserted; the party was inside the house. Shiny automobiles lined up along the curb, bumper to bumper.

The taxi let Lillie and Chiu off in front of the gate. Keeping yards apart like an estranged couple, they walked up the concrete rise.

"I'll make the introductions. After that, you're on your own," Chiu said tersely.

"Fine."

"Soong is leaving tomorrow. This is it. I won't arrange another meeting."

"If I want another meeting, you will arrange another meeting."

"Are you going to set him up and blackmail him too?"

"You are being dramatic, Mr. Chiu. There is no blackmail. You and I are exchanging favors."

"You don't know what you're up against. You are a fool to mess with Soong. I don't care what you do, just leave me out of it. If you did so much as breathe a word that I brought you here, I'll set fire to the Mayflower and have you deported back to China."

"The Mayflower has a new owner as of two days ago. I may not be as educated as you are, Mr. Chiu, but I know my rights. This is British soil. You can't deport me."

"The Brits can fly their Union Jacks on rooftops, but Hong Kong is a Chinese city. I don't need their help. My men can make you disappear. You will be wiped off the face of the earth. It will be like you never existed and the police will have no clue what happened."

"Your threats are getting tedious."

"*My* threats? What have you been doing to me?"

"You did it to yourself, Mr. Chiu. You killed a girl and then you made a full confession. Willingly."

"When am I going to get the tape back?"

"I was going to let you have it after tonight if things go well. Now that I find out you plan to do me harm, I am keeping it. As insurance."

"Where is it?"

"Somewhere safe."

"Where is it?"

"Do you seriously expect me to tell you?"

"You would, if you wanted to stay alive."

"If I could be scared that easily, I wouldn't be here. And just so you know, if something happens to me, the tape will go to the authorities. Along with the crime scene photos, your tie, and statements from eyewitnesses."

"You are out of your mind."

"I am not stupid."

"I'll find them."

"I'm sure you will try and your men will have fun looking. Now shut up and ring the damn bell."

They had reached the double mahogany door. Chiu jammed his thumb on the button like he was crushing a bug. The door opened at once. Seeing Chiu, a manservant in a white jacket suit bowed and stepped aside. They entered a marble foyer illuminated by a cascade chandelier. A sweeping staircase ran up along the side. An amah stepped forward and helped Chiu with his coat. Lillie signaled she had nothing to check in.

The party was an international gathering: Chinese, Caucasians, Malays, and Indians. The host and his wife were receiving the guests under a beam of light in the living room. Lillie had seen his photograph in newspapers, a Shanghai merchant who'd made his fortune exporting Chinese herbs. He was in his fifties, tall with a slight stoop, an unremarkable face except for the confidence the eyes exuded. He was the only man in the room not wearing black. His gray suit matched his hair; a diamond stickpin blinked from his tie.

"Mr. Yu, may I present Miss Lee?" Chiu said when it was their turn. "She is the friend of a business associate. She always wanted to see your house, so I brought her along. Hope you don't mind."

"Not at all. Welcome, Miss Lee."

"Thank you."

"You must be from Shanghai."

"Yes. This is such a beautiful house, Mr. Yu. You've built a landmark."

"The architect did an excellent job. We are pleased with how it turned out."

His wife was a tiny woman in green silk and black pearls. She nodded at them without a word. Chiu broke off from Lillie and moved to the other side of the room, quickly ensconced in a group of fellow bankers. A buzz of talk and laughter hummed over soft music from a gramophone. Lillie sensed an air of anticipation, a stirring when new guests appeared. Soong, the guest of honor, had not yet arrived.

Edging back to the foyer, she headed to the other side of the floor. Most of the space was taken up by a formal dining room. Servants were laying out utensils on a long buffet table. Through a swinging door, she glimpsed a white-tiled kitchen and cooks busy at the stoves. The aromas suggested dinner was to be European fare. She moved on. At the end of the hallway was a solarium, half enclosed in glass with a red-tiled floor and white wicker furniture. Potted palms and hanging ferns lent an air of tropical elegance. The glass partition overlooked a courtyard surrounded by brick walls ten feet tall. She couldn't climb over even if she weren't wearing heels and a tight dress. Recalling European mansions in Shanghai, she knew there had to be a separate entrance for servants in a house like this. She returned to the foyer and located a narrow stairwell near the front door, leading down to a pair of doors at basement level. She descended uncarpeted steps. One door opened to servants' quarters, revealing a short hallway with rooms on both sides. She looked into cubicles furnished with bunk beds and folding chairs. The other door was locked. She released the bolt and stepped out into the open.

It was the twilight hour when light and shadow merged. The streetlights had been turned on. Pinpoints of yellow glowed on the hillside. A thin moon peered from behind the clouds. She felt a rush of wind on her face, carrying the brine of the South China Sea. She stayed close to the wall, ducking at windows to avoid being seen by people in the house. By rows of empty clotheslines, she found a wooden gate in the middle of the tall hedge surrounding the property. It was secured by a rusty chain, no lock. On the other side was a path, wide enough for two people to walk side by side, winding down to the beach. Tumbleweeds and ratty shrubs grew wild and tall, providing natural camouflage. She looked across the sand to the hotel on the edge of the water. The brightest lights shone from the second-floor balcony. Silhouettes of dancing couples swayed under chandeliers; she could hear the band. The nightclub was a popular spot with the local elite. There would be a constant flow of guests and cars. No one would give a second glance to a woman dressed up for a party. It would be easy to find a taxi there and return to the city. At dawn tomorrow she and Pierre would take the first ferry to Lantao Island. She had rented a cottage near the Trappist monastery high up in the mountains. It was one of the remotest areas in the Colony; the location had not been recorded by land surveyors. The monks kept to themselves. They grew their own food and paid little attention to the outside world. She had told them she and her son needed a quiet place to restore their spirits after an acrimonious divorce. They would stay there until it was safe to make the next move.

A plan. Just in case something went wrong tonight.

Confident of having identified an escape route, she rejoined the party. Chiu was in the hallway talking to an attractive woman in a red velvet dress. Laura Soong, former Shanghai debutante, now Mrs. T. V. Soong and reigning socialite, was smiling at something he said. Catching Lillie's sight, Chiu stared down at her for a good minute, and then unexpectedly winked.

She walked on.

T. V. Soong was holding court in the foyer. A ceiling light cast his profile in sharp relief. The face was a mass of acne scars, with grayness under the eyes. He had put on weight and looked ten years older than his age, not the dapper gent in the public photographs she had seen in Shanghai. Guests circled him three and four deep. The conversation was polite small talk. Soong's manner was circumspect; he spoke haltingly, not making eye contact with his audience. Lillie edged up and stood behind a woman with a high hairdo.

Someone was watching her.

He was on the other side, outside the circle, leaning against the wall, with one arm across his waist and the other supporting his chin. There was no doubt that she was the object of his attention. The man was tall and broad-shouldered, wearing the obligatory dark suit and white shirt. The hair was over greased; the bow-tie was of the clipped-on variety bought from a street vendor. There was a light bulk in the pocket of his jacket and she wondered if it was a gun. She wouldn't be surprised if Chiu had sent someone to keep her from Soong. How far would the man go to stop her? He was twice her size. If he wanted to do her harm, she wouldn't have a chance. With minimum movement she unclasped her handbag and reached inside. The metal of the pistol stung like ice; her fingers trembled. She gripped the handle of the gun.

Soong made a wave with his hand, signaling the end of the chat. The group dispersed obediently, heading to the dining room. Lillie's watcher didn't move, head cocked, hand brushing back a forelock; a small smile played across his mouth. She had seen the same smile, on hundreds of men. He's on the prowl. She was the only single female guest and he had made her his target. Relieved, she dropped the gun back into the handbag, snapped it shut and tucked it under her arm. She took a glass of champagne from a passing waiter, lifted for a toast and emptied it in one gulp. He stepped forward, smile broadening. She realized she had just encouraged him; worse, she had made sure the man wouldn't forget her. Why did she make that stupid toast? Why did she need to show she had nothing to hide? She hurried away, tightening her grip on the handbag in case the gun should fly out, feeling weak at the knees. She shouldn't have drunk the champagne; she hadn't eaten a thing since breakfast. If she passed out, Chiu wouldn't waste a minute in calling the guards. Yu must have a team patrolling the estate. They would bundle her up and throw her into the sea.

Why did Chiu wink at her? Like he'd got things figured out and was ahead of the game.

She took a deep breath and joined the queue to the buffet.

Bowls of orchids and candles decorated the long dining table. Every inch of the surface was laden with food: warm canapés, turkey, lobster, smoked ham, salads. At one end of the table, a chef was slicing slabs of roast beef. Chatter, clanking of silver, laughter and music, all added up to a noise like a waterfall. Soong's wife was at the head of the buffet line, chatting with other wives. Any moment her husband would be joining her, and the couple would once again be surrounded by admirers. Lillie looked around the room full of guests and servants. How could she have expected to have a private talk with Soong? And even if she could find a way to corner him, she doubted that he would confess what he had done to Victor to someone he had never met, a stranger, a nobody. How naïve of her to have thought she would get the truth out of Soong by showing up at a party?

She had come this far. She had to try.

She edged away from the buffet line and moved to the door. She wanted to be the first to see Soong. The moment he showed up, she'd offer a friendly greeting so he wouldn't be on guard, then she'd move behind him. She'd press the gun in his back and order him to follow her. Everyone would be too busy with the food to notice. She'd get him out of the house and then ask him about Victor. With a gun pointing at him, he would talk.

She waited.

The buffet line was shrinking. Most guests had gotten their food and found seats at the table. No sight of Soong.

She slipped back into the foyer. Empty. In the living room a Caucasian couple was doing a fox-trot in the corner. An amah was straightening cushions on the long sofa. Lillie returned to the hallway and walked to the other end of the house. In the garden room, Yu's wife and another woman were sipping brandy in the dark. She lifted her gaze at the intruder at the door, cast a bored look at Lillie and returned to her companion.

Soong wouldn't have left without his wife, Lillie thought. He has to be in the house. Maybe he's resting upstairs. He did look worn out.

She mounted the carpeted stairs. A library and two bedrooms made up the second floor. She peered into the library. A soft lamp shone on bookcases lined with leather volumes. A group of armchairs, neatly tucked under a round card table. The doors of the bedrooms were open. They had been turned into powder rooms for the guests. She inhaled a potpourri of expensive scents in the first room. Cigar smoke lingered in the next.

She went up another floor. The moment she reached the landing, she sensed a presence. She softened her steps. There were only two doors on this floor. The first was a child's room, painted in bright yellow and containing more toys than a kindergarten. The other room, located right above the library, had an ornate double door and seemed equally spacious.

The master bedroom.

The door was opened a slit. Persian rug. Brocade wallpaper. Tall windows with an unobstructed view of the sea. A leather armchair with matching ottoman. A marble fireplace dominated one wall; a pile of chopped logs stacked neatly inside the cavity. She nudged the door inch by inch. Corner of a four-poster bed. Tapestry bedspread. Desk with a brass lamp shaded in green glass. A man slumped over on the desk.

Soong.

She couldn't believe her luck. She took a deep breath, stepped in and closed the door behind her.

"Honey," Soong mumbled without looking up. He had taken off his glasses; they lay on the desk. "I had to get away. My heart's bothering me."

She took another step.

"I can't find my pills."

"I am not your wife. She is downstairs."

He looked up. He was breathing through the mouth. The neck muscles tightened; his face was pale and pulled thin. "Did my wife send you?" His voice had the blurred quality of someone with a toothache.

She didn't reply.

He tried to lift himself out of the chair, one hand pushing down the armrest, the other clutching his chest. He fell back, face red.

"Help me," he said, wincing as if the words hurt.

Lillie moved forward. He leaned on her. She felt the heaving in his chest and his dependence. They negotiated the few steps to the bed. She eased him down. He couldn't raise his legs onto the mattress; she helped him. He tried to unbutton his shirt, but his fingers were shaky. She did that for him too. He lay on one side of the enormous bed. She propped pillows under his head and pulled a blanket to his chest, performing the tasks by instinct. He closed his eyes. After a while his breathing became even.

She went back to the door and turned the bolt to lock it. She walked to the other side of the room and closed the drapes.

She stood at the foot of the bed.

The set-up was a dream. They were alone. No one knew she was here. She would make him tell her what had happened to Victor. If Victor had been harmed, she would walk up to the bed and shoot Soong through the blanket.

A small pressure on the trigger and she would have performed the ultimate act of homage to the man she loved.
Everyone else was on the ground floor; they wouldn't hear
the shot. She would go back downstairs and leave quietly.
By the time they discovered Soong's body, she would be
out of their reach. Chiu would know it was her, but he
wouldn't dare say anything.

She took out the pistol and pointed it at Soong.

She tried to hold it steady, but her hands were trembling.

Somewhere a clock chimed, like a gong inside the
room. She started and dropped the pistol. It hit the edge of
the rug with a thud.

"What was that?" Soong asked, opening his eyes.

She was about to pick up the gun, but straightened up.
"Nothing."

"I'm thirsty."

"I can't help you."

"Please…"

She shouldn't deny a man's last wish. She poured a
glass of water from the carafe on the nightstand, then eased
him up and put the glass to his lips. He choked, recovered,
then drank gratefully.

"You have trouble with your heart?" she asked.

"Now and then."

"Is your condition serious?"

"I hope not."

"Have you told anyone you are here?"

"Yu."

"Anyone else?"

Soong shook his head.

"What about your bodyguards?"

"Who?"

"Your bodyguards. Are they here?"

"Yes."

"How many?"

He seemed to gain back some strength. His breathing was deeper, pushing some color into his face. He took over the glass and drank more. "Why do you want to know?"

She didn't answer.

For the first time since she entered the room, Soong looked at her. "Have we met before?"

"I wouldn't think so."

"Your Shanghainese is perfect. You're from there?"

"Yes."

"Are you sure we haven't met? You look familiar."

"I would have remembered if I met you. Anyone would."

Soong wasn't convinced. "I never forget a face. Where did you live in Shanghai?"

"The French Concession."

"I must have seen you in the neighborhood."

"Our house is a quite a distance from yours."

"Did you work in one of the banks?"

"No."

"A restaurant? A hotel?"

"I was a housewife."

"When did you leave Shanghai?"

"A few months ago."

"Why?"

"The war. And other reasons. I didn't want to leave."

He nodded. "There is no city like Shanghai, and I have seen more than a few."

"I would go back if I could."

"You know what I like most? The streetlights after dark, the jazz clubs, the fried dumplings at Three Six Nine—they are best with warm sake."

"Beer."

"A woman who likes beer. That's unusual."

"Not if she's from Shanghai," she said.

"We are an adventurous people. No surprise that half the Chinese overseas are from Shanghai."

Talking like this, Soong seemed to be no different from anyone and the day was like any other day.

"You feel better now?" she asked.

"A little."

"I want to ask you some questions."

"Can they wait? I'll have a nap. We can talk later."

"I cannot wait. I have put myself through a lot of trouble to be here. To see you."

He smiled. "I hope you are not disappointed, seeing me like this. What can I do for you? An autograph?"

"I am not a fan. I am here to settle a score."

"Come again?"

"Settle a score."

"What are you talking about?"

"Today is your day of reckoning, Soong Tse-ven. Time to pay for your crimes."

"What are you? Nuts?" He sat up. "What do you want?"

"Someone I love is missing and you are responsible."

"Someone you love? I don't know you..." His voice climbed a scale of disbelief. "Who are you?"

"You remember Victor Maurier?"

"Victor? Of course I remember him."

"What have you done with him?"

"What have *I* done with him?"

"Your men tried to kill him in Shanghai."

"If you know that, you must also know Victor escaped."

"And disappeared again."

"Last thing I heard, Victor was the guest of honor at Gold Fox Han's palace in Shansui."

"You sent your people there. To kill him. This time they succeeded."

"I didn't send anyone to Shansui. My men had better things to do than chase a former employee halfway across the country."

"If you didn't kill him, what happened?"

"If Victor disappeared in Shansui, it had nothing to do with me. I wasn't pleased that he reneged on his promise and gave away confidential information to my brother-in-law's rival. But under the circumstances, I'm willing to give him the benefit of doubt. Han had to have pointed a gun at his head, and Victor didn't have a choice."

The conversation revived Soong. He looked around the room. Lillie saw him catch sight of the pistol on the floor.

"What are you to Victor?" he asked.

"We were engaged to be married. He was going to take me and his son to Europe."

Soong shone the bed light on Lillie's face.

"No wonder you look familiar. You are the girl from the ballroom. Victor kept your photograph in his office. He let his wife go because of you. I thought it was foolish and told him so. Why ruin a perfectly sound marriage for someone he met at a nightclub?"

"We fell in love."

"That's what he said, he wanted to be with the woman he loved. I told him he was doing that already. But being with you a few hours in the day wasn't enough; he wanted to share everything with you. Typically French. They believe finding true love should be the core of a man's aspirations—the gospel according to nineteenth-century radicals of the Romantic persuasion. Couldn't stand them when I had to read them at Harvard. Sissy stuff."

Lillie teared up. "Victor is ten times the man you are."

"Is he? I heard size is a big deal with Caucasian men. Who would know better than the number one girl from Shanghai's number one ballroom?" Soong said unkindly. "How have you been coping with the space vacated by Victor? Make do with two men, three?"

Face flushed, Lillie picked up the gun and pointed at him. "I meant it when I said I am here to settle a score."

"Put that thing away. Silly histrionics don't scare me. All right, you are his fiancée. I can understand that you are concerned. But I wasn't responsible for his disappearance. That's the truth. In fact, I was looking for him myself."

"You wanted him out of China, why would you be looking for him?"

"Two reasons. The first has to do with the confidential papers Victor stole from my office in Nanking. All of them have been recovered, so I'm willing to let the matter rest. The second may interest you. It concerns the money I deposited in Victor's account here in Hong Kong. His pay and bonuses. It's still there. He didn't show up at the bank. He wouldn't have missed the appointment unless he was detained against his will."

"He is still in Shansui?"

"I doubt it."

"What made you think he isn't there?"

"I don't think Han would let him stay once he got what he needed."

"Has Victor made contact?"

He thought. "Well, yes and no."

"Did you hear from Victor or not?" She tightened the grip on the gun. "Tell me what you know."

"I didn't hear from him directly, but one of my aides reported that a few weeks after Victor disappeared from Han's compound, a Caucasian man used his passport to cross the border to Indochina."

"Indochina?"

"Shansui is not far from the border. If Victor had been able to find his way out of Han's fortress, he would want to get out of the country. The logical choice would be to head south. Indochina is right there. The French are in charge. It should be easy for a French citizen to make the connection to France or Hong Kong. But there was no way to verify the man was him. It could be coincidence that the man had the same name, or he stole the passport from Victor."

"It had to be Victor. He always has his passport with him. He escaped. He is alive."

Soong nodded. "If anyone could beat the odds, it would be Victor. He is a resourceful man."

"But, it's been so long. Where is he?"

"Hard to say. He may be stuck somewhere."

"I'll go there. I'll look for him."

"Have you been to Indochina?"

She shook her head.

"It's a dangerous place. The natives are fighting the French and the Japanese are moving in. It's worse than Shanghai. You might want to think twice before you go."

"Victor is there. That's all I care about."

"We don't know that for sure."

"But there is a good chance that's where he went."

"A good chance is still only a chance. You don't know the country. It won't be easy to find him."

"I know Victor. I know his habits. I know how he thinks. I'll keep looking until I find him. It's a chance I am willing to take."

"Like the chance you took with me?"

"Yes."

He regarded her with new benevolence. "It must have taken a lot of nerve to do what you did tonight. A woman, untrained and unconnected, confronts me. Maybe Victor was right to have given up his wife for you. This is what I think you should do. Hold off going to Indochina. Wait here. If Victor is alive, he will come to Hong Kong to collect the money. I'll leave word at the bank. If and when he shows up, he will be told where to find you."

"How long should I wait?"

"A month or two. Enough time for him to find his way out of Indochina."

"That's too long. I'll go mad waiting. I want to see Victor and make sure he's all right. I can go with bodyguards."

"He may have already left Indochina. Better if you stay put so you won't miss each other. That's what I would do. It's your decision, of course. Whatever you decide, you should take his money out of the bank. You are his fiancée and you are taking care of his son. I'll let you accept the money on his behalf."

"Victor's money."

"He earned it. You want to know how much?"

She nodded.

He told her the amount.

She tried to keep amazement out of her face. It was a fortune. Another trunk of gold peaches.

"I'll talk to Chiu about closing the account and handing the money to you. He is my man in these matters and he is here tonight."

"Chiu."

"You know him?"

She nodded.

"That should make things easy," he said.

"I'm afraid it won't. Not at all. Would it be possible to have someone else handle the matter?"

"This is a highly confidential transaction. I don't want to bring in someone new. Chiu can be a double-crossing bastard, but he always does what I say."

"Is there really no other way?"

"If you don't want to deal with Chiu, you can wait until Victor is here and let him make the withdrawal. It's up to you."

"What is the catch?"

"There is no catch."

"Why do you let me take Victor's money when I'm pointing a gun at you?"

"It's not about you. It's about Victor. The money is his due."

"That's it?"

"It may be a large sum to you; it isn't to me."

Lillie searched Soong's face. "Why should I trust you?"

"Because I am a man of my word."

She remembered the things Victor had told about Soong. She re-aimed the gun. "You don't keep your word."

"If my word is not good enough, so be it," Soong said dryly. "Let me tell you why you should accept my offer instead of threatening me. Look at you. You are scared to death. You weren't able to pull the trigger when it would have been easy. I was in pain and defenseless. But you didn't take advantage of the situation; instead, you helped me and chatted with me. You weren't interested in getting to know me; you were looking for an excuse so you wouldn't have to use the gun. Why? Because you are not a killer, and you don't want to be a fugitive for the rest of your life."

"You are willing to let me go?"

Soong nodded.

"Why?"

"Because Victor loves you and in spite of what happened at the end, he did risk his life for me."

"You won't hold a grudge against him? Or me?"

"I have more important things on my mind. Go to the bank. Tomorrow. Nine o'clock. Chiu will have the money ready. American currency, the way I promised Victor. If you want to redeposit the money in the bank, Chiu will give you a favorable rate. If you want to take the money with you, fine. The offer will expire at noon."

"Tomorrow."

"There is one condition. Whatever you find out about Victor, dead or alive, you will not tell anyone that he worked for me and you will not talk about what you know about the Airsea operation."

She nodded.

"Go back to the party. Find my wife and let her know where I am."

"Yes, Mr. Soong."

"Leave the gun on the nightstand. Right here."

31

Tonight's banquet would be the crowning achievement in Chef Wong's career. He had been supervising a team of seventy cooks in preparation for General Han's wedding feast. The menu was long and bountiful: 2,000 roast suckling pigs, 6,500 salt-baked chickens, 4,800 barbecued ducks, 5,000 smoked hams delivered by train from Hunan Province, 1,000 crates of seafood—shrimp, scallops, and oysters—10,000 gallons of sorghum wine, sacks of swallow's nests and shark's fins, delicacies ordinary people couldn't afford to taste. In addition to the party for invited guests, there would be a buffet for the public. It was expected to draw thousands. Peasants and laborers had begun heading for the Villa as soon as news of the free meal was out. Roads to Shansui had been jammed for miles. A crowd, swelling by the minute, had been gathering in the Villa's square.

The bride's joss must be phenomenal, Wong thought as he watched stacks of bamboo steamers move like floating chimneys out of the kitchen. Everyone knew that after Han's first wife died, countless women had shared his bed. None of them had held his interest. Except her. There was a rumor that Han was doing the unprecedented: he was holding off making Clouds and Rain until the wedding night when she became his Supreme Wife. Fu-jen. Pinnacle at seventeen. The reigning empress, Soong May-ling, had been nearly thirty when she married the Generalissimo, and she had to contend with vengeful ex-wives, concubines, and their children. This new Han Fu-jen wouldn't have such obstacles. She would be empress and her son the uncontested crown prince of the Han empire.

If there would *be* a Han empire.

Wong wouldn't bet on it. Han might be wealthy and powerful, but his ideas were, to be honest, a little mad. Emperors belonged to the history books. The world was moving on. Even someone who had little interest in current affairs could feel the change. Ways to do routine chores were taking on strange new forms. Who could have imagined the radio or the telephone or the automobile? Wong wouldn't have anything to do with these gadgets, of course. All that phantom power called electricity might blow up in his face. But young people were eager to experiment. Many were going abroad to study. They would bring back new skills and fresh ideas. In a decade or so, China would be a different country.

Whether or not there would be a Han empire, Wong didn't care. After tonight he would retire from Han's employ and the profession. What better time to hang up one's wok than on the heels of one's best performance? If he never cooked again, it would be fine. He was dead tired of coming up with thirty-eight varieties of dishes for every meal—only because "three" and "eight" rhymed with the words "longevity" and "wealth." And watching them go to waste. Day after day.

There were perks. No complaint there.

As head chef, he controlled the Villa's central pantry. He overstocked regularly and sold the surplus through the back door to restaurants. The proceeds plus commissions from suppliers had added up to a massive nest egg; interest alone would let him live the rest of his life in luxury. He would spend his golden years in tropical splendor. He would move to Singapore and buy a mansion with a garden and a view of the sea, and indulge in his two passions: orchids and pretty Malaysian boys. Nothing like sleeping in the nude with a lithe, brown body and waking up to a firm young yang sweetly plugged in the right place…

With that lovely picture in mind, Wong headed back to the sweltering kitchen.

Han surveyed the bridal chamber. It would rival the best room in the Forbidden City. The bed was placed on a marble plinth facing south, an optimal feng shui position to ensure marital harmony and conception of healthy children. A canopy of imperial yellow brocade draped the frame. Red was the traditional color for newlyweds, but he had decided to stay with the royal theme. He ran his hand over the smooth fabric, savoring the audacity. This shade of yellow and the dragon motif had been exclusive symbols for emperors. He would have been beheaded if this was still the Ching Dynasty.

Chiang Kai-shek, Mao Tse-tung, and other warlords might give themselves fashionable titles and hide their ambition behind fancy ideologies borrowed from the West. The truth is: Everyone wants to be emperor.

Only I dare to admit it.

He sat on the down-filled mattress. In a few hours Yunna would walk into the room. He would lift her bridal veil and she would look up at him with those luminous eyes. Warm wine would be poured into golden cups and they would drink to their union. He would take her hand and they would come to the bed where they would join as one. He would be her first and only lover. She would be his. Forever.

A few hours. An eternity.

He signaled a guard. "I want to see Ah Ching."

Moments later, the maid entered the suite.

"Good afternoon, General." She bowed. "Ah Ching is at your service."

"How is Miss Li?"

"She is fine, General. She was back in the east wing apartment since yesterday. Right now she's getting dressed and preparing for the ceremony."

"You were with her at the hilltop retreat?"

"Every moment, General. Ah Ching made sure Miss Li was comfortable and enjoyed complete privacy."

"How is her mood?"

"Excellent. It was lonely at the retreat. She is glad to be back."

"Has she asked for me?"

"Yes, she asked if you were in the Villa."

"What did you tell her?"

"We told her you were and there was nothing for her to worry."

"What else did she say?"

"Not much. She was satisfied with our answer." A smile. "It was obvious that the General was in her thoughts."

"Did she ask for anyone else?"

"Once she asked if she could see Mr. Lin. We told her it was your wish that she not be distracted."

"She didn't object?"

"She repeated the request an hour later. When she was given the same answer, she said she'd like a walk in the garden. Ah Ching offered to walk with her. She said she didn't want company. Ah Ching guessed maybe she had more than fresh air on her mind, and I had to remind her—very gently of course—that she was not to be left alone."

"How did she react?"

"She went back into the room and locked the door. When we brought food, she said she had no appetite. She didn't let us in. It was clear that she needed some quiet time. There has been so much excitement."

"How long did she stay in the room?"

"Through the night."

"Her room was guarded?"

"Every minute. Ah Ching sat by the door until the lights inside the room were turned off. And then the guards took over."

"No one came to see her?"

"No... Not exactly."

"I want a straight answer."

"A bouquet was placed outside Miss Li's room early this morning. But there was no evidence that she had contact with anyone."

"Who put it there?"

"It seemed to have appeared on its own–that's what the guards said. I told them that was not possible; they must have fallen asleep and didn't want to admit it. I asked around. No one owned up. They were flowers picked from the gardens. It had to be someone inside the Villa. Ah Ching guesses a maid wanted to send good wishes for her wedding day. Miss Li is popular with the staff."

"What did the guards do with the flowers?"

"They gave them to Miss Li."

"Did she make more requests to be alone?"

"No, General. She seems calmer."

"Is she happy?"

"We don't doubt that Miss Li is very happy, General."

"The truth, Ah Ching."

She kept her eyes on the floor. "Hard to see into someone else's heart, General. Harder for a stupid woman like your devoted servant here. Ah Ching can only describe what she has seen. Do forgive her if she chooses the wrong words."

"Go on."

"Something is bothering Miss Li. Perhaps a conflict in the heart. She seems to be torn by different feelings and she is doing her best not to show them."

"What sort of feelings?"

"Miss Li's feelings are too complicated for a simple-minded servant to understand. But Ah Ching has no doubt those feelings will go away once she becomes Han Fu-jen and realizes what an extraordinary role you are offering her." She added, "Maybe Miss Li's fretfulness has nothing to do with the heart. It could can be a simple matter of nerves, her being so young and marrying such a great man. It would be intimidating for any girl."

"Make sure she has everything she needs. No more untraceable deliveries."

"Yes, General."

"What about her mother? Did you do what I told you?"

"Yes, General. Mrs. Li has been moved to Contentment Hall."

"Did she make trouble?"

"It wasn't easy—Mrs. Li was unhappy about the move and she wasn't the least cooperative—but it wasn't anything Ah Ching couldn't handle."

"Good."

"May Ah Ching make a suggestion?"

Han nodded.

"It would be prudent to keep Mrs. Li far away from the new Han Fu-jen. Very far away."

"Why?"

"Mrs. Li hasn't been herself since the announcement of the wedding. She is acting like someone who has lost control of her mind. It wouldn't surprise us if she did something foolish. We pray she wouldn't disrupt the wedding ceremony. But who can tell?" She added, "She reminds Ah Ching of the late Han Fu-jen. The days before the end."

"Have her locked up for the rest of the day. Tomorrow I'll send her back to Nanking."

"That would be wise, General. Would you like Ah Ching to issue the order on your behalf?"

"Do that."

Ah Ching bowed and left the room.

It was unpleasant to talk about Su-chen, Han thought. The woman still refused to see that once she stepped inside Shansui, she existed at and for his pleasure. She had no right to behave as if she had a say in what he did. He should have sent her away as soon as he told her about Yunna.

Yunna.

What was on her mind? Why had she asked for Jong? How much did Jong matter? How much will Jong matter?

Since returning from Tsingtao, Jong had gone about his daily routine as if nothing had happened. He had not said a word about Yunna. Yet Han felt the strain under the calm. Felt it like his own heartbeat. The signs were barely detectable: a fleeting hesitation, a quick probing glance, extra inches of space when they walked alongside each other. For two people who had shared their lives for thirteen years, the small signs could have been war drums.

The boy he'd brought up had become a man he could no longer understand or control. If I can't have the man I molded, Han thought, I don't want a stranger in his place. Better to endure the pain of separation than the hazards of living with a potential traitor. He decided he would hold off announcing Jong's role as executor of his estate. A different order would be issued. Jong would leave China. Following-up with the American press would be the official purpose of the trip. After that, he would think of something else to keep Jong away. Long enough for him to forget Yunna.

The plan didn't calm Han.

Why did Jong make him doubt his loyalty? Didn't he see how much Han wanted things to be the way they were, and how much it hurt him that they weren't? How could the only person he trusts in the world become his archrival?

Ridiculous.

Mad.

Han picked up a vase and threw it across the room. It hit a jade figurine from the Tang dynasty. The figurine bounced against a shelf and cracked neatly into halves before breaking into bits on the floor.

To hell with irreplaceable things.

He picked up a bowl from the Ming Dynasty and broke that too. In a final rage, he swept the entire row of antiques to the floor before he stormed out of the room.

A breathtaking sight.

Hundreds of lanterns had been hung along roofs and garden walls, crisscrossing over treetops, a myriad of lights eclipsing the full moon above. From the top of the watchtower, Jong could hear the thrilled murmurings in the crowd, could feel their awe. To them the Villa must be like a dream, as it had been to him. And then innocence had waned, enchantment faded, until he saw the palace for what it was. A pompous structure built with a poisonous drug to satisfy one man's vanity. How many lives had been sacrificed? How many more for future Crescent Moon Villas if Han had his way? It came to Jong, surer than ever, that the Communists would win. Mao was the only leader bringing hope to the people. They would stand behind him.

Jong raised the binoculars for a wider view. Security was tightest where the crowds were. Four hundred of the five hundred guards were patrolling the square. Their shiny gear stood out among the tattered throng clustered around buffet tables. At Ceremonial Hall where the banquet for invited guests would be held, fifty guards were posted. The rest were placed at intervals throughout the compound. He shifted the view to the old soldiers' cemetery near the north gate. Deserted. No guard in sight—the omission was deliberate. He adjusted the focus and found what he was looking for: the glimmer of a metal fender behind the hedges. He had parked the truck there in the morning. It was out of the way. He hoped no one would wander that far and no one would notice the truck and the covered bulk on its bed: luggage and provisions for the long drive. But with a gathering this large, it would be impossible to predict the crowd's movements. Looking up, he was reassured by a clear sky. The good weather should hold. The road should be safe.

He hoped.

He pulled the binoculars back to the center of the compound. His timing was disconcertingly perfect. It was the moment to witness the launch of the wedding ceremony. In front of the east wing apartment, strings of firecrackers were blasting from the ground up, sending off showers of red confetti. Four coolies took their positions and lifted the bridal sedan chair off the ground. A band opened the way. Musicians in red suits were beating drums and clashing cymbals. Maids jostled behind, pulling swirls of colorful ribbons, cheering and clapping. A woman of vast girth in a flowing scarlet robe swaggered along, rounding up the procession.

He would give anything for a glimpse of Yunna. A nod would be enough, a signal that she had read the letter hidden in the bouquet and that she would be with him.

He hurried down the watchtower.

Inside Ceremonial Hall, three hundred guests waited. Chattering and cheers rose to a climax as the bridal procession arrived. Another cannonade of firecrackers went off. The sedan chair landed in front of the entrance. Two maids flipped open the red curtains. A second pair helped Yunna out of the sedan chair, flanking her as if they were supporting an invalid. She was draped in a golden gown. A crimson veil covered her face. Only her hands were visible. She folded them in front of her body, a pilgrim approaching a holy site. The way she had held them in the Frenchman's house when they met for the first time, Jong recalled with an acute pain in his heart. Half blindfolded, she let go of the maids' grasp, took small steps until she got her bearing. Standing alone, she paused for a moment, as if pondering whether to go forward. She fiddled with her hands, knotting and unknotting them.

She has read my message, he thought. She, too, needs a signal.

He wished he could run up to her and grab her hand. Take her away. From Shansui. From Han.

A maid tapped Yunna's elbow, nudging her on. Another lifted Yunna's skirt as she mounted the steps. The destination was the ancestral shrine in the center of the hall. Red plates carved with the names of Han's forefathers presided over pots of burning incense sticks. A long altar displayed platters piled high with pagodas of red buns. Two monks in saffron robes waited. Yunna stopped in front of the shrine, rigid like a golden mummy. The monks began to chant. She bowed to the plates. Three times to the gods in heaven and earth. Three times to the patron sages of the Han clan. Final round to the ancestors. The moment the bowing was completed, another set of firecrackers blasted off, louder this time, like artillery fire. Salvos of drums went off. Cheering roared in an avalanche as eyes once again turned to the door.

Han.

He was dressed in full military regalia with plumes in his headgear and medals on his chest, looking triumphant.

He stood in front of the crowd and raised his hands in a gesture of benediction, his face flushed with happiness and victorious pride. Jong had seen the same gesture hundreds of times, but the one tonight had no precedent. Han was a different man. He was a different man.

You may think you've won. But this is only a battle. You will not win the war.

Han stood next to Yunna. A red silk sash was presented to them; each held one end. The crowd quieted down, all eyes fixed on the pair. The monk made a wave with his hand. The new couple bowed to the ancestral plates and the gods. Once, twice...

Jong looked at his watch. 7:30.

He edged away from the gathering, keeping his movements inconspicuous, the sea of faces passing him by, dissolving into the festive throng. Once in the clear, he quickened his steps. Firecracker fumes filled the air; the feeling of battle intensified. He chose paths obscured from public view, heading to his apartment.

He entered and closed the door. Moments later he reappeared with a black box in his hands.

To Grand Hall.

The lanterns in the garden were the only source of light, silhouetting the furniture in wavering shadows on the walls. Jong didn't need any illumination. He could have found his way in the room with his eyes closed. For thirteen years this was where he and Han had spent the morning, always only the two of them. When he was young, this had been the classroom and Han the teacher. Later, it was where they talked about things on Han's mind, the province, the Party, his Grand Strategy. Jong stared at the chairs on both sides of the desk. Thirteen years. Almost half his life. Coming to an end tonight. He felt a profound sense of loss. How will my day begin after tonight? What will my life be without Han? And Han—what will he do when I'm gone? Will he find someone to take my place? Someone young and driven and idealistic. Someone who gives the unquestioning loyalty he demands. How to replace thirteen years?

This isn't the moment to reminisce. Get through the day first. There won't be any future if I don't let go of the past. When it's over, I'll find a way to make sense of it all.

Will I?

He stepped behind the desk and opened the second drawer on the left. He retrieved a key from a small box, then fitted it into the lock of the door behind the desk. He noticed a smudge of fresh fingerprint on the metal plate. Han must have gone down to the vault to burn incense sticks before the wedding, paying his customary respects to the gold before an important event. He turned the key. The door clicked open. He slipped the key in his pocket, took a flashlight from the shelf and switched it on. The beam of light revealed a narrow hallway. The walls and floor were unfinished concrete, like a tunnel to a bomb shelter. He knew where it led, though he had never been there. Han had never showed him the gold and Jong had not minded. He saw the vault as the defining boundary of their lives, Han's zone of privacy in their otherwise all-encompassing relationship.

Jong moved on with cautious steps, taking care not to touch anything. Reaching the end of the tunnel, he pushed the door and was surprised to find it wasn't locked. He entered. Pitch dark. He shone the flashlight. A window-less room. Small. Sparsely furnished. One desk with a dry inkwell and a volume of Confucius's Analects placed neatly on the corner. A chair tucked into the cavity of the desk. Two vases on the shelf. A map of China on the wall. A black metal door dominated one wall. He ran the light over the door. No knob, no keyhole, the entire piece seemed to have been welded into the concrete.

The entrance to the vault.

What he knew about the vault he had picked up from Han's passing remarks over the years. The warehouse was three stories deep below Grand Hall, accessible by a stair-well. Lethal traps had been set at the top of the stairs; the triggers would go off when an intruder approached within fifteen inches of the wall. If hit, he would be paralyzed in seconds and stay immobile for hours. The intrusion would set off an alarm wired directly to Han's bedroom and the head guard's quarters. Han was the only one who knew how to disarm the traps. With Han, one could never be sure if the information was complete; crucial details might have been held back. There might be triggers in the rest the room. Not knowing where they were, he shouldn't go further.

He placed the black box on the floor in the middle of the room. He lifted the lid, set the hands of the clock and pressed a switch. The ticking began, echoing like dripping water, louder with each beat.

He had passed the point of no return.

If things went wrong, he would destroy himself and everything he held dear. If not, he would be able to tell his grandchildren that he, half-breed foster son of a warlord, had made a small contribution to fashioning a safer future for China.

Rustle of moving air. Hurried footsteps. Behind him. Jong listened. No mistake, someone was following him. He took out his gun and stepped over to the shoulder of the lane.

A shadow. Twenty yards away. One person, slight build.

"Who's there?" He pointed the gun at the moving figure.

"Wait. Please don't shoot, Mr. Lin."

The shadow materialized in the clearing. A maid, a junior servant who waited on Han's concubines. She quickened her step, catching her breath.

"Why are you following me?"

"So sorry, Mr. Lin. We've been looking for you."

"We? Who?"

"The servants."

"Why?"

"There has been an emergency."

"What kind of emergency?"

"Mrs. Li. She... She is in Contentment Hall. We don't know what to do. We need you to take a look."

He put away the gun. "How did you know where to find me?"

"We didn't see you at the wedding ceremony. A guard said he saw you leaving the hall. I was told to try your apartment. You weren't there. I thought I would get the head guard, and then I saw you."

"What happened to Mrs. Li?"

"She... I can't say." She turned and started to run.

Contentment Hall was one of the cottages on the outer fringe of the compound. Small and with few amenities, they were used as accommodations for attendants of guests and as halfway houses for concubines on their way out. Gin-lin had been its last occupant before she left for Manchukuo. On the small front lawn, guards and maids had gathered, talking among themselves. Seeing Jong, they quieted down and stepped back.

He walked in.

The sitting room was empty.

The door to the bedroom was half open. Something on the wall.

A tall shadow.

He switched on the light. The slippers were the first things he saw. Black silk, embroidered with a red phoenix, lying on the floor next to an overturned stool. He lifted his eyes. Red trousers. Red tunic. Long black hair. The body was hanging from a ceiling beam by a sash. In the dimness it appeared suspended in midair. He was looking at her back. All he felt was relief at having been spared the sight of her face. He wanted to remember her as he had known her. A graceful, older Yunna.

He called the servants into the room.

"Who found Mrs. Li?"

A maid stepped forward. "I did."

"When?"

"Before the wedding ceremony."

"Say that again."

"I found Mrs. Li before the wedding ceremony, Mr. Lin."

"Are you sure?"

"It was about six o'clock. The others were setting tables for the banquet. I'd finished my work in the laundry room. I thought I should stop by and see if Mrs. Li was all right."

"She was already... like this?"

"Yes."

"Why was she in Contentment Hall?"

"Mrs. Li was to stay here. The General's orders."

"When were these orders received?"

"This morning. Mrs. Li was asked to move out of the east wing apartment. She had to do that before noon. There wasn't time to pack. I helped her to put together a few things. She didn't have anyone to serve her in her new quarters. I was told to keep an eye on her."

"What about Ah Ching?" Jong asked.

"She was reassigned to wait on Miss Li."

"Were you with Mrs. Li the whole afternoon?

The maid shook her head. "I had to help with the wedding preparations. I checked on her when I could. She was very upset. She kept pacing around the room with a scroll in her hand. Sometimes she stopped at the window and stared at the watchtower, and then without warning, she shrieked. It was scary. I didn't dare to go in; I wouldn't know how to do."

"What happened next?"

"Another order came from the General. Mrs. Li was not to attend the ceremony or the banquet. She was to be locked in the bedroom until tomorrow, and then she would be sent back to Nanking. Mrs. Li was beside herself when she found out. She demanded to see the General. She forced her way out the door. The guards put her back in the room. She was hysterical when we left. Right before the banquet, I thought I would bring her some herbal tea, to help her sleep. I knocked on the door. She didn't answer. There wasn't a sound anywhere. It didn't seem right. I looked through the window. I couldn't believe what I saw. I thought I had to make sure and found the guard who had the key. We unlocked the door. But it was too late."

"That was when you looked for me?" Jong asked.

"Yes."

"Has Miss Li been told?"

"There was no way we could reach her."

"General Han?"

"It's his wedding day. It would be bad luck. We didn't dare."

"Who knows about this?"

"Just us here."

"No one else?"

"No." She asked, "Mr. Lin, should we change Mrs. Li's clothes?"

A red suit.

Jong understood. There was a belief that anyone who committed suicide wearing red would be able to garner energy from the netherworld. She would have the power to come back and take revenge on those who hurt her.

"It was her choice to wear red. We must honor her wish," he replied. To the guards: "Take Mrs. Li down and put her on the bed."

Jong watched the body crumple into the arms of the guards. The sheen of her red silk tunic caught the light and shimmered like bloody metal. He tried to imagine the despair and the pain before the body became inert. She had loved and hated Han more than anything in the world, but she had given her life for nothing. Even if there was life after death, ghosts could not right life's wrongs. And Han wasn't worth the sacrifice, though to her he must have been the sum total of her dreams. But how well had she known him?

"Leave the body here. I'll decide what to do. Go back to your posts and stay there. Don't come back until I tell you to. And not a word to anyone about this."

"Yes, Mr. Lin."

They filed out of the room.

Alone, Jong knelt down and bowed to the woman who could have been the grandmother of his children. He hoped there would be a future occasion to express his gratitude in a proper ceremony. Su-chen would never know what an immense favor she had done for him. For China. Her death before the wedding ceremony had changed everything. Now a peaceful alternative would be possible.

Minutes ago, he had four hours. Now there would be three years.

"I need to see the General," Jong said to the sentries at Grand Hall.

"Now?"

"It's urgent."

"General has left strict orders not be disturbed."

"I wouldn't have come if it could wait. Something happened and he must be told."

"Mr. Lin, we can't…"

"Just let me through. You won't be blamed."

They exchanged a look before stepping aside.

Jong entered the dark foyer and walked along the atrium garden, his hurried footsteps echoing his heartbeats. The opening let in a rectangular view of the sky. Moonlight shone on the leaves and blossoms, blurring their outline with its luminous haze. New peonies had been planted for the occasion. Clusters of scarlet blooms on leafy branches; in the half darkness the petals looked bruised. They must have been put there before the wedding; he had not seen them before. Their presence was jarring, as if he had been away and seasons had passed in his absence. On the surface of the pond, lotus grew in clumps, breaking up a perfect reflection of the scenery. The veranda emptied into an enclosed corridor. Two rows of red lanterns marked the way to the bridal chamber. He was walking through a tunnel of red fog.

He kept his eye on the thread of light under the door.

They are not in bed yet.

At the door, he heard Yunna's voice. Soft murmurs. Han's. They were talking.

Let it be that I've come in time.

He knocked.

No answer.

He knocked again, louder.

"Who's there?"

"Me, General."

Silence.

"Can I have a word? We have a very urgent situation."

He waited. A long moment passed.

"Please, General."

Footsteps.

The door opened a few inches.

"Sorry, General, I must talk to you."

"Whatever it is, can't you handle it?" Han said irritably.

"It's Yunna's mother."

"What about her?"

"Better that we speak privately."

"We are alone here."

"I don't think you want Yunna to know about this."

Han cast Jong a long look before he stepped out and closed the door.

"Su-chen is about to kill herself," Jong said.

"What?"

"She has put a noose around her neck. In Contentment Hall."

"Stop her."

"I tried. She wouldn't listen. She said she must see you."

"Tell her I'll see her tomorrow."

"She is very distraught. If you don't go to her, she will follow through on her threat."

"I don't believe her."

"You would if you saw her."

"Ignore her. She'll get over it."

"I don't think we should do that, General. If things get worse, there will be a scene. We have a lot of people here tonight."

"She surely knows how to pick her moment," Han said unhappily.

"You don't want a funeral right after your wedding, do you, General?"

"All right. Tell her I'll be there."

"Better if you come with me?"

"Now?"

"Now."

"No."

"She won't wait."

"I said I'll come. Now go."

Jong tried to catch a glimpse of Yunna, but Han shut the door in his face.

32

A light bulb hung down from the ceiling, casting a yellow glow on the room. Two elongated shadows were mimicking their moves on the walls. The public persona and the private man, Jong thought. Every part of us is here tonight.

He pointed at the covered lump on the bed. "Want to see her face, General?"

Han didn't move. "That's her?"

"That's her. Su-chen. Yunna's mother."

"I don't want to see her."

"She died. For you."

"She took her own life."

"It's a shame, don't you think? A life wasted. For what?"

Han stiffened. "Shame is right and she brought it upon herself."

"You could have prevented this. Only you."

"Don't be ridiculous. If someone wants to kill herself, there's nothing anyone can do."

"You know what you meant to her. You know what you did to her. You were the reason she ended her life. I expect you to tell Yunna the truth."

"What is wrong with you? Why are you talking to me like this? Why is it so quiet around here? Where are the guards?"

Jong ignored Han's questions. "Do you see the ramifications of her death?"

"What ramifications?"

"Yunna's mother died before the wedding ceremony. Tradition decrees that when a parent passes away, a child must not marry for three years. The marriage has to be annulled. Yunna cannot be your wife."

"I see. So this is what it's about," Han said calmly. "Su-chen killed herself *after* the ceremony. Our marriage is legitimate and irrefutable."

"A maid found her body while the staff were preparing for the banquet. Before the wedding ceremony. There were witnesses."

"She was dead when you came to see me?"

"Yes."

"You lied?"

"Yes."

"Just so you could get me out of the bridal chamber and save Yunna before the marriage was consummated." Han stepped forward, reassessing Jong in light of this revelation. "What are you planning to do? Take her from here? From China?"

"I will do what is right for us."

"Us. Do you mean you and Yunna, or do you include me in your idiotic scheme?"

"All of us."

"Then obeying my orders is what is right for you."

"That is no longer a guiding tenet of mine."

Han crossed his arms. "When did you decide to go against me? Twenty days ago when I told you I was marrying Yunna? Eight months ago when she moved here? Thirteen years ago when I brought you here from Shanghai?"

Jong didn't answer.

"Did you coerce Su-chen into killing herself so you could stage your rebellion?"

"She was devastated by your marriage to her daughter and humiliated by how she herself was treated. She couldn't face the world and she couldn't live with a broken heart. You backed her into a corner. You should have expected this is what she would do."

"I have never considered suicide an option for anyone, no matter what the circumstance. This is a total surprise to me. However, I'm aware of her propensity for hysterical behavior. I am willing to accept that there was no conspiracy between you and my late mother-in-law. For now."

"What about the marriage?"

"What about it?"

"Are you going to have it annulled?"

"No."

"Will you honor a mourning period?"

"If that's another way of telling me to stay away from Yunna, the answer is no."

"Isn't preserving tradition the core of your beliefs? What will the rest of China think when they find out about this blatant defiance?"

"I have the Mandate of Heaven. I am not subject to the customs of the common folk."

"You are a regional government official. You don't have the Mandate of Heaven."

"The Mandate is mine. And Yunna is mine."

"You and she participated in a ceremony. That's all. You will not have your way with her. I won't let you."

"That's a curious thing to say, considering who is in charge here."

"Yunna won't give in to you."

"How do you know? Did you tell her not to?" Han searched Jong's face. "You did, didn't you? You sent a message to her. Those damn flowers. I thought they were from you when Ah Ching told me. Do you think a few words from you will be enough to convince her to give up being my wife?"

"She is not your wife. She will never be your wife. Not in her heart."

"How do you know what is in her heart?"

"I know. As she does mine."

"Yunna doesn't have much regard for the heart. Yours, hers, or anyone's. She is not a sentimental girl. If you don't believe me, it just shows how little you know her." Han headed to the door. "This is my wedding night. I am not wasting another moment on this foolishness."

Jong blocked the way.

He enunciated every word. "Before you leave this room, General, you should know that a bomb has been placed on top of the vault. It's set to go off at midnight."

"What?"

"A bomb. It is not as powerful as the one marketed by Ganz, but it will demolish the entrance to your gold mine."

"Are you out of your mind, Jong?"

"Your gold will be exposed for the world to see. You can order the troops to guard it, but they will be outnumbered by the looters. They are already here. You invited them, remember? It's too late for them to go home after the free meal. They are sleeping in the square and in the forest. It will take them minutes to get here. And they will get here. They are poor and desperate, with nothing to lose."

"I'll get a guard to defuse the bomb."

"He wouldn't know where it is."

"I'll tell him."

"He would need the key to the secret room. I have the key."

"Give it to me."

"If you do as I say, I'll defuse the bomb."

"You are threatening me?" Han said, unbelieving.

"I want you to take seriously what I'm about to say."

"Say it."

"Let Yunna go. Use the gold to improve people's lives. Stop your opium trade. I cannot stand by and watch you destroy the country, with drugs and with bombs. China has no use for your reactionary scheme. It must go forward and join the rest of the world. The new China should be free and democratic."

"You think you have the last word on China's future?"

"It isn't my word, or yours. Open your eyes. Look around. The world is moving on. China is moving on."

"This isn't about China or the world, is it? This is about you and me. You resent that I took your girl and you ask me to hand over everything I have."

"I am asking you to do the right and moral thing."

"I do what I want to do. It's *my* gold, *my* China."

"China isn't yours. It belongs to the people. People. The millions out there, beyond these walls. They are the country. Not one man. Not Chiang. Not Mao. Not you. You will never win. You don't have support from the people. The gold is all you have. It buys you things and people who can be bought, but it will not buy you the country." In an emphatically casual tone, Jong added: "Incidentally, General, you will have to find other means to attain the Mandate of Heaven. Ganz won't be delivering the bomb to you."

"How do you know?"

"I investigated Ganz and his claims. He has as much information about the atomic bomb as anyone who reads foreign journals. As for his connection to the Berlin leadership, he knows some people, a trade commissioner, ministry secretaries, but no one who has the power to approve the sale of the new atomic bomb—if there is one. Things are still in the research phase; Germany is nowhere close to producing the weapon. The deal was a sham from the start. You told Ganz about your imperial dream. So he made up a dream weapon and sold it to you."

"That can't be true," Han said with a note of uneasiness. "Ganz has always come through."

"Looks like he's been holding out for the deal of his life. Even if the bomb is for sale, he wouldn't have been able to negotiate with the current regime in Germany. Ganz is a Jew."

"Ganz—a Jew?"

"It's on his parents' birth certificates. Check with the registrar in Bremen."

"I've known him for years. He never said anything about being Jewish. He doesn't live like a Jew."

"There are two thousand miles between Tsingtao and Shansui. What you know about him came from word of mouth, his mostly. Did you look into his background? Verify his contacts? Investigate his record?"

"There has never been any reason to doubt him. We've done business for years; he has never failed me. Sure, there are gaps in my knowledge. It would be impossible to know everything about a person." A sober awakening. "I trusted him. I thought he was my friend."

"He was your friend all right. He knew you well enough to tell you what you wanted to hear, make the moves you wanted to see. Didn't you find the timing of his sales pitch just a little too perfect? The bomb would be ready when you are, and it would do the things you wanted it to do. He counted on you to buy the whole lie. And you did."

Silence.

"Bastard. I'll kill him."

"You'll have to find him first. He had sold his house before we arrived in Tsingtao. As soon as we left, he took off in a plane heading west. Probably to South America. He didn't need to wait for the deal to close. You agreed to give him two-thirds of the sum before delivery. The money would see him through nicely."

"I'll stop the payments."

"Too late. The first installment has been transferred."

The bad news was sinking in. Han decided to make a mental separation from Ganz. "I'll get the bomb from someone else."

"The Americans will have the bomb. But they won't sell to you."

"Everything is for sale. At the right price. If I can't get the atomic bomb, I'll find something else. There is always something else. With my gold I can buy anything, outbid anyone. I am going to have the country no matter what."

"No matter what."

"That's right. I will be emperor. I don't care what it takes."

"Is that your last word on the topic, General?"

"You are damn right it is."

Jong took out a revolver and pointed it at Han. "You are leaving me with no choice."

"Of course you have a choice. You can choose to return to sanity. Put that thing down, I don't like it," Han said, very agitated.

"I will press the trigger if you don't do as I say."

Han looked at Jong, amazed. "You are going to kill me because of some ideological difference between us?"

"It's more than ideology. It's the country, the future, the millions of lives you plan to destroy."

"What has gotten into you? You have known my plan all along. You were the first person I told. All these years. You helped to shape the strategy, calculate the moves, recruit the people. We talked about it every day. If you didn't believe in it, why didn't you say so?"

"No, I didn't. That was my mistake. I will have to live with it for the rest of my life."

Han ignored the contrite remark. "And the battles we fought together. Don't tell me your heart wasn't in them. If you tried to fool me, Jong, you also fooled yourself. You were too good at what you did to be disingenuous. Best military strategist I have ever worked with. I taught you, sure, but you have taken my training further. You have genuine talent. You will go far."

"Not in China. It must have crossed your mind that it was safe to put someone like me in my position. I could never be a threat. China will never accept a half foreigner for a leader."

As if all along he had anticipated one day he would hear the complaint, Han nodded knowingly. "You don't want to play second fiddle anymore. You want to be boss. Call the shots. Is that it? I can make it happen. After I've won the country, I'll let run you a province or a city. Shansui. Canton. You can have your pick."

"That's not what I want."

"You want money. You want to live comfortably for the rest of your life. Power, money, either or both. Your choice. I promised I won't stand in your way when you want to leave; I will keep the promise. Looks like the time is now. Let's work it out. All the gold you can take. Go as far away as you wish. No strings attached."

"I don't want your gold."

"Gold is gold. It's a universal currency. You will be free to do the things you want. Live where you want."

"I don't need the gold to be free. Neither do you."

"Is that so?"

Han began to pace around Jong, appraising him. Jong's aim followed. Han ignored it.

"I've always marveled at your indifference to my wealth. Here you are, living on top of the world's largest gold mine, and having my trust like no other person alive. Yet you aren't tempted. You aren't even curious. I thought, either he is a first-rate actor or a rare man. Tell me, have there been moments you wondered how it would be to own the gold?"

"No."

"Not even a fleeting second?"

"No."

"Yet you stay loyal to me. At least until now. Why?"

"The gold has nothing to do with us."

"Nice to have one's belief confirmed. I should congratulate myself on my astute judgment of character, shouldn't I?" he remarked dryly. "All the orphans in China and I picked the one who is incorruptible. You don't want power or money. What do you want?"

"Yunna."

"You want her enough to give up all this?"

"I want her more than anything, and she wants me. We are meant to be together. We are going to leave Shansui before you launch your war. Everyone in the Villa knows about us. Except you. You were so engrossed in yourself and your Grand Strategy that you didn't see we have been together."

"I knew about your attachment. That was why I kept her away from you. I admit I didn't expect you to go this far to get her back."

"I'll go further."

"Yunna is not indispensable to me. If you want her, you can have her. Not now. Later. After I've grown tired of her. Going by my experience with women, it will be inevitable. I'll let you enjoy her at our mutual convenience, on the condition that she stays married to me. And she will bear my children—that must take precedence over everything else. Other than that, you can have her as often as you wish. You couldn't ask for more, could you?"

"How can you speak about Yunna glibly as though she were a singsong girl?" Jong cried. "I don't want to have her. I want to be with her."

"I speak any way I choose about anyone. I was willing to share my dynasty with you. Why not a woman?"

Jong moved behind the bed, the covered corpse a barricade between them.

"Here is the widow of your best friend. You took advantage of her at a time when she was most vulnerable. After you were done with her, you cast her aside. She killed herself because of you. Still you don't care. Not about her. Not about the hundreds of women, other men's wives, daughters. Their lives ruined because you must have your moment of pleasure. Do you know how many of them killed themselves after they were dismissed from your bed? The rest have to live with this terrible shame since, according to the feudal canon so sacred to you, a violated woman is damaged goods. What about the bastards you've fathered? Your own flesh and blood. Without a name. Without a father. They may be hungry and helpless. You've never bothered to track them down. But they are a small number compared to the lives you have destroyed with opium. Have you seen what the drug does to a man? When you add another gold bar to your collection, have you asked yourself what it is made of?"

"You sound just like that damn American," Han said under his breath.

Jong's eyes blazed. His voice trembled. The pent-up agony of the years was choking him. "Yet all that carnage isn't enough. Not for the great Han Tang-ming, next emperor of China. After dispensing poison for a quarter of a century, you are ready to slaughter an entire population because you won't fight a fair war."

They stood motionless. Face to face. Each holding his own.

Han's voice was surprisingly calm. "I take it this is only the prologue to the litany of my sins. Go ahead. Get them off your chest. They must have been festering while you pretended to be loyal."

"There was no pretense. I was loyal to you. It would have been a lot easier if I weren't."

"Good to know. Against my better judgment, I believe that."

"What does it matter what I say? You don't want to see the truth. You are blinded by the gold."

"Am I?" Han said, amused. "Or are you the one who is blinded? By a pretty face. For your entire adult life, I have been the center of your life. Now you are pointing a gun at me, ready to pull the trigger. You always said you would stand by me no matter what. What happened to that promise? Don't let your infatuation with a woman cloud your judgment. Look at past dynasties. Many careers have been ruined by women. If you want a place in history, you must put personal sentiment aside. Greatness demands a price. A woman is a small one to pay for what we will achieve together."

"I don't want what you want. I don't want a place in history. I want a simple life. I want to be able to live with my conscience."

"You would rather live with this so-called conscience of yours than with me?"

"Yes."

"You shouldn't have come to Shansui thirteen years ago."

"I was a child. I didn't know."

"You regret having been a part of my life?"

"Every day of it."

"That's too bad. I wouldn't have kept you here if I had known. Now it's too late; we cannot undo the years."

"We can do something about the future."

"*We*," Han repeated, holding his gaze. "I think you still care about me, Jong. Even now, after I took the girl you love, after I disappointed you with my reactionary dreams. We have a place in each other's life no one can match. I felt it when I met you in Shanghai. I still do. You were the son I should have had. Haven't I treated you as such? My son. For thirteen years we were each other's family. Can you throw that away?"

Jong resented the truth of what Han said. Even more he resented the love he himself felt. He *was* Han's son. In every way that defined the bond.

"Don't destroy what we have because of a girl. Or because you are momentarily caught up in some belief that disagrees with mine. They will pass. We are more than them."

Jong stared at the hand that gripped the gun, the hand Han had held when he introduced him to his staff when Jong first arrived at the Villa, when he taught him how to fire a gun. Jong's will was slipping.

"I promise all this will be forgotten as soon as you defuse the bomb. I will not punish you for this act of treachery. We will part ways. That will be it."

"I will leave. But you must agree to the conditions."

"You are a stubborn man." Han shook his head. "Let's pretend for a moment I agreed. What guarantee would you have?"

"Your word now. If you renege on it, I'll find another way to kill you."

"What if I agreed to your demands now and then killed you later? You know how easy it would be for me to do that."

"I'll take my chances."

"Then you do trust me," Han concluded quietly. "Another man would promise anything now and take it all back later. I have never lied to you and I don't want to start now. I'll tell you exactly what I am willing to do. I will give you Yunna—if she means this much to you, you can have her. Between the two of you, I value you over her. Keep that in mind for the rest of your life, Jong. Think about it when you look at her. I will let you two go with as much of my gold as you can take with you. You will be free to live anywhere. I give you my word that I will leave you alone, as you will give me yours to do the same. But what I do with my gold, the opium, and how I fight my war, they are for me to decide."

"Not acceptable. Everything or no deal." Jong cocked the gun.

Han's face broke into a smile. "That's what I wanted to hear. Up until now I thought Yunna was the only cause of this outrageous behavior. That would have been a pity. The years you spent with me wasted. How many times have I told you one should never involve women with the important matters of life? What could be more important than being the ruler of the Middle Kingdom? After your infatuation wore off— it will wear off, you'll look back and laugh at what you did tonight. She is more precious to you now because she has become unattainable. Most men are fools; they desire what they can't have. I'd like to think you are different."

"I love her, whether she is attainable or not."

"Of course you believe that; you have to. But if this would help to get her down from your pedestal, let me tell you what you don't know about her. Yunna might not love me but she worships me. Partly it's her youth; mostly it's her ambition. She is the type of woman who finds power more alluring than any other attribute in a man. I saw it the moment she came on my boat. There was no question that I was on her mind. Not Han Tang-ming her father's best friend, but Han Tang-ming the richest man in China. The light in her eyes—you should have seen it. I am the god she has been waiting for. She made the pilgrimage to show up at my feet. If I'd encouraged her, she would have given herself to me. It would have been an offering..."

"Stop!"

"She sees in me a grander, more heroic version of her father. I am the man who can make her dreams come true. And Yunna's dreams are no ordinary girl's. They are as big as mine. She wants to remake China with me. She wants to conquer and rule the world with me. Can you do that with her? For her? Can you satisfy her with your conscience and your simple life? Will your love be enough for her?"

"You don't know a thing about love."

"And you do? Tell me."

"Being selfless. Being there when she needs you. Being there when she doesn't. Caring about her more than you care about yourself."

"Is that so? Then you've chosen the wrong woman to love," said Han in a tone of simple regret. "But maybe it isn't Yunna whom you love so selflessly. Maybe it's me you want to hurt. Deep down inside you resent that you can never be my real son, you can never achieve what you want to achieve in China. You thought the best way to get even was to take her away from me. You didn't count on me giving her up."

"You heard my terms. Agree to them or I will pull the trigger."

Han stepped forward, presenting his chest as the target. "Can you pull the trigger? Can you, Jong? I gave you everything. I made you who you are."

"If I killed you, I would rid the world of a menace, a criminal, a terrorist. It would be the best thing I could do for China." Jong's voice was shrill, filled with despair. "Do you hear me? You are a menace, a criminal, a terrorist…"

Han's face went through a change, turning dark and dangerous.

"How dare you to talk to me like this. I am Supreme Commander-General of Southwest China. As your liege lord and commanding officer, I order you to surrender your weapon."

"I am no longer under your command."

"This is mutiny. You are committing treason."

"You have made it impossible to be loyal to you."

"How?" Han fixed his eyes on Jong's. "By caring about you more than I care about anyone else?"

"You are wrong, General. You care about your gold more than you care about anything or anyone."

"Is that what you believe?"

"It's what I see. How I feel."

Han was hurt to the heart. "I should have left you in Shanghai."

"There are many more things you should regret, General. Would you like me to go over the list? How far back should I take us? How much detail should I provide?"

"Get that smirk off your face." Han's own was white. His throat throbbed as he squared up to his adoptive son. No longer a son but an enemy. "Who are you to judge me? Let me tell you where you came from. The two people who were your parents. You should know what you are made of."

The turn of the conversation was unexpected. Jong was stunned.

"My parents?"

"Yes."

"You knew them?"

"Yes."

"Who were they?"

"Your mother was a prostitute. Your father was a small-time thug, uneducated, crass, the kind of foreigner that swaggered around town, bullying the weak with a rusty gun and the insufferable arrogance of the white race. What his countrymen have been doing to China on a grand scale, he did in pittance. Miserably. The stories about him being an American missionary and your mother a princess were made up by Nan-fei. She didn't want you to carry the shame of being the child of a thug. She wanted you to feel special."

"Nan-fei knew all along?"

"Oh yes. She was there, before and after you were born."

"Why didn't she tell me?"

"She hated your father. She didn't think he deserved you. He abandoned you and your mother before you were born. Nan-fei thought if you knew who he was, you would want to look for him. She didn't want you to have anything to do with the man."

Jong said weakly, "How do you know what Nan-fei thought?"

"She was a prostitute I used to bed when I was in Peking. So was your mother. Your father was their pimp. There were other girls who worked for him. He liked your mother best; she was the prettiest. He took her off the roster and made her his exclusive bedmate. When she became pregnant, she tried to have an abortion. She didn't want to have a child with the man she despised. The quack botched the operation. She had to live out the pregnancy. She was going to find a family who would adopt you as soon as you were born, but she died giving birth to you. The midwife took you to your mother's best friend. That was Nan-fei. After she buried your mother, she didn't have the heart to give you away. Over the years she came to love you as her own child. That's the plain history of your pedigree."

A long silence.

"I don't believe you," Jong mumbled, reeling. "You are making this up. Nan-fei wouldn't have lied to me."

Han said dryly, "Ask her yourself. She has your birth certificate."

Jong stared at him, speechless.

"She's kept it," Han continued. "She knows the truth would eventually have to come out."

"My father... What happened to him?"

"About the time you were born, he offended someone important in Yuan Shih-kai's army. He had to leave Peking in a hurry. One night he robbed his girls, took their money, their jewelry, anything he could sell, and vanished. Hasn't showed his face since. He could still be in China, if his enemies haven't found him."

"I can look for him..."

"He might not want you to do that. He didn't bother to take a look at you when you were born. He didn't care that he had a child and that your mother died. Your father was a real good-for-nothing. No backbone. No conscience. Not an iota of loyalty." He pauses before delivering the punch line. "As it turns out, Jong, you are more his son than mine."

"How could you have known?" Jong protested miserably. "You said when you found me in Shanghai, it was the first time we met."

"I never set eyes on you when you were an infant. I learned about the connection in Shanghai. After I offered to take you to Shansui, Nan-fei came to see me. She knew who I was, of course. She wanted to speak to me in person, make me promise to take good care of you. I recognized her when she walked into the hotel suite. She told me your story and she asked me to keep it secret. The link confirmed my belief it was destiny that you should come into my life. I was right. I am right."

"No. *No!*"

"What are you objecting to? That you have been part of my life? That I am your joss?"

"We shared a past. That is a fact I cannot change. But you are not my joss. I don't owe you anything. Even if I did at one time, I have paid up." Jong's voice cracked. "With thirteen years of my life. I have paid up."

"Were the thirteen years your penance? Have they been unbearable? Did I make you suffer? Have I ruined your life? Is that what you really believe, deep in your ungrateful little heart? Do you want me out of your life, Jong? Do you? Look me in the eye. Tell me."

Tears filled Jong's eyes. A myriad of wavering images appeared before him. Places and people and scenes from his past. His recollections and his fantasies of what might have been. All were nothing. Except Han. Han was the only genuine fairy tale in his life.

For the rest of his life, Jong wondered what would have happened if there had been more time. A few moments would have been all that was needed. He would have backed away from the edge of the precipice and given in to Han. He would have defused the bomb and left the Villa, alone, never to return. Han would have lived out his dream of being emperor. Or he wouldn't have.

Love got in the way.

The truth of his past overwhelmed and confused him. He felt wounded and lost. He gazed at Han, wanting his guidance, his forgiveness, his love.

Han sensed his faltering and seized the moment. He lunged at him, grabbing at the weapon. Jong wasn't prepared; he backed away, barely avoiding Han's outstretched hands and managing to hold on to the gun. Han didn't give him any reprieve. He landed a sharp blow on Jong's arm, trying to shake the gun loose. Jong stumbled. He did what he could to hold his body steady. A drowning man clutching at straws. The gun was the only thing in his grasp. His finger gripped it, pressing the trigger.

The shot reverberated through the walls. The sound roared through his head and shut down his hearing. In the longest second of his life the world became silent. There was nothing in his sight except the blinding light that streamed from Han's eyes. In a moment that had no space in time, he wished he had never confronted Han, that he could go back to being a boy of fifteen and choose a different future, that he had never fallen in love with Yunna. The force of the bullet lifted Han off his feet. Blood sprouted from his chest. He staggered. His eyes, filled with disbelief, were fixed on Jong. Two pairs of eyes locked in a shocked silent scream until Han could no longer stand. Scrambling for support, he grabbed the sheet covering Su-chen's corpse. At the sight of her grotesque face, he shrieked. His legs buckled; his body teetered and fell.

Han breathed in painful gasps. And then the breathing stopped.

Dead quiet.

Jong stared at the gun in his hand and then at the slumped shape on the floor.

"Generalllll!"

In the ensuing second, the whole universe shook. The room jumped. The world convulsed. A thundering explosion shattered the night, sending off tremors like an earthquake.

Jong raced to Grand Hall, knowing already that he was too late.

The bomb had gone off.

Blackness. As if an unexpected peace had returned. Only for a moment.

A rocket of fire shot up from the center of the Villa like a meteor. It exploded and split into hundreds of fragments in midair. A roof fell with a vast thud. Splinters of fire exploded and showered down on the rest of Grand Hall. Flames everywhere. They licked the structures and quickly became blazing tributaries, gathering velocity as they consumed rooftop after rooftop.

Epilogue

Yunna had named the place The Milky Way, an allusion to the celestial bridge where two lovers in a folktale reunited after a lifetime of travail. She had planted white ginger and jasmine bushes; on a moonlit night the blossoms glowed like a tiara of stars. The compound sat on the edge of a forest, the tall trees providing shade and camouflage. The buildings had thick concrete walls painted in drab green and iron grille over the windows. There were offices, conference rooms, barracks, a spacious garage, and a storeroom where there were enough provisions and supplies for a troop to live on for months. A stream flowed from the top of the hill into the valley; a tributary ran through the forest and supplied them with the water they needed. Behind the main building was a shed where Jong kept the truck he had driven from Shansui, and cylinders of fuel in the event they had to leave unexpectedly. Their home had been the living quarters for the commanding officer. It had three rooms, a bath and a kitchen. The windows were on one side and they faced the sea. On clear days, the view was one of the loveliest in Kwantung Province: northward to Canton's White Cloud Mountain, southward to the Pearl River estuary. Refugees looking for shelter climbed the steep path to the hilltop. Seeing the barbed wire fence and the military base behind it, they turned around and hurried away.

Jong and Yunna managed to keep the war out. Most of the time.

There were sporadic sounds and spectacles. At odd hours, fighter planes roared over the compound; combat fire flew out of the sky like flashes of distant lightning, followed by rockets landing on the hillside. The next day they saw smashed structures through binoculars. When they thought things had quieted down, small explosions hit up the mountain side like campfires; ricocheting bullets tore into the stream, flinging up mud and pebbles. The noises were accentuated by the hollow of the valley, sending a crescendo of sound through the air. Blare of sirens, thud of grenades, crackle of machine guns. They seemed closer than they were, but Jong and Yunna didn't dare to take a chance. At the smallest sign of threat, they stopped what they were doing and hurried down to the bunker.

Life went on.

In the morning Jong woke up to the chirping of birds. Families of them had built nests under the eaves. They sang at the first rays of the sun, a chaotic cacophony like players tuning up before a concert. Yunna arose before he did. Sleep brought troubled dreams; she preferred to have few of them. She brewed tea and cooked rice porridge on the woodstove. Not wanting to share their life, they had no servants. They didn't mind the chores; they provided a familiar rhythm to the day. The routines were molecules of predictability assuring them that their small world was safe from the chaos outside. After breakfast, they tended to the vegetable garden. The provisions in the storeroom were canned meats, bags of rice and dry noodles. They would last years for the two of them. For fruit and vegetables, they had to rely on a market down the hill. Supply was at best intermittent. It was necessary to grow their own produce. Jong enjoyed the work. It invigorated him, as did the sights of flowers, trees, clouds. He was aware of the irony that he had spent thirteen years in the most scenic spot in China and he had paid little attention to its natural beauty. Shansui's landscape had been a spectacular mural and Han its creator. Like everything Han had touched, the place became out of scale.

In the afternoon he read books on architecture and English laws, trade journals for builders and newspapers from China and abroad. From the compound's office, he had gathered topographical maps of Hong Kong Island, Kowloon Peninsula and the New Territories. He studied them, identifying potential sites for residential and commercial development. He envisioned building comfortable apartments for middle-class families, office and shop spaces for young people starting their first business ventures. When he needed a break, he listened to radio broadcasts and his favorite recordings of classical music. On sunny days he left the confines of the fortress and climbed the hill. Surrounded by sky and open sea, he lay flat on the grass, without a thought of battles, of cries of soldiers and refugees, and of feelings unresolved.

He tried to keep the past out of his mind.

For an hour every day, he tutored Yunna English with textbooks she had ordered from London. Since Hong Kong was going to be their home—she was convinced Japanese occupation of the British colony would not last—she wanted to learn the language of the government. Twice a month, she put on peasants' clothes and hiked down the hill to the closest town. There were errands to run: picking up mail from the post-office, buying the latest newspapers and magazines, shopping for essentials. Jong had offered to go with her, but she reminded him that his Eurasian features would attract attention and it would be best for her to go alone. The excursion required half a day, but she seldom returned home before dark. She never told him what she did with the extra time and he never asked. He understood her desire to get away; their secluded world on the mountain top could be confining.

When he needed fresh vistas, he took out the truck and drove on the mountain roads, with the compass as his only companion. The solitary sojourns restored his spirit. They reminded him how much he cherished what they had, being together, being safe, free of the burden and the strife of the past. A part of him wouldn't mind if they stayed here for the rest of their lives. Life was as close as to paradise as he could imagine. Every day was filled with wondrous moments of having her in his sight, sharing routines, touching her. When they come out of their seclusion, he knew he would look back and think of these years as the best in their lives. He was aware that she would be less nostalgic; and that this difference between them was as fundamental as who they were and how they saw their place in the world. She wouldn't have put her life on hold; in spite of the dangers, she would have chosen to take ownership of the gold, along with it, Han's big dream. He wondered if she kept in touch with her relatives who had relocated to Chungking, if she made new friends on her trips to town. He wouldn't mind if she did. He knew she missed the attention of people, missed being part of the events that were reshaping the country.

He wished there were ways to let the outside world in, but he didn't want the risk of exposing themselves to the many who were looking for Han's gold. They were widely believed to be the only two people who knew where the vault was. If their whereabouts was discovered, Jong had no doubt that they would be hounded. Their life would change from that of recluse to fugitive. As the months passed, there was no indication that interest in the gold had abated; their hiding might go on indefinitely. The waiting began to wear on her. Inevitably he became the recipient of her frustrations. At moments he caught her staring at him with cold hostility. Her face transformed into an old woman's—he could see how she would look in thirty years. An aging beauty haunted by bitterness and suspicion. Sometimes he found her sitting in a corner of the bedroom, drapes drawn, without lights. Her knees pressed together, her arms wrapped around her body, as if she needed to protect herself. He touched her. She was stiff and unresponsive. So he let her be.

We are in a limbo, he reminded himself. Even in normal times, uncertainty causes anxiety. We are living in the shadow of war, waiting for peace that may take a long time to come. And she is still recovering from the cataclysmic events that brought them here. How could she have anticipated that for the second time since that morning in Nanking, her life would be turned upside down in a span of hours?

All things considered, she seemed content. He was happy that she was.

News of the outside world was seldom good. The United Front of the Kuomintang and the Communist Party, as expected, fell apart. In spite of the Kuomintang's impending exile to Formosa, the civil war was escalating. Both sides fought poorly. Military and civilian casualties were rising in staggering numbers. The Japanese were branching into Southeast Asia, engulfing countries in their path: the Philippines, Malaysia, Hong Kong, Singapore. In Europe, the war raged on. Poland fell in thirty days. The Soviet Union attacked Finland. Norway gave in to Germany. The Netherlands, Belgium, France followed. Hitler seemed unstoppable. The Allies were floundering...

On December 7, 1941, Japan attacked Pearl Harbor. Four days later, Germany declared war on the United States. The war, which had been fought on two continents, merged.

On August 6, 1945, the United States dropped the first atomic bomb on Hiroshima. Three days later, the second on Nagasaki.

On August 15, 1945, Japan surrendered.

August 29, 1945.

A message arrived from Shansui. The Japanese had been trying to locate Han's buried gold since they occupied the province last November. They had ransacked what was left of the compound, uprooted the gardens and drained the ponds. They had hunted down the Villa's former staff, tortured and interrogated them. They still hadn't been able to find the passageways to the vault. On the eve of their evacuation, they had set fire to what's left of the Villa. The message enclosed photographs showing views of a vast charred terrain.

That night, Jong and Yunna sat by the stream to watch fireworks celebrating Hong Kong's liberation. He told her the news.

"The Villa is gone. There isn't a home for us anymore," she said quietly.

"Even if it's there, we couldn't claim it back. The Communists would condemn the Villa and what it stood for. They don't take kindly to people like us."

"What do they call us? Imperialists? Enemies of the people?"

"They believe that since we owned more than our share of privilege and property, we must have exploited the less fortunate and caused their suffering. They want us to pay for our sins."

"The new ruling class punishes the old ruling class. How long can they stay above the fray?"

"Not long. Power corrupts. That we know."

She thought. "I didn't."

"You were very young."

She raised her eyes to the sky as though it was where the past was kept. "I took to heart that 'a hero can make an era.' China was weak because the government was weak. All the country needed was strong leadership. We suffered enough at the hands of weak men. A strong leader would put the country on the right track, and we would prosper. Why shouldn't we? Big country, old culture, rich in natural resources, resilient people. I wanted to find that man and help him. That was my dream. I would have given anything for it."

Me. You gave me up for the dream when you decided Han was the man who would save China. But then, Jong reminded himself once again that he, too, had harbored foolish dreams of his own.

"I was watching the world from the inside of a hothouse," she said.

"So was I. For thirteen years."

The fireworks dwindled. The quiet returned and the world seemed at peace. Jong could only hope that this was indeed the end of the war. Since the second half of the Ching Dynasty, the few sustained periods of peace had been brief. Perhaps Communism would give the country a fresh start. Perhaps Mao would turn things around.

Perhaps.

Yunna didn't want to look at the ruins any more. She turned the photographs face down. "The country has changed so much. Hard to believe."

It didn't matter where his father had come from, China was his country. But except for Yunna, everything he cared about in China was gone: Han, Nan-fei, hope.

"You are my country now," he said.

She came to him and he embraced her. She locked her forearms around his neck, like someone clutching a life-saver. Her skin was cold. She was trembling. He kissed her, wanting to share her fears and her hopes.

She pulled back.

"You should have seen it. The place was immense. I couldn't tell where it began or where it ended. Rows and rows of gold, shining like layers of light. There will never be anything more beautiful."

He could almost see the gold in her eyes, along with yearning, disappointment, and sadness all at once. He was relieved that she wasn't expecting a response from him, because he didn't know what to say. He belonged nowhere near her dreams. Nowhere near the past.

"The vault is deep underground. It must have survived the fires," she said.

"Looks like that's what happened."

It had survived the bomb he planted. The blast had blown away the roof in the center of Grand Hall and started the fire. The burning had obliterated part of the frame before Han's soldiers put it out. Torn pillars and charred rubble piled on top of the marble base. They must have concealed the stairwell to the vault. When the guards cleared the debris, they must have inadvertently filled up the tunnel to the vault.

"The Japanese had months. Doesn't it seem strange that they couldn't find the gold?" she said.

"Maybe it wasn't not meant for anyone to find it."

"I wish there was a way we could go back and secure the area."

"We don't have the authority. The land belongs to the state now."

"We have to leave the gold there?"

"Yes."

After a moment, she said, "Someday, someone will find the gold."

"Someday."

"We can claim it. As the General's heirs, we have the right. He was going to do so much with it. We can too. It's possible. Isn't it?"

The gold doesn't belong to us, he replied in silence. And Han's success would have meant calamity for China. But he had come to accept her way of remembering Han. How could he blame her? He had held back the truth. His own culpability was one reason. Another was the wish to keep her memories intact, as he would have wanted his to be. Deep in him burned embers of love for the man who had destroyed everything and everyone in his path. For all that was corrupt and abhorrent in Han, Jong was achingly aware that he had imparted to him only the good and the wise. He was Han's son. As long as he lived, Han would be with him. There was absolutely nothing he could do about it. Nor did he want to.

"Did you have anything to do with the opium business?" she asked unexpectedly.

"The General kept me out of it."

"Why?"

"He said I didn't have the temperament. He was right."

"He was protecting you."

"Yes."

"Do you miss him?"

Jong was not sure he could find the words to give shape to his chaotic memory. "Yes, I miss him." A pause. "Do you?"

"I hardly knew him; there is little to remember him by. Those days before the wedding, I was dazed and bewildered. So much happened that was too fantastic to believe, even now. Sometimes I can't even remember his face. Yet I know I will never forget him."

"We will never forget him."

"He chose me when he could have had any woman. He gave me his name. And his legacy. He made me Han Fu-jen."

"He did."

Between the two of you, I value you over her. Keep that in mind for the rest of your life, Jong. Think about it when you look at her.

"Did you mind?" she asked. "Do you?"

"It was a fact that you and he took part in a marriage ceremony."

"Have you forgiven me, for letting myself be tempted?"

"That's in the past. There's no point in talking about it now."

"But it's on your mind."

He didn't answer.

"It's there. I can feel it."

"I can't help it." He added, "But it isn't the only thing on my mind."

"I need to know if I have your forgiveness, if you have made peace." She found his eyes. "Have you, Jong?"

"Peace. I don't know what it means."

"Have you accepted what happened?"

What *did* happen? Would he ever find out? Would he want to find out? Had Yunna orchestrated the encounter on the beach and made Han fall in love with her? Had she decided to do that after he told her about Han's Grand Strategy? What did she and Han do during the days when he was in New York? What happened in the bridal chamber? Would she have left with him willingly if Han were alive?

"We lived in his world. He was in control. It wasn't up to us," he summed up. "That's what I have learned to accept."

A taillight shot up from the Pearl River, indicating the finale of the fireworks. Her head was in profile to him, dark except for a beam of the faraway light. She gazed once again at the sky.

She began her queries, as she did whenever she needed assurance.

"That night, you came to the bridal chamber, and then the General left me. Where did he go?"

"To Contentment Hall. Your mother had hanged herself. I wanted him to see so he would annul the marriage."

"When you wrote the letter, you couldn't have anticipated my mother's suicide."

"No."

"You had something else planned to get him away from me?"

"The bomb."

"You never planned for it to explode?"

"I was going to defuse it when he agreed to let us go. The situation went awry."

"The assassins?"

"They intercepted my plan."

"They followed the General to Contentment Hall?"

"They must have. They appeared as soon as he walked into the room."

"How many men were there?"

"Things happened very fast. Hard to be sure. A few."

"They shot the General?"

"One of them did."

"They didn't shoot you?"

"No."

"Did you know why?"

"I could only guess. I wasn't their target. They were in a hurry to get away."

"You didn't see their faces."

"They wore masks."

"You thought they bypassed the guards, sneaked into the compound and hid near Grand Hall," she said.

"It seemed that was what happened."

"How could they have known the General would leave the bridal chamber on his wedding night?"

"Maybe they were prepared to wait till the morning."

"Why didn't they kill him as soon as he left Grand Hall?

"It would have been difficult. It was the heaviest guarded spot inside the compound."

"There weren't any guards near Contentment Hall?"

"No."

"You didn't go after them when they killed him. Why?"

"I had to make a choice. To go after the assassins or to save you. The bomb was planted in Grand Hall. It was set to go off. I didn't want you hurt."

"That's why you were there after the first explosion. Just in time to get me out."

"We were lucky."

"The truck and the provisions. You had them ready. How?"

"The preparations were made earlier. I told you in the letter."

"What about this place?"

"It's one of our safe houses. I chose it because it's close to Hong Kong."

A moment. "Who wanted the General dead?"

"He had many enemies. He did things that were harmful to many people."

"Who?"

"The Kuomintang, the Blue Shirts, other warlords. Every one of them would have benefited from his demise."

"Why did they choose that day to kill him?"

"There was the convenience of the crowds. They could find their way into the compound with little chance the guards would pay attention to them. They probably also wanted him dead on the happiest day of his life."

"Happiest day—you think so?"

He didn't answer.

"You thought it was part of a bigger plot to take control of Shansui?"

"There had been similar plots before. Everyone was after the gold."

"What happened to the General's body?"

"The guards must have buried it."

"The General was dead. No one was in charge. We didn't have to run away. We could have stayed and taken ownership of the Villa and the gold. But you decided not to. Why?"

"I didn't know how much danger we were in. The assassins could have come back. Maybe not right away, but they might show up when we least expected and with more people. Once news of the General's passing got out, there would be others who wanted to seize the opportunity to raid the Villa. The gold was a big target. It would have been risky to be there."

"You preferred not to face the risk?"

"I preferred to keep us out of danger."

"There is nothing more dangerous than wars, yet you fought for the General," she insisted.

"Neither the General and I had been in combat. We planned and we gave orders." He added, "They were skirmishes. Shansui never took part in the major conflicts."

"The real thing was going to happen after the wedding, wasn't it? It was going to win the country. Begin the new Han dynasty."

"That was what he thought would happen."

"You didn't think it would?"

"No."

"But you could have been wrong. Things could have happened his way. He could have won."

His response would not be what she wanted. He kept quiet.

"Could you have been wrong?"

"All of us have been wrong one time or another," he said after an age, his voice was an old man's, resigned to dismissing the impossible. "Whatever could have happened, or might have happened—it's not relevant anymore."

A flash shot up from the Pearl River. It could be strayed firework or a shooting star.

"Why did the British grant us asylum?" she asked.

"On my way back from New York, I stopped in Hong Kong. I negotiated a settlement with the Liaison Office. I thought it might be an option in case things didn't turn out the way the General planned."

"You would have preferred America?"

"Yes, but it would have to involve official channels. The British were close by and they had a relationship with the General."

"Only passports for us? Not for the General?"

"He would never have left China."

"Not even for his life?"

"He never thought he would fail."

"Why did you lose faith in the General?"

He thought. "I did, didn't I?"

"Was it because of me?"

He looked at the same beautiful face he had seen countless times. The same indefinable quality that had shaken his soul and broken his heart. Had it been for her that he did what he did? Had she been the cause or the catalyst?

"I didn't lose faith in the General because of you. I lost faith before I met you."

"When did you start to doubt him?"

"There wasn't a precise moment, but the culmination of thoughts and observations." His voice turned inward. "In the beginning I believed in him. How could I not? His vision was compelling. I was young, in awe of him. He was my world. I knew no other. I wanted no other. As time passed, I got to know him. And myself. I realized he and

I saw the world differently, wanted different things out of life. If I'd stayed, I would have had to become someone I was not, would have done things I didn't believe in. I had to find a way out. Then he launched his Grand Strategy. I had to act. Before he chose power over reason."

"What do you mean?"

"Had he lived, many innocent lives would have been sacrificed."

"It was a good thing that he was stopped."

"I believe so. Given what I knew at the time."

She held him in her gaze. "You haven't told me everything."

"No."

"Would it change us if you did?"

"I hope not."

"Will you tell me, someday?"

"Yes, someday I'll tell you."

"But not now?"

"No. Not now."

He heard her sigh. He was aware that this small sound, let out at yet another turning point in their lives, would be etched forever into his memory.

A thin rain was falling. Stars glowed big and pale in the drizzle. At the foot of the hill, a smattering of vehicles rumbled southward. People who could were leaving Mao's China, heading for Hong Kong.

A tiny island on the South China Sea. A British colony made possible by opium and an unfair treaty. In a few hours it would be their home. It came to Jong that this would be a new beginning for her, but a wrap-up for him. For better or worse, the prime of his career had passed with Han.

"What are we going to do in Hong Kong?" she asked.

"Live. Do the things we want to do."

"If the General had lived, what would he do?"

"Build a second Crescent Moon Villa. Build a new empire. Use his wealth to produce more wealth."

It would have meant more gold. Han had been obsessed by the precious metal; it hadn't mattered that his method of accumulating wealth was impractical and archaic. An adroit investor would not have let his assets sit idle in the basement. But then, Han had been a man of a bygone era.

"You said the General deposited money into accounts overseas?"

"In England and Switzerland. The account in the British bank was for profits from the opium trade. The money in the Swiss account was intended as deposit for a newly invented weapon. He ordered the transfer when we were in Tsingtao. I had doubts about the deal. I held off payment and put the money in a transit account."

"You didn't want the General to have the weapon?"

"It turned out there was no weapon for sale."

"Even if there was, you would have done what you could to stop the General."

"Yes."

"There is a lot of money?"

"A staggering sum."

"It's ours now?"

"Yes."

"We are young," she said with renewed hope. "We will begin in Hong Kong. We will build our empire."

He was not sure if that's what he wanted to do. Having learned painfully the price one had to pay for power, it was not an experience he would wish on someone he loved. But he reckoned things had a way of sorting themselves out, it was not his role to decide for her.

༄

The sea was steel blue and the wind ripped over it. An untidy fleet of junks, ferryboats, and sampans jammed the narrow strait between Hong Kong Island and Kowloon Peninsula. After three and a half years of Japanese occupation, people were coming out to celebrate the Colony's liberation. The foreshore was pulsating with activity. Buildings on the waterfront were festooned with Union Jack streamers. Families lined up by the railing, waving and cheering. The sun shone through the morning fog, casting shafts of light on the city.

Jong and Yunna were at the prow of the cross-harbor ferry to Hong Kong Island. The boat was running into the wind, spray flying on the sides, cooling the hot summer day.

He pointed at a spot on the Peak. "There."

She shaded her eyes for a better look. "Seems tiny from here."

"There is enough land to build a main hall and two wings."

"It would be a start."

At Queen's Pier they boarded a taxi. The trace of a painted Japanese flag bled on the hood; the inside reeked of gunpowder. The Japanese had confiscated all the vehicles in the Colony, the driver told them, his car had been recovered in the garage of the Peninsula Hotel, where the

Japanese had set up administrative headquarters. He had reclaimed it—one of the fortunate few who were able to start earning a living on the first day of peace.

They drove by the row of stately European buildings on Des Voux Road. Jong remembered one of them was the bank owned by the Soong family. The clan had moved with Chiang Kai-shek to Formosa—calling the island the Republic of China. A small consolation prize for the party that lost the country. Yunna gazed at the Kuomintang flag hoisted above the entrance until it was out of sight. Going up the Peak, the taxi passed Government House with Japanese gables added to the roof. Piles of debris high as a bus surrounded the compound; workers were clearing them. In a few hours, an English colonial officer would reclaim the premises.

The taxi climbed past the Mid-levels and turned on Old Peak Road. Jong told the drive to pull up to the vacant lot.

"It's even smaller up close," Yunna said.

Jong took her hand as he brushed aside the weeds. "Look at the view."

Ahead were Kowloon Peninsula, the mountains of the New Territories, and the small islands on the South China Sea. The sun had burned away the morning fog. The harbor shone like an immense blue crystal.

"Imagine the lights when the city is rebuilt," Jong said.

There were tears in her eyes. He hoped they were for joy.

"We'll rent a place close by," he continued, enthusiasm rising. "I'll oversee the construction, make sure it's built the way we want. Let's give it a new name."

"Why a new name?"

"We don't want people to make the connection with the one in Shansui."

"I don't want another name. Let people think what they want."

The day was getting warm. They sat under a tree. Yunna leaned against the trunk, hands resting on her knees, staring at the clouds. She must be tired from the trip, Jong thought. They had woken up in the middle of the night, driven two and a half hours to the Canton-Hong Kong border. They didn't have the papers to bring the truck into the British colony; they had left it behind and crossed the border on foot. In the crowded train station, they had joined the long queue boarding the first train to Kowloon, and then the cross-harbor ferry to Hong Kong Island.

He took out a notebook and began to make a list of things to do. Rent an apartment. Hire servants, secretaries, and chauffeurs. Interview architects to draw up the building plans. Assemble a construction crew. Activate the transit account in the Swiss bank and close the one in the London bank. Move the funds to Hong Kong. He had clear ideas what to do with the money, having spent years planning for this day. Fifteen percent would go to building the new Crescent Moon Villa. Thirty percent invested for a stable income. The rest would be capital for his new company. He would buy land and put up apartments and offices. The refugees from China would be needing space to live and work. A building boom was inevitable. His company would help rebuild Hong Kong. Turn it into a world-class city.

"Yunna? Is this really you?" a male voice said in Shanghainese. "Mr. Lin?"

A tall blond boy was standing in front of them.

"You don't remember? It's me. Pierre. Pierre Maurier. You came to my house in Shanghai, and then you brought me to Shansui."

"Pierre. Oh my goodness. I didn't recognize you." Yunna stood up. He was taller than her by a head. "You've grown up."

"I'm a few years older and you are more beautiful." His handsome face was wreathed in smiles, his blue eyes taking her in fondly.

She reached for his hand. He had already pulled her to him and wrapped her with his arms.

"This is unbelievable," Yunna said, cupping his face. "My little Pierre. So handsome. So grown up. In Hong Kong."

"We just arrived. How did you know we would be here?" Jong asked.

Pierre released Yunna but held her hand. The link caused Jong a small pang of jealousy. They sat in a circle on the grass.

"I rented a room across the street when I found out this lot belonged to General Han. I was hoping one day you would come. You are my only friends in the world. I watch from the window everyday. I didn't know how long I would have to wait. I couldn't believe my eyes when I saw you."

"You have been in Hong Kong all this time?" Jong asked.

Pierre nodded.

"Didn't your mother meet you here and she was going to take you back to France?"

"She wasn't the one who sent the wire to Shansui. It was Auntie Lillie."

Pierre told them how he had found Lillie at the airport and how she had made a home for them, managed the Mayflower and looked for his father. She was worried the worst might have happened to him, but she never lost hope. One day she told Pierre she had to attend a party in Repulse Bay. Mr. Soong would be there. He would know where Victor was and she would ask for his help. And then she started to pack. He asked if they were taking a trip. She said there's a chance they might have to hide so Mr. Soong's people wouldn't be able to find them. He couldn't understand why she would have to prepare for something like that, but she wouldn't say more. He didn't have a good feeling, so he waited up for her, made sure she got back all right. She was home earlier than expected, wildly excited and happier than she had been for months. She said she'd found out Victor had left Shansui and he could be on his way to Hong Kong. Pierre wanted to know more, but she said that was all the information she had. It didn't seem much, but it was enough for her to believe the wait would be over. The next day, she went to the bank. She was going to withdraw the money his father had earned working for Mr. Soong—there's a lot of it. Her appointment was at nine. She promised Pierre she would be back before noon. He waited and waited. She never came home. He thought about what she had said the night before. His father had talked about Mr. Soong and he knew he wasn't a nice man. He started to panic. At five o'clock he went to the police station. The policeman said there hadn't been enough time to consider her missing. Pierre returned the next morning, refused to leave until they agreed to look for her. Weeks passed; they couldn't find a trace of her anywhere.

"You were all alone?"

"We had an amah. But Auntie Lillie dismissed her before she went to the party in Repulse Bay. She said it would be easier in case we had to lock up the apartment and go into hiding."

"It must have been dreadful. All by yourself. You were only a child," Yunna said as she brushed back a forelock from his face.

The water in the blue eyes had pooled. Pierre made an effort to contain it but didn't succeed. He broke into sobs.

"I wanted to find her. And my father. But I didn't even know where to look. Two people who loved me. Gone."

"How did you manage?"

He wiped away the tears and took a deep breath. "I went to school, did my homework, and carried on like before. I thought if I kept doing what I'd been doing before, it would be easier to believe things would be all right. Social Services assigned a worker to keep an eye on me. There were other children in her care, but I was the only one living on my own. She took extra care to make sure I was all right. She visited me every week and accompanied me on occasions when a parent was needed. The teachers at the missionary school helped where they could. Money wasn't a problem. After Auntie Lillie sold the Mayflower, she put half the money in the bank and half in the safe at home. She liked to have cash on hand. I took out a set amount every month for the expenses. She taught me to be careful with money and I was."

"It must have been lonely."

"It wasn't too bad during the week when I was at school. It was the evenings and the weekends that were hard. The apartment was empty; I felt I was alone in the world. But I tried not to be sad. I told myself my father and Auntie Lillie loved me, and they wouldn't abandon me... A few months later, the Japanese came. The city turned into a war zone. Lucky for me, they left me alone, being Caucasian might have helped. But I saw the cruel things they did to women, old people, and little children, right in the streets. I still have nightmares about them."

"The war is over," Yunna said gently. "You will be safe."

Pierre nodded. "Didn't the newspapers report Japan has surrendered unconditionally? People are saying there will be peace for a thousand years."

"Let's hope so."

"You never found out what happened to Lillie?" Jong asked.

Pierre shook his head. "According to the police, the last time she was seen, it was at Mr. Soong's bank in Central. The receptionist said Auntie Lillie had an appointment with the managing director, Mr. Chiu. She arrived on time and she was shown to his office. As soon as she walked in, he told the receptionist to hold his calls and closed the door. Half an hour later, the staff saw her come out with a bag. She didn't say a word to anyone and headed straight to the door. That was it. No one saw her come out of the bank. The police didn't find any trace where she might have gone. Maybe they didn't try hard enough. Maybe Auntie Lillie didn't want to be found. I can't believe she could have vanished like that."

"All these years. Nothing?"

"Nothing from her, but there were rumors."

"Tell us."

"A group of thugs were waiting for her outside the bank. They forced her into a car and drove to a remote area. They killed her, buried her body, and made off with the cash. The whole thing was nothing more than a random crime of abduction and robbery." He shook his head. "How could the thugs have known? Auntie Lillie found out only the night before and she told only me. She had arranged a car for the appointment. It took her there and it was waiting outside the bank while she went in to see Mr. Chiu. The driver was someone she knew. It was broad daylight in Central District. There were guards at the door and people walking by, lots of people. How could she have been abducted without being seen? Auntie Lillie wouldn't have let anyone bully her. She would have fought back, made a scene and cried for help. She is smart and brave; if you only knew the things she had been through…" His voice quivered as memories returned in a rush. "There was another story. Her troubles had begun in Shanghai. She had offended a high-ranking Kuomintang official. That was the reason she had to run away, not saying goodbye to us. You remember, Yunna? You were there that morning. The official found out she had come to Hong Kong and sent his people here. They arrested her at the bank, took her back to China, and put her in prison. If that were true, why would they have waited this long to make the arrest? We had been here for months, living at the same address. She went to work every day. We ate at restaurants, shopped at department stores. There was no sign that Auntie Lillie was worried about being pursued. And why would a high-ranking government official set up such an elaborate trap for a woman who had little means to defend herself?" He had mulled over the scenarios many times and had worked out an explanation. "This story doesn't make sense unless the appointment at the bank was a trap. She was lured there by a false promise of money—it was just too good to be true that someone like Mr. Soong would be willing to give away that much money to someone he had only met at a party. She found out after she got to the bank. Maybe she was able to make a deal with Mr. Chiu to spare her life. But

Mr. Chiu worked for Mr. Soong. She couldn't really trust him; she had to get away. She only planned to stay in hiding for a while, but then the Japanese came." His eyes followed a plane lifting off from the tip of Kowloon Peninsula. "If she escaped, she would have found a way to come home and take me with her. Even if she couldn't show up in person, she would have made contact. Get someone else to bring me to where she was. She isn't my mother, but she loves me." Pierre took something wrapped in a handkerchief out of his pocket. "She left behind a lot of these."

A gold peach.

"When I realized it wasn't likely that Auntie Lillie would be home soon, I went through her things. I thought I might find something that would give me a clue where she had gone. An address. Name of a friend. Travel itinerary. I didn't find anything like that, but there was a bunch of keys in the suitcase she had packed before she went to Repulse Bay. They didn't fit the locks in the house. I thought they had to mean something; she had made a point of bringing them along if we had to hide. I took them to a locksmith. He told me they would open safe deposit boxes in banks. I went to the banks and showed them the keys. It turned out she had safe deposit boxes in European and American banks—she didn't want to have anything to do with the Chinese ones. She had put my name on the accounts, like she had done with everything she owned. I was able to open the boxes. They were filled with these. There were more than a hundred. I didn't know what to do and left them where they were. When I heard the Japanese would take over the banks and confiscate everything, I took them out and kept them with me. I didn't tell anyone in case they might be real gold. Do you think they can tell me where Auntie Lillie is?"

Jong looked the peach. It all came back to him: the gift from Han to Henry, Victor and Yunna taking the trunk out of the house on Purple Gold Mountain, Victor escorting Su-chen and Yunna to Shanghai, Lillie making off with the trunk, Victor's search for her that led him to Shansui... Incredible that so many lives had been linked to these gold peaches.

Time to put the past behind them.

"I doubt that they can tell you more than you already know," Jong said, rewrapping the gold sphere that reminded him of everything he abhorred. "They are precious metal made into the shape of a fruit, that's all. They have no significance other than their monetary value."

"Is it real gold?"

"Yes."

"There is a small scratch on each one. I wonder if it means anything," Pierre said.

"A personal seal was carved on the surface. It was removed."

"Would it be a way to trace the original owner?"

"The original owner may not be the rightful owner," Jong replied. "They were your Auntie Lillie's. Now they are yours."

"Why did Auntie Lillie have so much gold?"

He could tell Pierre the story. But where should he begin—how Han had amassed his gold or what had happened on the day of the Nanking Massacre? What would be the point?

"It could have been a gift," Jong replied.

"From whom?"

"You would have to ask her, or your father."

"Why didn't my father come to Hong Kong? Where is he?"

Jong was reluctant to tell the boy how his father had disappeared. He would have to reveal the identity of the man who had been responsible. He didn't want to talk about Han and the crimes he had committed. With the passage of time, he hoped he would remember only the kind side of him—friend, teacher, father. A flawed man defeated by his own dreams. Not the monstrosity he had become. And something about the boy endeared him to Jong. He saw his younger self in Pierre. The sad independence of orphans. The precocious wisdom of the dispossessed. He wanted to protect him. He knew Yunna felt the same.

"I don't know. I never saw your father again after his stay in Shansui."

"Where could he have gone?"

"Lillie might have the right information. Your father had found his way out of the Villa and the province. After that, it wouldn't have been difficult for him to leave China. He could have gone anywhere."

"Why did he leave me in Shansui?"

"He didn't have a choice. If he came back for you, he might not have been able to get out at all."

"Why did he have to run away?"

"He was caught between General Han and Mr. Soong. It was an impossible situation."

"You think my father is alive?"

"Didn't Lillie say he was?"

"But she disappeared. Right after she found out."

"They may be waiting for the right moment to come back. It could be soon." Jong added, "One thing we can be sure of. Wherever they are, they would be glad to know you are safe."

"I want to find my father and Auntie Lillie, and then I'll go to France to see my mother. I don't want to be alone."

"You won't be alone. We are building a house here, like the one in Shansui, though not as grand. Nothing will be as grand," Yunna said. "It will be our home. And yours. We want you to live with us. We'll take care of you."

"Do you really want to live here?" Pierre looked around. "Hong Kong is so small."

"After China, anywhere else would be small."

"Don't you want to go back? Shanghai, Shansui—I miss everything."

"We hope to go back. But it will be for the best that we put China out of our thoughts. For now." Jong stepped out of the tree's shadow, letting the sun warm his face. "China is going through changes. It's a different country now. It may stay that way for a long time, or it may not. We will go back if and when we can. But if we can't go back, and all we'll have are memories, that'll be all right. There is much to cherish." He smiled at the glistening harbor below. "This is home."

"Home," Yunna echoed as she looked to the north. The endless landmass that was China.

Overhead a flock of birds lifted out of the trees and flew toward the sky.

Kate Zeng was born in China and grew up in Hong Kong. She lives in Northern California.

Katezeng15@gmail.com

www.ingramcontent.com/pod-product-compliance
Lightning Source LLC
Chambersburg PA
CBHW032248020726
47495CB00001B/21